THE AVENGERS

Dave Rogers

Designer   Geoffrey Powell
Editor   Jane Struthers
Chief Editor   John Doyle

Published by
Independent Television Books Ltd
247 Tottenham Court Road
London W1P 0AU

In association with Michael Joseph Ltd

First published 1983
Reprinted 1984

© The Avengers, EMI Film Distributors
   Ltd 1983
© Text, Dave Rogers 1983
© Photographs, copyright remains with
   original copyright holders 1983

Typeset by The Yale Press
Norwood, London SE25

Printed in Great Britain by
Butler & Tanner Ltd
Frome and London

ISBN: 0 907965 09 1

THE AVENGERS

by Dave Rogers

All 161 Original Episodes – Story Cast Pictures

ITV BOOKS
in association with Michael Joseph

Although articles on *The Avengers* have appeared in numerous publications throughout its 21 years of television life, no one, it seems, has seen fit to research and publish a complete volume on the series.

This book will hopefully rectify that omission, and give The Avengers aficionado a full reference guide to the 161 episodes that make up *The Avengers* story.

I have refrained from offering any personal opinions on the show and stuck to the facts as printed in the studio files. However, I have (in an effort to clarify some details which have been misrepresented over the last 14 years) included information which, though at variance with the generally accepted version of events, should help clear up one or two misconceptions regarding the show's history. These are offered not as *fact,* but as an alternative to those printed elsewhere.

Also included is previously unpublished material on the series, plus reviews of the ill-fated Avengers stage show and South African radio series. In short, this is the complete history of one of Britain's most popular and successful television series.

Wherever possible, through correspondence and interviews with the stars, production staff and television companies, the information in this book has been checked and cross-checked for its authenticity, and can, therefore, be taken as 99% correct.

Five of the synopses of the first season's episodes are of shorter length than the rest. The official studio material for these is unfortunately, lost and consequently I've had to rely on my own notes for these.

One fallacy I would like to dispel at the onset is the belief that the 1960 production *Police Surgeon* and *The Avengers* are connected! Throughout my research, I've found *no* evidence to support this theory. Admittedly, Ian Hendry took the role of a doctor in both series, and both series were produced for ABC/TV by Sydney Newman and Leonard White. However, as the character Hendry played in the former was called Geoffrey Brent, while in *The Avengers* it was David Keel (and as Patrick Macnee never appeared as Steed in *Police Surgeon*), I believe I can safely say that no such connection exists, and that *The Avengers* began with the introduction of John Steed in 1961.

Dave Rogers

I would like to thank the following individuals and organisations for their cordial (and invaluable) help during the preparation of this volume.

In particular, Bud Payton, of EMI, whose co-operation was incalculable, and without whose support and encouragement this book would not have been written. Miss Anjna Patel and Bernard Heywood (both of EMI), for whom nothing was too much trouble. A special thanks to Bob Norris, for his kind (and helpful) comments on the manuscript. John Doyle and Jane Struthers, of ITV Books, for having faith in the project. Jack Breckon and his staff of Thames Television. Brian Clemens, Albert Fennell and Laurie Johnson, of Avengers (Film & TV) Enterprises. The directors and staff of Eurotel Distribution. The management and staff of Nostalgia & Comics, Birmingham. The Brookes (Josie, Lewis and Carl) for their unfailing support. Paul Jackson, Richard Hollis and Colin for 'easing the burden'. Dave McCulloch for his 'Bizarre' imput. The staff of Birmingham and Manchester Reference Libraries.

I would also like to thank the following companies for allowing me to use extracts from their publications: The London Express News & Features Service; The Mirror Group Newspapers; World International Pub Ltd; and Harmsworth Pub Ltd.

Finally, a big thank you to my wife Celia and family, for putting up with the 'bouts of silence' and the constant tapping of the typewriter keys.

This book is respectfully dedicated to Honor Blackman, Diana Rigg, Linda Thorson, Joanna Lumley, Gareth Hunt and Patrick Newell and, in particular, one man, who more than any other helped to make *The Avengers* unique: Avenger extraordinaire – Patrick Macnee.

CONTENTS

CONTENTS

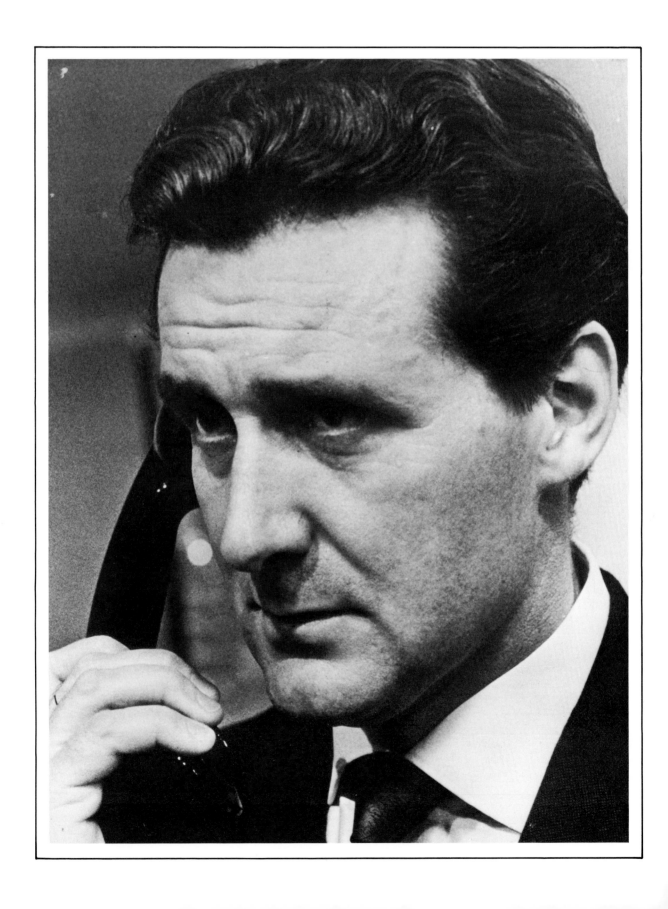

Ian Hendry/Patrick Macnee
1961

Enter
John Steed

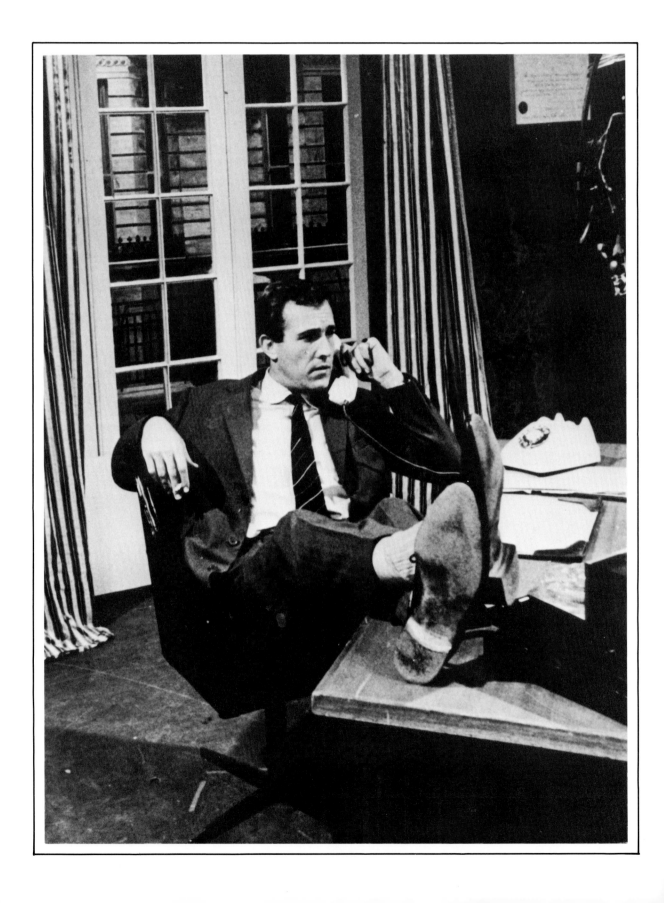

BACK in the dawn of the 1960s when England was just beginning to swing, hemlines were rising and the Beatles had yet to change the world, Sydney Newman, Head of Drama for the long since departed ABC Television, had lunch with an actor named Patrick Macnee. There was a role he wanted to discuss. 'This character I have in mind is a sort of George Saunders type,' said Newman. 'He's to be sardonic, suave and cynical, with a flair for elegant clothes, an eye for the women and a not too fastidious ruthlessness in getting his own way. You'd be perfect for the part.'

Any actor would have been interested but Patrick Macnee was not sure that he wanted to remain an actor. He'd just completed producing a television documentary series based on Sir Winston Churchill's memoirs, *The Valiant Years,* and he believed that his future lay in television production. On the other hand, the role did sound appealing. Unsure what to do, he decided to ask a ridiculously high fee and let fate take its course. To his astonishment, Newman agreed, and Macnee signed to play John Steed in a new series called *The Avengers.*

The rest is history. Twenty years later Patrick Macnee was still playing the key figure in a series that had become cult viewing all over the world.

Perhaps one of the secrets of the great success of *The Avengers* is that the series evolved over those two decades, so that the most recent episodes bear very little resemblance to the series that first went on the air in January 1961.

It all began when Sydney Newman was asked by ABC's Managing Director, Howard Thomas, to find something light-hearted to liven up their drama schedules. At the time a new type of thriller was all the rage. Popularised by film directors like Alfred Hitchcock and novelists like Ian Fleming in his James Bond books, these new thrillers were as tough and exciting as ever, but they were also sophisticated and tongue-in-cheek. Audiences were being invited to laugh as well as gasp, and they showed every sign of enjoying the experience.

It was Sydney Newman's daring idea to try this new formula on television for the first time. He already had one actor in mind. He had been producing a series called *Police Surgeon,* a standard cops-and-robbers crime series which had failed to make much impression on viewers, but he couldn't help noticing that their letters indicated they liked the brash appeal of its young star, Ian Hendry. If Ian Hendry could be combined with this new formula Sydney Newman was sure they'd have a success. With this in mind, Newman, together with *Police Surgeon's* co-producer Leonard White, came up with the idea of teaming Hendry with another actor. Hendry, again playing a doctor, would set out to avenge the death of his fiancée when she is shot by a drug gang, and the newcomer would be a sort of undercover agent who co-opts the doctor into his crusading role against the pluguglies. The series would be called *The Avengers,* because the stories would concern the efforts of the doctor and his partner to avenge the death of his fiancée and 'because it's a great title,' said Newman.

Ian Hendry was enthusiastic about the idea. On the face of it Dr David Keel was rather similar to Dr Brent in *Police Surgeon,* but this time the doctor would have a private practice and no outward connection with the police. 'Keel is a most attractive character,' Hendry said at the time. 'He combines toughness with compassion, and serves as the conscience of the team. The role will be a kind of extended version of the police surgeon, because Keel will be more directly involved with fighting crime. And as he tangles with villains himself, he'll have more of the action. The accent is on authenticity, with vigorous, fast-moving action and well-researched stories.

The role of the 'mysterious' undercover agent, (the cynicism to Keel's conscience) was crucial, and that was when Sydney Newman remembered an actor he'd met in Canada. Old Etonian Patrick Macnee had just the sort of smooth charm he'd envisaged for John Steed, and Macnee, like Hendry, was captivated by the role he was asked to play.

'He is a wolf with the women and revels in trouble,' said Macnee. 'He doesn't think so much about saving hoodlums as just getting them out of the way. By the same token, he doesn't follow the Queensbury Rules, and though he works indirectly with the police, he is not too popular with them.' During the early episodes, it was never made clear whether Steed was a 'loner' or worked for some secret Ministry department. In later episodes, however, he was often seen receiving orders from a mysterious establishment figure called One-Ten.

Television programmes in those early days went out 'live', so if something went wrong during transmission, there was nothing anyone could do. Nevertheless, Hendry and Macnee managed to evolve an off-beat approach to the characters of Keel and Steed and the series proved very popular with the public. Incidentally, Macnee was wearing his 'city-gent' style of dress as early as mid-way through the Hendry series, but it wasn't until the Honor Blackman episodes that the now familiar Edwardian image began to evolve.

HOT SNOW

Teleplay by Ray Rigby
Based on a story by Patrick Brawn

Dr Tredding	Philip Stone
Peggy	Catherine Woodville
Dr David Keel	Ian Hendry
Spicer	Godfrey Quigley
Charlie	Murray Melvin
Johnson	Charles Wade
Det-Supt Wilson	Alister Williamson
Stella	Moira Redmond
Sgt Rogers	Astor Sklair
Steed	Patrick Macnee
Mrs Simpson	June Monkhouse

Designed by Alpho O'Reilly
Produced by Leonard White
Directed by Don Leaver

THE episode opens with Dr David Keel feeling on top of the world. He has just announced his engagement to his secretary, Peggy. Later that day, however, a gang of drug peddlers mistakenly deliver a packet of heroin to Keel's surgery. Realising their mistake, the gang sends two of its members to retrieve the package, but Peggy disturbs them. They escape but, because Peggy can identify them, lie in wait and gun her down in the street. Keel calls in the police, only to find they have insufficient evidence on which to act. Heartbroken at Peggy's death, Keel vows to find the killers himself. He follows the trail to the consulting rooms of a shady medical practitioner (who should have received the heroin in the first place) but he, too, has been murdered by the gang. As he leaves, Keel is stopped and questioned by a mysterious stranger who introduces himself as John Steed. Steed tells Keel that he is after the gang and enlists his help to track them down. Using a fake package of heroin as bait, Keel contacts the gang but tells them that he will only deal direct with their boss, Vance. The gang, however, are suspicious and decide that Keel must be killed. They lay a trap for Keel, but as they are about to dispose of him, Steed arrives and rescues him. A furious fight breaks out, in which the police arrive and arrest the gang, but the gang leader, Vance, is able to escape.

BROUGHT TO BOOK

Teleplay by Brian Clemens

Prentice	Lionel Burns
Lale	Redmond Bailey
Pretty Boy	Clifford Elkin
Bart	Neil McCarthy
Nick Mason	Charles Morgan
Spicer	Godfrey Quigley
Dr David Keel	Ian Hendry
Dr Tredding	Philip Stone
Carol Wilson	Ingrid Hafner
Chinese Girl (Lila)	Joyce Wong Chong
John Steed	Patrick Macnee
Ronnie Vance	Robert James
Det-Supt Wilson	Alister Williamson
Det-Sgt	Michael Collins
Jackie	Carol White

Designed by Robert Fuest
Produced by Leonard White
Directed by Peter Hammond

ONCE again, Dr David Keel meets the mysterious John Steed. Steed invites him to ingratiate himself with Vance, leader of a notorious gang of protection racketeers. Steed explains that he has managed to become a member of a similar gang led by Mason, who wants to poach Vance's territory. When Steed explains that Peggy's killer is implicated with Mason, Keel accepts the challenge, and a police raid is staged in Vance's presence, which makes Keel appear crooked. To test Keel's loyalty, Vance asks him to attend to his brother, Pretty Boy, who has been razor-slashed by Mason's gang. Keel does this, and is readily accepted by Vance. Keel is then told that one of Mason's gang, Spicer, has been hired to kill the Vance brothers. Keel tells Steed, who arranges for the police to be present at the killing. Mason, however, suspects Steed and, instead of Spicer, arrives himself and warns Vance that there are traitors in both camps – adding that he has sent Spicer to kill Steed. Keel overhears and rushes to rescue Steed. In threatening Spicer with instant death by an injection from his hypodermic needle in revenge for his fiancée's murder, he extracts a confession which the police arrive in time to hear. Spicer successfully dealt with (by a trick – there was nothing harmful in the hypodermic), Steed enlists Keel's permanent help in the undercover police's constant fight against organised crime.

SQUARE ROOT OF EVIL

Teleplay by Richard Harris

John Steed	Patrick Macnee
5	Heron Carvic
Secretary	Cynthia Bizeray
Bloom	Michael Robbins
Hooper	George Murcell
Warren	Vic Wise
The Cardinal	Alex Scott
Lisa	Delphi Lawrence
Carol Wilson	Ingrid Hafner
Dr David Keel	Ian Hendry

Designed by Patrick Downing
Produced by Leonard White
Directed by Don Leaver

STEED finds that a corpse and the 'Cardinal' lead him into an adventure in which the lovely Lisa may prefer him dead.

Patrick Macnee and Ian Hendry, who played the crime-busting original Avengers, John Steed and Dr David Keel.

Steed and Dr Keel devise a trap which will outwit the drug-pushers in Brought To Book.

NIGHTMARE

Teleplay by Terence Feely

Williams	Gordon Boyd
Dr David Keel	Ian Hendry
Carol Wilson	Ingrid Hafner
Faith Braintree	Helen Lindsay
Commander Reece	Michael Logan
John Steed	Patrick Macnee
Dr Brown	Robert Bruce
Dr Jones	Redmond Bailey
Dr Miller	Robert Sansom

Designed by Robert Fuest
Produced by Leonard White
Directed by Peter Hammond

AN eerie telephone call from one of his patients, Faith Braintree, leads Dr Keel to investigate the disappearance of her husband, an eminent scientist engaged on top secret work. While he is attending Faith, a fake MI5 man arrives and, assuming Keel to be the professor, tries to kidnap him. Keel is saved, but recovers from the attack in hospital where Steed persuades him to impersonate Braintree and draw the enemy's attention from the real professor (who is still missing). The ruse works, and a second attempt is made to kidnap Keel. He escapes, but during the ensuing fight is shot in the chest. A minor operation is needed but Carol, Keel's receptionist, learns that the anaesthetist is one of the enemy. But, before she can tell Steed, she is caught and tied up by the assassins. During the operation, Keel's oxygen is tampered with and he is dying when Steed arrives and unmasks the anaesthetist. Carol is freed and Keel recovers. The real Braintree, suffering from amnesia due to overwork, is found and Steed, Keel and Carol have a celebratory drink with the professor and his wife.

In **Nightmare**, **Dr Keel** receives a strange telephone call from Faith Braintree, one of his patients.

CRESCENT MOON

Teleplay by Geoffrey Bellman and John Whitney

Senora Mendoza	Patience Collier
John Steed	Patrick Macnee
Bartello	Harold Kasket
Carmelite Mendoza	Bandana Das Gupta
Luis Alvarez	Nicholas Amer
Paul	Eric Thompson
Fernandez	Jack Rodney
Vasco	Roger Delgado
Carlos (policeman)	George Roderick
Dr David Keel	Ian Hendry

Designed by Alpho O'Reilly
Produced by Leonard White
Directed by John Knight

STEED is sent to a Caribbean island, to investigate the kidnapping of a young girl, Carmelite Mendoza. Although the family jewels are missing, Steed suspects a political motive, for the girl's father, pro-Western General Mendoza, was officially reported killed in a mysterious accident only a week earlier. Steed's questioning of Senora Mendoza and her family retainer, Vasco, reveals nothing. Later, however, Vasco is seen killing Carmelite's kidnapper and abducting the girl himself. Having intercepted a police report about the murder, Steed beats the police to the scene of the crime and follows up a clue naming the man behind the abduction as Senor Paul. Meanwhile, in London, Dr Keel is told to expect a new patient – General Mendoza! By clever questioning of Vasco, Steed discovers where Carmelite is being held prisoner, but when he attempts to rescue her, Paul attacks him. Steed soon overpowers Senor Paul and takes him and the girl to the police. Paul admits being behind the original kidnapping, but states that he only wanted to take her to her father, who had to flee and fake his own death to escape the plotting of his wife. Senora Mendoza and Vasco wanted his vast fortune to bring their political party to power. Back in London, Keel tells Steed that when the General was in England he was ill and he had attended him.

GIRL ON THE TRAPEZE

Teleplay by Dennis Spooner

Vera	Delena Kidd
Anna Danilov	Nadja Regin
Dr David Keel	Ian Hendry
Carol Wilson	Ingrid Hafner
Policeman	Ian Gardiner
Zibbo	Kenneth J Warren
Supt Lewis	Howard Goorney
Stefan	Edwin Richfield

Designed by Paul Bernard
Produced by Leonard White
Directed by Don Leaver

A GIRL jumps into the Thames but the body which is rescued and which Dr Keel tries to revive is that of another girl, whose face seems familiar to Keel. The girl dies, having murmured the word 'Danilov', and Keel is convinced that she is the victim of foul play. With the help of his receptionist, Carol, Keel finds the dead girl's photograph in a newspaper and they discover that she was the trapeze artist with the Radeck State Circus, now on the last night of its visit to Britain. They visit the circus and discover that one of the performers, Vera (the girl who jumped from the bridge), is guarding a girl whose face is masked by bandages. The owner tells them that the trapeze girl had a slight accident during her performance but is now recovering in her dressing room. Suspicious, Keel calls in the police, who tell him that Professor Danilov, a Radeck scientist, has fled to the West with his young daughter, Anna. Keel investigates the trapeze girl's dressing room and finds the heavily bandaged figure. But before Keel can question her, Zibbo the clown traps him, and he and Carol are held prisoner. Zibbo informs them that Anna Danilov, bandaged to avoid recognition, will take the place of the dead girl and be smuggled back to Radeck to compel her father to return. Keel is told that unless he tells the police that he has made a mistake, Carol will be shot. Keel does so, but the police sergeant remains suspicious, and has the circus secretly surrounded. That night, Keel arranges for Carol to escape by having her swathed in bandages and pretending to be Anna. Then he himself escapes and takes the real Anna to safety. Carol, however, is trapped by Zibbo, who threatens her at gunpoint. As he is about to shoot her, the police close in and the gang is arrested.

DIAMOND CUT DIAMOND

Teleplay by Max Marquis

John Steed	Patrick Macnee
One-Ten	Douglas Muir
Fiona Charles	Sandra Dorne
Dr Collard	Hamlyn Benson
Carol Wilson	Ingrid Hafner
Dr David Keel	Ian Hendry
Stella Creighton	Joy Webster

Designed by Robert Fuest
Produced by Leonard White
Directed by Peter Hammond

DR KEEL and Steed hunt for a gang of diamond thieves, and Steed joins an airline to find a murderer, but two beautiful women make it difficult for him to keep his mind on his work.

Steed is faced with death and forced to fight desperately for his life in The Radioactive Man.

Carol hopes to do some clever detective work when she visits the Beronne Hair Salon, in Ashes Of Roses.

THE RADIOACTIVE MAN

Teleplay by Fred Edge

Marko Ogrin	George Pravda
Mary Somers	Christine Pollon
Carol Wilson	Ingrid Hafner
Dr David Keel	Ian Hendry
John Steed	Patrick Macnee

Designed by Alpho O'Reilly
Produced by Leonard White
Directed by Robert Tronson

STEED and Dr Keel search for a killer whose touch spells death. The man is using a newly discovered radioactive isotope as a murder weapon, bringing death to anyone making contact with it. They desperately continue their search, knowing that every second makes the danger more deadly, death more certain.

The injured Frank Preston is quickly treated by Dr Keel and Carol, in Hunt The Man Down.

ASHES OF ROSES

Teleplay by Peter Ling and Sheilagh Ward

John Steed	Patrick Macnee
Olive Beronne	Olga Lowe
Jacques Beronne	Mark Eden
Johnny Mendelssohn	Peter Zander
Dr David Keel	Ian Hendry
Carol Wilson	Ingrid Hafner
Denise	Hedi Erich

Designed by Patrick Downing
Produced by Leonard White
Directed by Don Leaver

WHEN a watchman dies in a warehouse fire, Steed is convinced that it was murder and that the fire was started deliberately – one of several recent cases of suspected arson. Steed has only one lead – a telephone number – and it belongs to a hairdressing salon run by Olive and Jacques Beronne. Steed asks Dr Keel to let Carol have some time off to go to the hair salon. Carol, eager for adventure, and what she imagines is some smart detective work at the salon, does so, but finds nothing of interest. Sitting under her hairdrier, she presses the heating switch. Suddenly, there is a loud explosion and the hairdrier bursts into flames. Steed, waiting outside in his car, hears the explosion and rushes to Carol's rescue. He takes her back to his apartment and when she revives he tells her that fortunately, the extra current had blown the hairdrier's fuses and saved her life. He has also discovered that Jean, one of the salon assistants, and not Carol, was meant to be the next under the hairdrier. Visiting the salon, Steed questions another of the assistants, Denise, and learns that the salon is near bankruptcy. Leaving, he spots Jacques Beronne talking to a man called Mendelssohn, a convicted criminal. Carol questions Jean, who tells her to come to her flat later that evening. But their conversation is overheard by Olive Beronne, and when Steed and Carol arrive at Jean's flat they find she has been strangled. When he discovers that the Beronnes are about to leave for Paris, Steed intercepts them at the station and Jacques confesses that the salon will be set on fire that evening so that the Beronnes can collect the insurance. Meanwhile, Denise has told Carol that she suspects Mendelssohn of intended arson, and together they drive to the salon to stop him. They are both saved from being burned alive when Steed arrives and knocks out Mendelssohn as he is about to light the fuse to an incendiary bomb.

HUNT THE MAN DOWN

Teleplay by Richard Harris

John Steed	Patrick Macnee
Paul Stacey	Maurice Good
Dr David Keel	Ian Hendry
Carol Wilson	Ingrid Hafner
Stella Preston	Melissa Stribling
Nurse Wyatt	Susan Castle

Designed by Robert Fuest
Produced by Leonard White
Directed by Peter Hammond

WHEN Frank Preston is released after a long prison sentence for robbery, the proceeds of which (more than £100,000), have never been traced, he drives to a sewer in which he had hidden the money, but is disturbed and attacked by two thugs, Stacey and Rocky, who then try to force him to reveal where the money is hidden. Preston is rescued by John Steed, who has been assigned to follow Preston and find the stolen loot. Steed takes the injured man to Dr Keel's surgery, and under anaesthetic and in delirium, Preston murmurs 'That's where we hid it'. Unknown to Keel and Steed, Stella, Preston's wife, who has been brought to the surgery by Steed, has joined forces with Stacey and Rocky and tells them she thinks Keel knows where the money is buried. The two thugs kidnap Keel's receptionist, Carol, and tell Keel that she will be killed unless he divulges the whereabouts of the money. Keel tells Steed of the threat, and he promises to use his department's resources to find the thugs' hideout. Before he can do so, however, Preston, worried about his wife, breaks out of hospital and arrives home to see her kissing Stacey. He goes to Keel's surgery and, at gunpoint, forces Keel to give him further medical attention and then enlists his help in finding the money. He and Keel then drive to an entrance to the sewer and go down, followed by Stacey and Rocky, who have brought Carol along as hostage. When Preston finds the money, there is a chase through the sewers and finally Preston and Dr Keel are cornered by the thugs. Steed arrives with the police in tow, the thugs are arrested and Carol is freed.

PLEASE DON'T FEED THE ANIMALS

Teleplay by Dennis Spooner

John Steed	Patrick Macnee
Felgate	Tenniel Evans
Carol Wilson	Ingrid Hafner
Dr Keel	Ian Hendry
Christine	Carole Boyer
Kollakis	Harry Ross
Renton-Stephens	Alastair Hunter
Yvonne	Catherine Ellison
Sarah	Genevieve Lyons
Barman	Mark Baker

Designed by Patrick Downing
Produced by Leonard White
Directed by Dennis Vance

FELGATE, a minor Whitehall civil servant dealing with secret cyphers, is being blackmailed by the owner of a Soho club. He is being watched by Steed, who has been planted in the same office. Steed and Dr Keel follow Felgate to a private zoo in the country where he throws a packet of the blackmail money into the reptile pit. Though Steed keeps close watch on the package, it mysteriously disappears. The next day, the blackmailer, finding Felgate has no money left, orders him to steal a top-secret file from his office. Felgate refuses and the club owner has him beaten up, but Dr Keel saves the civil servant from serious injury. Later at the club, Steed, knowing the conversation is being recorded, allows himself to be put into an embarrassing position with one of the club hostesses. He is soon contacted by the blackmailer who threatens Steed about the recording and orders him to steal the secret file. Acting on written instructions, Steed throws the package (containing false secret information) into the reptile pit of the zoo. Keel, keeping watch, sees a small monkey enter the pit and make off with the package. Questioning the zoo manager and his daughter, Steed decides that though they have no knowledge of the affair the girl's pet monkey was the one used to collect the packages. He discovers that a girl who runs the drinks kiosk next to the reptile pit, is friendly with the daughter, and the monkey plays party tricks for her and her customers at the kiosk. Steed discovers that the girl is the ringleader behind the blackmail gang and she is arrested.

DANCE WITH DEATH

Teleplay by Peter Ling and Sheilagh Ward

Dr David Keel	Ian Hendry
Carol Wilson	Ingrid Hafner
Elaine Bateman	Caroline Blakiston
Trevor Price	David Sutton
Beth Wilkinson	Angela Douglas
Major Caswell	Ewan Roberts
Valerie Marne	Pauline Shepherd
Mrs Marne	Diana King
Philip Anthony	Geoffrey Palmer
John Steed	Patrick Macnee
Porter	Norman Chappell

Designed by James Goddard
Produced by Leonard White
Directed by Don Leaver

ELAINE Bateman, the owner of a ballroom dancing school, is gassed. When Dr Keel revives her, she insists that someone is trying to murder her. The police say that though she has already reported one attempt on her life, they have been unable to prove her story. Keel, however, is sympathetic and puts her under his care. Visiting the dancing school, he meets Elaine's partner, Major Caswell, and the school pianist, Anthony, and is forced to intervene when one of the pupils, Price (who is in love with Elaine), gets jealous. During the rumpus, Keel drops his scarf but next day when he returns to collect it, he finds it has been used to strangle Elaine. Steed, when told, promises to help clear Keel's name. Steed enrols as a student at the school and meets the rich Mrs Marne and her spoiled young daughter, Valerie. Anthony's face seems familiar to Steed, who checks the files and tells Keel that the man was acquitted years ago of murdering his wife. Steed, however, is convinced that the man was guilty. He is also wanted by the police for a more recent crime. However, when Steed and the police go to arrest Anthony, they find he has eloped with Valerie — and her mother's diamonds. Steed tells Keel that the man is suspected of electrocuting his victims in the bath, and they set out to find him. Meanwhile, in a hotel room, Anthony, having first confirmed with the infatuated Valerie that the diamonds are in her possession, suggests that she has a nice hot bath. Keel visits the dancing school and catches Price searching Anthony's belongings for evidence that Anthony has been blackmailing him. Fortunately, Price has discovered where Anthony has taken Valerie, and Keel drives frantically to the hotel. He meets Steed there, who, having had Anthony's taxi traced, has arrived before him. They break into the room just in time to save Valerie from electrocution and arrest Anthony.

ONE FOR THE MORTUARY

Teleplay by Brian Clemens

Benson	Peter Madden
John Steed	Patrick Macnee
Dr David Keel	Ian Hendry
Carol Wilson	Ingrid Hafner
Scott	Ronald Wilson
Pallaine	Dennis Edwards
Yvette Declair	Malou Pantera
Dubois	Frank Gatliff
Maid	Irene Bradshaw
Bernard Bourg	Toke Townley

Designed by Robert Fuest
Produced by Leonard White
Directed by Peter Hammond

STEED has to get an important new medical formula to a health conference abroad. Unknown to Dr Keel, Steed conceals the formula, in microdot form, on a document belonging to one of Keel's partners. Keel will take it with him when he attends the conference in Geneva. On the flight, Keel meets a girl who is taken ill and after attending to her, he invites her to go to the conference with him, unknowingly giving her the invitation card on which the medical formula is hidden. When Steed arrives in Geneva, he finds Keel is under arrest. He has been accused by the police of murdering a man who was actually killed by one of the thugs seeking the formula. Keel is released into Steed's custody and Keel takes him to meet the girl at his hotel, but when they arrive she has gone. Keel remembers that the girl said she was going to visit her uncle, and he goes to the address, but finds only a weird taxidermist who says he has never heard of the girl. He suggests, however, that Keel has confused his name with that of a nearby town. Keel traces the girl and makes an appointment to see her. Steed and Keel visit the girl's room and Keel is astonished when Steed informs them of the importance of the invitation card. Steed then phones a doctor to whom the formula was meant to be delivered. But the doctor arrives accompanied by two heavies. He confesses that he is behind the attempts to steal the formula and intends to sell it to the highest bidder. His plans are foiled by the arrival of the police, and Steed takes possession of the formula until a new, safe, contact can be made.

THE SPRINGERS

Teleplay by John Whitney and Geoffrey Bellman

John Steed	Patrick Macnee
Dr David Keel	Ian Hendry
One-Ten	Douglas Muir
Pheeney	David Webb
Straker	Charles Farrell
Haslam	Brian Murphy
Mr Groves	Arthur Howard
Caroline Evans	Margo Andrew
Neame	Donald Morley

Designed by Alpho O'Reilly
Produced by Leonard White
Directed by Don Leaver

STEED asks Dr Keel to impersonate a convict who he believes will shortly be helped to escape from a particular prison. Steed is anxious to trap the organisers of the escape route who will help any prisoner, even the dangerous ones, providing they have the funds to pay their price. Keel enters the prison and he soon receives a message giving a date for the escape. Believing that the escape route is by water, Steed visits a town served by a canal. A clue leads him to a girls' finishing school, and masquerading, with a young female agent, as father and daughter, they visit the school. However, Steed cannot be sure that this is to be Keel's destination. Later, Keel, helped by a warder, makes his escape, while at the finishing school, Neame, the gang's organiser, catches Steed trying to break into the school to find information. When Steed fails to return to his hotel room, his female partner informs Steed's superior, One-Ten, but he tells her that to rescue Steed at this point would jeopardise the whole project. Meanwhile, Steed tries to convince Neame that he is simply a thief, but he is locked in a room at the school. When Keel is brought there, they devise an escape. When one of the gang recognises Keel as an impostor, however, it is left to Steed's quick-thinking to get them out of their predicament. The super-cool Steed soon outwits the gang and Neame is placed under arrest.

THE FRIGHTENERS

Teleplay by Berkely Mather

Moxon	Philip Locke
Deacon	Willoughby Goddard
John Steed	Patrick Macnee
Carol Wilson	Ingrid Hafner
Dr David Keel	Ian Hendry
Jeremy de Willoughby	Philip Gilbert
Nigel	David Andrews
Sir Thomas Waller	Stratford Johns
Marilyn Waller	Dawn Beret
Mrs Briggs	Doris Hare

Designed by Robert Fuest
Produced by Leonard White
Directed by Peter Hammond

STEED and Keel are on the trail of an organisation which arranges the beating-up of subjects for money, and intercept two thugs who have been hired to beat-up a young society man, Jeremy de Willoughby. When de Willoughby refuses to press charges, Steed and Keel try to learn something from one of the thugs, but he refuses to divulge anything. Keel, however, tricks him into leading him to the hideout of the organiser, who is known as the Deacon. Keel learns that the Deacon has been paid by a business tycoon, Sir Thomas Waller, to prevent de Willoughby from marrying his daughter. Steed, meanwhile, makes enquiries about de Willoughby and discovers that he is a 'professional marrier'. Meanwhile, Waller refuses to pay the Deacon his fee because de Willoughby has not been frightened off. The Deacon now decides to settle with Waller. Dr Keel invites de Willoughby and his fiancée, Marilyn Waller, to his home to arrange their elopement. While they are there, a scruffy woman appears, claiming to be de Willoughby's mother. Now, faced with Marilyn's disenchantment and the threat of arrest by her father, de Willoughby flees. Keel pays off de Willoughby's 'mother' — an actress hired for the occasion — and the police arrest the Deacon before he and his men can carry out their threat on Waller.

Steed burns the formula, which he had initially secreted on an invitation card, in **One For The Mortuary.**

THE YELLOW NEEDLE

Teleplay by Patrick Campbell

Sir Wilberforce Lungi	Andre Dakar
Dr David Keel	Ian Hendry
Carol Wilson	Ingrid Hafner
Inspector Anthony	Eric Dodson
Jacquetta Brown	Margaret Whiting
John Steed	Patrick Macnee
Chief Bai Shebro	Bari Johnson
Ali	Wolfe Morris

Designed by Alpho O'Reilly
Produced by Leonard White
Directed by Don Leaver

AN attempt is made on the life of Sir Wilberforce Lungi, an African leader visiting London for friendly negotiations leading to independence for his country, Tenebra. Steed asks Dr Keel, an old friend of Lungi's, to help his investigations of Lungi's secretary/companion, Jacquetta Brown. Steed flies to Tenebra, in the guise of a journalist, to meet Lungi's rival and enemy, Chief Bai Shebro, a passionate tribal nationalist. Keel finds Steed was right to suspect Jacquetta Brown. In Africa, Steed is befriended by a servant, and one of Shebro's wives, Judith, both of whom know and like Keel. Steed gathers more information which points to Jacquetta's unreliability. Shebro discovers Steed's impersonation is false and has him arrested and held prisoner. Judith helps Steed escape, and tells him that a final attempt is to be made on Lungi's life some time during the next 48 hours. In London, Jacquetta (who is a member of a sinister African secret society) substitutes a dose of yellow fever for the insulin with which Lungi has to inject himself. Steed rings Keel to say that he is not to leave Lungi for the next 48 hours. The call, however, is overheard by Jacquetta, and she drugs Keel. Steed returns the following morning, and overpowers Jacquetta as she tries to give Keel a second dose of the drug.

DEATH ON THE SLIPWAY

Teleplay by James Mitchell

Kolchek	Peter Arne
Dr David Keel	Ian Hendry
John Steed	Patrick Macnee
Sir William Bonner	Frank Thornton
Liz Wells	Nyree Dawn Porter
Sam Pearson	Paul Dawkins
Fleming	Sean Sullivan
Geordie Wilson	Redmond Bailey
Jack	Robert G Bahey
Insp Georgeson	Barry Keegan
PC Butterworth	Tom Adams
One-Ten	Douglas Muir
Pardoe	Gary Watson
PC Geary	Patrick Conner
Sgt Brodie	Hamilton Dyce
Chandler	Billy Milton

Designed by Robert Fuest
Produced by Leonard White
Directed by Peter Hammond

STEED is sent, masquerading as a metallurgist, to a dockyard where a nuclear submarine is being built. A secret service man has been murdered there by a foreign spy, Kolchek, an old enemy of Steed's, who wants the plans of the submarine's reactor and is being helped by Fleming, the yard's personnel manager. Kolchek recognises Steed and arranges an accident for him but to no avail. Worried that time is running out, Kolchek orders Fleming to place a time-bomb in his briefcase and leave it on board the submarine during his next inspection. Steed returns to his hotel room to find Liz, Fleming's secretary, searching his suitcase — she believes he is a snooping detective. She explains that Fleming was once her lover and that a year ago his drunken driving killed a child. Steed now suspects that Fleming is being blackmailed into treachery by Kolchek and when an astute policeman observes that Fleming has left his briefcase behind, Steed realises that a bomb may be on board, and goes to search for the briefcase. Meanwhile, Kolchek, believing that Liz suspects him, locks her in a cupboard. Steed manages to find the deadly briefcase and hurries to confront Fleming with the evidence, only to see Kolchek pull a gun on Fleming. Kolchek turns the gun on Steed as he enters, but Fleming knocks the gun from his hand. Steed then throws the briefcase into the water, where the bomb explodes, harming no one.

Steed faces Death On The Slipway *when he visits a dockyard where a nuclear submarine is being built.*

Dr Keel is asked by Steed to impersonate a convict who is going to escape from prison, in The Springers.

DOUBLE DANGER

Teleplay by Gerald Verner

Mark Crawford	Charles Hodgson
Harry Dew	Robert Mill
Al Brady	Peter Reynolds
Bert Mills	Ronald Pember
Dr David Keel	Ian Hendry
Carol Wilson	Ingrid Hafner
Lola Carrington	Vanda Hudson
John Steed	Patrick Macnee
Bruton	Kevin Brennan
Bartholomew	Gordon Phillott

Designed by James Goddard
Produced by Leonard White
Directed by Roger Jenkins

STEED is investigating the theft of a fortune in diamonds from Hatton Garden. He believes that the raid was carried out by a well-organised gang of diamond thieves who have recently pulled off major robberies in all the diamond centres of the world. When one of Dr Keel's patients, dying from gunshot wounds, whispers the words 'Hot Ice', Steed and Keel are soon in earnest pursuit of the gang.

Dr Keel stumbles into the thick of a call-girl racket and asks Steed to help him, in Toy Trap.

TOY TRAP

Teleplay by Bill Strutton

John Steed	Patrick Macnee
Dr David Keel	Ian Hendry
May Murton	Hazel Graeme
Henry Burge	Tony van Bridge
Alice	Nina Marriott
Bunty Seton	Sally Smith
Mrs McCabe	Ann Tirard
Freddie	Brandon Brady
Johnnie	Brian Jackson
Photographer	Lionel Burns
Lennie Taylor	Tex Fuller
Ann	Mitzi Rogers

Designed by Douglas James
Produced by Leonard White
Directed by Don Leaver

BUNTY, daughter of a country doctor, who is a friend of Dr Keel, is working in a large department store. Worried by the disappearance of her friend May, she asks Keel for his help. Keel believes May is involved in a call-girl racket and enlists Steed's help in finding her. The trail leads to an ex-shop girl, Chrissie, and when she is murdered, Keel tells Steed he is worried about Bunty's safety. Steed visits the department store and learns from the supervisor, Hearn, that Chrissie had recently stopped working there. Meanwhile, Keel visits the hostel where the shop girls live, and is warned off by the housekeeper, Mrs McCabe. Steed learns that one of the store's assistants, Lennie, has a criminal record, and he and Keel trail him to his apartment. When Lennie leaves, they enter and find Bunty's friend May. May says that Lennie has been hiding her from the boss of the call-girl organisation. Steed asks Bunty to act as a decoy and pretend that she is interested in the gang's offer to work as a call-girl. Bunty is soon approached by the boss of the gang – Mrs McCabe. Steed arrives with the police and Mrs McCabe is arrested.

THE TUNNEL OF FEAR

Teleplay by John Kruse

Maxie Lardner	Stanley Platts
Jack Wickram	John Salew
Dr David Keel	Ian Hendry
Carol Wilson	Ingrid Hafner
Harry Black	Murray Hayne
John Steed	Patrick Macnee
One-Ten	Douglas Muir
Mrs Black	Doris Rogers
Madame Zenobia	Nancy Roberts
Claire	Miranda Connell
Billy	Douglas Rye
Sergeant	Morris Perry

Designed by James Goddard
Produced by Leonard White
Directed by Guy Verney

WHEN an escaped convict, Harry Black, appears at Dr Keel's surgery bearing injuries caused by broken glass, Steed investigates and discovers that Black, who insists he was framed, has recently been working in a funfair at Southend. Steed tells Keel that top-secret information has been leaked to foreign countries, and it seems that Southend is the source of the leaks. He tells Keel to go to the funfair and make enquiries about Black, while Steed gets a job at the fairground. When Black returns to the funfair, his former colleague, Maxie, tips off the police. Keel, having visited Black's mother who also says that her son was framed, helps Black, who takes refuge on board the boat of his girlfriend, Claire. Maxie soon becomes suspicious of Steed and informs his boss, Wickram, who sets a trap. Maxie knocks Steed out in his hotel room. Steed is then hypnotised by a fairground hypnotist, working for Wickram, but he will not divulge any information. Keel, meanwhile, has realised that Black must have been hypnotised and framed, in order to get him out of the way. He drives to Claire's boat, where Black tells him that Claire has been kidnapped by Wickram and his henchmen. They rush to the funfair and find Claire and Steed trussed and gagged in the tunnel of the Ghost Train, with a machine which is tapping information from a telephone line to Europe. Disturbed and threatened by Wickram, they are saved when Steed conducts a gigantic bluff with an apparently explosive cigarette. Keel and Steed soon overpower the rest of the gang and end the leaks.

THE FAR DISTANT DEAD

Teleplay by John Lucarotti

Zun Garcia	Reed de Rouen
Dr David Keel	Ian Hendry
Dr Ampara Alverez	
Sandoval	Katharine Blake
Hercule Zeebrugge	Francis de Wolff
Rayner	Tom Adams
Godoy	Andreas Malandrinos
Mateos	Michael Mellinger
Inspector Gauvreau	Guy Deghby

Designed by Robert Fuest
Produced by Leonard White
Directed by Peter Hammond

RETURNING to England from Chile, Dr Keel's flight stops over in Mexico City and, learning that a cyclone has struck a small Mexican sea-port, he volunteers to help the victims. En route, he meets a young Mexican woman doctor who is also going to help the disaster victims. Keel and the woman soon decide to continue their journey together. At the emergency hospital in the town, a patient is brought in suffering from severe food poisoning, and Keel discovers that the cooking oil flown in as rations is, in fact, hydraulic fluid. He learns that the oil was donated by an old warehouseman who had been storing the tins for an unknown customer. Returning to his hotel room, Keel finds an anonymous letter, informing him that the first victim of the cooking oil died in Vera Cruz two years before. In Vera Cruz, Keel and the woman doctor visit the victim's widow, who tells them that her husband stole the oil from a tramp steamer. A check with the shipping company shows that the oil came from Marseilles. In Marseilles, they meet a man named Caron who tells them that the oil came from Zeebrugge. Keel's companion discovers that this is not the port of Zeebrugge, but the name of a financier and, making an excuse to Keel, she leaves. Keel soon discovers his mistake and finds the financier's address. He drives to Zeebrugge's home in time to stop the woman doctor taking revenge for the deaths of the villagers by killing the financier. Sympathetic to her cause, however, he allows her to escape before calling the police to arrest Zeebrugge.

KILL THE KING

Teleplay by James Mitchell

King Tenuphon	Burt Kwouk
Prince Serrakit	James Goei
General Tuke	Patrick Allen
Mei Li	Lisa Peake
John Steed	Patrick Macnee
Crichton-Bull	Peter Barkworth
Dr Keel	Ian Hendry
Carol	Ingrid Hafner
Zoe Carter	Moira Redmond
Major Harrington	Ian Colin
Ingrid Storm	Carole Shelley
U Meng	Andy Ho
Suchong	Eric Young

Designed by Paul Bernard
Produced by Leonard White
Directed by Roger Jenkins

KING Tenuphon, who is in London to sign an oil treaty, is threatened with assassination by dissidents in his country, and Steed is instructed to guard him until the treaty is signed. An attempt has already been made on the King's life when, on the plane carrying him to England, a steward tried to shoot him, wounding instead Prince Serrakit, the King's adviser. The steward was killed by Tuke, the royal bodyguard. Meanwhile, a Major Harrington arrives at a flat opposite the King's hotel suite and tells the owner, Mrs Carter, that her husband – a missing secret service agent – will be shot unless she lets him use her window to shoot the King. Steed discovers that U Meng, leader of the dissidents, has paid someone to carry out the killing. Worried that the King may be shot by a sniper close to the hotel, Steed checks for possible sniper points. But when he arrives at Mrs Carter's boarding-house, she tells him nothing of Major Harrington. Later that day, a low-flying helicopter attracts the King and his entourage to their hotel balcony. Suspicious, Steed throws himself at the King just as Major Harrington shoots from across the street. Prince Serrakit is killed, and the King's bodyguard, Tuke, shoots the major.

Juno, a Great Dane trained by Barbara Woodhouse, was a regular member of the cast of the first series.

DEAD OF WINTER
The Case of the Happy Camper

Teleplay by Eric Paice

Harry	**John Woodvine**
Syd	**Blaise Wyndham**
Schneider	**Carl Duering**
John Steed	**Patrick Macnee**
Dr David Keel	**Ian Hendry**
Dr Brennan	**David Hart**
Inez	**Sheila Robins**
Carol Wilson	**Ingrid Hafner**
Willi	**Michael Sarne**
Margarita	**Zorenah Osborne**
Weber	**Neil Hallett**
Ted	**Norman Chappell**
Kreuzer	**Arnold Marle**

Designed by Robert Fuest
Produced by Leonard White
Directed by Don Leaver

STEED investigates when the body of Gerhardt Schneider, a wanted Nazi war criminal who had tried to raise a new Fascist party to be called Phoenix, is discovered among the deep-frozen consignment of meat unloaded at the London docks. Having questioned the dockers and Weber, the head of the meat importing firm, about the body, Steed and Dr Keel go to the mortuary where Dr Brennan, a friend of Keel's, is to do the autopsy on Schneider's body. On arrival, however, they find the body gone and Brennan murdered. Steed persuades Keel to impersonate a doctor member of Phoenix who is about to arrive in London. Willi, a young member of Phoenix, takes Keel to the distinguished Dr Kreuzer, who shows him Schneider's body. To Keel's amazement the body blinks and sits up. Kreuzer explains that he can suspend life by deep-freezing and later resuscitate his patients. But he knows Keel to be a fraud, and has him bound and gagged and made ready for his next experiment. Steed meanwhile receives a visitor – Margarita, Willi's girlfriend, and she takes him to Keel. They arrive at the docks, where Steed is attacked by Kreuzer's henchmen. The dockers, however, have been primed by Steed and make a surprise rescue. Steed is in time to prevent his friend from being used in Kreuzer's experiment and releases him from his cold-room prison. Phoenix is totally destroyed and Keel's only after-effect is a cold.

THE DEADLY AIR

Teleplay by Lester Powell

Barbara Anthony	**Ann Bell**
Dr Philip Karswood	**Michael Hawkins**
Heneger	**Keith Anderson**
John Steed	**Patrick Macnee**
Herbert Truscott	**Richard Butler**
Dr David Keel	**Ian Hendry**
Dr Hugh Chalk	**Allan Cuthbertson**
Dr Owen Craxton	**John Stratton**
One-Ten	**Douglas Muir**
Carol Wilson	**Ingrid Hafner**
Dr Harvey	**Cyril Renison**
Keo Armstrong	**Anthony Cundell**
Professor Kilbride	**Geoffrey Bayldon**

Designed by Robert Macgowan
Produced by Leonard White
Directed by John Knight

STEED and Dr Keel are called in when Heneger, a scientist working on top-secret experiments to prove a vaccine for a serious disease, is attacked and a whole batch of the precious vaccine wasted. Two other scientists, Chalk and Craxton, decide on a final test of the vaccine, but one of the doctors enclosed in a hygienic test room collapses with a fatal dose of the disease. It is suspected that the vaccine is faulty, but when a monkey is injected, it remains healthy, leading Dr Keel to suspect sabotage. Investigating the machinery used in the test, Steed finds traces of glass inside the air duct that feeds sterilised air into the test chamber. He tells Keel he believes the man was murdered by a phial of the vaccine being broken and introduced into the air-feed to the room. Steed and Keel volunteer to carry out the next test when, unaccountably, the air intake fan begins to work, and the door is locked from the outside. An engineer in charge returns to find that Heneger is responsible for the murder attempt. Heneger, however, shoots the engineer and makes his escape. Fortunately, the engineer manages to shut off the air to the test room and release the door, before dying. Steed finds an unbroken phial of the vaccine taped to the fan blade and has it analysed. The vaccine is proved to be over 100 times more potent than the rest of the batch, and Steed seeks the help of Professor Kilbride. Then the remaining six phials of the vaccine are stolen. Heneger next tries to kill the Professor, but Keel prevents him by throwing the contents of a test-tube in his face. Heneger now admits his part in the crime but says that Dr Craxton is the mastermind behind the murders. He wants to discredit the vaccine so he can sell it, suitably disguised, elsewhere. Craxton, meanwhile, has trapped Steed in the test room, taped a new phial to the intake fan, and set it working. Keel manages to rescue his partner, who now believes that this time he has received a fatal dose, and hasn't long to live. Truscott, head of the project, says the phial used by Craxton was harmless – he had taken the six lethal ones home and replaced them with phials of pure water. Craxton is arrested by the security guards.

In **Dead Of Winter***, Willi introduces Dr Keel to Dr Kreuzer, who deep-freezes his patients and later resuscitates them!*

A CHANGE OF BAIT

Teleplay by Lewis Davidson

Archie Duncan	**Victor Platt**
Lemuel Potts	**John Bailey**
Peter Sampson	**Henry Soskin**
Carol Wilson	**Ingrid Hafner**
John Steed	**Patrick Macnee**
Herb Thompson	**Robert Desmond**
Nat Fletcher	**Graham Rigby**
Dr David Keel	**Ian Hendry**
Barker	**Gary Hope**
André	**Arthur Barrett**
Bryan Stubbs	**Norman Pitt**
Ivy	**Gillian McCutcheon**
Charlie	**Harry Shacklock**
Steed's helper	**Michael Hunt**

**Designed by James Goddard
Produced by Leonard White
Directed by Don Leaver**

ARCHIE, an elderly man seriously ill with a heart disease, has bought a cargo of bananas which he hopes to sell at a profit. But Potts, a crooked businessman, knowing Archie's difficulty in finding a buyer, organises a sale. But he then tells Sampson, a shop steward at the docks, to organise a strike so that Barstow, another businessman to whom Potts offers the bananas, will be able to claim insurance when the fruit goes rotten. Keel, called in when Archie has a heart attack, discovers that Steed already knows about Potts' scheme. Steed blackmails Sampson into calling off the strike, and arranges that when Potts telephones Barstow to warn him that the fruit will be delivered after all, Steed himself takes the message. Barstow is now forced to accept delivery of the rotten bananas, and it seems that Potts will now have to pay Archie for the consignment. Potts, however, decides to delay payment until Archie's heart gives out from the suspense. Steed, realising this, decides to take part in another of Potts' shady deals – a plan to set alight an antique shop for the owner, who needs the insurance money. Steed and Keel conceal themselves in the shop and extinguish the flames. The shop keeper, furious, telephones Potts, who hurries to the shop, and is photographed by Steed as he is about to re-start the fire. Once arrested, he is invited by Steed to telephone Barstow, incriminating him. Steed explains that if he does this he will be allowed to telephone the bank and stop Archie's cheque. Potts telephones Barstow, but when he tries to phone his bank, discovers that Steed has put the clock forward, and the bank is not yet open. As the police take Potts away, Steed gives Archie his cheque while Keel breaks into laughter.

DRAGONSFIELD

Teleplay by Terence Feely

John Steed	**Patrick Macnee**
Lisa Strauss	**Sylvia Langova**
Saunders	**Alfred Burke**
Redington	**Ronald Leigh-Hunt**
Susan Summers	**Barbara Shelley**
Jack Alford	**Thomas Kyffin**
Technician	**Keith Barron**
Secretary	**Amanda Reeves**
One-Fifteen	**Eric Dodson**
Boris	**Steven Scott**
Landlord	**Michael Robbins**
Peters	**Herbert Nelson**
Second Technician	**Morris Perry**

**Designed by Voytek
Produced by Leonard White
Directed by Peter Hammond**

STEED is sent to a research centre at which a team of scientists is working against time to produce a material which will shield space travellers from radiation. One of the scientists has recently been badly exposed to radiation, and cannot work. Steed discovers that Saunders, the unpopular security officer, has warned Dr Alford, one of the team, about fraternising with Susan Summers, his pretty assistant. Alford takes this badly, but Susan believes that Saunders is simply jealous. Later, Steed overhears a quarrel between Susan and another female member of the team, Lisa Strauss, whom Susan accuses of being in love with Dr Reddington, the head of the project. When Alford is attacked by an unknown assailant, Steed rescues him, though Alford receives injuries and is put out of action. Meanwhile, unknown to Steed, Saunders has managed to break the code used by the saboteurs, and sends a message making a rendezvous at the local pub. Arriving for the showdown, Saunders is captured and held at gunpoint by two thugs. In the meantime, Steed, having volunteered to act as a guinea-pig in an experiment, is almost killed when someone tampers with the laboratory equipment. From Saunders' report, Steed learns of the trap he has set and arrives at the pub to find Saunders has been taken away by two gunmen. He tracks them to a disused flour mill and arrives in time to disarm the gunmen and rescue Saunders. Steed forces one of them to reveal that the saboteur is Susan Summers and Steed quickly drives back to the research centre, while Saunders rings the authorities to arrest the gunmen. However, Lisa and Dr Reddington have just discovered a fatal error in their calculations. They agree to run one final test, assisted by Susan Summers. Steed arrives, to be told by Dr Reddington that Susan and Lisa have gone to the laboratory ahead of him to set up the experiment, and he gets there in time to stop Susan strangling Lisa.

Steed and Boris fight it out when Steed investigates an atomic research centre, in Dragonsfield.

Steed, Carol and Dr Keel discuss an important clue concerning a consignment of bananas in A Change Of Bait.

*Steed had three female colleagues to help him in the Department
– Mrs Cathy Gale, Mrs Emma Peel and Tara King – each of whom
were very different.*

*Above: Mrs Peel was very feline and dressed
in clothes which accentuated her cat-like
appearance and movement.*

*Right: Emma Peel worked with Steed in the
fourth and fifth series and is shown here in
Something In The Nursery.*

Above: Wearing her famous Emmapeelers, Emma Peel disposes of an opponent in The Living Dead.

Left: Mrs Catherine Gale shared her role of co-Avenger with Dr King and Venus Smith in the second series.

Left: Tara King was more likely to knock out her opponents with a champagne bottle than with karate and judo.

Above: Unlike her predecessors, Tara King was single. She lived by herself in a very fashionable flat.

Patrick Macnee/Honor Blackman
1962

A Licence To Thrill

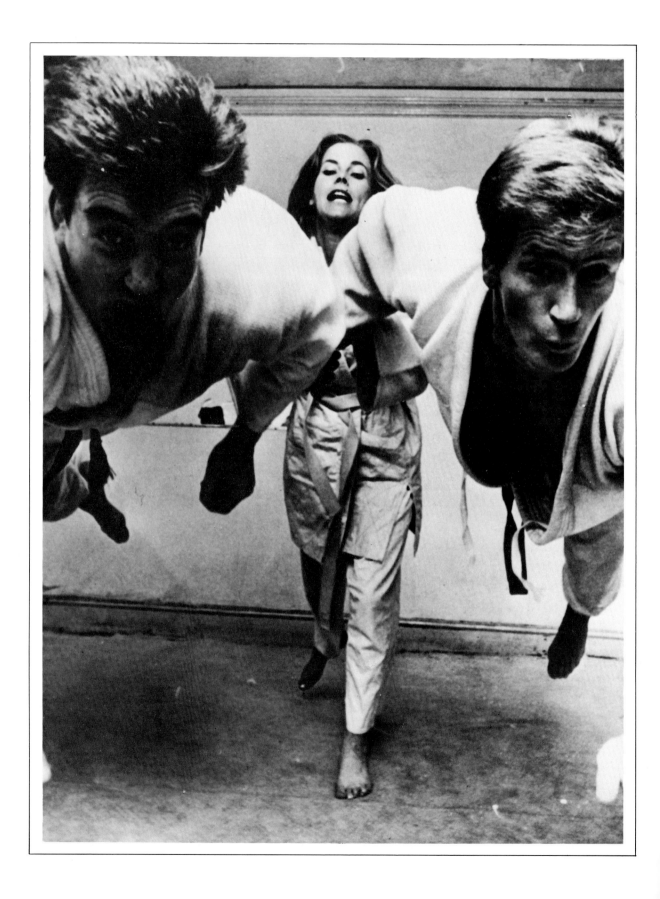

AN Equity strike interrupted the first year's run (Equity, the actor's union, forbade any of its members to appear in film work) and during the break Ian Hendry, having no wish to be typecast in a regular television series, dropped out. Finding that he had a half-dozen or so unused scripts commissioned for the first series, producer Leonard White decided to change the Keel role to that of a woman. He invented a character called Mrs Catherine Gale (based, so the story goes, on two famous women: Margaret Mead, the anthropologist, and Margaret Bourne-Smith, the photographer for *Life Magazine*).

Cathy Gale was to be a cool blonde with a PhD in anthropology, who had spent several years on an isolated Kenyan farm with her husband. When he was killed during a Mau Mau raid, she returned to Britain to take up a position at the British Museum. Unlike Steed, she was not a professional undercover agent, but her existence was known and accepted by Steed's superiors. Her resourcefulness and scientific knowledge, not to mention her skill at judo, were often in demand by Steed, but her attitude to any mission was totally different. The end could never justify the means to her, and she disliked Steed's cavalier treatment of people. Nevertheless, she assisted him as a crusading amateur with a genuine desire to help the victims of crime. An official writer's directive described her:

> *Cathy is an expert mechanic and photographer and drives a car (and motorcyle) fast and well — has a thorough knowledge of fire-arms and is highly skilled in their use. She is loyal, honest, compassionate, and essentially humanitarian — and in as much as she is quick-witted and very well able to look after herself, she is more than a match for anyone, including Steed. Unlike Steed, she finds it necessary to carry a gun, but when she has to tackle a criminal, she prefers to fight according to the rules, closing with him to use the classic judo methods in which she has been trained.*

After ABC had spent six months considering the right girl for the part, Honor Blackman was chosen to join Patrick Macnee in his fight against crime. Prior to the series being screened in September 1962, Honor said 'I'm a first for television. The first feminist to come into a television serial; the first woman to fight back. Cathy is all anthropologist, an academic, all brain and what she doesn't have in the way of brawn, she makes up for in motorbikes, black boots, leather combat suits and judo. We had enormous problems with re-writes at the beginning. Cathy was so wet I had to say "Look, write my part as if I were a man and I'll turn it into a woman's part."

Macnee's role was also revamped. Athough he had been wearing his Edwardian-style clothes for the final episodes of the Hendry series, the producer asked him to dandify the role more than ever. A return visit to his tailor brought him embroidered waistcoats, and a visit to a well-known London hatter brought a variety of bowlers.

'I design all my own Avenger suits,' Patrick said. 'I like the idea of velvet for the collars, it helps mould and complement the suits. There are no breast pockets and only one button to give the best moulding to the chest. Plus a deliberately low waist, to give the effect of simplicity, but with an individual style.' Expensive shirts, many of them striped, elegant embroidered waistcoats, expensive cuff-links and tie pins, plus hand-made Chelsea boots, completed the wardrobe. 'I visualised Steed as a modern-day Beau Brummell — with an iron exterior,' he said, 'and based him on a combination of Leslie Howard's Sir Percy Blakeney in *The Scarlet Pimpernel*, and a performance by Ralph Richardson in a film called *Q Planes*. In developing Steed's character, I considered one of the most important facets was to give him good manners. You did not complain about the food, you always opened doors for ladies. You could bash someone over the head but you always observed the social proprieties.

One of the contributing factors to the programme's success was the judo-influenced fighting style of Cathy Gale. Prior to the Blackman series, women who were in distress, or being attacked by thugs, had always been shown struggling or screaming. Suddenly, the viewer was confronted by a woman who not only stood her ground but, when attacked, frequently gave her assailant a sharp kick in the solar-plexus. Not to mention the occasional over-the-shoulder judo throw, and giving an all-systems-go display of self defence. Apparently, it wasn't a calculated plan on the part of the producers.

Originally, Cathy was to have carried a small .25 calibre pistol in her handbag. But after two or three weeks of Cathy reaching into her handbag yet again, they got bored with the gun's limitations and decided to change the format. They first tried fitting Cathy with a garter holster, but feminine though the garter proved, it made Honor walk bow-legged. (There was also the added drawback of Cathy having to raise her skirts every time she met a possible assailant.) Next they tried concealing firearms about her person. Under-arm holsters are fine for men, but they don't have breasts or tight-fitting sweaters. Miniature swords and daggers were the next idea, but they also proved no good — too many cut or broken bra straps. So they were left with purely physical attacks. Honor and Patrick were sent to see René Burdet, ex-head of the Resistance in Marseilles during the war, who taught them how to throw people. Later, Douglas Robinson, a Black Belt of the 9th Dan, taught Honor and Patrick the art of judo, and slowly, defence expertise was worked into their parts.

Right from the start of the new-style *Avengers*, ABC Television was convinced of one thing — that Cathy Gale should be a leader of fashion. So, when recording began in May 1962, fashion expert Michael Whittaker was asked to advise on how Cathy's clothes could keep ahead of current fashions throughout the coming winter season. He designed four basic outfits for Cathy, and predicted that tailored styles and high boots were coming into vogue. As this was absolutely in line with Cathy's character and the job she had to do, her entire wardrobe was planned with an eye to these trends. But her leather fighting gear came about by accident.

Honor Blackman told the press at the time, 'The leather thing was extraordinary. The fact that I happened to choose leather for my fighting kit was a pure accident. Cathy led a very active life and I soon realised that skirts were out of the question. When your legs are flying over your head, the last thing you want to worry about is whether your stocking-tops are

showing. It happened that right at the beginning of the series, I split my trousers in close-up, with my rear in full view of the camera. So it became obvious that I had to find some tougher gear. Somebody suggested suede, but we found that suede doesn't "light" on television. Then someone, Patrick, I think, suggested leather and after trying it, the producers said "Great", so I wore it throughout the rest of the show. The only things you can wear with leather trousers are boots, so they kitted me out with calf-length black boots, and the leather thing was born.'

Whereas the formula remained the same – a fast-moving crime hunt with plenty of off-beat twists and a strong vein of wacky humour, laced with an undercurrent of social conscience – this time Steed was to share his exploits with *three* new partners. They were all unofficial, and all much more concerned than he was with man's behaviour towards his fellow man.

Julie Stevens was signed to play Venus Smith, a bargee's daughter who had become a successful night-club singer. In this job she met and became friendly with Steed (whom she regarded as a somewhat eccentric older brother) and she was occasionally co-opted by him to help his fight against crime. Very different and much less sophisticated than Cathy, Venus was intrigued by the aura of mystery surrounding Steed, and helped him for the excitement of going places and doing things not otherwise possible to her. A natural brunette, Julie wore a blonde wig for the first few episodes, but later had her own hair dyed to a platinum blonde. She appeared in six of the 26 episodes.

When Dr David Keel went abroad on a fellowship, Steed co-opted the third new face, Dr Martin King. He was played by Jon Rollason. King was very like his predecessor – a determined young idealist with a strong sense of humour. But he did not have as much time as Keel for extramural activities, and featured in only three of the stories. It does, however, seem that the producers intended to continue the theme of the doctor and undercover agent format. Official studio information sheets show that the three Rollason episodes – *Mission To Montreal*, *Dead on Course*, and *The Sell-Out* – were made prior to the Blackman stories. The first Honor Blackman episode to be made was *Death Despatch*, perhaps due to Honor having prior commitments.

In the previous (Hendry) series, Steed was occasionally seen receiving orders from the mysterious One-Ten, played by Douglas Muir. One-Ten returns in this series, and in one episode is joined by One-Twelve, played by Arthur Hewlett.

Last in the 'new' team, was Freckles, a two-year-old dalmatian puppy, which replaced Juno, the Great Dane who was Steed's regular companion in the Hendry series. Juno was unfortunately killed in an accident on London's underground, while en route to film an *Avengers* story *Death Of A Great Dane*. The Great Dane used in the episode was Juno's sister, Junia. Both dogs were trained by Barbara Woodhouse.

MR TEDDY BEAR

PROPELLANT 23

Teleplay by Martin Woodhouse

Interviewer	**Tim Brinton**
Col Wayne-Gilley	**Kenneth Keeling**
John Steed	**Patrick Macnee**
Dr Gilmore	**John Horsley**
One-Ten	**Douglas Muir**
Catherine Gale	**Honor Blackman**
Henry	**Michael Robbins**
Mr Teddy Bear	**Bernard Goldman**
Café girl	**Sarah Maxwell**
Dr James Howell	**John Ruddock**

Story Editor John Bryce
Designed by Terry Green
Produced by Leonard White
Directed by Richmond Harding

COLONEL Wayne-Gilley is publicly murdered during a television interview. The method used is so diabolically clever that One-Ten is certain that the killer can only be Mr Teddy Bear – a professional assassin, of no political allegiance, who works for the side that pays him best. Steed's department has long been after the killer, and to finally trap him, One-Ten tells Cathy Gale to commission him to murder John Steed. Contact made, Cathy is summoned to a remote country house where she meets a toy teddy bear. The assassin's voice is relayed through the toy, and he agrees to kill Steed for £200,000. Cathy is asked to leave something as surety and places a diamond pendant on the desk, at the same time smuggling a cigarette case into her handbag. But it provides no clue to Teddy Bear's identity – it bears only the fingerprints of a chimpanzee. Via a false newspaper advertisement, Steed is lured to the apartment of an informer who has been helping in the hunt for the assassin, but he finds the informer dead. Disturbed, he returns to his flat. The telephone rings. It is Mr Teddy Bear, who informs Steed that he is dead – the phone has been smeared with a deadly poison which enters the skin's nerve endings. Steed struggles to inject the antidote and falls to the floor. Cathy now receives a bill for £200,000. She begins to wrap up the money but is interrupted by an old professor friend who tells her that he has been asked to collect a package and deliver it to a man named Bruin. As she hands over the package, the phone rings. It is Steed, who tells her to disregard the professor and meet him at a warehouse. Unknown to her, the caller is not Steed, but Steed's voice recorded earlier by Teddy Bear. At the warehouse, Cathy is held at gunpoint by the assassin. He tells her that although he knows she has tried to trick him, he couldn't kill a woman and offers Cathy a knockout pill to give him time to get away. Steed, now fully recovered, enters the warehouse and throws the bolt on the steel doors. Cathy snatches the assassin's gun and forces him to swallow one of his own knockout pills. Teddy Bear has, however, tricked them both. The knockout pills contain a fast-acting poison and he falls to the floor, dead.

Teleplay by Jon Manchip White

Jules Meyer	**Frederick Schiller**
Jeanette	**Justine Lord**
Capt Legros	**Nicholas Courtney**
Co-pilot	**Michael Beint**
Paul Manning	**Geoffrey Palmer**
Catherine Gale	**Honor Blackman**
John Steed	**Patrick Macnee**
Laure	**Catherine Woodville**
Jacques Tissot	**Trader Faulkner**
Lieut 'Curly' Leclerc	**John Crocker**
Siebel	**John Dearth**
Roland	**Ralph Nossek**
Pierre	**Barry Wilsher**
Gendarme	**Graham Ashley**
Shop assistant	**Deanna Shendery**
Baker	**John Gill**

Story Editor John Bryce
Designed by Paul Bernard
Produced by Leonard White
Directed by Jonathan Alwyn

STEED and Cathy are told to meet a passenger en route from Tripoli to Marseilles. He will be carrying a sample of a new liquid rocket fuel, Propellant 23. At Marseilles airport, they await the courier's arrival but as the man enters the airport customs centre, he collapses and dies. A silver liquor flask in his hand falls unnoticed among some flowers. The man's briefcase is confiscated by the customs officials, and a bottle of hair-restorer in it is given to a police officer, Curly, who suffers from baldness. Later, Steed breaks into the room where the briefcase is hidden. He finds the case but is attacked by Siebel, a foreign agent, already there. Steed soon overpowers the man and escapes with the briefcase. Meanwhile, Manning, an English passenger on the plane, has been questioning the stewardess about the dead man, and is told that he died from poisoning. Cathy has learned that Jacques, a hotel tout, was seen picking up a silver liquor flask. Then, the customs official tells her of the hair-restorer given to Curly. She goes to his flat, where she is disturbed by Siebel. She knocks him out and finds the bottle of hair-restorer – empty. Cathy reports to Steed and together they visit Jacques' apartment. On the floor they find the dead body of the air stewardess. Frantically, they search for the missing Jacques and he is finally found drinking in a bakery. Their recovery of the flask is interrupted by the arrival of Siebel and Manning. Cathy holds Siebel at gunpoint while Steed neatly disposes of Manning with a sharp tap from his umbrella.

Steed and Mrs Catherine Gale ponder over Mr Teddy Bear's next move when he is commissioned to kill Steed.

THE DECAPOD

Teleplay by Eric Paice

Girl in shower	Pamela Conway
Yakob Borb	Paul Stassino
Stepan	Philip Madoc
John Steed	Patrick Macnee
Bodyguards	{ Douglas Robinson { Valentine Musetti
Venus Smith	Julie Stevens
Cigarette girl	Valerie Stanton
Edna Ramsden	Lynne Furlong
Ito	Wolfe Morris
Harry Ramsden	Raymond Adamson
Guards officer	Harvey Ashby
and	The Dave Lee Trio

Story Editor John Bryce
Designed by Terry Green
Produced by Leonard White
Directed by Don Leaver

STEED is assigned to ensure the safety of Yakob Borb, President of the Balkan Republic, who is in London to negotiate a huge loan. When Borb's English secretary is murdered, Steed arranges for Venus Smith to take her place, allowing Venus to believe that Borb might grant her a singing tour of his country. Borb is a wrestling enthusiast, and he and Venus go to a fight where one of his bodyguards is wrestling The Decapod, a ten-limbed squid whose emblem is used by an old professional, Harry Ramsden. The bout is over in minutes, for The Decapod deliberately kills his opponent and escapes. Steed is told by Stepan, the Balkan Ambassador, that the bodyguards' death was meant to isolate Borb and warn him off completing the loan. Steed visits Ramsden's wife, who works at Venus' club. She says her husband is innocent. He then appears and says he was paid to keep away from the fight. The Decapod in the ring was an impostor. Borb and his second bodyguard, closely followed by Steed, are at the club watching Venus' cabaret act, when suddenly the lights go out. Borb and the bodyguard leave, and when Steed follows them, he finds Borb safe, but a Decapod mask is hanging in the cloakroom and the bodyguard is dead. Although he believes the bodyguard's death was his final warning, Borb insists on completing the loan. He then tells Venus that he has become infatuated with her, proposes to buy a luxury yacht and cruise the world, and will she join him? Venus says she will consider his offer. Steed, meanwhile, has accused Stepan of the murders and forces him to confess – he had engaged the bodyguards, not to protect Borb but to prevent him abandoning the Presidency. (Borb now wants only to live the life of a playboy.) Steed goes to the club, and finds himself face to face with the Decapod. As they begin to fight, Ramsden arrives and challenges The Decapod to one final bout. Ramsden wins and Steed lifts his mask to reveal Yakob Borb. Stepan, having followed Steed, learns of Borb's treachery and exacts his own justice on him by shooting the President.

BULLSEYE

Teleplay by Eric Price

Jean	Mitzi Rogers
Miss Ellis	Judy Parfitt
Brigadier	Charles Carson
Foreman	Robin Wentworth
Catherine Gale	Honor Blackman
Young	Felix Deebank
Reynolds	John Frawley
Shareholder	Graham Bruce
Karl	Bernard Kay
John Steed	Patrick Macnee
Dorothy Young	Laurie Leigh
Inspector	Fred Ferris

Story Editor John Bryce
Designed by Robert Macgowan
Produced by Leonard White
Directed by Peter Hammond

BRITISH weapons are being smuggled to trouble-spots abroad, creating a dangerous political situation. Steed arranges for Cathy, armed with 20 per cent of the shares, to join the Board of Anderson's Small Arms Ltd – a firm whose chairman has just been killed, and which is fighting a take-over bid from Calder, a tycoon. Cathy meets other board-members, including a Brigadier, and the super-efficient Miss Ellis. Cathy is invited to visit the butts and fire one of the new Anderson rifles. When she goes to collect her target, she finds the shot body of one of the directors. Though the death occurred before Cathy entered the butts, the murder bullet came from her rifle and hers are the only fingerprints on it, so the police are suspicious. Young, another board-member, invites Cathy aboard his powerful motor launch and tries to persuade her to sell him her shares. She refuses. Meanwhile, Calder visits the Brigadier and makes him a substantial offer for his shares. Later that day, the Brigadier is found in his office, dead. Suspecting Calder, Cathy visits his sumptuous office, and when he offers her a large sum for her shares, she accepts. He then informs her that the three dead directors sold out to him but they had been killed before they could implement the sale. Someone is desperate to stop his takeover. That evening, when Miss Ellis calls a shareholder's meeting, Calder (Cathy's shares giving him the necessary advantage) interrupts the meeting and calls for an immediate inventory and sales check. This move panics the criminals, Young, his wife, and their accomplice, Karl, into escaping in Young's boat. But before they can depart, Cathy denounces Miss Ellis as the ringleader and murderer. The rest of the gang are arrested and Steed is delighted at the outcome – Cathy's shares are now showing a handsome profit.

Venus Smith entertains Yakob Borb with her cabaret act at the nightclub where she works, in The Decapod.

Cathy becomes a shareholder of an arms firm but finds one of the directors has a mercenary target, in Bullseye.

MISSION TO MONTREAL

Teleplay by Lester Powell

Carla Berotti	Patricia English
Film director	Harold Berens
Peggy	Pamela Ann Davy
Brand	Alan Curtis
Receptionist	Angela Thorne
Pearson	Eric McCaine
Nicholson	Mark Eden
Stewards {	Peter Mackriel
	William Swan
Budge	Gerald Sim
Marson	John Bennett
Reporters {	Malcolm Taylor
	Terence Woodfield
	Leslie Pitt
Photographer	William Buck
Sheila Dowson	Iris Russell
Dr Martin King	Jon Rollason
Judy	Gillian Muir
John Steed	Patrick Macnee
Passenger	John Frawley
Barman	Allan Casley

Story Editor John Bryce
Designed by Terry Green
Produced by Leonard White
Directed by Don Leaver

STEED takes advantage of the fact that his friend Dr King needs a holiday, to put him aboard a luxury liner cruising to Canada, as private doctor to Carla Berotti. She is a beautiful but neurotic film actress whose stand-in was murdered, in London, in mistake for her. Steed also joins the crew as a steward. Dr King witnesses a secret meeting between Carla and the ship's Second Officer, Nicholson, which reduces Carla to tears. When telling Steed of this, he is informed that a microfilm of the Dew Line – the early-warning system in North America – has been stolen and Carla is suspected of carrying it for a group of agents. This disturbs King, for he likes Carla, and she has come to rely on him. Carla is frightened when Nicholson tells her that Brand, who murdered her stand-in, is on board. She hides the microfilm in a bottle of tablets and puts them in King's medicine bag. That night one of the guests passes out from too much drink and he is put into King's cabin to sleep it off. Next morning, he is found dead. While investigating, Steed discovers the microfilm in the medicine bottle, but Carla refuses to answer Dr King's questions, except to swear she meant him no harm. Later, Steed receives a message giving him the identification code used by the agents to contact each other. The code is used by Brand, and Sheila, Carla's secretary. Steed now tells Sheila, in confidence, that he has the microfilm and Carla is willing to divulge the necessary information to implicate the rest of the gang. Sheila and Brand decide Carla must die, and Nicholson is persuaded to do the deed. That night on deck, he takes Carla in his arms and attempts to throw her overboard, but Steed and King are waiting and save her. The gang are taken into custody. So is Carla, and a sad Dr King watches as she is taken down the gangplank at Montreal.

THE REMOVAL MEN
The Most Expensive Commodity

Teleplay by Roger Marshall and Jeremy Scott

Jack Dragna	Reed de Rouen
Bud Siegel	Edwin Richfield
Godard	Donald Tandy
John Steed	Patrick Macnee
Cecile Dragna	Patricia Denys
Binaggio	George Goderick
Venus Smith	Julie Stevens
One-Ten	Douglas Muir
Waiter	George Little
Jailer	Hugo de Vernier
Nicole Cauvin	Edina Ronay
Charlie	Hira Talfrey
Harbour officer	Ivor Dean
and	The Dave Lee Trio

Story Editor John Bryce
Designed by Patrick Downing
Produced by Leonard White
Directed by Don Leaver

WHEN an eminent British politician is murdered, Steed flies to the Riviera on the trail of a gang which kills for money. To be accepted into the gang, Steed gives himself a criminal record and robs the home of the gang boss, Dragna. But there is no vacancy, so Steed arranges for one of the gang members to be arrested. Dragna now admits Steed into the gang and tells him that in order to ensure the prisoner's silence one of the gang has entered the prison and killed him. At a local nightclub where Venus is appearing, Steed receives his first assignment – the murder of a young French film actress. Steed visits the girl, tells her of the murder plot, and says he knows of a safe hiding place. As they climb into the actress's car, Steed sees Venus. Not wishing to answer questions, Steed snubs her. Once the girl is safely hidden, Steed drives her sports car off a cliff and reports her successful killing to Dragna. He believes Steed, but next day Venus mentions her chance meeting with Steed and the actress to Siegal, the club owner. Siegal reports to Dragna that Steed was seen with the actress moments before her death and Dragna orders Venus to be silenced. Rebuked by Dragna for his carelessness in allowing Venus to see him with the actress, Steed is ordered to kill Venus. Meanwhile Siegal, suspicious of Steed, makes his own investigation to find out if the actress really is dead. Later that

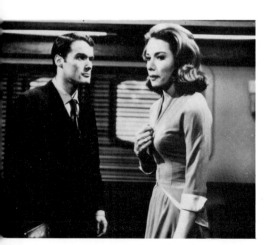

When Dr King is sent on a Mission To Montreal, his task is to protect the actress Carla Berotti.

When Juno was killed in an accident, Freckles took over the role of Steed's best canine friend.

THE MAURITIUS PENNY

day, he shows Dragna photographs he has taken that afternoon of the actress, alive and well, at the hideout, and Dragna orders the killing of both Steed and Venus. At the nightclub, Steed tries to warn Venus, but is unable to do so as Siegal keeps a close watch on both of them. Dragna enters and orders the club to be emptied. Once alone, Siegal pulls a gun on Steed. Dragna, however, not wishing to rush, orders Venus to make her final curtain call, and Venus is forced to sing for the gang boss. During one of her numbers she distracts his attention sufficiently for Steed to break free and in the ensuing fight both Siegal and Dragna are killed.

Teleplay by Malcolm Hulke and Terence Dicks

Goodchild	Philip Guard
Percy Peckham	Harry Shacklock
John Steed	Patrick Macnee
Catherine Gale	Honor Blackman
Boy	Anthony Rogers
Gerald Shelley	David Langton
Maitland	Edward Jewesbury
Brown	Alfred Burke
Lord Matterley	Richard Vernon
Porter	Raymond Hodge
Burke	Alan Rolfe
Andrews	Edward Higgins
Charlady	Grace Arnold
Lorry driver	Edwin Brown
Lorry driver's mate	Anthony Blackshaw
Miss Power	Delia Corrie
Sheila Gray	Sylvia Langova
Foreign delegate	Theodore Wilhelm

Story Editor John Bryce
Designed by Philip Harrison
Produced by Leonard White
Directed by Richmond Harding

WHEN the Mauritius Penny, a very rare stamp, is offered for sale in an ordinary sale catalogue, a stamp collector informs Steed, and is killed for his trouble. Steed visits the stamp dealer's shop and gets a lead to the stamp auction room where he meets Lord Matterley, a rich collector, and Shelley, owner of the auction room – and secretly second-in-command of a secret organisation. Shelley decides that Goodchild, the stamp dealer's assistant, who has panicked after the murder, is a risk, and has him killed during the auction. Steed and Cathy find more dealers' lists in the dead man's pockets and realise that all the stamps offered form a coded message. Cathy gets a job at the stamp shop but Brown, Goodchild's murderer, discovers she is working for Steed and tries to kill her. Cathy overpowers him and in his pocket finds an invitation to a philatelic convention at the auction room. Meanwhile Steed keeps an appointment written in Goodchild's diary, and finds himself at a lady dentist's. She doesn't know Goodchild, but

when she checks his dental chart against Steed's teeth, she realises he is a fake and anaesthetises him. Steed recovers, and is questioned and threatened by Shelley. But a lorry driver who has come to collect a packing case rescues him. He tells Steed that he has been carrying packing cases to and from the shop all week. One case fell open and it was full of guns. Cathy has discovered that the convention is really a planning meeting for an extremist political group, heavily armed, which plans to take over the country and begin New Rule. Brown, recovered, arrives and Cathy is caught and questioned. But Steed has been delivered to the convention by the driver and he breaks out of the packing case in time to rescue Cathy. The head of the organisation arrives – it is Lord Matterley. Steed and Cathy overpower him, and when he rises to address his followers, they both have guns trained on him – and Matterly announces the unavoidable postponement of New Rule.

As well as being a cabaret singer in a nightclub, Venus Smith was one of Steed's accomplices in the second series.

A tense moment from The Removal Man, when Steed hides from Siegal, one of Dragna's thugs, in a nightclub.

There is more to The Mauritius Penny than meets the eye when Steed decides to investigate a philatelic code.

DEATH OF A GREAT DANE

Teleplay by Roger Marshall and Jeremy Scott

Minister	**Billy Milton**
Gravedigger	**Herbert Nelson**
Gregory	**Leslie French**
Catherine Gale	**Honor Blackman**
John Steed	**Patrick Macnee**
Mrs Miller	**Clare Kelly**
First assistant	**Dennis Edwards**
Second assistant	**Anthony Baird**
Getz	**Frederick Jaeger**
Miller	**Frank Peters**
Policeman	**Michael Moyer**
Sir James Arnell	**John Laurie**
First winetaster	**Eric Elliott**
Second winetaster	**Roger Maxwell**
Man from kennels	**Kevin Barry**

Story Editor John Bryce
Designed by Patrick Downing
Produced by Leonard White
Directed by Peter Hammond

STEED is on the trail of a gang that smuggles fantastic sums of money out of the country. When he is told that Miller, a man badly injured in a road accident, is carrying a great number of diamonds in his stomach, he is sure that there is a connection with the gang. Steed sees Miller's wife, who says her husband was working for Alex Litoff, a multi-millionaire financier and renowned philanthropist. Steed visits Litoff, and is received by Gregory, Litoff's butler, who is about to walk a Great Dane – the companion, he says, of a similar dog which died some weeks before. Litoff is apparently ill, so Steed meets Getz, his assistant. Producing the diamonds, Steed tries to blackmail Getz, who immediately agrees his price, saying that Litoff would dislike the publicity of taking Steed to the police. When Cathy discovers that Litoff has withdrawn all his financial support from numerous charitable organisations, most of which he had founded, Steed is convinced that Getz is unloading all Litoff's assets, and realising millions of pounds in the process. Steed visits Sir James Mann, Litoff's personal doctor, who admits his patient is seriously ill with a bad heart. When Steed tells him about Getz selling off Litoff's assets, Sir James, certain of Litoff's ignorance, is horrified. Steed breaks into Litoff's home. The millionaire's bed is empty, and Steed finds Sir James Mann waiting with a loaded gun. Cathy meanwhile discovers that Miller has been murdered, and decides to call on his wife – whom she finds dead at her practical joke shop. Cathy finds a Great Dane locked in a back room and takes it home with her. The captive Steed is told by Gregory about Getz's plan, conceived when Litoff died of thrombosis, to seize the financier's fortune and divide it between himself, Gregory and Sir James. They pretended that Litoff was still alive, but he was secretly buried in a pets' cemetery, in the supposed grave of the Great Dane. Miller was ordered to destroy the dog, but gave it to his wife. When Cathy arrives – on the pretext of collecting the remaining dog for the kennels – she is recognised and taken prisoner. Getz decides to kill them, but they turn the tables and as Steed and Cathy escort the three out at gunpoint Gregory, butler to the end, holds the door open for them.

The basic plot of Death Of A Great Dane *was re-used in* The £50,000 Breakfast, *an episode of the fifth series.*

THE SELL-OUT

Teleplay by Anthony Terpiloff and Brandon Brady

Dr Martin King	**Jon Rollason**
John Steed	**Patrick Macnee**
M Roland	**Carleton Hobbs**
Policeman	**Anthony Blackshaw**
Gunman	**Storm Durr**
One-Twelve	**Arthur Hewlett**
Fraser	**Michael Mellinger**
Harvey	**Frank Gatliff**
Lilian Harvey	**Anne Godley**
Judy	**Gillian Muir**
Customer	**Cyril Renison**
Workman	**Richard Klee**
Reporter	**Henry Rayner**

Story Editor John Bryce
Designed by Terry Green
Produced by Leonard White
Directed by Don Leaver

STEED is assigned to guard a United Nations official, M Roland, secretly in London for high-level talks. An assassination attempt on Roland's life is made and although it fails, an innocent man is killed. Dr King, having seen the killing, is enraged at Steed's apparent casualness about the murder. Steed tells his superior, One-Twelve, that he believes the assassination attempt, and the failure of several others, has been the work of an informer. Steed suspects Harvey, an associate who is also responsible for the security of the talks. Before the next meeting, at which Steed pretends to be M Roland, he asks King to help him, but he says he is tired of the bloodshed which is involved in Steed's job. As Steed arrives at the hotel for the

Steed is assigned to protect M Roland, a United Nations official, pictured here in The Sell-Out.

DEATH ON THE ROCKS

talks, a workman tries to shoot him. Dr King is passing and helps. Meanwhile Harvey tells another associate, Frazer, that he believes that Steed is the informer, and learns that Frazer has been ordered by One-Twelve to follow Steed. At the next session of talks – which masquerade as a cocktail party – Steed, suspecting that Harvey's health is bad, dopes his drink, having first ensured that Mrs Harvey will call on Dr King, who will then report to Steed on Harvey's illness. One-Twelve is called away from the party and Steed follows him. He finds Frazer dead, and One-Twelve knocks Steed unconscious. Meanwhile, Harvey discovers it was Steed who suggested that his wife call in Dr King, and he holds the doctor at gunpoint. Harvey tells King that because he was dying he'd turned informer to secure what future he had left. One-Twelve meanwhile tells Steed that although he'd always suspected Harvey of being the informer, he had knocked Steed out hoping to convince Harvey that Steed was the one under suspicion. One-Twelve leaves to ensure the safety of M Roland. Steed goes to King's surgery, rescues the doctor and takes Harvey into custody.

Teleplay by Eric Paice

Mrs Ross	Annette Kerr
Liza Denham	Ellen McIntosh
Diamond dealers	{ Jack Grossman
	{ Vincent Charles
John Steed	Patrick Macnee
Max Daniels	Hamilton Dyce
Van Berg	Richard Clarke
Catherine Gale	Honor Blackman
Painter	Haydn Ward
Fenton	Gerald Cross
Nicky	David Sumner
Samuel Ross	Meier Tzelniker
Jackie Ross	Toni Gilpin
Sid	Douglas Robinson
Mrs Daniels	Naomi Chance

Story Editor John Bryce
Designed by James Goddard
Produced by Leonard White
Directed by Jonathan Alwyn

WHEN Mrs Ross, the wife of a diamond merchant, is murdered by a beautician who smothers her with a quick-hardening face pack, Steed – having heard that an enormous influx of illegal stones is swamping Hatton Garden – enters the diamond business. He buys Ross' house and persuades Mrs Gale to move in and pose as his wife. Fenton, part of the illegal smuggling ring, tells Nicky, one of his henchmen, to investigate Steed's activities. This is easy, as Steed has entered into partnership with Ross, whose daughter, Jackie, Nicky is courting. At a party held in Steed's new house, Nicky suggests he buys some illicit diamonds, but Steed is non-committal. Meanwhile Cathy breaks into Nicky's cellar, and discovers some crystals on the floor, but is interrupted and attacked by one of Fenton's men, whom she fights off. Nicky arrives and she persuades him that she had come about a business matter. She invites him to leave the gang he was blackmailed into joining but Nicky declines. After she has left, Nicky notices that the wires to the alarm system have been cut. He does not tell Fenton of Cathy's visit. Cathy is later visited by Mrs Daniels, the wife of another diamond merchant, who tells her that her husband is being threatened by the gang. Steed has made Ross admit that his wife was killed so as to

blackmail him into buying from the gang. He is now afraid for Jackie's safety, as Fenton plans to drive the Diamond Federation out of business. Cathy arrives and shows Steed what she found in the cellar – rock salt crystals, in which the diamonds are smuggled into the country. Meanwhile, Mrs Daniel's body is found in Cathy's flat. Steed accepts the diamonds from Nicky, and is given a few hours to produce the cash. Ross has refused to join the gang, so Fenton has Jackie kidnapped. When Fenton's man tries to kill both Ross and Jackie, Steed – who has found them in Fenton's salt warehouse – intervenes. Fenton arrives, but with Ross and Nicky's help (the latter wants to protect Jackie) Steed captures him. Meanwhile Liza, the beautician who killed Mrs Ross and Daniels and is the real leader of the gang, tries to murder Cathy. But Mrs Gale throws Liza in the way of Daniels' gun and knocks him cold with a stuffed animal's head.

Steed enters the diamond business and Cathy gets a piggy-back ride in Death On The Rocks.

No matter what danger befell him, Steed remained debonair, sophisticated and unruffled – the perfect English gentleman.

TRAITOR IN ZEBRA

Teleplay by John Gilbert

Escorting Officer	Richard Pescud
Nash	Noel Coleman
Crane	Danvers Walker
Maggie	June Murphy
Catherine Gale	Honor Blackman
John Steed	Patrick Macnee
Mellors	Ian Shand
Wardroom steward	Michael Browning
Graham	William Gaunt
Franks	Richard Leech
Rankin	John Sharp
Linda	Katy Wild
Thorne	Jack Stewart

Story Editor John Bryce
Designed by Terry Green
Produced by Leonard White
Directed by Richmond Harding

INVESTIGATING reports that an officer on HMS Zebra – a shore establishment – is giving secret information to the enemy, Steed joins the unit as a naval psychiatrist and Cathy goes undercover in the control room. Crane, the suspected officer, is accused of leaking information so the enemy can jam the navy's new device for tracking enemy missiles and satellites.

At the base, Steed meets Captain Nash, his secretary, Lieutenant Mellors and Sub-Lieutenant Graham – a friend of the accused, who says he has submitted a report which proves that people other than Crane had access to the formula. This alarms Mellors, who is using a code (via a dartboard at the local inn) to pass on information to Rankin, a local artist. He collects the information and uses his dog to convey the message to a local sweet shop, where it is received by Linda, a counter assistant. Mellors anxiously consults Rankin, who in turn phones someone else, and that night Mellors is strangled in his car. Cathy forms a friendship with Franks, a local newspaper proprietor, and he invites her to his offices. While there, she notices a piece of paper bearing a darts score. When Franks next visits the sweet shop to collect the information from Rankin, Steed follows him. At the shop Steed questions Linda, but she reveals nothing. When the next tracking test is jammed, it becomes obvious that Crane is not guilty. Graham, believing his friend's innocence is proven, receives a message from Linda asking him to meet her but Franks, suspecting that Linda might give him away, slips a pill into Graham's drink, and within minutes, the officer is dead. Steed questions Linda again and she confesses her guilt, but refuses to disclose Frank's name. Cathy searches Rankin's room when he arrives and attacks her. Steed arrives but Rankin escapes through the window and goes to warn Franks. Franks, believing that the game is up, murders Rankin and booby-traps his office, then sets out to plant a bomb at the base. Steed narrowly escapes death from the booby-trap and follows Franks to the naval base. He reaches the control room just as Franks has planted his bomb. By locking Franks in with his own device, he forces him to defuse it, and saves the day.

Cathy befriends Franks, who is the Traitor In Zebra, *when she and Steed investigate a shore establishment.*

THE BIG THINKER

Teleplay by Martin Woodhouse

Dr Clemens	Walter Hudd
Catherine Gale	Honor Blackman
Dr Farrow	David Garth
Dr Hurst	Tenniel Evans
Janet Lingfield	Marina Martin
Dr Kearns	Anthony Booth
John Steed	Patrick Macnee
Broster	Allan McClelland
Clarice	Penelope Lee
Blakelock	Ray Brown

Story Editor John Bryce
Designed by James Goddard
Produced by Leonard White
Directed by Kim Mills

THE final tests on Plato, the largest and most advanced computer ever built, are being sabotaged. When the computer breaks down a second time, and a dead professor is found frozen stiff inside it, Cathy, posing as a language specialist, is sent to investigate. She meets Dr Clemens, head of the project, an old friend, Professor Farrow, and Kearns, a brilliant mathematician. Steed – posing as a government official – appears and tells Cathy that Plato could be a major advance in missile interception, and encourages her to become friendly with Dr Kearns. Kearns takes Cathy to Broster's gambling club, and joins a poker game, but soon runs into debt through his opponent's skilful play. Steed believes that getting Kearns into debt is an attempt to soften him up and enlist him into treachery. Later, Broster and his girlfriend, Clarice, are surprised when Cathy offers to pay Kearns' debts. When Broster tries to intimidate Cathy, he is defeated by her expert judo. Next day, Clemens dismisses Kearns, but Kearns insists he is valuable and stays for the next test on Plato. But someone has tampered with the

Kearns may be a mathematician but he finds it hard to count his drinks in this scene from The Big Thinker.

DEATH DISPATCH

fuses and Cathy is almost killed when they blow up. When Cathy and Kearns enter Plato to check, they find the dead body of Dr Clemens. Kearns is immediately suspected, but disappears. Later that night, Cathy returns to the Plato project and finds Kearns hiding inside the building. He says Clemens was killed because he had evidence that the murderer was one of his own staff. Kearns believes that Clemens may have fed the information into the computer before he died, so they enter Plato and Kearns begins the test. But someone has locked them in, the refrigeration system has been sabotaged and the temperature is falling rapidly. Kearns sends out an SOS through the computer which Steed picks up, as he has been keeping an eye on Cathy. Steed rescues them and Kearns checks the tape for Clemen's message. Professor Farrow arrives and tries to stop the computer. In his attempt to destroy the evidence of his crime, he accidentally switches on the main fuses and is electrocuted.

Teleplay by Leonard Fincham

Baxter	Hedger Wallace
Pasco	Alan Mason
John Steed	Patrick Macnee
One-Ten	Douglas Muir
Catherine Gale	Honor Blackman
Thugs	Geoff L'Cise / Arthur Griffiths
Miguel Rosas	Richard Warner
Anna Rosas	Valerie Sarruf
Monroe	David Cargill
Chambermaid	Bernice Rassin
Rico	Michael Forrest
Singer	Maria Andipa
Customer	Jerry Jardin
Travers	Gerald Harper

Story Editor John Bryce
Designed by Anne Spavin
Produced by Leonard White
Directed by Jonathan Alwyn

A BRITISH courier is murdered in Jamaica but he manages to prevent his diplomatic bag, containing dispatches, from being stolen. Steed and Cathy are flown to the scene of the crime, but Steed cannot understand why it happened, as the bag contains only routine information. Steed masquerades as the replacement courier and, with Cathy keeping watch, sets out to complete the dead courier's itinerary. When they arrive in South America, Steed is attacked and an attempt made to steal the bag, but Cathy is at hand and the attempt fails. Rosas, an ambitious South American politician, is angry when his assistant, Pasco, fails to get the bag, and orders another man, Muller, to get rid of Pasco and intercept Steed. Steed and Cathy meanwhile have flown to Santiago and Steed leaves the bag in his hotel room as bait, should another theft be attempted. That night he observes Pasco enter his room but when Steed goes in

after him, he finds Pasco dead and the bag's contents disturbed. Steed realises that the murderer must have entered his room through the window, having climbed down from the balcony of the room above, so Cathy impersonates a chambermaid and checks the room, to find it occupied by Muller, but she gets away safely. When Steed arrives at Buenos Aires – the last stop on the courier's route – the police question him about the body in his hotel room. Meanwhile, Cathy has followed Muller from Santiago, but she is spotted and taken to Rosas' home. When Steed discovers Cathy's fate, he goes after her but Muller is waiting for him and at gunpoint takes Steed to Rosas. Muller then explains that Rosas wants the itinerary of the visit of an American envoy, whose assassination will trigger a revolt planned to put Rosas in power. Just then, Rosas' young daughter arrives and Steed disarms Muller and arrests Rosas. Their mission accomplished, Steed and Cathy are invited to the reception for the visiting envoy.

Patrick Macnee and Joe Robinson, one of his judo teachers, go through their paces for an episode of The Avengers.

Steed chats to Anna Rosas, the daughter of a crooked South American politician, at a reception, in Death Dispatch.

DEAD ON COURSE

Teleplay by Eric Paice

Pilot	Trevor Reid
Bob Slade	Bruce Boa
Margot	Margo Jenkins
Freedman	John McLaren
John Steed	Patrick Macnee
Deidre O'Connor	Elisabeth Murray
Dr Martin King	Jon Rollason
Sister Isobel	Janet Hargreaves
Mother Superior	Peggy Marshall
Hughes	Nigel Arkwright
Michael Joyce	Liam Gaffney
Vincent O'Brien	Donal Donnelly
Gerry	Edward Kelsey
	Wilfred Grove
	Mollie Maureen
	Denis Cleary

Story Editor John Bryce
Designed by Robert Fuest
Produced by Leonard White
Directed by Richmond Harding

STEED and Dr King investigate a suspicious plane crash on the Irish coast. The bodies have been taken to a nearby convent and while King is there, the sole survivor of the crash, the stewardess, is brought in, still unconscious. Steed has discovered that the plane's load of bank notes has disappeared. He visits the convent and King tells him that the pilot of the plane was strangled. At the local inn, King meets a villager, Vincent, who hints at knowing something about the crash. He tells King he saw a man in pilot's uniform after the crash. Suspicion now falls on the missing co-pilot. Steed discovers that the co-pilot is secretly married to an airhostess, Deidre. She tells him nothing, but Steed is not convinced and believes that the crash was no accident, even though there is no sign of any sabotage. At the convent, the injured stewardess recovers consciousness but is strangled before she can be questioned. The Mother Superior, however, refuses to allow a search for the murderer – or let her nuns break their vows of silence – so Steed taps the telephone lines to the convent and overhears Deidre telling someone in the convent the call sign of the aircraft which is to carry the remainder of the bank shipment. At the inn, King finds a nun's habit and a concealed passage leading to the convent. He asks Vincent to tell Steed, which he does, but begs an air passage to America on a plane carrying Deidre, and piloted by Steed. Meanwhile, King goes to the convent and is held at gunpoint by the Mother Superior – one of the gang who has been using the convent as cover. King is locked in a cell with the missing co-pilot, who says Deidre was told he would be killed if she did not reveal the plane's call sign. The gang then talk-down the plane on a crash course, but it is Steed's plane which responds to the call sign. Realising they are heading for a crash, Vincent breaks down and confesses to being the ring-leader. Steed lands the plane safely and he and Dr King, helped by the co-pilot, round up the rest of the gang.

Cathy and Steed discover a hidden cache of arms, and Cathy is engaged as a professional assassin by Intercrime.

INTERCRIME

Teleplay by Terrance Dicks
and Malcolm Hulke

Palmer	Donald Webster
Sewell	Rory MacDermot
Moss	Alan Browning
John Steed	Patrick Macnee
Catherine Gale	Honor Blackman
Hilda Stern	Julia Arnall
Trusty	Charlotte Selwyn
Prison officer Sharpe	Bettine Milne
Felder	Kenneth J Warren
Lobb	Jerome Willis
Manning	Patrick Holt
Pamela Johnson	Angela Browne
Kressler	Paul Hansard

Story Editor Richard Bates
Designed by Richard Harrison
Produced by John Bryce
Directed by Jonathan Alwyn

TWO petty thieves are caught rifling a safe by Moss, who represents Intercrime, the international crime organisation for which they work, and he shoots them. One of them, Palmer, survives and tells Steed that a woman, Hilda Stern, is arriving in England to work for the gang. Steed has her arrested at London Airport, and Cathy follows her to Holloway, where she learns that Hilda's escape is already planned. Steed persuades Cathy to take the woman's place in the escape and Felder, the British organiser of Intercrime, accepts Cathy as Hilda, and tells her she has been engaged as a professional assassin. Palmer meanwhile has had a change of heart and telephones Felder to warn him about Steed. Deciding that Palmer is a risk, Felder orders Cathy and Moss to kill Palmer and Steed. Cathy soon returns and tells Felder that Moss was ambushed by Palmer, but she has dealt with him and Steed. Meanwhile, Pam Johnson, a girlfriend of Manning, one of Felder's business associates, learns about the gang and Steed warns her that Felder will try to kill her. Cathy attends a trial held by Intercrime in which one of its members, Lupescu, is accused and found guilty of stealing £500 out of the proceeds of a robbery. Then the real Hilda Stern, having escaped from Holloway, arrives. Cathy says that the new Hilda is the impersonator, but when Felder orders her to shoot Lupescu, she can't, and is discovered. Manning – now revealed as the supreme organiser behind Intercrime – is told that Felder intends to take over from him. During the ensuing dispute, Steed arrives and manages to free Cathy. A fight takes place, in which Cathy grabs Hilda's gun, and Steed subdues Manning and the rest of the gang. Unfortunately, Steed is mistaken for one of the gang and is taken away by the police. Visiting him in his cell, Cathy promises to put matters right – soon!

Steed keeps One-Ten informed of all new developments when he and Cathy investigate some Immortal Clay.

IMMORTAL CLAY

Teleplay by James Mitchell

Catherine Gale	Honor Blackman
Allan Marling	Gary Watson
Mara Little	Didi Sullivan
Richard Marling	Paul Eddington
John Steed	Patrick Macnee
One-Ten	Douglas Muir
Miller	James Bree
Anne	Rowena Gregory
Josh Machen	Bert Palmer
De Groot	Steve Plytas
Blomberg	Frank Olegario

Story Editor Richard Bates
Designed by James Goddard
Produced by John Bryce
Directed by Richmond Harding

WHEN Allan Marling claims to have created an unbreakable ceramic, One-Ten tells Steed to see if such a thing really exists. Knowing Cathy is writing a book on china, Steed sends her to the Marling factory. She is being shown round the factory by Allan's brother, Richard, when the body of a man, Lander, is found dead in a slip tank of clay. Cathy discovers that Lander had been seeing Richard's wife, and that Marling was jealous. She meets a man named De Groot, who says he is buying Marling ware to show at the Leipzig Trade Fair. Steed arrives and, entering the laboratory, finds De Groot's right-hand man, Blomberg, searching the premises. He overpowers Steed and escapes. Meanwhile, in another part of the factory, Miller, the Marling's chief designer, is offered £20,000 by De Groot to steal the ceramic. Miller, wanting to impress his beautiful assistant, Mara, accepts. De Groot tells him to remould

the tile into a cup, so it can be smuggled out in the consignment of pottery meant for the Leipzig Fair. Next day, Allan Marling arranges to demonstrate the unbreakable ceramic to Steed. He is about to hand it to Steed, when his brother arrives. Richard scoffs at Allan's claim and knocks the tile from his hand. It falls to the floor and shatters. Miller gives De Groot a glove marked with Allan's name, which he found near the slip tank in which Lander was killed. De Groot phones Allan and tells him he has the glove and Allan agrees to meet him in the laboratory. De Groot arrives with Cathy, who has said she is interested in the tile. They are joined by Blomberg and Miller, and as Miller hands over the cup, and demands his £20,000, De Groot shoots him. The cup falls from Miller's hands – and shatters! De Groot turns the gun on Cathy and Allan. Steed meanwhile has been told by Mara that she loves Allan and wants to steal back the glove. She introduces him to Richard's wife, who confesses that Lander offered her a vast sum for the tile. But when Lander tried to make love to her, Allan fought to protect her, and Lander struck his head and fell into the slip tank. Steed dashes to help Cathy, and arrests De Groot and Blomberg. As they depart, Josh, the night-watchman, arrives – carrying the real unbreakable cup. He explains that he saw Miller making it, then stole it and locked it in the firm's safe.

BOX OF TRICKS

Teleplay by Peter Ling
and Edward Rhodes

Gerry	Ian Curry
Venus Smith	Julie Stevens
John Steed	Patrick Macnee
Henrietta	Jacqueline Jones
Manager	Dallas Cavell
Denise	April Olrich
General Sutherland	Maurice Hedley
Kathleen Sutherland	Jane Barrett
Dr Gilham	Edgar Wreford

Story Editor Richard Bates
Designed by Anne Spavin
Produced by John Bryce
Directed by Kim Mills

NATO secrets are being leaked and Steed is convinced that this is tied up with the death of a magician's girl assistant during a vanishing cabinet trick at the club where Venus is working. He gains entrance by pretending to be a masseur and meets General Sutherland, a NATO Commander, who agrees that there has been a serious leakage of secrets within his command. Meanwhile, in the cabaret room, Denise, the new assistant, has a row with the magician. Later, when Denise is demonstrating the vanishing cabinet's workings to Venus, she too, is killed. Venus tells Steed that she overheard a conversation between the General and his daughter Kathleen, in which the General told off his daughter for consulting a faith-healer, Dr Gilham. Kathleen believed that Gilham could cure her ill father with one of his sealed healing boxes, which contain a balanced assortment of minerals. Steed, posing as a rich hypochondriac, calls on Dr Gilham, who agrees to send one of the healing boxes to Venus for Steed to collect. The box arrives but is stolen from Venus' dressing-room. When Steed discovers it, hidden in the well of a lift that forms part of the cabinet apparatus, Venus and Steed are nearly killed by a concealed trip-wire hidden in the lift. Meanwhile Kathleen has been told by Gilham to take the latest healing box to the club and replace the one she had previously concealed in her father's wheelchair. As she is about to change the box, Steed intervenes and, breaking open the seal, reveals a portable tape-recorder, which has recorded all her father's conversations. Wander, the magician, is in league with Gilham, and kidnaps Kathleen, but Steed sees it and follows them to the magician's dressing-room. He arrives to witness Wander forcing Kathleen into the vanishing cabinet and overpowers the magician, then he and Venus leave to arrest Dr Gilham.

Steed is able to question General Sutherland, a NATO Commander, when he poses as a masseur in Box Of Tricks.

Venus Smith provides light relief when she sings in Box Of Tricks, *accompanied by the Dave Lee Trio.*

WARLOCK

THE GOLDEN EGGS

Teleplay by Doreen Montgomery

Cosho Gallion	Peter Arne
Neville	Alban Blakelock
Mrs Dunning	Olive Milbourne
John Steed	Patrick Macnee
Markel	John Hollis
Julia	Pat Spencer
Mogam	Philip Mosca
Catherine Gale	Honor Blackman
Doctor	Brian Vaughan
Pathologist	Gordon Gardner
Miss Timson	Christina Ferdinando
One-Ten	Douglas Muir
Barmaid	Susan Franklin
Pasco	Herbert Nelson

Designed by Terry Green
Directed by Peter Hammond

Teleplay by Martin Woodhouse

Dr Ashe	Donald Eccles
Elizabeth Bayle	Pauline Delaney
DeLeon	Gordon Whiting
John Steed	Patrick Macnee
Catherine Gale	Honor Blackman
Diana	Irene Bradshaw
Hillier	Robert Bernal
Redfern	Peter Arne
Campbell	Louis Haslar
Hall	Charles Bird

Story Editor Richard Bates
Designed by Douglas James
Produced by John Bryce
Directed by Peter Hammond

Steed becomes worried over Cathy's disappearance and breaks into Gallion's home to find her, in Warlock.

WHEN Neville, a scientist who has perfected a new fuel formula, is found in a state of coma, Steed is assigned to the case, and One-Ten takes the formula for safe-keeping. Steed and Cathy discover that Neville was associated with a black magic circle, but before they can question him further, Neville is kidnapped and taken to Gallion, the head of the circle. Gallion is being paid by Markel, a foreign agent, to interest scientists in black magic and then extract their secrets. Markel tries to question Neville and when he realises that the scientist no longer has the formula, he angrily rouses him to ask further questions. The shock is too great for Neville and he dies. One-Ten tells Steed and Cathy that two other security leaks were connected with the circle. They search Neville's library for clues, and find a dated reference to the circle's next meeting. Steed and Cathy attend the meeting and Cathy is introduced to the circle's leader. Gallion asks if he may cast Cathy's horoscope and she agrees. Gallion finds that Cathy would be ideal for one of his experiments. Returning to his room, Gallion is accused by Markel of being a fraud because he failed to produce Neville's formula. Gallion appears to put a 'hex' on Markel – and he falls to the floor, dead. The following morning Steed finds that Cathy has been kidnapped. Suspecting that the circle is involved, he goes to Gallion's home, and arrives to find the experiment in progress. He is cornered by Gallion's henchmen, and Gallion uses all his powers to make Cathy appear. She arrives, and holds Gallion at gunpoint. Steed overpowers his guards and he and Cathy round up Gallion's supporters. When Gallion realises that his evil powers are finished, he mysteriously collapses – and dies?

DR ASHE, an experimental scientist, is attacked by a burglar, De Leon, and a refrigerated case containing two gold-plated eggs is stolen. Cathy investigates but on questioning Ashe, he denies the theft and the attack. De Leon is taken ill with a mysterious disease. Hillier, the man who engaged him, and who works for the immensely wealthy Redfern, told De Leon that the job contained no risk and there was nothing extraordinary about the eggs. Because of this, De Leon refuses to reveal where the case is hidden. Ashe's assistant, Elizabeth (also in Redfern's pay), warns him that De Leon must be treated immediately for he caught the fatal virus which Ashe has developed and keeps in the eggs. Redfern arranges for a fake ambulance to collect De Leon from hospital, but on its way to Redfern's it is involved in a road accident. Though the ambulance has been cremated in the crash, Steed identifies De Leon's safe-cracking tools and Cathy takes Ashe to De Leon's home in the hope of finding the missing case. After a fruitless search, Ashe goes home, but Cathy continues and finds the case buried in the ground. She takes it home but Redfern and Hillier arrive. They kidnap both her and the case. Imprisoned, Cathy is visited by Elizabeth, who now realises that when she is no longer of any use to Redfern, she can expect little mercy. She frees Cathy but they are discovered by Redfern and held at gunpoint. Cathy threatens to drop the eggs unless he surrenders. He refuses and Cathy throws the eggs into his face. Instinctively, he tries to catch them, and Cathy is able to disarm him. After Redfern and Hillier are rounded up, Cathy and Steed discover that the eggs are dummies. They visit Dr Ashe who explains he was so convinced of the potential evil of the virus that he destroyed all his experiments and the real, deadly, golden eggs.

A star is apparently hurtling towards the Earth, which it will destroy so Steed and Cathy investigate The White Dwarf.

SCHOOL FOR TRAITORS

Teleplay by James Mitchell

East	John Standing
Venus Smith	Julie Stevens
Claire Summers	Melissa Stribling
Roberts	Richard Thorp
Higby	Reginald Marsh
John Steed	Patrick Macnee
One-Seven	Frederick Farley
Dr Shanklin	Anthony Nicholls
Professor Aubyn	Frank Shelley
Green	Terence Woodfield
Proctor	Ronald Mayer
Barmaid	Janet Butlin

Story Editor Richard Bates
Designed by Maurice Pelling
Produced by John Bryce
Directed by Jonathan Alwyn

WHEN a university tutor who had been working on important research is found dead, suicide is suspected and Steed is sent to investigate. He is sure the man was murdered and hints that the dead man has left a letter addressed to Venus, who is appearing at the University during Rag Week. Meanwhile, Claire, a girlfriend of Roberts, who now has the dead tutor's job, tells him she is in financial trouble and persuades him to forge a cheque – thus placing him in the hands of Higby, a local pub owner. Venus is contacted and ordered to leave the letter in the college quadrangle. But on Steed's instructions, her envelope contains blank paper. While Steed waits to see who collects the letter, a man named East diverts his attention and Green, an undergraduate, makes off with it. Steed follows Green, only to find him dead and the letter gone. When Claire discovers that Venus has tricked her, she sends a pot of beauty cream containing acid to Venus. But Venus does not use the cream and, as she prepares to meet Steed, Roberts breaks into her room and demands the real letter. Steed arrives and questions Roberts, who admits that Higby has blackmailed him into getting the letter, and he agrees to help. Higby, however, suspects Roberts as a risk, and when Roberts discovers that Claire is working for Higby, he is shot. Claire now decides to blackmail East, a promising graduate, with the same technique she used on Roberts. East apparently falls for the trick and Higby orders him to kill Steed. East now confides in his tutor, Professor Shanklin – the master-mind behind the scheme – and he gives him the gun with which to murder Steed. But East has been co-operating with Steed and, together with Venus, they round up Shanklin, Higby and Claire.

THE WHITE DWARF

Teleplay by Malcolm Hulke

Professor Richter	Keith Pyott
John Steed	Patrick Macnee
Catherine Gale	Honor Blackman
Minister	Daniel Thorndike
Henry Barker	Peter Copley
Cartwright	Philip Latham
Fuller	Vivienne Drummond
Rahim	Paul Anil
Luke	George Roubicek
Maxwell Barker	George A Cooper
Johnson	Bill Nagy
Miss Tregarth	Constance Chapman
Butler	John Falconer

Story Editor Richard Bates
Designed by Terry Green
Produced by John Bryce
Directed by Richmond Harding

PROFESSOR Richter, an astronomer, is murdered while observing a star called The White Dwarf. The Ministry of Science, however, refuse to allow his assistant, Cartwright, to reveal the news of Richter's death. Steed tells Cathy that Richter believed The White Dwarf is heading straight for our solar system, and will destroy the Earth. Cathy arrives at the observatory, posing as an astronomer, and is shown around by Richter's son, Luke. They enter the telescope chamber and discover the body of Rahim – an Indian astronomer who was sent to confirm Richter's observations. Meanwhile Steed discovers that Maxwell Barker, a financier, in conjunction with an American financier called Johnson, is selling the bulk of his stocks and shares. Realising that Barker's brother, Henry, works for the Ministry of Science, Steed accuses Henry of leaking information about The White Dwarf to his brother. Henry threatens to tell the Minister and resign his post. Johnson overhears and decides Henry must be killed. Later that evening, Johnson is discovered dead in Maxwell's apartment. Meanwhile, Luke, enraged by the Ministry's reaction to his father's death, tells Cathy about his father's findings and when Cartwright arrives to make the final observation, Cathy has changed the plates in the telescope. Cartwright focuses on The White Dwarf and is horrified to see that Richter was right – the star is heading towards Earth. When Maxwell appears, Cartwright accuses him of defrauding him over the deal. Steed and Cathy arrive and take Cartwright into custody but Maxwell escapes onto the roof of the observatory where, during a chase, he is shot dead by Steed.

MAN IN THE MIRROR

Teleplay by Geoffrey Orme and Anthony Terpiloff

Betty	Daphne Anderson
Strong	Ray Barrett
Brown	Julian Somers
John Steed	Patrick Macnee
Venus Smith	Julie Stevens
Jean	Rhonda Lewis
Trevelyan	Hayden Jones
Iris	Frida Knorr

Designed by Anne Spavin
Produced by John Bryce
Directed by Kim Mills

STEED investigates the suicide of a cypher clerk, Trevelyan. Venus, taking photographs in a funfair, has her camera and films stolen by Betty, a girl who works at the café there. One roll of film, however, is not stolen and when developed it shows Trevelyan's face reflected in the Hall of Mirrors. But the film was taken *after* the clerk's death! Strong, who owns the café, tries to persuade Betty to leave Brown, the owner of the funfair, but Brown warns off Strong, reminding him that he is an accessory to treason. When Steed and Venus visit the funfair, Steed deliberately lets Brown see the photograph of Trevelyan. Steed visits Mrs Trevelyan, who admits that she identified another body as her husband's. He had been kidnapped, and in order to preserve his life she had agreed to co-operate with the criminals. Meanwhile, at the café, Venus recognises a brooch worn by Betty as being one stolen from her at the same time as the camera. She tries to reclaim it, but is caught by Strong. Betty now tries to blackmail Mrs Trevelyan and says she will reveal the whereabouts of her husband for a fee. Mrs Trevelyan agrees to pay £500, but Steed interrupts them and is held at gunpoint by Strong. Strong shoots Brown, who was going to show Steed where Trevelyan was hidden. Mrs Trevelyan takes Strong's gun and trains it on Steed and Venus. She and her husband are, in fact, traitors. Strong ties Venus and Steed up and a time-switch bomb is set to kill them. As Strong leaves, Betty, who loves Brown, turns on him and shoots him. Steed is able to call her, and she turns off the mains supply, which defuses the bomb.

CONSPIRACY OF SILENCE

A CHORUS OF FROGS

Cathy visits the animal quarters of the circus, which she is investigating, in Conspiracy Of Silence.

Teleplay by Roger Marshall

James	Arro Morris
Sica	Alec Mango
Carlo	Robert Rietty
John Steed	Patrick Macnee
Rickie	Sandra Dorne
Catherine Gale	Honor Blackman
Gutman	Roy Purcell
Leggo	Himself
Terry	John Church
Arturo	Tommy Godfrey
Professor	Willie Shearer
Rant	Ian Wilson
With	Elizabeth and Collins

Story Editor Richard Bates
Designed by Stephen Doncaster
Produced by John Bryce
Directed by Peter Hammond

WHEN two Italians are brought together in the office of a circus artist agency, one, Carlo, knows that the other is a complete stranger to him. The second Italian, Sica, is a member of the Mafia and has been ordered to kill Steed. Sica knows that Carlo joined the Mafia when young, and is still bound by the sacred oath. Sica now orders Carlo to carry out the assassination. When Carlo attempts to kill Steed, his own panic and reluctance make him fail, but he does escape. Steed tells Cathy that the Mafia are smuggling drugs via London to Canada and the States, and that the assassination attempt was meant to silence him. When Cathy discovers that Carlo is a clown, she visits the circus as a photographer/journalist. The proprietor welcomes the publicity and arranges for Cathy to share the caravan of Carlo's wife, Rickie. Later that day Sica arrives and threatens Rickie, demanding to know where Carlo is hiding. Rickie is rescued when one of the stage-hands, Terry, intervenes. Rickie tells Cathy that when Carlo was in the Italian Air Force, one of his bombing raids hit a school and killed 80 children. Unknown to Cathy, Carlo is at the circus dressed as Beppo, another clown. The real Beppo has had an accident. Rickie tells him that he must kill Steed, so the Mafia will leave him alone. Steed receives two tickets, sent anonymously by Carlo, for the next performance. After the show, Carlo confronts Steed — together with Terry, who works for Sica — and says he must die. Meanwhile Cathy has discovered Sica in the clown's quarters and holds him at gunpoint. Sica boasts that Steed cannot escape both his enemies and Cathy swears that if he dies, she will kill Sica. Two shots ring out and Sica is exultant. Footsteps draw near and Cathy is relieved to hear Steed calling her name — Carlo had shot Terry instead of Steed.

Teleplay by Martin Woodhouse

Staphanopoulus	Makki Marseilles
One-Six	Michael Gover
Mason	Eric Pohlmann
Anna	Yvonne Shima
Venus Smith	Julie Stevens
Ariston	John Carson
Pitt-Norton	Frank Gatliff
Helena	Colette Wilde
Jackson	Alan Haywood
John Steed	Patrick Macnee

Story Editor Richard Bates
Designed by James Goddard
Produced by John Bryce
Directed by Raymond Menmuir

STEED, holidaying in Greece, is asked to investigate the mysterious death of a deep-sea diver, Staphanopoulus. Steed stows away on a luxury yacht, The Archipelago, owned by Mason. Experiments are being made on board with a bathyscaphe designed by Pitt-Norton, a scientist in Mason's employ. Venus has been invited on board to entertain Mason's guests, one of whom is a foreign agent, Anna. Three other guests, Jackson, Helena and Ariston — all close friends of the dead diver — decide to dive under the yacht and spy on Mason's laboratory, so as to discover the cause of Staphanopolus' death. When Jackson and Helena are confronted by Steed, he is held at gunpoint and told to keep out of the way. As Jackson prepares to dive, Anna appears and kills him with a harpoon gun. Mason says that Jackson has drowned while skin-diving and Helena wants to kill Mason in order to avenge the death of her two friends, but Ariston persuades her to talk to Steed first. Venus tells Steed that Mason has a secret laboratory, where delicate fish are kept. They leave to investigate but Mason appears and Steed is questioned. Meanwhile, Ariston and Helena discover the experimental bathyscaphe in which Stapanopolus died. Ariston goes down in it and when it resurfaces he is unconscious. Steed tells Ariston that he suspects Mason of experimenting with different gas mixtures in the bathyscaphe, in order to discover a mixture that will prevent compression sickness. Anna has taken Venus prisoner and she forces Pitt-Norton to face the truth about his experiments — that Mason is only interested in the bathyscaphe because of its use as a midget submarine. Helena threatens to kill Mason but Steed intervenes. Together they enter the laboratory in time to see Anna and Pitt-Norton forcing Venus to make one final test in the bathyscaphe. Helena overpowers Anna and Steed makes short work of Pitt-Norton.

Steed, on holiday in Greece, stows away in Venus' cabin aboard Staphanopoulus' yacht, in A Chorus Of Frogs.

SIX HANDS ACROSS A TABLE

Teleplay by Reed R De Rouen

Julian Seabrook	Philip Madoc
Sir Charles Reniston	John Wentworth
George Stanley	Campbell Singer
Oliver Waldner	Guy Doleman
Butler	Ian Cunningham
Brian Collier	Edward de Souza
Lady Reniston	Freda Bamford
Catherine Gale	Honor Blackman
Rosalind Waldner	Sylvia Bidmead
Miss Francis	Gillian Barclay
Draughtsman	Stephen Hancock
Bert Barnes	Frank Siemen
John Steed	Patrick Macnee
Receptionist	Ilona Rodgers

Story Editor Richard Bates
Designed by Paul Bernard
Produced by John Bryce
Directed by Richmond Harding

CATHY is invited to spend the weekend at a house party given by an old school friend, Rosalind Waldner, whose father, Oliver, is a member of the powerful Reniston Group of shipbuilders. Rosalind tells Cathy that Herbert Collier, a shipbuilder planning to build a nuclear-powered liner with French collaboration, has been killed in a road accident, leaving his son Brian in control of the shipyards. The Reniston Group is against combining with the French and wants to win the order for the new liner to be built in their yards. Steed meanwhile visits Brian Collier, who intends to continue his father's policy. He admits that the situation is very difficult for him because he is in love with Rosalind. Brian calls Waldner and the other board members – Sir Charles Reniston and George Stanley – to his office and tells them of his intentions. Afterwards, as Cathy and Brian leave together, a heavy block and tackle falls from the roof of the works section, narrowly missing them. Sir Charles is worried about Waldner's attitude to Brian's proposal and suspects that he may be planning something but Stanley says there is nothing wrong. The following day, however, Seabrook, financial adviser to the Reniston Group, tells Brian that his company will shortly be taken over. Brian says he will fight the take-over bid, and Cathy – quite fond of Oliver Waldner – offers her support. Seabrook and Sir Charles resign from the Reniston board and join Brian, so he can buy back control of his own company. That night as Cathy is trying to open the safe in Waldner's study, Waldner finds her. He explains that he and Stanley are trying to take over enough companies to control the British shipyards but only to prevent orders being given to foreign companies. At the next board meeting, the take-over bid is defeated and Cathy and Steed arrest Waldner and Stanley.

Cathy is attracted to shady tycoon Oliver Waldner, the father of one of her friends, in **Six Hands Across A Table.**

Cathy fights Pancho Driver, the owner of a gymnasium frequented by her protégé boxer Joey Frazer, in **Killerwhale.**

KILLERWHALE

Teleplay by John Lucarotti

John Steed	Patrick Macnee
'Pancho' Driver	Patrick Magee
Harry	Morris Perry
Catherine Gale	Honor Blackman
Joey Frazer	Kenneth Farrington
Willie	John Tate
Sailor	Frederick Abbott
Fernand	John Bailey
Angela	Julie Paule
Receptionist	Lyndhall Goodman
Laboratory assistant	Christopher Coll
Brown	Robert Mill

Story Editor Richard Bates
Designed by Douglas James
Produced by John Bryce
Directed by Kim Mills

WHEN Cathy introduces Steed to a young boxer named Joey Frazer, Steed suggests that he should start training at a gymnasium run by Pancho Driver. Cathy agrees and decides to manage Joey herself. Joey is introduced to Driver and given a trial bout in the ring against the formidable Tiger. After the fight Joey borrows a bar of soap from a visiting sailor's locker. Pancho enters and takes away the soap, warning Joey not to interfere with other people's property. Next day, when Cathy is binding Joey's hands, she notices a peculiar smell and realises that the soap was, in fact, ambergris. That night she visits the gymnasium and finds a dead sailor's body in the dressing room. She tells Steed, who is very interested, and had suspected that ambergris was being smuggled from the Caribbean to Pancho's gym – now he has the proof. Steed follows Pancho's assistant, Harry, to a courturier's owned by Fernand. While he is there, pretending to buy an outfit for his niece, two men enter and demand money from Fernand. He pays half his debt and they promise to return the next day for the rest. Joey, anxious to help Cathy, searches the dressing room for the silver paper the soap was wrapped in. He has found it in the cellar when Pancho appears and holds him at gunpoint. Cathy arrives at the gym. Worried by Joey's absence, she goes to the cellar and finds Pancho sitting on a vaulting box. She forces Pancho to take the box to pieces, and inside finds the unconscious Joey. Cathy tries to revive Joey but Pancho attacks her and takes her and Joey to Fernand's laboratory and locks them in a storeroom. In the meantime, Fernand has discovered the body of the sailor, hidden in the couturier's by Steed. Pancho panics and tries to escape. However, Steed has released Cathy and Joey and they are able to stop Pancho's escape attempt. After a fight, Fernand and Pancho are arrested.

The Avengers *rapidly became known for being in the forefront of fashion, and the clothes worn in the series were an important part of the show's image.*

Patrick Macnee wears his own clothes, while Honor Blackman wears a Mary Quant two-piece and cloak by Michael Whittaker.

Left: Honor Blackman wears a full-length leather dress and matching cape, designed by Frederick Starke.

Above: Honor Blackman wears her world-famous leather flying suit designed by Michael Whittaker for her part as Cathy Gale.

Right: It was intended that Cathy Gale should carry her gun in a garter holster, but the idea proved impractical.

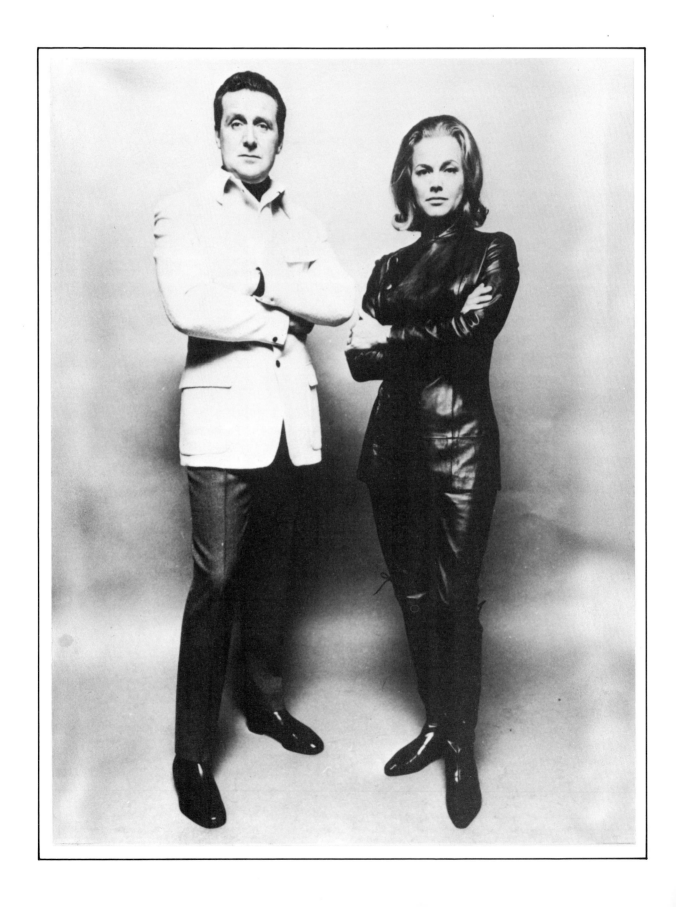

Patrick Macnee/Honor Blackman
1963-64

First Of The Super Heroines

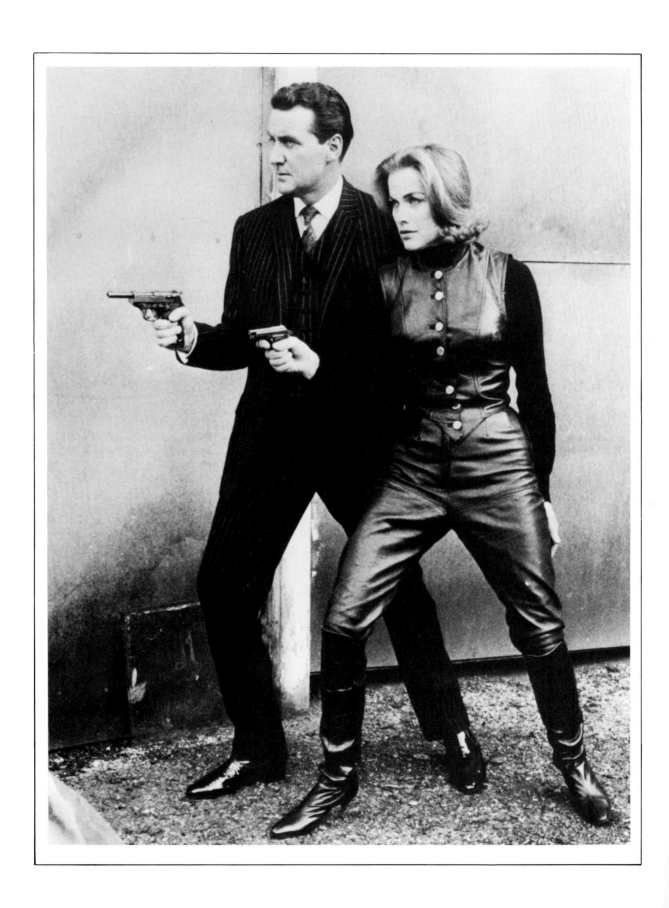

B Y 1963 everyone was talking about *The Avengers*. 'It's trivial and I love it without reservation because it's shrewdly calculated and played with great style,' said *The Spectator*. 'It's the darling of the Primrose Hill set,' said another newspaper. 'It keeps the Bright Young Things of Belgravia and Chelsea at home on Saturday nights.' The programme received critical acclaim and the accolade of television's most fashionable drama programme. When it was screened for the first time in Scotland it immediately scored the highest viewing figures of any television contractor for the time of day. In Fleet Street, photographers were taking down their scantily clad pin-ups and substituting the sexy Honor Blackman, and even as the final episodes of the first Blackman series were being screened, plans were being made for a further 26 episodes.

But not everyone applauded *The Avengers*. A distinguished writer speaking on *The Critics* radio programme deplored 'this silly excellence' and worried about the effect that working on a series 'as empty as a dry skull' must have 'on the soul of the man who makes it'. But critical critics were in the minority. Most people enjoyed the show's originality, and the Cathy Gale character, as one of the screen's earliest liberated women, was a revelation. At the time, Honor Blackman said 'I'd been used to playing women of the sweet, fair-haired English rose variety. So when the opportunity of playing a character like Catherine Gale came my way, it was like a breath of fresh air. The first few weeks were extremely difficult and for a time I wondered if I'd bitten off more than I could chew. But then I began to cope with the task of licking Cathy into the beginnings of what she is now. Everybody had ideas of what she was going to be like. And all of us, including Leonard White who was then the producer, wondered how the public were going to receive this "way-out" woman who was starting to evolve. As far as we were concerned, the more she took shape, the more our image of her crystallised, the more we liked her. Imagine our extra delight then when we found that people were thrilled by her way-outness – were even prepared to take more.'

Leonard White, who shaped the first two series, had transferred to ABC's *Armchair Theatre*, and the series' former story editor, John Bryce, was now heading the production team. Gone too were Venus Smith – Julie Stevens had left the show to have a baby – and Dr King, One-Ten, Freckles and company were quietly forgotten.

Bryce and story editor Richard Bates (son of novelist H E Bates), gathered together the finest writing talent available. Writers of the calibre of Brian Clemens, Roger Marshall and Malcolm Hulke were asked to devise new and amusing situations and dialogue for Steed and Cathy. They were also urged to attend readings, rehearsals and recordings, and encouraged to regard themselves as key figures in the shaping of the final production. Under Bryce's guidance, *The Avengers* team became keener than ever. They saw their programme as a punchy, well-laced brew of the old thriller format – an up-to-the-minute shake-up of a cocktail that had delighted high and lowbrow ever since it was first devised. They relished its bizarre, tongue-in-cheek quality, and refused to treat it seriously – except in their own terms, which was as an hour of slick, sophisticated, and highly entertaining television.

However, when a national newspaper called Steed 'a marshmallow Scarlet Pimpernel', and further research indicated that viewers felt that Steed was becoming too much of a humorous 'feed' to Cathy Gale, steps were immediately taken to toughen up his character and restore the cultivated callousness which first endeared him to his fans. Similarly, Cathy's role was changed to allow her more opportunity to show the feminine and fallible side of her nature. (Towards the end of the first Blackman series, Cathy was allowed to fall for a tycoon who turned out to be a bad lot. She was shown kissing the man and since then Bryce had vetoed all embraces.)

To this end, producer John Bryce issued a revised directive to both writers and directors:

> *Steed is a thoroughly professional and efficient secret agent, expert at murder, arson, burglary, forgery and the use of explosives, codes and poisons. He is trained to withstand torture and brainwashing. Steed is dedicated, ruthless, unscrupulous. His mission is all-important to him and in his eyes its success justifies whatever methods he has to use. Unlike Cathy, he carries no obvious symbol of his vocation, such as a gun-holster, and in fact he uses a gun infrequently. When tackling criminals he fights like a cad and uses every dirty trick in the book to knock them out with the least inconvenience to himself. Steed is a man-about-town with a private income. He patronises the best tailor, bootmaker, hatter and wine merchant, frequents the best clubs, plays bridge, bezique, polo and croquet, and reads the Royal Edition of The Times. Cathy trained as an anthropologist, she is now an undercover agent, and as much of a professional as Steed. Direct in all her dealings, she cares about people and clashes frequently with Steed over the callousness of his methods. Cathy is avant-garde in all her tastes. Her clothes are designed to suit her own individual style of cool, uncluttered elegance, masculine in the manner that emphasises femininity and always practical for the life she leads.*

Steed and Cathy's wardrobes were also changed for the new series. Patrick Macnee's clothes became more Edwardian than ever. Braided pin-stripe suits; embroidered waistcoats in brocade and silk; cummerbunds, a variety of furry and smooth curly-brim bowlers; evening coats in mohair, with black velvet collars and gold satin linings; a single-breasted tuxedo, with lapels and cuffs faced with black satin and edged with braid; a chain-striped suit and waistcoat edged with black satin and black braid buttons; Hardy Amies blazers in rough Irish tweed – they all formed part of his new wardrobe. He also had specially-made umbrellas that contained swordsticks and hidden compartments for maps, a sextant and compass – and even one that served as an effective rifle.

Cathy's leather, though not entirely forgotten, gave way to garments that had either a military or Chinese influence. Suits, hats and boots took their flavour from the officers' uniforms of

the Napoleonic period, with fobs, waistcoats and cravats. Dresses and jackets had a simplistic Chinese line. Frederick Starke, one-time chairman of the London Fashion House Group, was given the task of designing Cathy's new fashions, and Honor wore Starke creations in 15 out of the 26 episodes. The other stories were completed before Mr Starke's designs became available. For one episode, *Don't Look Behind You,* Honor's outfits were designed by ABC Television.

During the court scenes of the season's opening episode, *Brief For Murder,* many interesting facts about Steed's background emerged. Steed is the younger son of a younger son, a scion of a noble family, but he is the black sheep of the family. He was sent to Eton, but spent most of his time in amateur theatricals. He left Eton shortly before war broke out and had a fine war record, which was distinguished when, as a lieutenant in the Royal Navy, he commanded a motor torpedo boat. After 1945 he ran an ex-Naval launch in and around the Eastern Mediterranean ports at a time when cigarette trafficking was in full swing. Later, he turned up in London and, to some extent, re-established himself with his family by taking a respectable job with the Civil Service. Shortly afterwards, he appeared in the Middle East as economic adviser to Sheikh Akbar Ben Sidi Ben Becula, ruler of an oil-rich state. While he was there the Sheikh became involved in a quarrel with two neighbouring states. Some people say this row nearly started World War III, but others say it averted it. However, the Sheikh became richer through oil royalties and Steed returned to England with an award from the Sheikh, the Order of the Golden Ram (Second Class) and life royalties from two of the oil wells. From this income he lived the life to which he had accustomed himself. At about this time he is said to have done some work for the State, but no official record exists of such work...

To give an added dimension to the characters of Steed and Cathy, they now had resident addresses, and many of the stories opened and closed with Steed and Cathy meeting at home – something which would be continued in later episodes. Steed's flat, at 5 Westminster Mews, was furnished with Victoriana collected during his frequent trips up and down the country. Polo cups and hunting trophies adorned the shelves, complemented by Steed's collection of military paintings. The hearth had a tiger-skin rug and over the fireplace hung a magnificent portrait of his great grandfather, RKJJ de V Steed (known in his day as 'Stallion'). The flat was furnished with red leather upholstery. Concealed behind a false row of books was a secret radio receiver. The spacious window overlooking Parliament Square was built of bullet-proof glass.

Cathy's flat, at 14 Primrose Hill, was modern and functional, predominantly press-button controlled. Her kitchen was superbly equipped and all the rooms had sliding doors. There was a concealed cocktail cabinet in the sitting-room, which was furnished with uncomfortable-looking backless chairs and a sofa. To make life that much easier, a television monitor screen showed her who was at the door, and her photographic studio contained the most modern equipment. One unusual feature was a magnetic chessboard which, when reversed, revealed a telephone.

BRIEF FOR MURDER

By Brian Clemens

Wescott	Alec Ross
Dicey	June Thody
Marsh	Fred Ferris
John Steed	Patrick Macnee
Catherine Gale	Honor Blackman
Wilson	Anthony Baird
Barbara Kingston	Helen Lindsay
Miles Lakin	Harold Scott
Jasper Lakin	John Laurie
Judge	Robert Young
Bart	Michael Goldie
Maisie	Pamela Wardel
Miss Prinn	Alice Fraser
Foreman of the Jury	Walter Swash

Story Editor Richard Bates
Designed by James Goddard
Produced by John Bryce
Directed by Peter Hammond

WESCOTT, charged with treason at the Old Bailey, is pronounced not guilty. Cathy, however, is certain of his guilt and discovers that Wescott's contact – a man called Jonno who was never caught – is in fact Steed. When Cathy asks him about it, Steed refuses to discuss the matter and threatens to silence her 'once and for all'. Cathy responds by publishing her accusation in the newspapers. Steed contacts Wescott and asks him to put him in touch with the solicitors whose brief got Wescott acquitted. The solicitors are Jasper and Miles Lakin, two elderly brothers. They are glad to help Steed and happily agree to defend him on the murder charge when he commits the murder of Mrs Gale. The brothers tell Steed exactly how to commit the murder. Steed shoots Cathy and the body falls into the Thames. As Steed leaves, he is seen by the principal of a yoga school where Cathy practises. Steed is soon arrested and sent for trial. The prosecution case goes exactly as arranged by the Lakins and Steed is pronounced not guilty. As he leaves the court, he looks up into the public gallery – where Cathy sits. Steed and Cathy meet later at Miss Prinn's yoga school and Steed tells Cathy that her murder is not sufficient to arrest the Lakins. They have safeguarded themselves too well and must be caught out at their own game. Cathy visits them posing as a Miss Patchett, wishing to commit a fraud involving two business partners who must be caught while she goes free. The Lakins are surprised at having to work for a conviction, but agree to help. They carefully arrange all the details, but Steed, by pretending to have been re-arrested, operates their plan so that they become the two business partners and they are caught in the very trap which they so expertly arranged.

THE UNDERTAKERS

By Malcolm Hulke

Green	Howard Goorney
Madden	Patrick Holt
Catherine Gale	Honor Blackman
John Steed	Patrick Macnee
Mrs Renter	Lally Bowers
Lomax	Lee Patterson
Wilkinson	Ronald Russell
Paula	Jan Holden
Daphne	Mandy Miller
Mrs Lomax	Marcella Markham
Mrs Baker	Helena McCarthy
Reeve	Denis Forsyth

Story Editor Richard Bates
Designed by David Marshall
Produced by John Bryce
Directed by Bill Bain

STEED tells Cathy that he is disturbed because Professor Sayer – with whom Steed was going to promote a new invention – has apparently gone into meditation at a rest home, The Adelphi Park. Steed has visited the home but was refused entry by the Matron, Mrs Lomax. He shows Cathy a copy of the local electoral register which contains the names of the occupants of Adelphi Park. Cathy realises that they are all millionaires. Meanwhile, Marshall, a multi-millionaire, is murdered by a man called Green, and the body is taken away by three undertakers. Apparently all the millionaires at the rest home have recently signed over their fortunes to their next of kin, to evade death duties. Cathy wonders if the owners of Adelphi Park have discovered a way of keeping the millionaires alive, at least on paper, for the required five-year period after the signing. Cathy applies for the position of Assistant Matron at the home while Steed, posing as a representative of a firm of funeral directors, visits the local undertakers which is run by Green. There

in the Chapel of Rest he finds the body of Mrs Lomax. Cathy arrives at Adelphi Park and meets the new Matron, Mrs Sayer – wife of Professor Sayer – who confirms that Adelphi Park is being run by an organisation to help millionaires evade death duties. Meanwhile Marshall, who is still alive, and his 'murderer' Green, are talking in the funeral parlour. Marshall tells Green that he is waiting to take revenge on Lomax – husband of the former matron – who had ordered Marshall's death. Daphne Marshall now arrives from Switzerland and is told by her stepmother, Paula, that her father is staying at Adelphi Park. Daphne calls at the rest home and demands to see her father but is held captive by Mrs Sayer, Paula and Lomax. They take Daphne away, but they are seen by Cathy who immediately informs Steed. Steed returns to the funeral parlour and sees Marshall and Green leaving. He forces an entry and is attacked by one of Green's undertakers, but he makes short work of him and leaves for the rest home. At Adelphi Park, Cathy has found Daphne locked in a closet. She releases her and they are about to depart when Lomax arrives and holds them at gunpoint. He is disturbed by the arrival of Marshall and Green and Marshall, swearing vengeance, shoots Lomax. Steed arrives and in the confusion Marshall and Green escape into the grounds – to be pursued and caught eventually by Cathy and Steed.

Steed and Cathy meet at Miss Prinn's Yoga School, of which Cathy is a member, in Brief For Murder.

THE MAN WITH TWO SHADOWS

By James Mitchell

Gordon	Daniel Moynihan
Charles	Paul Whitsun-Jones
John Steed	Patrick Macnee
Borowski	Terence Lodge
Catherine Gale	Honor Blackman
Rudi	Douglas Robinson
Sigi	George Little
Julie	Gwendolyn Watts
Dr Terence	Geoffrey Palmer
Miss Quist	Anne Godfrey
Cummings	Philip Anthony
Holiday camp official	Robert Lankesheer

Story Editor Richard Bates
Designed by Paul Bernard
Produced by John Bryce
Directed by Don Leaver

STEED is summoned by Charles, his superior, to meet a man named Borowski who has been brainwashed by the 'opposition'. During brief moments of sanity, Borowski speaks of the 'doubles' that the opposition are going to smuggle into the country. Steed and Charles realise that all the men hold top positions in the Ministry of Security. Cathy and Steed watch the newspapers closely for any suggestion of a scientist or politician being murdered. Their first clue is a brochure for a holiday camp found amongst Borowski's possessions. A few days later a man is run over by a car, and since his description fits a scientist called Gordon who is visiting the holiday camp, Steed visits Gordon's doctor and dentist. But the body is so badly damaged that they are unable to confirm that it is Gordon. Cathy meanwhile visits the holiday camp and meets a man named Gordon. She returns convinced that he is the real Gordon. Steed visits the man and tells him that he must have a medical check-up. Gordon agrees and both doctor and dentist say that the man is the real Gordon. Steed, however, is unconvinced. Gordon returns to the camp, calls his superiors and relates what has happened. They decide to put the next part of their plan into action – the new double will be John Steed. Steed books into the camp and that night he is attacked by his double. There is a fierce fight and 'Steed' tells Gordon and Cummings (a visiting politician and the third doppleganger) that the real Steed is dead. Cathy is summoned by Charles and told that if the real Steed is dead, she will have to kill his double. At the same time, Steed is told by Cummings that if Cathy suspects anything, Steed will have to kill her. When Cathy learns that Gordon has left the camp and returned to his research station, she approaches Cummings and asks for his help. At Steed's chalet Cathy pulls a gun on Steed and asks Cummings to keep him under surveillance while she goes for help. When she has left Steed immediately attacks Cummings. The following day, Cathy returns home to find Steed waiting for her. He tells her he disposed of his double and went along with the plan to discover the identity of the gangleader – Cummings. He has since been placed under arrest, along with his associates, and Gordon is now feeding back secret information to the opposition supplied by Steed!

THE NUTSHELL

By Philip Chambers

Elin Strindberg	Edina Ronay
Catherine Gale	Honor Blackman
John Steed	Patrick Macnee
Laura	Patricia Haines
Military policeman	Edwin Brown
Disco	John Cater
Venner	Charles Tingwell
Susan	Christine Shaw
Anderson	Ian Clark
Jason	Jan Conrad
Alex	Ray Browne

Story Editor Richard Bates
Designed by Philip Harrison
Produced by John Bryce
Directed by Raymond Menmuir

STEED and Cathy are called to The Nutshell – a vast underground shelter to be used by the security forces in the event of World War III – where the Director of Operations (Disco) tells them that a file listing double agents, codenamed Big Ben, has been copied. They have photographs taken by hidden cameras during the break-in, and the thief is an attractive young girl. Cathy is sent to Central Security to find out from Venner if the girl is on their files. Steed is ordered to Special Branch but instead visits a rehearsal room where he meets the girl, Elin. She gives him the microfilm she has taken of Big Ben and Steed tells her to leave the country. He then telephones Disco to say he has found the girl. Disco sends Venner to arrest Elin but when he reaches the rehearsal room she is dead. Venner returns to Disco with several photographs of Elin. Steed is seen in the background of one of them. Disco suspects him of being a traitor and Venner is ordered to bring him in for questioning. Venner visits Steed's flat but Cathy refuses to believe that Steed is a traitor or to help, other than telling him that Steed is meeting a man called Jason at an airfield. Venner and his assistant, Anderson, go there and try to arrest Jason but Steed orders them to release him. As Jason hurries to the waiting aircraft Steed gives himself up. He is taken back to The Nutshell and questioned, but refuses to say what has happened to Big Ben and is finally put in a cell. Cathy arrives and, apparently convinced of Steed's guilt, tells Disco that she will try to persuade Steed to tell the truth. As she enters Steed's cell, he attacks her. During the fight, she surreptitiously hands him a gun, then the guards rescue Cathy. Venner arrives and offers Steed his freedom in exchange for the microfilm. That evening, Steed escapes, captures Venner and restores the microfilm to Disco. Steed admits that he bribed Elin to copy Big Ben in order to trap the real traitor – Venner.

In The Nutshell, *Steed and Cathy encounter Disco, who tells them that a top-secret file has been copied.*

Steed in his flat at 5 Westminster Mews, standing in front of the portrait of his great-grandfather, RKJJ de V Steed.

DEATH OF A BATMAN

by Roger Marshall

Edith Wrightson	Kitty Attwood
John Wrightson	David Burke
John Steed	Patrick Macnee
Catherine Gale	Honor Blackman
Lord Teale	Andre Morrell
Eric Van Doren	Philip Madoc
Cooper	Ray Browne
Lady Cynthia	Katy Greenwood
Gibbs	Geoffrey Alexander

Story Editor Michael Bates
Designed by Paul Bernard
Produced by John Bryce
Directed by Kim Mills

WHEN Steed attends the reading of the will of Wrightson, his one-time batman, he is surprised to find that he is repaid £10 owed since 1942. Lord Basil De Witt, an influential merchant banker, is left Wrightson's war medals. To his son John, Wrightson leaves £100 – and £480,000 to his wife Edith. Steed is astonished by the sum and he and Cathy ponder how Wrightson, a draughtsman for a printing firm, could have amassed such a fortune. Steed suspects forgery. Lord Basil and his partner, Van Doren, are also concerned at the amount left by Wrightson and fear that the game is up unless they act quickly. A lovely, though scatterbrained, heiress, Lady Cynthia, arrives and is firmly advised not to sell her profitable investments. When she leaves, however, Van Doren and De Witt immediately make arrangements to sell them. Steed and Cathy attend an open day at an electronics firm and Steed tells Cathy that he is concerned about the security implications of Van Doren and De Witt having financial control of the firm. It seems they specialise in electronics companies. Steed visits Lady Cynthia, who gives him a list of her investments. Thorpe, a broker, tells Steed that the stock market price on Lady Cynthia's investments indicate selling. John Wrightson now contacts De Witt and blackmails him, because he knows that his father's fortune came from De Witt and Van Doren for services rendered. His father's firm printed new currencies, share certificates, etc, and Wrightson, as top draughtsman, was first to be told of any new order. Therefore he could inform De Witt before the public announcement. Steed, having gained proof from Thorpe of De Witt's crooked activities, calls on John and forces him to help him trap De Witt. De Witt swears his motives were solely patriotic – all his money was used to finance Britain's electronics industry. But Steed has no option but to inform the police and De Witt and Van Doren are arrested.

NOVEMBER FIVE

By Eric Paice

Returning	
Officer	John Murray Scott
Michael Dyter	Gary Hope
Mart St John	Ric Hutton
Gunman	Frank Maher
John Steed	Patrick Macnee
First lady	Aimee Delamain
Major Swinburn	David Langton
Arthur Dove	David Davies
Catherine Gale	Honor Blackman
Fiona	Iris Russell
Joe	Joe Robinson
Mrs Dove	Ruth Dunning

Honor Blackman's wardrobe
Designed by Frederic Starke
Story Editor Richard Bates
Designed by Douglas James
Produced by John Bryce
Directed by Bill Bain

AS the results of the Parliamentary by-election for South-East Anglia are being announced, the winning candidate, Dyter, is shot by someone in the crowd. Dyter had promised to expose a major security scandal. Steed visits the House of Commons, and sees Major Swinburn, MP, who had employed Dyter. Swinburn tells Steed that there is no substance to the scandal. Later, however, Swinburn hastily arranges a meeting between himself, St John, Dyter's publicity agent, and Arthur Dove, MP, a member of the opposition. They discuss the failure of the government to deal with the theft of a nuclear warhead and decide that Swinburn should put a question before the House to expose the security breach. Steed co-opts Mrs Gale into standing in the by-election caused by Dyter's death and together they visit a ski-school run by Fiona and Ernst. They meet Dove and Swinburn, and Steed tells Swinburn and St John that he is acting as Mrs Gale's election agent. Cathy says she will fight the election on Dyter's platform of exposing the security scandal but that she will do this before the campaign starts. This worries Swinburn. When they go to meet him at the House, they find him murdered. Later, Steed meets Dove and reveals that the government has received a blackmail note asking for £500,000 in return for the warhead. St John meanwhile visits Fiona and Ernst and tells them about Steed's activities. He then returns to his office and is confronted by Dyter, very much alive, who says he has abandoned the ransom threat in favour of a new plan. He will blow up the bomb, which is now hidden on the terrace of the House of Commons. Meanwhile, Steed and Cathy are going through the files in St John's office. They remove some photographs of the murder and realise that Dyter was not killed. That night, when Dyter goes to the House to set off the bomb, he finds Steed there, and then he and Cathy round up the rest of the gang.

How could Wrightson have made such a fortune? This is what perplexes The Avengers in Death Of A Batman.

Clad in Chinese-style leather, Cathy explains her theory about robbing a gold vault, in The Gilded Cage.

THE GILDED CAGE

By Roger Marshall

John Steed	Patrick Macnee
Catherine Gale	Honor Blackman
Groves	Neil Wilson
J P Spagge	Patrick Magee
Fleming	Norman Chappell
Manley	Frederic Abbott
Westwood	Alan Haywood
Wardress	Margo Cunningham
Benham	Edric Connor
Hammond	Martin Friend
Peterson	Terence Soall
Gruber	Geoff L'Cise
Barker	Douglas Cummings

Story Editor Richard Bates
Designed by Robert Macgowan
Produced by John Bryce
Directed by Bill Bain

CATHY has been working in a secret gold vault and when she tells Steed that it would only take six men to steal and remove the gold, he sees a way to put her scheme to good use. Steed's department has been on the trail of a man named Spagge, a millionaire from his criminal activities who is suspected to be the mastermind behind several recent big crimes. Steed visits Spagge and tells him that he and Mrs Gale are planning to steal £1,000,000 worth of gold. Spagge refuses to help. The following morning Cathy is arrested and charged with Spagge's murder. As she is led away, Steed arrives and assures her that he will soon have her released. In her cell, she desperately tries to recall what happened after her arrest, but her mind is a blank. Later that day she is visited by Benham, the prison chaplain, who asks why she killed Spagge and what part Steed played in the crime. Cathy continues to protest her innocence. She is called to see the Governor and is led away by a warder and left outside a large door. She finds herself confronted by six men, including Benham. They say that her arrest was a test, and having passed with flying colours, they are now prepared to hear her plans for stealing the gold. Steed is told that Cathy is safe and Spagge is not dead. He takes a case of clothes to Spagge and asks that they be passed on to Cathy. That night, at home, Steed answers his telephone. As he stands silhouetted in the window, somebody shoots him and he falls. The robbery is successfully carried out and the gold taken to Benham's home. Spagge then arrives and orders them to kill Cathy as he has discovered that Steed is working for the police. At this moment Steed arrives and rounds up the gang, leaving Cathy to fight it out with Benham and Spagge.

SECOND SIGHT

By Martin Woodhouse

Dr Vilner	Steven Scott
Neil Anstice	Peter Bowles
Dr Eve Hawn	Judy Bruce
John Steed	Patrick Macnee
Catherine Gale	Honor Blackman
Marten Halvarssen	John Carson
Dr Spender	Ronald Adam
Steiner	Terry Brewer

Honor Blackman's wardrobe
Designed by Frederick Starke
Story Editor Richard Bates
Designed by Terry Green
Produced by John Bryce
Directed by Peter Hammond

STEED hears that blind millionaire Halvarssen wants to bring two eye corneas from Switzerland. They are to travel in a specially sealed container designed by Dr Vilner. Steed tells Cathy that Halvarssen intends to use the cornea grafts on himself, to regain his sight. When Cathy visits Halvarssen's home, she is prevented from seeing him by his assistant, Anstice, but Cathy manages to make him reveal that the grafts are to be taken from a live donor. Steed calls in Dr Spender, a famous eye surgeon who, against Steed's wishes, demands that Halvarssen allows him to attend the operation. Steed decides that Cathy should go too, and Halvarssen agrees. Anstice accuses Halvarssen of jeopardising their plan, but he says that the complications are minor. Anstice can deal with Cathy and Spender later. At the Swiss clinic, Cathy and Dr Spender are told that they cannot see the donor, Hilda Brauer. However, Cathy finds Hilda's room - it is empty but for an unfinished portrait. She tells Spender and they both insist on seeing Hilda Brauer. Anstice finally takes them to her room. The bed is now occupied but the patient's face is totally masked by bandages. Anstice says she is under sedation and therefore no one can talk to her. That afternoon, Cathy receives a phone call from Steed and learns that Halvarssen lost his sight because of a head wound. New corneas are useless because it is physically impossible for him to regain his sight. Meanwhile Spender has been called to Hilda's room, but to his surprise finds only the patient there. He walks to the balcony to see if anyone is there. Hilda Brauer walks up behind him, and pushes him over the balcony rail. Arriving home, Cathy meets Steed at a private airfield where the sealed container is brought through customs by Anstice. Steed is convinced that Halvarssen is smuggling and though Cathy agrees, she is disturbed by Dr Spender's death and does not believe that Halvarssen would condone murder.

Cathy and Steed wait at the airfield for the sealed container, holding two eye corneas, in Second Sight.

She tells him of Spender's death and asks Anstice why he has not been told of the killing. Anstice replies that he is a professional and Spender was in the way. Steed now learns that Hilda Brauer died three years before. There was neither patient nor operation. At Halvarssen's home, Anstice hands him the container. The millionaire opens it and removes two large diamonds. He then draws one diamond across a mirror and feels for the scratch, but the mirror is smooth - Anstice has double-crossed him. As Anstice holds Halvarssen at gunpoint, Cathy arrives. Anstice grabs Cathy and, using her as a cover, tries to escape but Steed intervenes and the crooks are arrested.

THE MEDICINE MEN

By Malcolm Hulke

Catherine Gale	Honor Blackman
John Steed	Patrick Macnee
Geoffrey Willis	Peter Barkworth
John Willis	Newton Blick
Frank Leeson	Harold Innocent
Taylor	John Crocker
Fay	Monica Stevenson
Masseuse	Brenda Cowling
Miss Dowell	Joy Wood
Edwards	Peter Hughes

Story Editor Richard Bates
Produced by John Bryce
Directed by Kim Mills

A CHINESE girl is murdered in a Turkish bath and Steed asks Cathy to investigate. He visits a pharmaceutical company, Willis Sopwith, which has been badly hit by the sale of imitation products on their overseas markets. Steed learns from Geoffrey Willis that the imitators change the spelling of the brand name as protection against copyright action, and Willis Sopwith have redesigned all their cartons in an effort to get one jump ahead. The company's research scientist, Edwards, tells Steed and Willis

Cathy is a little tied up when Miss Dowell discovers her searching Taylor's printing shop, in The Medicine Men.

that there is a printer's trademark on one of the imitation cartons – if they can trace the printer he may lead them to the imitator. Cathy discovers that the Chinese girl often went to the Turkish bath and sometimes her pores oozed paint, as though she had taken a bath in it. At the baths a girl called Fay is covered in paint and Cathy discovers that she once advertised cosmetics for Willis Sopwith. Cathy gets a job as an efficiency expert at the firm. Miss Dowell, Willis' secretary, shows Cathy around and Edwards' body is discovered in a stationery cupboard. He has hanged himself. Cathy meets Willis' father, John Willis, chairman of the company and learns that Fay is his girlfriend and she models for Leeson, an artist. Meanwhile, Taylor, a printer, shows replicas of the new Willis Sopwith carton designs to Leeson. That night Steed and Cathy break into Taylor's print shop and discover the copies. Later Steed visits Leeson's studio and overhears him explaining to Fay that this time their cartons will be identical to the originals. They will contain various poisonous ingredients, causing illness and death in the Arabic countries, and so harm the goodwill there of Willis Sopwith and of Britain, thus endangering a forthcoming oil treaty. Fay is horrified and says she will tell John Willis. Steed and Cathy return to the printing shop and replace the printing block with one made by Steed. They discover Fay bound and gagged and release her. But as Cathy searches the rest of the building, she is discovered by Miss Dowell and Steed is held at gunpoint by Geoffrey Willis – the ringleader of the organisation. Taylor arrives with the new cartons but Miss Dowell realises that the Arabic wording on them reads 'Poison. This is an imitation'. Steed manages to break free and Cathy takes care of Miss Dowell while Steed overpowers the rest of the gang, using his bowler.

THE GRANDEUR THAT WAS ROME

By Rex Edwards

Bruno	Hugh Burden
Marcus	John Flint
Estow	Ian Shand
Catherine Gale	Honor Blackman
Octavia	Colette Wilde
John Steed	Patrick Macnee
Appleton	Kenneth Keeling
Lucius	Raymond Adamson
Barnes	Colin Rix

Story Editor Richard Bates
Produced by John Bryce
Directed by Kim Mills

W HEN there are reports of crop failures, unknown diseases in animals and frequent outbreaks of illness in all parts of the world, Steed and Cathy visit United Foods and Dressings Ltd (UFD), a factory which distributes fertilisers and insecticides. Cathy tells Estow, the public relations officer, of the reports and Estow shows them over UFD. Cathy can see no way the modern equipment could have been tampered with but Steed is not so sure. Meanwhile Sir Bruno Lucer welcomes Marcus Dodds, his right-hand man, who has been touring America on behalf of Sir Bruno's political party. Lucer lives in a villa designed like that of a Roman senator, and clearly has a Caesar fixation. He introduces Marcus to his attractive companion, Octavia. At Steed's flat, Steed and Cathy study specimens of grain and fertilizer from all over the country. Finally, Cathy discovers that some of the UFD grain is infected with ergot, which would account for some of the illnesses. Steed thinks that it is no accident but a deliberate attempt to infect the grain. He shows Cathy an unusual marking which he found on one of the sacks at UFD, but Cathy is unable to identify the marking. Lucer is preparing for the arrival of his deputies from all over the world, and he informs Marcus that the full 'senate' will soon meet to announce his plan to take over the world by spreading bubonic plague. Later, Marcus meets Octavia and tells her that he thinks Bruno is taking the Roman Empire idea too far. Together they plan to kill Bruno and become the new party leaders. Meanwhile Steed has told Cathy that the chairman of UFD is Sir Bruno Lucer, a one-time left-wing politician. Cathy produces some photographs she took at UFD and one of them shows the marking Steed found earlier – a Roman monogram. On the pretext of selling Roman figurines, Steed visits Bruno who confesses that in his opinion the Romans were the greatest civilization ever, but denies having any strong political feelings.

THE GOLDEN FLEECE

By Roger Marshall and
Phyllis Norman

Captain Jason	Warren Mitchell
Major Ruse	Tenniel Evans
Sgt Major White	Barry Lineham
Mrs Kwan	Yu Ling
Mr Lo	Robert Lee
John Steed	Patrick Macnee
Catherine Gale	Honor Blackman
Esther	Lisa Peake
Jones	Michael Hawkins
Private Holmes	Ronald Wilson

Story Editor Richard Bates
Produced by John Bryce
Directed by Peter Hammond

As Steed leaves, he bumps into Marcus and recognises him as Dodds, the organiser of The World Empire Party. That night Cathy breaks into the UFD laboratory but is caught and held prisoner by a security guard. He phones Marcus, who tells Bruno they now have a guinea pig for his experiment with the plague. The following morning, Steed, concerned at Cathy's disappearance, breaks into Bruno's villa. He is discovered by Estow and locked in the cellar with Cathy. Bruno prepares for the 'senate meeting' and his subsequent coronation. At the height of the celebrations Bruno sends Lucius, an American senator, to fetch Cathy. When he arrives at the cell with a guard, he is surprised to find Steed missing. The guard takes Cathy away, and Steed appears from his hiding place above the door. The senator draws his sword but Steed kills him. In the hall above, Marcus and Octavia prepare a goblet of wine, containing the plague toxin which is meant to be given to Bruno. But Bruno is suspicious, and changes the goblets around, giving the 'doctored' one to Cathy, and orders her to drink it. She hesitates – then throws the wine in his face. At that moment, Steed arrives and the senators flee, leaving Steed and Cathy to fight the guards. They quickly dispose of the opposition and set out in search of Bruno and Marcus, only to find Bruno dead. Marcus has killed him and the debt is paid. Together they arrest Marcus and his accomplice, Octavia.

AFTER dinner with Cathy at a Chinese restaurant, Steed deliberately gets the cloakroom attendant to hand him the wrong coat. When they reach Steed's flat he searches the coat pockets and finds a cheque for £2000 made out to Mr Jason and drawn against a Chinese bank. Steed decides to wait and see who collects it. Meanwhile at the restaurant, an elderly Chinese gentleman, Mr Lo, tells the owner, Mrs Kwan, to prepare for the arrival of three guests, one of whom is Mr Jason. During the meeting Mr Lo lets it be known that someone in the organisation has absconded with £10,000. Jason realises that it is one of his men, and promises to investigate. Next morning, Jason visits Steed, having traced him through the address in Steed's coat. When Jason has left, Steed tells Cathy why he is interested in the restaurant – it is being used as a cover by Mr Lo, an international gold smuggler. Jason confers with his associates, Sgt White and Major Ruse, who agree that the man responsible for endangering their relationship with Mr Lo and the success of the highly important Golden Fleece Fund, must be brought to heel. Jason visits the man, Jones, an ex-corporal who now runs a garage, and asks him to return the money. Jones refuses and that night Mr Lo kills him. Steed has found out that Jason is really Captain Jason and asks Cathy to investigate him. Cathy, however, explains that she cannot as she has been offered a job cataloguing an army museum. At the base she meets an officer named Black. He shows Cathy around the museum and she discovers that Captain Jason is stationed at the base. Cathy phones Steed and tells him. When Jason, White and Ruse discover that Jones has been murdered, they determine that the next assignment from Lo must go through without a hitch. They agree that the Golden Fleece Fund – the proceeds from their smuggling activities with which they are supporting deserving ex-comrades – is the most important thing in their lives. Cathy learns that there is to be a large shipment of ammunition that night and informs Steed. When the ammunition arrives, Steed and Cathy watch as White, Jason and Ruse pack it into specially marked boxes. Steed forces the men to open one of the boxes – the tips of the bullets are made from pure gold. After reassuring the men that the names of the ex-comrades they were helping will never be revealed, Steed and Cathy arrest them.

Bruno gets more than he bargained for when Cathy throws her poisoned drink at him, in The Grandeur That Was Rome.

DON'T LOOK BEHIND YOU

By Brian Clemens

Catherine Gale	Honor Blackman
John Steed	Patrick Macnee
Ola	Janine Gray
Young man	Kenneth Colley
Man	Maurice Good

Story Editor Richard Bates
Produced by John Bryce
Directed by Peter Hammond

CATHY is invited for a weekend at the Devon home of Sir Cavalier Resagne, an authority on mediaeval costume. Steed drives her there and on the way picks her a bunch of wild flowers. At the house they are welcomed by Ola, a young girl, who says that Sir Cavalier will not be back until later. Steed leaves to spend the weekend on the coast. By dark Sir Cavalier has not returned and Ola insists that Cathy eats without him. After taking a phone call, Ola says she has to visit a friend in the village and Cathy assures her that she does not mind being alone. Later,

Cathy is menaced by an unseen murderer, whom she and Steed helped to arrest years before, in Don't Look Behind You.

Cathy is disturbed by a noise which she traces to a room at the end of the landing. In the room is an empty rocking horse – still rocking. At this moment the front door bell rings. Cathy answers it to find a young man in dark glasses who says he has run out of petrol – could he use the phone? Reluctantly, Cathy lets him in, but when he picks up the phone the wires have been cut. As he cannot repair the phone, Cathy gives him the keys to the garage so he can find a can of petrol. The young man goes to the garage and a few moments later Cathy hears him drive away. Cathy returns to the room with the rocking horse but the door is locked. She goes to her bedroom and finds Steed's flowers strewn across the floor. She decides to read a book but when she opens it, cut-up pieces of a photograph flutter to the floor. She puts the pieces together – it is a picture of herself. Cathy is startled to hear the phone ringing downstairs and hurries down to answer it – only to find the wires are still cut. As she enters the kitchen she hears a scream from outside. She finds a torch and goes out into the garden to investigate, but finds nothing. In the garage she discovers a Rolls-Royce. She turns on the headlights and tries to start the engine, but without success. Then she sees written on the garage door 'Don't look behind you'. She immediately does so and discovers she is sitting in a hearse. As she jumps out she steps on something – the young man's dark glasses. She has just returned to the house when all the lights go out, and in the dining-room the candles are being snuffed out one by one. She hurries upstairs and hears again the noise of the rocking horse. Rushing to the room – now open – she discovers the young man on the rocking horse, dead. She then hears her name being called, coming from first one part of the house and then another. She runs down to the front door but it is locked. She turns to see the shadow of a man standing in the hall. As she approaches him she realises he is a man she helped Steed arrest years before. Now he has escaped and means to kill her. Cathy backs into the dining-room to find another man there – Steed. He explains he knew the man had escaped and suspected that he might try to avenge himself. Steed, in fact, had never left the house. As the murderer breaks into the dining-room they overpower him.

DEATH A LA CARTE

By John Lucarotti

Catherine Gale	Honor Blackman
Emir Abdulla Akaba	Henry Soskin
Mellor	Robert James
Ali	Valentino Musetti
Umberto	David Nettheim
Lucien	Gordon Rollings
Arbuthnot	Ken Parry
John Steed	Patrick Macnee
Dr Spender	Paul Dawkins
Josie	Coral Atkins

Story Editor Richard Bates
Produced by John Bryce
Directed by Kim Mills

CATHY is hired by a London hotel to organise the visit of Emir Abdulla Akaba, who is visiting London for his annual medical check-up. The penthouse and adjacent kitchens are put at his disposal. Steed, suspecting that someone will try to assassinate the Emir, gets a job in the kitchen as a chef. He meets two highly temperamental chefs, Lucien and Umberto, and the head of the kitchen staff, Arbuthnot. Lucien bakes a cake to celebrate the Emir's arrival and as it is presented to him, Pentner, the Emir's adviser, hides a packet under the silver cake cover. After the reception, a young girl, Josie, takes the silver away to be cleaned. That night Lucien breaks into the cleaning room and removes the package, which contains several mushrooms. When he learns that the silver room has been broken into, Steed is worried that his suspicions may be confirmed. Meanwhile the Emir's medical adviser, Dr Spender, confirms that the Emir is ill, but the Emir intends issuing a bulletin saying he is quite well, so as to ease

Steed exchanges his familiar bowler hat for rather more unusual headgear in this scene from Death A La Carte.

DRESSED TO KILL

the unrest in his country. Steed tries to make sure that he cooks the Emir's next meal by knocking over Umberto's specially-prepared lasagne. Pentner, however, urges Lucien to ensure that the Emir's next meal is poisoned. That night as the Emir is dining with Dr Spender, he collapses and dies. Steed and Cathy are summoned to the penthouse and when they learn that the Emir is dead, Cathy insists on calling for an ambulance. Pentner refuses, saying that if the news reaches his country there would be a revolt. Dr Spender is asked to wait in one room while Steed and Cathy go into the bedroom. Suspecting that the Emir's death may have been planned, Steed climbs out on to the roof and down to the kitchen. He finds Lucien searching for the mushrooms, now powdered, and overpowers him. Cathy fuses the penthouse lights and when Pentner comes in to investigate she knocks him out and releases Dr Spender. Steed reveals that the mushroom powder was poisoned, although the Emir died of natural causes. Because the poison would not have taken effect for at least ten days, the Emir has died too soon and so Pentner's planned coup is defeated.

A story of the New Year
By Brian Clemens

Newman	Leon Eagles
First officer	Peter Fontaine
John Steed	Patrick Macnee
Catherine Gale	Honor Blackman
Napoleon	Alexander Davion
Pussy Cat	Anneke Wills
Barman	Frank Maher
Highwaywoman	Anthea Wyndham
Policeman	Richard Leech
Sheriff	John Junkin
Robin Hood	Leonard Rossiter

Story Editor Richard Bates
Produced by John Bryce
Directed by Bill Bain

AN early-warning station is alerted for World War III, but just in time it is discovered to be a false alarm. Steed explains to Cathy that all the country's early-warning stations were alerted, but as yet, nobody knows how it happened. Steed has found out that land has been bought overlooking the stations, and he himself has bought a plot overlooking the newest early-warning station. Later, Steed arrives at a large railway terminus dressed as a gambler for a New Year's Eve party to be held on a train. He meets two other guests, one dressed as Napoleon and a girl dressed as a cat. More guests arrive, including a monk, who dodges Newman, the conductor, and boards the train unseen. When the train leaves, Steed finds himself in the company of Napoleon, Pussy Cat, a sheriff, Robin Hood, a policeman and a highwaywoman. As they chat, they realise their invitations are false. The coach stops, and they get out, but the train has gone on leaving their coach stranded at a derelict station. They discover they all have a business meeting in London the next day, taking up their options on plots of land overlooking the new early-warning station. The sheriff, an ex-railwayman, says that this station was closed years ago and he volunteers to go to the nearest village for help. Hearing a scream, they rush outside and find his dead body – an arrow projecting from his back. Robin Hood announces that he has lost his bow and quiver, but denies that he murdered the sheriff. Steed goes to the ticket office and meets the monk – who is Cathy. On the coach the highwaywoman is overcome by the barman and the conductor. Steed searches the coach without success and when he goes back to the station the highwaywoman is there. The policeman says there are six plots of land for sale and seven people who claim ownership. He produces a map of the site and numbers of the plots. They know that the sheriff

owned the plot containing the railway station, so if they all write down the number of their plots, someone will give himself away. Steed and the highwaywoman – who is Cathy – have the same plot. The policeman produces a gun and they are handcuffed together and locked in the station-master's office. They soon escape and, in the ticket office, discover Napoleon, Newman and the barman discussing their plans to take over the early-warning stations. Cathy deals with the barman and Steed calls Napoleon out onto the platform where they have a Western-style shoot-out. Newman appears behind Steed, a shot rings out, and Steed turns to see Cathy, horse pistol smoking.

Steed is invited to a fancy dress New Year's Eve party, but finds that all the guests are Dressed To Kill.

Always impeccably dressed, Steed's clothes became even more dandified and Edwardian in the third series.

THE WHITE ELEPHANT

By John Lucarotti

George	Martin Friend
Noah Marshall	Geoffrey Quigley
John Steed	Patrick Macnee
Catherine Gale	Honor Blackman
Brenda Paterson	Judy Parfitt
Fitch	Bruno Barnabe
Joseph Gourlay	Toke Townley
Madge Jordan	Rowena Gregory
Lawrence	Edwin Richfield
Lew Conniston	Scott Forbes

Story Editor Richard Bates
Produced by John Bryce
Directed by Laurence Bourne

WHEN Snowy, a white elephant, is stolen from Noah Marshall's Zoo, Cathy joins the staff as a big-game hunter. Noah tells her that Snowy was found by one of his hunters, Conniston, in the Burmese jungle. He brought the elephant home and Noah has kept it as a pet ever since. Cathy discusses Snowy's disappearance with her keeper, George. He is convinced that the elephant is dead since only one man could have

Cathy and Steed are trapped in a zoo when they become involved with ivory smugglers, in The White Elephant.

taken her from the zoo alive – Lawrence, who owned the Burmese camp where Snowy was found. But George tells Cathy that Lawrence was killed in the jungle. Brenda, Noah's secretary, seems to be running the organisation almost by herself and even chooses Noah's guns for him. Cathy tells Steed of this and he visits the gun shop and meets Fitch, the owner. While Fitch goes to get a gun to show Steed, Steed notices some fine white powder on the counter and deliberately brushes his sleeve against it. Meanwhile Brenda is inspecting a new supply of cases that have been delivered by Madge, who makes cages for the zoo. The cases contain secret compartments, in which Brenda and Conniston smuggle ivory into the country. The next day, when Cathy is feeding the animals, she goes into the meat cold-room and discovers George hanging from a meat hook. Steed confirms that George was murdered and shows Cathy the sample of dust from the gun shop. When analysed it was found to be ivory dust. Steed tells Cathy ivory smuggling has been on the increase for some time, and is damaging Britain's reputation in Africa. Conniston and Brenda are preparing to ship another consignment of ivory out of the country. As Noah will be on night duty, they decide to drug him. That night Steed breaks into Madge's cage-making factory. He discovers Snowy hidden in a cage and finds Fitch working on the smuggled ivory. A fight breaks out and Steed knocks Fitch unconscious. Cathy meanwhile has returned to the zoo and finds the drugged Noah, but before she can arouse him Lawrence, supposedly dead, arrives. He is, in fact, in league with Conniston and suspects that Conniston and Brenda may be trying to double-cross him. Cathy overcomes Lawrence and ties him up, but Conniston arrives and locks Cathy in a tiger's cage. Steed goes to the zoo and releases Cathy. They set out to find Conniston and Brenda, and find them in the cage-making factory. They try to escape but Cathy and Steed stop them. Once the rest of the gang are under arrest, Steed and Cathy return the elephant to a grateful Noah.

THE LITTLE WONDERS

By Eric Paice

Beardmore	Tony Steedman
Sister Johnson	Lois Maxwell
Bishop of Winnipeg	David Bauer
Catherine Gale	Honor Blackman
John Steed	Patrick Macnee
Gerda	Rosemarie Dunham
Hasek	Frank Maher
Porter	Alex McDonald
Harry	Harry Landis
Big Sid	John Cowley
Fingers	Kenneth Warren

Story Editor Richard Bates
Produced by John Bryce
Directed by Laurence Bourne

MR BEARDMORE, a Harley Street specialist, is visited by the Bishop of Winnipeg and his nurse, Sister Johnson. The Bishop enters the examination cubicle and removes his vestments, beneath which he's wearing two guns. Cathy meets Steed at London Airport, where he shows her a suitcase belonging to the Rev Harbottle who has just been arrested. It contains a gun, ammunition, and a large German doll. The head of the doll is loose and Cathy takes it to a doll's hospital to have it restrung. Steed meanwhile visits Beardmore and learns that the Bishop does not have long to live. Cathy visits the doll's hospital. The next day, Gerda, the owner, rings as promised, to tell Cathy that the doll is ready for collection. But she must pay a restringing fee of £20,000. Cathy refuses to pay, but Gerda insists that she take back the doll. Cathy collects it and goes to Steed's flat. Steed notices that the head is different and they discover it contains microfilm, listing top British secret agents. Steed discovers that the Rev Harbottle was due to attend a convention of the leaders of a criminal organisation called Bibliotek. Next day, the Bishop of Winnipeg receives his guests – the Vicar of Melbourne, the Archdeacon of Singapore, the Dean of Quebec and other gentlemen bearing clerical titles. Steed arrives wearing a dog-collar. He calls himself the Vicar of Salisbury and claims he has taken over from the ailing Harbottle. The Bishop informs the men that they are there to elect a new Bishop, as he is in poor health. That night Sister Johnson appears from behind a secret screen and mows everyone down with a machine gun. Steed is wounded in the leg and visits Beardmore to have the wound dressed. When Steed has left, Sister Johnson appears and asks why Beardmore let him go. He replies that he is not yet sure of Steed's true identity. Sister Johnson visits the doll's hospital and asks Gerda why

THE WRINGER

By Martin Woodhouse

Hal Anderson	Peter Sallis
Charles	Paul Whitsun-Jones
Oliver	Barry Letts
John Steed	Patrick Macnee
Catherine Gale	Honor Blackman
Lovell	Gerald Sim
Bethune	Neil Robinson
'The Wringer'	Terence Lodge
Murdo	Douglas Cummings

Story Editor Richard Bates
Produced by John Bryce
Directed by Don Leaver

Cathy did not pay the repair fee. At that moment Steed arrives carrying the doll – whose head has been broken again – and promises to pay the fee once the doll has been repaired. After Steed leaves, Hasek, Gerda's assistant, searches the doll and to his relief finds the microfilm. Steed is at Cathy's flat when he receives a visit from the Dean of Quebec (he mysteriously avoided the machine gunning), who suggests that together they kill the Bishop and take over Bibliotek. Steed promises to think about it. Beardmore meanwhile has discovered that the microfilm is really Steed's laundry list and plans to get rid of Steed, Cathy and the Bishop. That night as Cathy returns to the hospital for the doll, she is captured by the Dean and taken to the school where Beardmore and Sister Johnson are waiting. Just in time, Steed rescues Cathy and arrests the Bishop and his colleagues.

Charles, Head of Operations, tells Cathy that Steed is a traitor who has killed six agents, in a scene from The Wringer.

STEED is told by Head of Operations, Charles, that fellow agent Anderson has not returned from his last mission – investigating a series of mysterious deaths of agents on an escape route between Austria and Hungary. Steed's enquiries lead him to a fire-watching tower in Scotland. There he finds Anderson suffering from shock and unable to remember anything of the last six weeks. Anderson then produces a dossier on Steed and says he remembers now that he can prove that Steed caused the agents' deaths. Anderson takes Steed back to Headquarters, where Charles finds enough evidence to convince him that Steed is a traitor. He turns Steed over to the head of the brain washing unit, a man nicknamed The Wringer. It soon becomes apparent that The Wringer, with the help of a man called Bethune, captured and brainwashed Anderson and forced him to write up the dossier on Steed. The Wringer wants to sabotage the Service by creating suspicion and mistrust amongst its members. After a long interrogation, The Wringer decides that Steed's mind is ready to be fed false information. Cathy arrives at the unit and when she discovers that Steed is already suffering from the effects of the brainwashing, she overpowers the guard and drags Steed out of the cell through an air vent. She then returns to London and tells Charles that Steed has escaped. Steed returns to the fire-watching tower and tries to make Anderson remember that it was he who compiled the dossier under pressure from The Wringer, but Anderson cannot remember anything. The Wringer and Bethune arrive at the fire-tower and their arrival jolts Anderson's memory. As Charles and Cathy arrive, they are greeted by Steed and Anderson confirms that The Wringer is the traitor.

The Dean of Quebec visits the Vicar of Salisbury – otherwise known as John Steed – in the case of The Little Wonders.

MANDRAKE

By Roger Marshall

Rev Wyper	George Benson
Roy Hopkins	Philip Locke
Benson	Robert Morris
John Steed	Patrick Macnee
Dr Macrombie	John Le Mesurier
Catherine Gale	Honor Blackman
Sexton	Jackie Pallo
Mrs Turner	Madge Ryan
Judy	Annette Andre

Story Editor Richard Bates
Produced by John Bryce
Directed by Bill Bain

STEED attends the funeral of an acquaintance, Benson, at a lonely cemetery in Cornwall. He learns from Benson's son that his father died suddenly and was buried in Cornwall at his own request. Visiting Cathy, Steed shows her newspaper cuttings announcing funeral services at the cemetery. The cemetery has not been so busy for years as the villages nearby have become derelict. All the funerals have been for people who lived in London. Meanwhile, young Benson visits the London surgery of Dr Macrombie and together with Roy Hopkins, the doctor's assistant, celebrate the success of their venture. When Benson has left, Macrombie suggests that they should cease their activities and retire. Hopkins, however, says that he has a new client, a Mrs Turner. Cathy photographs some of the more recent headstones in the cemetery. She meets the local vicar, the Rev Wyper, and while they are talking Hopkins arrives with Mrs Turner. Hopkins hopes that Wyper will be able to find a suitable plot for Mrs Turner's husband when he dies. Cathy overhears Hopkins telling the Sexton to keep an eye open for further strangers. Cathy shows Steed her photographs and Steed reveals that out of the eleven names nine were in Who's Who and seven of them left estates of over £100,000. He has also discovered that Hopkins owns a cracker factory. It seems, however, that Hopkins has another source of income. Hopkins meanwhile introduces Mrs Turner to Macrombie and together they go over her husband's case history. He is elderly and wealthy and his sudden death would arouse no suspicion. Macrombie agrees to help and gives her a small bottle of arsenic for her husband. Steed discovers that Benson recently visited Dr Macrombie and, at his suggestion, Cathy pays the doctor a visit. She manages to leave a window unlatched so that Steed can break in and study the doctor's files. Cathy returns to the cemetery but is disturbed by the Sexton. They fight and Cathy knocks the Sexton into an open grave. But Rev Wyper appears and holds Cathy at gunpoint. Next morning, Steed visits Benson, who admits his part in the plot. Cathy tells Wyper that she thinks the recent burials have been caused through arsenic poisoning. The soil in the area has a very high arsenic content, so a few weeks after the burials a postmortem would be unable to prove that arsenic had been the cause of the deaths. Steed arrives in time for the funeral of Mr Turner, and once the service is over, he and Cathy tell Hopkins, Macrombie and Mrs Turner that they have buried a coffin full of sand. Hopkins tries to escape, but the Sexton — having been bribed by Cathy — stops him and the gang are arrested.

The Rev Wyper holds Cathy at gunpoint when she investigates the recent burials in his parish, in Mandrake.

THE SECRETS BROKER

By Ludovic Peters

Mrs Wilson	Avice Landon
Julia Wilson	Jennifer Wood
Bruno	Valentino Musetti
Frederick Paignton	John Stone
Catherine Gale	Honor Blackman
John Steed	Patrick Macnee
Marion Howard	Patricia English
Jim Carey	Brian Hankins
Cliff Howard	John Ringham
Allan Paignton	Ronald Allen
Waller	Jack May

Story Editor Richard Bates
Produced by John Bryce
Directed by Jonathan Alwyn

WHEN one of Steed's associates is murdered, Steed has only two clues — a wine list from Waller and Paignton's wine stores, and a reference to a research establishment called Bridlingtons. Cathy is sent to Bridlingtons while Steed, on the pretext of buying a crate of wine, visits the wine shop. He notices Waller's anxiety when Frederick Paignton knocks over a pile of wine lists, and Steed surreptitiously removes a copy. At Bridlington's, Cathy meets Marion and Cliff Howard, who are working on a secret underwater tracking device. Cathy learns that Marion has a lover but is unable to discover his name. Meanwhile we learn that the murderer, Frederick Paignton, was blackmailed into committing the crime

Cathy is shown the underwater tracking device when she visits Bridlingtons, in The Secrets Broker.

THE TROJAN HORSE

by Malcolm Hulke

Johnson	**Derek Newark**
Rt Hon Lucian	**Geoffrey**
Ffordsham	**Whitehead**
Kirby	**James Donnelly**
George Meadows	**Arthur Pentelow**
Major	
Ronald Pantling	**Basil Dignam**
John Steed	**Patrick Macnee**
Ann Meadows	**Lucinda Curtis**
Tony Heuston	**T P McKenna**
Lynton Smith	**John Lowe**
Catherine Gale	**Honor Blackman**
Tote girl	**Marjorie Keys**

Story Editor Richard Bates
Produced by John Bryce
Directed by Laurence Bourne

AT a deserted racecourse the Hon Lucian Ffordsham waits with Johnson, a bookie's collector, to interview Kirby, who refuses to pay his debts. Johnson beats up Kirby and Ffordsham drags him away. Kirby fails to get up and Johnson tells Ffordsham he is dead. Frightened, they run away. Kirby gets to his feet, smiles and walks away. Steed visits the stables of George Meadows, a famous racehorse trainer. He tells Meadows that he has been asked by the Foreign Office to keep an eye on a horse, Sebastian the Second, belonging to a wealthy Shah. Steed is introduced to one of Meadows' jockeys, Lynton Smith, who says he will leave the stable after his ride in the Crediton Cup. Steed explains to Cathy his interest in Meadows' stables. Recently there have been a series of apparently unmotivated killings of eminent politicians and businessmen. Watching the Crediton Cup race, Steed and Cathy see Lynton Smith fall. He is carried into the steward's office on a stretcher. Kirby appears, dressed as a doctor, and murders Smith. He then returns to the office of Heuston, owner of a large betting shop syndicate. As Kirby leaves, Cathy arrives and explains to Heuston that she has been swindled by one of his settlers. She gives him the details of an elaborate bet and Heuston agrees that she is right. He is so impressed by Cathy's mathematics that he offers her a job, which she accepts. That night Steed is at the stables and witnesses a secret meeting of the jockeys and stable hands, during which Johnson gives a lecture on the use of poisons and firearms. At the end of the lecture Heuston appears and pays the men off. Steed is seen leaving by one of the hands and when Heuston learns of this, he suggests that Johnson gets rid of Steed. The following morning Ann Meadows discovers that her father is missing – not even

by Mrs Wilson, a fake medium who holds seances in which she uncovers her client's secrets. That night, Mrs Wilson visits Frederick's brother, Allan – Marion's lover – and tells him that his brother is in trouble and unless he helps her steal the tracking device, she will go to the police. Allan persuades Marion to put the Bridlingtons' alarm system out of action the following Tuesday. If she does not help, Mrs Wilson will tell Marion's husband of their relationship. Reluctantly, Marion agrees to help. That night, Steed and Cathy break into the wine shop and discover an entrance to a photographic studio hidden behind a false wine barrel. Steed has the wine list examined – the full stops are, in fact, micro-dots containing the stolen plans of new military weapons. He returns to the wine shop the following morning and is invited to a wine-tasting party on Tuesday night. On Tuesday, Marion persuades her husband not to work late, and then goes to the party with Allan. During the party, Steed deliberately leans on the false barrel and to Waller's embarrassment, 'discovers' the photographic studio. Meanwhile Frederick breaks into Bridlingtons but a moment later Cliff returns and sounds the alarm – which still works. In his panic, Frederick shoots Cliff. That night Steed breaks into the wine shop again and discovers Frederick's dead body hidden in a wine barrel. Marion is invited to Mrs Wilson's next seance, where she is forced at gunpoint into the cellar, and meets Waller. Waller tells her that she must bring her husband's plans to him immediately. Allan now tells Steed that Marion is missing and Steed hurries to the seance room. When he arrives, he is held at gunpoint by Julia, Mrs Wilson's daughter, who takes him into the cellar. Waller suggests that Steed be dropped into the Thames in a barrel of cement. At this moment, Allan arrives and Steed overpowers Julia. As Waller turns his gun on Allan and Steed, Cathy appears from out of a wine barrel and knocks Waller out.

Major Pantling, her father's close friend, knows of his whereabouts. Later, Johnson tells Heuston that he was forced to kill Meadows because he threatened to expose Heuston's crimes. Heuston is then confronted by Ann who says she knows her father and Heuston were running a racket together. Heuston confesses to this and tells Ann her father is dead. Ann pulls out a gun, but Cathy appears, disarms Ann, and tells her to call the police. Meanwhile, Steed finds Meadows' body in the back of a horsebox. He is discovered by Johnson who pulls a gun on him and takes him to Heuston. Heuston tells Johnson to carry out his orders and kill Steed. Johnson hesitates, and at that moment Cathy enters the room. Steed is able to disarm Johnson and covers the rest of the gang while Cathy and Major Pantling take Heuston into custody.

BUILD A BETTER MOUSETRAP

By Brian Clemens

Dave	Donald Webster
Catherine Gale	Honor Blackman
Ermintrude	Nora Nicholson
Cynthia	Athene Seyler
John Steed	Patrick Macnee
Harris	Harold Goodwin
Col Wesker	John Tate
Caroline	Alison Seebohm
Stignant	Allan McClelland
Jessy	Marian Diamond
Gordon	David Anderson

Story Editor Richard Bates
Produced by John Bryce
Directed by Peter Hammond

CATHY, having joined a motorcycle gang, calls on two elderly ladies, Ermintrude and Cynthia, who own a watermill and the surrounding meadows, to ask their permission for the gang to use one of the fields for scrambles. Ermintrude refuses and threatens to put a spell on the gang unless she leaves. Meanwhile, Steed, staying at a local inn, learns from the barman, Harris, about the mysterious jammings of all mechanical and electrical devices in the neighbourhood. He meets Stignant, a security officer at the nearby atomic research station, who admits that sometimes all clocks, engines, refrigerators and other apparatus have refused to function. But this has only happened since the arrival of the motorcycle gang. Steed arranges a rally and sends off each of the motor bike riders, including Cathy, across separate parts of the country. All the riders break down, and when she returns, Steed shows Cathy a map of the area and points out where each bike stopped. In the middle of the affected area is the watermill. Steed asks Stignant to find out anything he can about the two sisters. He discovers Ermintrude is the daughter of the late Professor Peck who, at the time of his death, had been working on several interesting experiments. Steed arranges to meet Stignant at the mill that night. Meanwhile at the mill, Ermintrude is working on two experiments. When Steed arrives at the mill, he finds Stignant murdered, in the bushes outside the mill. At the inn, Cathy tells Steed that Dave, leader of the gang, has offered to show her round the mill. Steed says he will follow her later and Cathy leaves. Caroline, the niece of Wesker, a retired army man, insists that Steed has a drink with her. She tries to drug him, but Steed, realising what's happening, pours the drink away. Caroline, believing she has been successful, leaves for the mill. Steed is about to follow her, when Jessy, another member of the motorcycle gang, brings him a letter posted by Stignant before his death. This reveals that Professor Peck had been working on a long-range jamming device, the plans of which he had left with his daughter. Steed hurries out of the inn and bumps into Harris who has just found Dave bound and gagged in the loft of his barn. Steed realises that Cathy has gone off with the wrong man. Meanwhile Cathy has discovered what she believes to be the jamming device but at that moment 'Dave' removes his helmet and goggles to reveal himself as Wesker. Caroline arrives and she and Wesker are about to leave when their exit is blocked by Ermintrude and Cynthia. Wesker escapes and runs out with the jamming device as Dave and Steed appear. In the ensuing fight, the other equipment is destroyed and Cathy is puzzled when Steed explains with a smile that the jamming device Wesker had stolen was really Ermintrude's attempt to build a better mousetrap.

When Cathy joins a motorcycle gang she and Steed become involved in plans to Build A Better Mousetrap.

THE OUTSIDE-IN MAN

By Philip Chambers

John Steed	Patrick Macnee
Catherine Gale	Honor Blackman
Mark Charter	James Maxwell
Alice	Virginia Stride
Quilpie	Ronald Radd
Jenkins	Ronald Mansell
Edwards	Anthony Dawes
Ambassador	William Devlin
Major Zulficar	Basil Hoskins
Helen Rayner	Beryl Baxter
Michael Lynden	Arthur Lovegrove
Sharp	Philip Anthony

Story Editor Richard Bates
Produced by John Bryce
Directed by Jonathan Alwyn

STEED is put in charge of the security arrangements for the forthcoming visit of Sharp, an Englishman who five years previously started anti-British propaganda and brought about revolution and bloodshed in Abarain. Sharp, termed traitor by the British, was awarded a military title in Abarain, and has now returned to Britain for trade talks, with diplomatic immunity. Steed points out to his superior, Quilpie, the irony of protecting a man they were trying to kill five years earlier. Two agents died in the attempts on Sharp's life – Rayner and Charter. Now, Charter turns up alive. Two days earlier he had been released after five years in prison. Steed is uneasy at the coincidence of the release of a man ordered to kill Sharp, and Charter's visit to England. Steed reads Charter's files and believes that he will still try to kill Sharp. Realising that he will need a car, Steed arranges for Cathy to sell one to Charter. Charter visits Helen Rayner, and obtains a list of their agent friends. He then drives to the garage of one of the agents, Lyden, and makes him respray the car. Cathy calls at the Abarain Embassy but they refuse to cancel Sharp's visit. She next calls on Helen Rayner and discovers that Charter has had the car resprayed. The car is soon traced to a remote cottage in Sussex. Charter meanwhile is caught trying to break into the Abarain Embassy. He is taken to the Ambassador, who tells him that should he be reluctant to kill Sharp, they will help. Sharp arrives in England. At a reception given in his honour, Steed tells Sharp that he has persuaded Charter to pretend to seek revenge on Sharp, in order to confirm his suspicion that Sharp had outlived his usefulness to Abarain and they wanted him dead. Charter had been released in the hope that he would do the job for them – and in so doing, put the British government at a disadvantage. Convinced that Steed's suspicions are correct, Sharp tells Steed that once the trade talks are over, he'll return to Abarain.

THE CHARMERS

By Brian Clemens

John Steed	Patrick Macnee
Catherine Gale	Honor Blackman
Martin	John Barcroft
Keller	Warren Mitchell
Kim Lawrence	Fenella Fielding
Betty Smythe	Vivian Pickles
Sam	John Greenwood
Harrap	Frank Mills
Horace Cleeves	Malcolm Russell
Mr Edgar	Brian Oulton

Story Editor Richard Bates
Produced by John Bryce
Directed by Bill Bain

STEED and Cathy discuss the mysterious death of Vinkel – a member of the opposition. Steed thinks they are purging the organisation, but then a man, Martin, tries to kill Steed in revenge for Vinkel's death. Steed protests his innocence and Martin is finally persuaded to take Steed to his superior, Keller. Keller and Steed discover that various acts of sabotage which each attributed to the other's side, have, in fact, been initiated by a third party. Steed suggests they work together to expose the other group but Keller insists that as an act of good faith they should each supply a hostage. Steed agrees to give Keller Cathy, and in return is presented with an attractive woman called Kim Lawrence. Martin and Cathy retrace Vinkel's movements and end up at a dentist's. Cathy goes in to make enquiries and when she returns, Martin has disappeared. Meanwhile Steed and Kim call at an exclusive tie shop, but the owner insists he has never heard of Vinkel. That night, they return to the shop and find Martin dead, in a crateful of bowler hats. Next day, Steed follows the crate, which is carried away by four elegantly-dressed young men. They go to a charm school, where Steed meets Mr Edgar, who tells him that he is training the men to become gentlemen. Steed notices the crate in Edgar's office, but now it only contains bowler hats. Meeting Kim outside, she suggests that maybe they followed the wrong crate, as she saw another one addressed to a dentist's. At the dentist's, he meets Cathy. Cathy tells him that Kim is not a member of Keller's staff but merely an actress hired to play the part. Rushing into the dentist's surgery, where Kim is supposed to be having treatment, Steed finds her gone and the dentist dead. Kim has been bound and gagged and hidden in a crate. As the young men arrive to remove the crate, Steed knocks one of them out and takes his place. Arriving at the charm school, they are greeted by Edgar and Steed discovers that the young men are really being taught how to kill, and all their umbrellas are swordsticks. Steed releases Kim but is interrupted by the arrival of Keller, who unmasks Steed and admits that he runs the third party. Cathy arrives and has a fencing match with one of the young men, and Steed knocks out Edgar. Keller is about to shoot Steed when Kim throws a fencing foil at him, killing him. Her mother, she tells Steed, used to be in a knife-throwing act.

Steed and Cathy are told by their superior, Quilpie, to protect a man whom they once wanted to kill, in The Outside-In Man.

Cathy is given to Keller as a hostage, but it is not long before the tables are turned on him, in The Charmers.

CONCERTO

By Terence Dicks and
Malcolm Hulke

Peterson	Bernard Brown
Catherine Gale	Honor Blackman
Polly White	Valerie Bell
Burns	Geoffrey Colville
John Steed	Patrick Macnee
Zalenko	Nigel Stock
Stefan Veliko	Sandor Eles
Darleen	Dorinda Stevens
Receptionist	Carole Ward
Robbins	Leslie Glazer

Story Editor Richard Bates
Produced by John Bryce
Directed by Kim Mills

IMPORTANT trade talks are taking place in London between representatives of the Russian senate and their British counterparts. To reinforce goodwill during the talks, a brilliant young pianist, Stefan Veliko from behind the Iron Curtain, is giving his first concert in London. When it is discovered that someone is trying to break up the talks, Steed puts Cathy in charge of security. She acts as a representative of the British Cultural Council and calls on Veliko with Steed. They discover that an attractive young girl, Polly, has accused Veliko of assaulting her and the girl has since been killed. Steed believes that her murder is part of an attempt to blacken Veliko's name and thus create an international incident which would affect the trade talks. Steed and Veliko's manager decide to keep the incident from the press. Steed discovers that Polly worked at a strip club, and visits a friend of hers there called Darleen. Darleen says she knows nothing of Polly's last job, but afterwards rings Steed and says she has some information for him. When Steed goes to her flat, he is knocked unconscious by Burns – Polly's murderer – who then forces Darleen to phone Stefan and invite him to the club. Steed discovers from Cathy what has happened and hurries to the club with Zalenko. They arrive in time to save Stefan from being compromised, with Darleen, in some photographs. Steed and Zalenko check the recital room in which Veliko is to give his concert before a distinguished audience – including the Minister responsible for the trade negotiations. Meanwhile at the club, Darleen overhears Burns and Peterson, his assistant, discussing how they plan to murder someone at the recital. She tells Cathy she will provide the name of the person to be murdered for £500. Cathy goes to the club with the money but finds Darleen dead. Before she can escape, she is threatened by Burns. At gunpoint he says he will kill her if she doesn't reveal what she knows. Cathy is rescued by Steed's arrival at the club. He overcomes Burns and they leave for the recital. During the interval, Peterson tells Stefan that he must pretend to shoot the Minister – otherwise he will be involved in another incident, thus ruining his reputation. As Steed and Cathy watch the Minister closely, wondering who will try to kill him, Cathy notices Stefan has a gun and, realising that Peterson is responsible, attacks and overcomes him before anyone is harmed.

In Concerto, Honor Blackman wore one of the distinctive outfits specially designed for her by Frederick Starke.

ESPRIT DE CORPS

By Eric Paice

Capt Trench	John Thaw
Sgt Marsh	Douglas Robinson
Pte Jessop	Roy Kinnear
Major Gen Sir Ian	
Stewart-Bollinger	Duncan Macrae
John Steed	Patrick Macnee
Mrs Craig	Pearl Catlin
Catherine Gale	Honor Blackman
Lady Dorothy	
Bollinger	Joyce Heron
Pte Asquith	Anthony Blackshaw
Admiral	Hugh Morton
Signaller	James Falkland

Story Editor Richard Bates
Produced by John Bryce
Directed by Don Leaver

AT Marroon Barracks, Captain Trench, of the Highland Guards, commands the execution by firing squad of Corporal Craig. After the execution, Steed meets Private Jessop, a member of the firing squad, who tells him that the regimental post-mortem on Craig will show that he died as a result of an accident while cleaning his rifle. Steed tells Cathy that he knows Craig was killed by bullets from three different rifles, and asks her to check the military establishment. She visits the local civil defence centre to meet Captain Trench and is invited by him to attend a regimental cocktail party that evening. Cathy arrives at the party with Steed, and while she heads for the Mess, Steed breaks into the Barrack Room and discovers huge amounts of ammunition. As he leaves, Jessop arrives and holds him at riflepoint. Steed offers the man a bribe to release him and Jessop accepts. Next day, on the pretext of writing the history of the regiment, Steed meets Lady Bollinger. She says that since her husband's retirement, he has devoted himself to Scottish history and has discovered that his step-son is the rightful heir to the throne of Scotland. The son, however, is a bookmaker in Halifax and is uninterested in making a claim. The final plans for an army exercise are taking place in Trench's office. Also present are an Admiral, a Marine Colonel and an Air Vice-Marshall. They all pledge their support for Operation Claymore, an exercise in capturing London. Listening outside, Steed waits for the men to leave, then climbs into the office and tries to read the secret papers relating to the exercise, but he is caught and arrested by Trench. Cathy is visited by Colonel Bollinger and he tells her that he has traced her family history and ·discovered that Cathy – after the Colonel's step-son who has disclaimed the title – is in direct line to the throne of

LOBSTER QUADRILLE

By Richard Lucas

Bush	Gary Watson
Quentin Slim	Corin Redgrave
John Steed	Patrick Macnee
Catherine Gale	Honor Blackman
Dr Stannage	Norman Scace
Mason	Burt Kwouk
Capt Slim	Leslie Sands
Katie Miles	Jennie Linden

Story Editor Richard Bates
Produced by John Bryce
Directed by Kim Mills

Scotland. He tells Cathy to be ready to take up accession. Steed meanwhile has been charged with treason by a court martial and Trench orders his execution. Lady Bollinger visits Cathy and explains that she believes her husband is planning a military coup and for his own sake must be stopped. Steed now faces the firing squad led by Captain Trench. They fire and Steed falls to the ground. The firing squad – with the exception of Jessop, who is left to dispose of the body – is marched away. As they leave, Jessop, having decided to accept a further bribe from Steed, tells Steed to get up. That night, at the Mess dance, Bollinger appears and denounces the military coup which he says Trench planned. Trench is placed under arrest but Cathy and Steed know that Bollinger means to continue the coup. They capture him as he leaves the Officer's Mess. Bollinger protests his innocence and tries to bribe them, telling Cathy that she could have been the Queen of England. Cathy smiles and replies that she made Steed fake her family tree.

Steed and Cathy discuss the protection of Stefan Veliko, a brilliant young Russian pianist, in Concerto.

THE Avengers visit a hospital mortuary where Steed identifies the body of an agent, Williams, discovered in the ashes of a burnt-out fishing hut. Among the dead man's belongings is an unusual chess piece. They visit the scene of the crime and as Steed pokes about in the ashes, he is discovered by Bush, who says he is trespassing. The hut belongs to his partner, Captain Slim. Steed visits Captain Slim, but is unable to discover how the fire started. He also meets Slim's daughter-in-law, .Kate, who tells him that Slim's son, Quentin, was recently drowned when his boat capsized in a sudden storm. Cathy takes the chess piece to Mason, the owner of a chess shop, who says the chess piece is one of a set bought by a man named Williams. When Steed returns to his flat, he finds Cathy trying to solve a list of chess moves that she has found in some letters addressed to Williams – she realises that they don't make sense. Meanwhile Bush phones Mason and tells him of Steed's visit. When Mason tells him about Cathy's visit to the shop, Bush asks Mason to find out her identity. Later that evening, Steed receives a phone call confirming his suspicions about Quentin Slim. Before his death he was under suspicion of smuggling. Steed leaves Cathy working on the chess moves and promises to return soon. Cathy continues her work, convinced that the moves form a code. She breaks the code but is interrupted by a knock at the front door. She answers it and finds herself confronted by Mason with a gun. When Steed returns to the flat Cathy has gone. He notices the original unusual chess piece standing alone on the board and, under a cushion, he finds Cathy's notes. He heads for the chess shop and breaks in. During his search he finds a small quantity of dope hidden in a drawer. As he leaves, Kate arrives and tells him that her husband is not dead but had moved to France. Together they visit Captain Slim and try to convince him that his son is still alive. Slim refuses to believe that Quentin wasn't drowned or that his son

was guilty of smuggling dope. Just then Quentin and Bush arrive and, although Steed disarms Bush, Quentin escapes. He goes to the fishing huts and orders Mason to prepare a boat for their escape. He ties Cathy to a rowing boat and as they leave sets fire to the hut. The following morning, two charred bodies are found among the ashes of the burnt-out fishing hut. Steed is concerned about Cathy's disappearance – until she finally arrives to say that she spent the night at the local police station.

Captain Trench talks to Steed and Cathy at a party, but they find that he has a very curious notion of Esprit de Corps.

In search of clues to solve the riddle of the chess piece, Steed breaks into Mason's shop, in Lobster Quadrille.

The Avengers *was one of the most car-conscious of all television shows and is remembered for its use of expensive, exclusive and elegant cars.*

Above: Steed forsakes his usual mode of transport for a bicycle ride by the river, in Brief For Murder.

Right: Steed stands beside his elegant yellow 1926 vintage Rolls-Royce Silver Ghost, a more suitable vehicle.

Right: Tara sits on the wing of her red Lotus Europe MK 1, which was considered to be a more feminine car for her.

Above: Cathy Gale often preferred two wheels to four, and is seen here riding on her powerful Triumph motorcycle.

Left: Emma Peel drove a 1966 Lotus Elan in a silvery powder blue in both the fourth and the fifth series.

Above: Steed drives his fully-restored 1929 vintage 4.5 litre Bentley in racing green, with Vanden Plas coachwork.

Left: Tara King's first car was a 7,014 cc AC 428, but it was too powerful and was replaced by a Lotus Europa.

Patrick Macnee/Diana Rigg
1965-66

M-Appeal

SO successful was the video-taped Blackman series that ABC Television decided to mount a 'new improved' 26-episode series, to be filmed for the first time, and to be produced by well-known British film producer Julian Wintle. (The third series had been the first *Avengers* series to sell to an international market – though, due to the lack of technology at the time to convert successfully a 405 line recording to a 525 line US transmission, it was never sold to America. He assembled a team of experienced telefilm professionals including Albert Fennell and Brian Clemens, who was appointed Associate Producer and Story Editor for the new series, and commissioned 26 scripts from the best British writers in this field.

It was then that Honor Blackman dropped her bombshell. She would not be continuing the Cathy Gale role after the end of the current series. If the producers had become hysterical at this point no one would have blamed them. Not only did they now have to find a new female lead for Steed, they also had to invent a new character, because Honor Blackman had so made the role of Cathy Gale her own, it would be almost impossible for another actress to take over. Auditions were held to find a partner for Patrick Macnee and well over 60 actresses were tested for the as yet un-named part. It was then that Marie Donaldson, a press officer working on the programme, had a brainwave. She realised that the new character had to have man appeal, and as she played around with the phrase in her head she couldn't help thinking Man Appeal, *M* appeal – Emma Peel. She liked the sound of the name and the producers leapt at it.

Emma Peel quickly became the beautiful young widow of test pilot Peter Peel and the daughter of a wealthy shipowner. A woman of independent means, she was the complete one-jump-ahead jet-set female, and the perfect partner for Steed in the espionage and counter-espionage game. (The fact that these two activities are covered by separate departments, MI6 and MI5 respectively, didn't deter the producers. They cheerfully explained that Steed was an employee of 'MI5 and a half'. Outwardly Emma was cast in the same image as Cathy Gale. She had the same streamlined life, same ultra-modern man-tailored leather clothes and the same propensity for dealing with thugs. But the relationship between Emma and Steed became much warmer and gayer than the one Steed had shared with Cathy. Whereas Steed had always used every trick in the book in commanding help from his amateur assistant, Emma was always aware that Steed's charm was a cloak for each attempt to involve her in some dangerous mission. Her innocence of what was going on was often·her best protection, and she accompanied Steed gracefully, but frequently gave him the sharp edge of her tongue before succumbing with a smile.

However, it was vital to find the right Emma, and after months of searching it began to look as if she didn't exist. Then they found a beautiful actress called Elizabeth Shepherd, and she was signed for the role. However, Miss Shepherd didn't impress the producers, because after seeing rushes of the first episode, they decided that, although an accomplished actress, she didn't give the character the light comedy they were looking for. Having spent over £120,000, they stopped produc-

tion and the search for a new girl began. A further 20 or so actresses were tested before Dodo Watts, the programme's casting director, asked the producers to look at an actress she'd just used in an *Armchair Theatre* production, 'The Hothouse'.

After viewing a tape of the play, the production team sensed that this could be the girl they'd been searching for and they invited her to take a screen test with Patrick Macnee. The results were first-class. Macnee and the young actress seemed to find an immediate rapport and she was signed to a long-term contract. The actress was, of course, Diana Rigg.

If Emma represented the future of Britain, Steed, as before, stood for the best of the past. He still embodied tradition and all that people associated with the British way of life – gracious living; a London home full of family heirlooms and handsome antiques; a cultivated appreciation of food, wine, horseflesh and pretty women; proficiency at gentlemanly sports such as fencing, archery and polo; exquisite tailoring; a high-handed way with underlings and an endearing eccentricity which manifested itself in such things as driving a vintage Bentley convertible and fighting with a swordstick, rolled umbrella or any handy implement, rather than the more obvious weapons.

In the best British stiff-upper-lip tradition, however, this rarified exterior camouflaged a highly-efficient operator, who quietly got his man while his opponents were still being distracted by his amusing ways – just as Emma's wit and femininity concealed a cool resourceful woman who was at her best in a crisis. Emma's mode of fighting was different, too. Cathy had been the judo expert. Emma's fighting technique was karate-influenced. Villains were attacked with the edge of the hand (palm and fingers held rigidly flat), the elbow, fingers and thumbs, and the foot, which, in action, became part of a graceful, but deadly, balletic movement. A jolting, stiff-legged kick was delivered as high as an adversary's jaw, to great effect. The fight sequences became more ambitious – choreographed mayhem – meticulously planned and arranged by one of Britain's top stuntmen, Ray Austin.

As the previous Blackman series had made a breakthrough in setting fashion trends, ABC were determined that the new series would once again lead the way, and called in top designer John Bates to produce a new and daring wardrobe for Emma. Bearing in mind that a filmed series has a screen-life expectancy of five years or more, and that the more extreme the fashions are, the quicker they date, Bates created designs that were as modern as her character, yet timeless enough to remain acceptable when the series was shown in some foreign country two or three years later. Since Emma was to be a younger, gayer and more feminine character than her predecessor, Bates designed a number of day and evening dresses which were both demure and daring, in materials such as lace, silk, plastics, lamé and crêpe. Emma's fighting suits largely discarded the leather image for a different kind of sex appeal based on form-fitting stretch jersey, or (where leather was used) on an animal look conveyed through snakeskin, or a soft-centred look achieved by wearing leather over a crêpe blouse. A recurring target motif was used to symbolise the op-art space-age design. Thigh-length skirts, catsuits, hipster pants and white berets completed the new look. ABC commissioned tie-ups with 14 British fashion manufacturers and soon major stores and

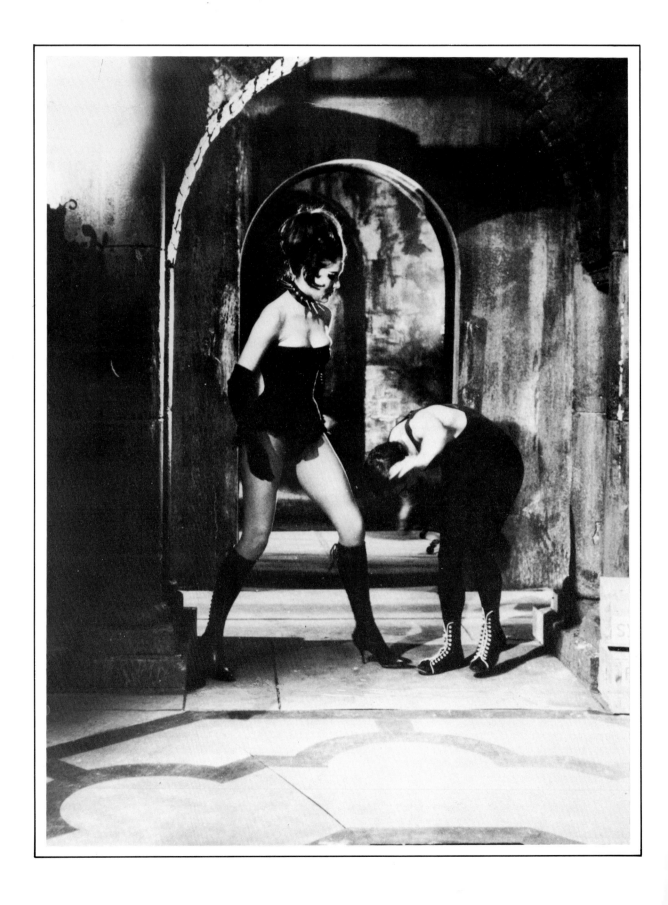

boutiques in Britain and overseas were selling what became known as the Jean Varon/Avengers pack.

Steed's address for the series remained the same, but this time we are treated to more interior views. He now had a tape machine that automatically recorded all telephone conversations (in and out). The apartment was on two levels, and the bathroom was reached by climbing three steps which led from the sitting-room. Added to his antique collection were a barrel clock, an 18th-century desk, a fox umbrella stand and a cast-iron Victorian juicer. A wrought iron staircase led from the kitchen to the underground garage.

Emma lived in a roof-top penthouse in Hampstead. The flat was basically one large room, which could be sitting-room, bedroom, or whatever she desired. All the furniture was concealed behind sycamore panelling. The room was full of gadgets, with everything operated by a master-control console mounted on the wall. With the press of a button, Emma could operate the sliding panels to reveal her wardrobe, bed, etc.

Clemens introduced certain ground rules. Interviewed at the time, he said, 'We admit to only one class . . . and that is the upper. Because we are a fantasy, we will not show a uniformed policeman or a coloured man. And you will not see anything so common as blood in *The Avengers*. If we did introduce a coloured man or a policeman, we would have the yardstick of social reality and that would make the whole thing quite ridiculous. Alongside a bus queue of ordinary men-in-the-street, Steed would become a caricature.' The show could contain sex, but it was never blatant. It was psychological sex – a salaciousness at the back of the mind rather than through the eye.

'We don't kill women in *The Avengers*. There may be hundreds of bodies scattered about, but we don't dwell or linger on them. We don't regard ourselves as a violent show. Perhaps that is why psychiatrists have said we have the ideal presentation of violence for children. We try to achieve the effect that once an actor has been killed, he gets up, collects his money and goes home.'

Albert Fennell (who, with Brian Clemens was to become the guiding light throughout the next five years of *The Avengers'* screen life) was responsible for adding that extra touch of gloss to the finished series. An experienced film technician, he put the stamp of technical expertise on the series and (though he has stayed somewhat in the background as far as the media is concerned) deserves as much credit for shaping the series as Clemens.

Clemens quickly realised that the only way to break into the American market (and thus ensure a profit) was to create something with which the Americans themselves could not compete. So the formula was to set the stories against a tongue-in-cheek panorama of the picture postcard Britain illustrated in tourist brochures. Every aspect of British life was incorporated as it was promoted overseas; from atom-stations, bio-chemical plants and modern industry on the one hand to fox-hunting, stately homes and the Olde Englishe Inne on the

other. It was all gently sent-up as a good-humoured counterpoint to the dangerous adventures of the two secret agents who hid their iron fists beneath the velvet gloves of high living and sophisticated luxury.

'We became terribly British,' said Clemens. 'A car is a car, and not an automobile. A lift is a lift, never an elevator. It is this Britishness that fits the fantasy world so appealing to the Americans.'

The theme music, previously a monotonous jazz theme, was revamped under the talented Laurie Johnson. The producers felt that the new direction the show was to take needed a more distinctive theme to complement the way-out situations they had planned. The new *Avengers* theme was composed after long discussions between Brian Clemens, Albert Fennell, Julian Wintle and Laurie Johnson, during which the style of the show was established. Subsequently the theme was recorded and the visual titles then cut to synchronise with certain pre-planned points in the music. Johnson then viewed the fine cuts of the films and decided which sections were to be covered by music. These were measured and converted to seconds by the music co-ordinator, Paul Clay, who then compiled music measurement sheets for each section. Johnson would then compose, and later record, the music to the film projected on a screen in the recording studio. If the film unit got behind in their shooting schedule and the amount of music he was able to compose was less than needed, appropriate sections composed for previous episodes were re-cut to fit. Laurie Johnson would then write the music which covered aspects indigenous to that episode. (Wherever possible, however, new music was used for each episode.) The films were then dubbed in the usual way. Throughout the series, producer, writer and composer would work closely at every stage so that all aspects developed or varied simultaneously.

Whereas most of the Honor Blackman stories had been standard thriller adventures, the new series became more science-fiction orientated. Plots concerned the efforts of power-mad scientists hell-bent on taking over the world, using such outrageous devices as a giant man-eating plant; steel robots; torrential rainstorms; and even agents being brainwashed in a Manchurian concentration camp – situated in the heart of London's West End!

The shooting schedule was long and arduous. (Diana Rigg and Patrick Macnee were required to learn over 60 pages of dialogue per week, and work a 14-hour day.) Each episode cost £30,000 to produce and had a 10-day shooting schedule. Because the series was being filmed for the first time, greater use was made of outdoor locations such as old country inns, deserted airfields and weapon research establishments. The principal shooting was done at EMI's Elstree Studios (known at the time as Associated British).

THE TOWN OF NO RETURN

By Brian Clemens

John Steed	Patrick Macnee
Emma Peel	Diana Rigg
Brandon	Alan MacNaughtan
Smallwood	Patrick Newell
Piggy Warren	Terence Alexander
Vicar	Jeremy Burnham
Saul	Robert Brown
Jill Manson	Juliet Harmer
School Inspector	Walter Horsbrugh

Diana Rigg's Wardrobe
Designed by John Bates
Music by Laurie Johnson
Directed by Roy Baker
Produced by Julian Wintle

WHEN four special agents in succession vanish without trace in Bazeley-by-the-Sea, a remote village on the Norfolk coast, near a derelict RAF base from World War II, The Avengers are alerted. John Steed, posing as a property dealer, and Emma Peel, as a school-mistress, arrive at the local inn, where they meet the proprietor, 'Piggy' Warren, a Battle of Britain veteran, Mark Brandon, who is the local headmaster, and Jill Manson, one of his staff. That night Steed and Emma are disturbed by strange sounds – the tramp of an army on the march; the far-off braying of hounds. Their initial attempts to investigate are thwarted, but later they find a mass of bootprints leading up from the sea, and then the body of Jimmy Smallwood, a recent arrival in the village, who has been savaged by the dogs. Smallwood had been visiting his brother, Tom, the blacksmith, but when Steed and Emma go to the forge they realise that the man claiming to be the blacksmith is a phoney. Emma calls in at the village church, but all recent entries in the parish records have been removed. She tells the vicar, but, to her amazement, he holds her at gunpoint. Meanwhile, Steed, touring the derelict airfield, discovers evidence that shows Piggy Warren is also an impostor. When he finds that Emma has disappeared, Steed forces Piggy to talk. The trail takes Steed back to the forge, where Saul, the blacksmith, lashes out at him with red hot steel. Steed eventually wins the fight and finds Emma trussed up. They now realise that the whole village has been over-run by subversive elements who have been training a pocket army to make a take-over bid of all Britain. At the airfield they discover a well-equipped arsenal in the disused underground shelters. They are about to leave when they are cornered by Brandon, Jill Manson and the vicar. The would-be invaders are eventually shut in behind the heavy emergency doors.

THE GRAVEDIGGERS

By Malcolm Hulke

John Steed	Patrick Macnee
Emma Peel	Diana Rigg
Sir Horace Winslip	Ronald Fraser
Johnson	Paul Massie
Miss Thirwell	Caroline Blakiston
Sexton	Victor Platt
Fred	Charles Lamb
Nurse Spray	Wanda Ventham
Baron	Ray Austin
Sager	Steven Berkoff
Miller	Bryan Mosley
Dr Marlowe	Lloyd Lamble

Music by Laurie Johnson
Directed by
Quentin Lawrence
Produced by Julian Wintle

A SUDDEN fault develops in the nation's early-warning radar system. Steed and Emma suspect deliberate jamming by hostile forces, but they are told that no blocking device that powerful yet exists. However, a Dr Marlowe had been working on such a system until his recent death. Steed goes to Pringby, a village lying in the path of the radar block, where Marlowe was buried, and arrives at the cemetery just as Marlowe's exhumed coffin is being loaded onto a hearse. He follows it to the Sir Horace Winslip Hospital for Retired or Ailing Railwaymen, and while making enquiries there, is astonished to recognise a passer-by as the dead Marlowe. It becomes apparent that Marlowe, obsessed with his work, has been frustrated by the lack of government funds and equipment and has sold out to enemy agents. Steed's arrival causes panic, and Johnson, who controls the set-up under the guise of head surgeon, decides that because of Marlowe's premature activation of the device, which has alerted the authorities, he must be eliminated. Enter Mrs Peel, posing as a nurse allocated by the Ministry. She soon befriends Nurse Spray, who says she will have little to do as Johnson performs his operations behind locked doors, with only the senior staff. Steed investigates the hospital's patron, Sir Horace Winslip, an eccentric who lives at Winslip Junction, a house completely full of railway ephemera. Steed notices there is a miniature passenger-carrying railway in Sir Horace's grounds that has a direct line to the hospital, plus a locked signal box inside Winslip Manor. That night, Steed and Emma secretly watch Johnson's latest operation. However, Johnson is soon asking Matron Thirwell to pass the blow-torch... Steed discovers that all the burials have been arranged with a local undertaker up to six weeks ahead. Each one is at a

Emma Peel and Steed make themselves comfortable during their train journey in The Town of No Return.

Diana Rigg wears Blackboard, Jean Varon's grey wool trouser suit designed by John Bates to form part of her wardrobe.

THE CYBERNAUTS

By Philip Levene

John Steed	Patrick Macnee
Emma Peel	Diana Rigg
Dr Armstrong	Michael Gough
Benson	Frederick Jaeger
Jephcott	Bernard Horsfall
Tusamo	Bert Kwouk
Sensai	John Hollis
Lambert	Ronald Leigh-Hunt
Hammond	Gordon Whiting

Music by Laurie Johnson
Directed by Sidney Hayers
Produced by Julian Wintle

Emma is tied to the track of a private railway line, with a steam engine bearing down on her in The Gravediggers.

A cybernaut menaces Emma Peel in Armstrong's factory, attracted to her by the pen she is carrying, in The Cybernauts.

A KILLER of fantastic strength wipes out a number of executives in violent succession. Steed and Emma discover that all the men were negotiating for the rights to a new circuit system developed by a Japanese company. Emma suspects that the men were killed by karate and she visits a leading karate school in search of a lead. Steed discovers that, of all the companies interested in the concession, the representatives of all but two of them have been murdered. Emma visits one, a mechanical toy manufacturer, owned by Jephcott. At the other company, United Automation, Steed, posing as a science reporter, meets the head of the company, Dr Armstrong, a cripple confined to an elaborately-automated wheelchair, from which he controls a complex web of gadgetry and automata. Armstrong realises that Steed is not really a reporter and suspecting him of being a spy, gives him a special pen – identical to the ones found on the murder victims. Later, Steed and Emma discover Jephcott dead. His violent assassin apparently reached him by walking through his office wall. Armstrong, the remaining bidder, seems to be guilty. Steed returns to Armstrong's hideaway and is trapped there just as he learns that the killings were performed by a radio-controlled robot, so that Armstrong could get the new circuit system – which would enable him to build an empire of robots under his supreme control. These were controlled by a radio transmitter housed in each of the pens given to the representatives. Steed realises that he left his pen with Emma... But she, fearing for Steed's safety, sets off for Armstrong's factory – unaware that the unstoppable killer is on her trail, guided by the pen she has clipped in her pocket. Steed has distracted Armstrong and his assistant, Benson, and escaped. He reaches Emma just as she is cornered by the robot, and shouts to her to throw the pen away. Emma does so – escaping death by seconds – but Armstrong now turns loose an advanced robot which can think for itself. The new robot advances on Steed and Emma, but Steed clips the pen to this robot, leading the first robot to attack its superior counterpart. In an effort to stop the mayhem, Armstrong dies at the hands of his own creations.

different cemetery in a site at which the coffin-encased devices would completely surround the radar station. Wondering how they would be triggered off, Steed sets off to investigate the signal box at the Manor. Meanwhile Johnson discovers Emma's true identity and wants to kill her. He will incriminate Sir Horace by strapping Emma to his private railway line and driving a steam engine over her neck. Steed is greeted at Winslip Manor by an irate Sir Horace. Steed explains that his wish to prolong the life of the railways was being used for more sinister intentions. Through Sir Horace's telescope, Steed sees Johnson's henchmen start up the engine which will kill Emma, who is tied helpless at the far end of the track. He leaps on the train and fights a furious battle with the men as the train speeds along the track. Finally, Steed switches a vital set of points and the train narrowly misses decapitating Emma. As Steed unties her, Johnson tries to kill them but Emma's karate skill saves the day.

DEATH AT BARGAIN PRICES

By Brian Clemens

John Steed	Patrick Macnee
Emma Peel	Diana Rigg
Horatio Kane	Andre Morell
Wentworth	T P McKenna
Farthingale	Allan Cuthbertson
Massey	George Selway
Marco	Harvey Ashby
Jarvis	John Cater
Professor Popple	Peter Howell
Glynn	Ronnie Stevens
Julie	Diane Clare

Music by Laurie Johnson
Directed by Charles Crichton
Produced by Julian Wintle

Steed rarely used firearms, preferring his swordstick and bowler, but in Death At Bargain Prices, *he fired ping-pong balls!*

Emma swings into action in her inimitable and graceful style in a fast-moving fight scene from Castle De'ath.

AN agent friend of Steed's is shot dead and dumped in an alleyway. A receipt from Pinter's Department Store, dated on a Sunday, is found on the body. Emma decides to take a job at the shop. At work in the lingerie department, she is approached by Jarvis, the house detective, who remarks on the apparent inexperience of most of Pinter's staff – a fact which dates only from the recent take-over by Horatio Kane, a tycoon known as King Kane, who lives in a penthouse over the store. Kane tells Steed, posing as an efficiency expert, that the store manager, Wentworth, will attend to him. Wentworth does just that, by forcibly evicting Steed. When Emma overhears about plans for the third night meeting of all the senior staff in one week, she asks Jarvis about them. Jarvis says that he, too, is suspicious of the management, and intends to eavesdrop at the meeting that night. He overhears Wentworth finalising a sinister plan, at the crux of which is a Professor Popple, who is being held in enforced detention. Jarvis is discovered by the gang and killed. The next day, Marco, a store executive, makes a play for Emma, and she asks him about the Sunday receipt. He says she must talk to Wentworth and, on the way to do so, Emma discovers a laboratory. In it is a shackled old man whom Emma recognises as Professor Popple, a missing atom scientist. As she leaves, Wentworth and Marco corner her. Steed calls at Pinter's and is told that Emma has been sacked. Suspecting that she is in trouble, Steed hides in the store until it closes. He then disposes of the nightwatchman and releases Emma, who is trussed up in a carpet in the furniture department. They enter the laboratory, where Popple lies in a drugged stupor, and discover that the receipts are, in fact, feed cards for an atomic computer. The whole store has been converted into a giant atomic bomb! Kane enters with Farthingale, his assistant, and at gunpoint, Steed and Emma are told

Kane's plans for the biggest take-over bid of all – he is about to hold all Britain to ransom under the threat of the bomb. A fight breaks out and Steed and Emma soon dispose of the villains. Kane, however, makes one last bid to detonate the bomb and sets a disused lift in motion. The descending lift will operate the detonator mechanism exploding the bomb. The Avengers struggle to open the lift gates and jam the progress of the deadly lift in time. Steed finally halts the lift inches from the detonator, using his umbrella.

You can find bear-skin rugs in the strangest places. Diana Rigg, wearing an outfit called Flash, *in* Castle De'ath.

Another scene from Castle De'ath, *in which Emma follows the sound of bagpipes, and finds herself trapped in the dungeons.*

CASTLE DE'ATH

By John Lucarotti

John Steed	Patrick Macnee
Emma Peel	Diana Rigg
Ian	Gordon Jackson
Angus	Robert Urquhart
McNab	Jack Lambert
Roberton	James Copeland
Controller	Russell Waters

Music by Laurie Johnson
Directed by James Hill
Produced by Julian Wintle

EMMA arrives at Castle De'ath in Scotland as a member of Aborcasha-ta (Advisory Bureau on Refurbishing Castles and Stately Homes as Tourist Attractions). She is ill-received by Ian, the 35th Laird, and McNab, the head gillie, even though Ian's cousin, Angus, has invited her. Another guest is Mr John McSteed, researching a book on the 13th Laird, Black Jamie. Steed enquires about the fishing but Angus warns him about the loch. The previous week, an amateur frogman's body was washed up on the banks. Steed tells Emma that the frogman was four inches taller dead than when he was alive. It seems he had been put on the rack and stretched... Steed leaves to walk around the loch, but is followed by McNab and another gillie, Roberton. Emma investigates the dungeons, where she discovers various instruments of torture. There, a seaman attacks her and another seaman crashes a blackjack over her head. She recovers and makes her way back to the main hall where she meets Steed and Ian. Emma says she slipped on the stairs. At dinner, Ian tells them the story of Black Jamie, who was walled up in the East Tower. Often, his ghost walks playing the Lament of Glen De'ath. Steed, however, is more interested in the vibrations shuddering through his brandy glass. Steed goes to his room, only to find Roberton has moved his things to the Lord Darnley Room, where the howling West wind will not bother him. Steed admires the magnificent canopy bed in the room and prepares to sleep. Silently, the canopy over the bed moves down on an enormous threaded screw, gathering momentum as it sinks lower until it crushes everything in the bed... Emma, meanwhile, has heard the sound of pipes and gone to investigate. She is going down the dungeon steps when the heavy door slams behind her. Next morning, Emma is drowsing on the steps when the door opens to reveal Steed, who tells her what happened the previous night. Steed goes fishing in the moat – watched by Roberton through binoculars – and Emma returns to the dungeon again, armed with a map she has found. McNab is just about to descend too, when Roberton calls him. Emma steps into an iron maiden, to hide. As she does so, the back opens to reveal a long corridor, which in turn leads to a room full of complicated electrical equipment. McNab goes to the moat but only finds Steed's clothes draped over a pole. Nearby are spare frogmen's clothes and oxygen tanks. When Emma returns, Ian tells her he has decided not to open the castle to the public, so Emma leaves. Meanwhile Steed surfaces from the moat, is seized by two men and taken to the control room beneath the castle. There, a controller sits before a fantastic complex, including a television screen, on which can be seen three midget submarines in a pen. McNab confronts Steed and tells him how they intend to corner the market in fish by driving them into their underground base with the submarines. Throughout the conversation, McNab is constantly interrupted by the phone and talks to someone he calls Chief. Steed manages to escape. That night, Emma returns to the castle to search for Steed. She is crawling across the battlements when she meets the ghost (McNab), blowing the pipes to deaden the sound of the turbine below. After a brief skirmish, Emma throws him over the battlements. Steed arrives in the main hall to do battle and is joined by Emma. Angus now reveals himself as the Chief and grabs a claymore to finish off Steed. Seizing a dirk from the wall, Steed soon disarms Angus who runs into the dungeon to escape. He enters the iron maiden, but the door jams and the maiden's spikes pierce into his body.

Holly Trent, giving an archery class, decides to use Steed as target practice, in The Master Minds.

THE MASTER MINDS

By Robert Banks Stewart

John Steed	Patrick Macnee
Emma Peel	Diana Rigg
Sir Clive Todd	Laurence Hardy
Holly Trent	Patricia Haines
Sir Fergus Campbell	Ian McNaughton
Davinia Todd	Georgina Ward

Music by Laurie Johnson
Directed by Peter Graham Scott
Produed by Julian Wintle

AN eminent government official, Sir Clive Todd, is suspected of treason. Heavily guarded, he lies at home badly wounded after his surprise role in a raid on top-secret files. Emma is brought in to act as his nurse and Steed learns from Sir Clive's daughter, Davinia, that her father was a member of Ransack, a club for intellectuals. When Sir Clive begins to respond to questioning, Emma urgently calls Steed to his bedside. But before they can make further headway, Sir Clive's doctor, Fergus Campbell, gives his patient a fatal injection. Appearing to come out of a trance, Dr Campbell is as appalled by his action as those around him. He reveals that he, too, is a member of Ransack. Steed joins the mysterious Ransack Club, and goes to the country boarding school where the club conducts special courses. Emma arrives there, too, as a secretary. Giving an archery class in the grounds is Holly Trent, who speaks to Steed somewhat scornfully about Ransack and its members. The hub of Ransack's activities is the gymnasium, where its members exercise on the equipment and work on highly intellectual papers. Steed manages to gain a high IQ rating with a little help from Emma. That night, Steed discovers Emma in a trance, watching military training films and going out on some form of combat training. When he mentions it to her, she at first denies all knowledge of it, but then realises that she and the Ransack members were obviously victims of mass hypnosis, induced by a voice over the radio speakers in each bedroom. This also explains Sir Clive's unusual behaviour and his murder by Campbell. Steed has escaped hypnosis because the speaker in his bedroom was disconnected. Steed decides to feign hypnosis and attend the next indoctrinations, but the Ransack officials see through his hoax and order his disposal. A seemingly entranced Emma volunteers to do it, but when she reports Steed is dead, they realise her complicity and a fight breaks out. Steed rescues her, and using the gym equipment as weapons, they defeat the Ransack members. At the climax of the fray, Holly Trent is revealed to be the mastermind, and Emma knocks her out.

THE MURDER MARKET

By Tony Williamson

John Steed	Patrick Macnee
Emma Peel	Diana Rigg
Mr Lovejoy	Patrick Cargill
Dinsford	Peter Bayliss
Barbara Wakefield	Suzanne Lloyd
Mrs Stone	Naomi Chance
Robert Stone	John Woodvine

Music by Laurie Johnson
Directed by
Peter Graham Scott
Produced by Julian Wintle

WHEN an outbreak of baffling murders commands the attention of The Avengers, Emma visits the widow of the latest victim, Jessica Stone, while Steed, posing as a potential husband, visits the Togetherness Marriage Bureau. Emma successfully finds a number-one suspect, Robert Stone, the widow's brother-in-law; and, in the sickly sweet atmosphere of Togetherness, Steed overhears a client called Henshaw in a sinister encounter with the management. Fearing that Henshaw may prove to be the next victim, Steed asks Emma to go to his flat. As Emma arrives at Henshaw's, she bumps into a woman called Barbara Wakefield, making a rapid departure. Emma enters the flat and finds she is too late – Henshaw is floating dead in his bath. The first partner Togetherness suggest for Steed turns out to be Barbara Wakefield. Steed hints that only a cousin stands in the way of his acquiring a massive inheiritance. The bait is taken and the Togetherness match-makers Lovejoy and Dinsford reveal that their bureau runs a murder racket on the side. If Steed will do a murder for them, they will kill his cousin. Meanwhile, Emma's investigation of Robert Stone has led her to the marriage bureau, where the two partners recognise her as an enemy. Togetherness now tell Steed that he must murder Emma Peel. Emma plays 'dead' for Steed's benefit and is shown laid out in her coffin. Pleased with Steed's apparent efficiency, the match-makers offer him more work, but he insists on first meeting the organisation's boss. Togetherness now receive a tip making them doubt Steed's word, so they make him watch Emma's coffin being buried. Steed looks on unflinchingly. Having passed the test, Steed now meets the boss – Jessica Stone. The widow had used the bureau against her own husband when he became too interested in its female clients. Meanwhile, Emma, having escaped burial alive, discovers that Robert Stone is innocent and only wants to find his brother's killer. At that moment, the gang arrive and corner Emma and Robert. But Steed soon arrives and together they tear Togetherness apart.

A SURFEIT OF H₂O

By Colin Finbow

John Steed	Patrick Macnee
Emma Peel	Diana Rigg
Jonah Barnard	Noel Purcell
Dr Sturm	Albert Lieven
Joyce Jason	Sue Lloyd
Eli Barker	Talfryn Thomas
Sir Arnold Kelly	John Kidd

Music by Laurie Johnson
Directed by Sidney Hayers
Produced by Julian Wintle

WHEN a village poacher is drowned in the middle of a field during a freak thunderstorm, his strange death seems to support the belief of local eccentrics that the Great Flood is coming again to Earth. Steed, however, looks for a more feasible explanation. Steed calls on Jonah Barnard, the village carpenter, who is building an ark. He points to a cloud hanging motionless in the sky which visibly increases in size every day. The cloud is in the vicinity of Grannie Gregson's wine-making factory. When Emma tries to enter the factory, as a reporter, she is rebuffed by Dr Sturm, but she later persuades Eli, the dead poacher's brother, to let her into the factory that night. When Emma arrives at the rendezvous she finds Eli is another victim of the mysterious rain. Posing as a vintner, Steed manages to gain admission to the factory. He learns from Joyce, the receptionist, that Dr Sturm has installed a lot of new equipment in his two years at the factory. When Joyce shows Steed around the cellars, she suddenly becomes alarmed when he hears the sound of heavy rain falling from somewhere in the premises. She hurries Steed away and he is astounded to discover that it is a fine day outside. Emma, meanwhile, alarmed by the weird readings she has had on her portable weather equipment, calls in Sir Arnold Kelly, a meteorological expert. He is working alone in a field, when the torrents suddenly begin and he is washed into the ground. Later Sturm's henchmen carry off his body. Realising that Emma called in Sir Arnold, Sturm decides to put an end to her. He invites her to look over the plant, and Emma is forced to accept – at gunpoint. Sturm straps her under the giant pulping press, hoping to force a confession as he steadily increases the pressure. Having told her that he intends to sell his deadly rain-making device as a military weapon, able to bog down whole armies, Sturm leaves Emma strapped on the press and only fractions of an inch from death. Meanwhile, Steed has convinced Jonah that the freak storms were man-made and he agrees to go with

Avengers fight arranger Ray Austin takes the toss when he and Diana Rigg run through a sequence.

him to the factory. They enter by a secret tunnel and free Emma, then find the rain-making machine, but are confronted by Sturm and his henchmen. A fight breaks out in the rain, which steadily increases in merciless intensity. They quickly finish off the gang and Sturm's diabolical scheme is washed away.

Emma and Steed make plans to outwit the rain-makers in a scene from A Surfeit of H₂O.

THE HOUR THAT NEVER WAS

By Roger Marshall

John Steed	Patrick Macnee
Emma Peel	Diana Rigg
Geoffrey Ridsdale	Gerald Harper
Philip Leas	Dudley Foster
Hickey	Roy Kinnear
Porky Purser	Roger Booth
Corporal Barman	Daniel Moynihan
Driver	David Morrell
Wiggins	Fred Haggerty

Music by Laurie Johnson
Directed by Gerry O'Hara
Produced by Julian Wintle

Left: Diana Rigg wears Jean Varon's black and white crêpe catsuit, designed by John Bates for her role as Emma Peel.

Above: *Emma will soon be wreathed in smiles again, but she is pretending to be dead in* **The Murder Market.**

STEED is invited to the closing-down party of RAF Camp 472 – Hamelin, a camp at which Steed saw service during the war. He takes Emma as a guest. Nearing the camp by car, they are involved in an accident when a dog rushes blindly across the road. The dashboard clock stops at 11 o'clock. Recovering, they walk to the camp. In the distance they can hear the sound of a tinkling piano, but when they arrive at the camp, the place is deserted. The camp clocks have stopped at 11 o'clock. In the bakery they find a cake bearing the unfinished inscription 'Goodbye Hameli'. They hear the sound of a milk float being started up and decide to climb the camp control tower to gain a better view. On the runway they see a man, dressed as a milkman, running for his life. A rifle shot rings out and the man falls. They edge over to the hangar from which the shot came and once again hear the sound of the milk float, which then stops. They can see it, and bundled on the rear platform is the body of the milkman. As they cross the now disused children's playground, Steed begins to stagger like a drunken man. The chains of the swings begin to rattle and vibrate loudly – the sound is terrifying. As the noise diminishes, Steed recovers his balance and hurries on to find that the milk float, the body and Emma have disappeared. He desperately searches the camp and finds a filthy man called Hickey. He tells Steed of the strange sound that made him feel drunk. Deciding the man is harmless, Steed sets off for the main gate where he has seen a uniformed figure. The sentry-box is empty except for a uniform hanging from a peg. As Steed leaves, the striped barrier pole across the entrance falls and knocks him unconscious. Recovering, he finds that he is sitting in his car on the grass verge where it crashed. There is no sign of Emma! He sets off for the camp and once again hears the sound of a tinkling piano being played in the Officer's Mess. He bursts inside to find the place jammed with his wartime comrades – Ridsdale, Wiggins, Porky Purser, and the new camp dentist, Leas. The time is three minutes past 12. Baffled, Steed goes outside for some air. He sees the dog that caused the accident whimpering by a dustbin. Stuffed among the rubbish by the bin is the dead body of Hickey. Once again he hears the milk float and following it, he sees a powerful man carrying the body of a Sergeant into the bakery. He crosses to the window and is amazed to see the Sergeant busy icing the cake. Dumbfounded, Steed hurries after the milk float in time to see the powerful man put the body of an Officer on the milk float, before driving off. Steed arrives at the medical centre, goes inside and sees a guard. They fight, and, taking off the man's helmet, Steed finds that the guard is wearing an elaborate pair of earmuffs. He hears muffled sounds from the dentist's surgery, where he finds Emma, bound and gagged. He releases her and together they search the surgery. In a locked room they find an oscilloscope, which, when pitched correctly, would affect the brain and render people unconscious. They also find the drug C11, used in brain-washing. Obviously, the camp personnel are made unconscious, then taken to the surgery, where their secrets are divulged. As Steed and Emma leave, they are confronted by Leas, and the giant who drove the milk float. In the ensuing fight Steed knocks over a cannister of laughing gas, and he and Emma guffaw their way to victory. Outside, they get in the milk float and drive off to a new adventure.

DIAL A DEADLY NUMBER

By Roger Marshall

John Steed	Patrick Macnee
Emma Peel	Diana Rigg
Henry Boardman	Clifford Evans
Ruth Boardman	Jan Holden
Ben Jago	Anthony Newlands
Fitch	John Carson
John Harvey	Peter Bowles
Frederick Yuill	Gerald Sim

Music by Laurie Johnson
Directed by Don Leaver
Produced by Julian Wintle

Sudden death strikes big business executive, Todhunter, during a board meeting – the sixth recent fatality in the financial world. Suspecting more than just coincidence, The Avengers decide to play the stock market. Steed calls on Henry Boardman, banker to all the deceased executives, and says he has £2,000,000 to invest. On Boardman's advice, Steed visits a broker, Frederick Yuill, who explains how money could have been made out of the sudden deaths. He also deduces that one of those to cash in was an investor called Jago. Meanwhile,

Steed is attacked at night in his underground garage by two men, one of whom he recognises, in Dial A Deadly Number.

Emma is following another lead. Todhunter's bleeper, which meant he could always be reached, is missing. It was operated by remote control through an answering service. Emma calls at his office to investigate. Steel learns that the key mechanic on the bleep operation is Fitch, a nasty man who immediately arouses his suspicion. At a dinner party, Boardman introduces Steed to his wife, Ruth, whom Steed knows is involved with Jago. Returning home that night, Steed is attacked in his underground garage by two men wearing motor-cycling outfits. Steed wins and recognises one of the men as being Yuill's butler. When Steed and Emma call on Yuill for an explanation, he is dead, with evidence that he, too, had a bleep device in his pocket. At a wine-tasting party in the cellar of Boardman's bank, Steed is unaware that he and Emma are being filmed by a hidden camera – enabling Fitch to make a pocket-watch identical to Steed's. At their next meeting, Ruth Boardman plants the lethal watch in Steed's pocket. An enlightened Emma is about to warn him when she is detained at gunpoint by Fitch. The maniacal mechanic now reveals that he was responsible for the bleep deaths. Steed detects the watch device and hurries to Fitch's workshop in time to rescue Emma, and, in the struggle, the evil Fitch is killed by one of his own devices. Emma examines the bleepers and discovers that each has been loaded with a capillary needle, which a call through the answering service would trigger off. The murder method now explained, Steed plants harmless bleep devices on all the suspects he has met, including Boardman, Jago and Boardman's partner, Harvey. In the ensuing mayhem, Boardman proves his innocence and his wife Ruth exposes herself as the guilty party. Jago shoots Boardman, and hurries down to the bank's cellar to join Harvey. However, Steed and Emma are waiting for them and soon stop the villains in typical Avengers style.

THE MAN-EATER OF SURREY GREEN

By Philip Levene

John Steed	Patrick Macnee
Emma Peel	Diana Rigg
Sir Lyle Peterson	Derek Farr
Dr Sheldon	Athene Seyler
Laura Burford	Gillian Lewis

Music by Laurie Johnson
Directed by Sidney Hayers
Produced by Julian Wintle

Steed and Emma set out to help botanist Alan Carter when his fiancée Laura Burford goes missing, thereby joining the ranks of several eminent horticulturists who have recently disappeared in Surrey. Steed discovers that all the missing scientists are working at an establishment run by Sir Lyle Peterson, a plant specialist who likes exotic insect-eating plants. Peterson tells him that all the scientists are working on a new flowering shrub. Rather surprisingly, Laura Burford is introduced to Steed. She seems happy enough, but casual about the forsaken Alan. Leaving the premises, Steed spots a giant oil derrick in the grounds. He later learns that Peterson has ordered a second derrick to be delivered to his farm. Steed and Emma investigate the farm and find the charred remains of a manned space craft. They are later told by the authorities that it was a space-shot which failed, and the craft, after a year in orbit, must have returned to earth, undetected, several months before – the very time when the first scientist went missing. Found attached to the space craft is a giant vegetable seed, and Steed asks a friend, Dr Cynthia Sheldon, to investigate. She says that not only has the plant got a brain and the capacity to grow to enormous size, but it is man-eating. Steed and Emma are horrified and set off with Dr Sheldon for Peterson's estate, equipped with an acid plant-killer. Steed fears that another space seed is being germinated there under the mysterious derrick. By now, Steed has realised that the few Surrey scientists to have resisted the call to Peterson's establishment all wear hearing aids. Conjecturing that the aids must be protection against the plant's unearthly hypnotic influences, he gets a set of aids for himself. When Steed and Emma reach the estate, they find pandemonium has broken out. The plant is growing rapidly and summoning local inhabitants with its hypnotic call to satisfy its hunger. They search for the control room. By now, the plant is covering the whole house. In the control room is Peterson,

TWO'S A CROWD

By Philip Levene

John Steed	Patrick Macnee
Emma Peel	Diana Rigg
Brodny	Warren Mitchell
Alicia Elena	Maria Machado
Shvedloff	Alec Mango
Pudeshkin	Wolfe Morris
Vogel	Julian Glover
Ivenko	John Bluthal

Music by Laurie Johnson
Directed by Roy Baker
Produced by Julian Wintle

Ray Austin explains a move to Diana Rigg during rehearsals for a fight scene in Dial A Deadly Number.

The Avengers equip Dr Sheldon with a hearing aid in case she is hypnotised by The Man-Eater of Surrey Green.

STEED believes that a notorious spy, Colonel Psev, will attempt to infiltrate a conference of defence chiefs in London. They are alerted to Psev's presence by the sudden arrival of four agents known to work for him. The quartet establish themselves at the national Embassy, where they use Brodny, the Ambassador, as a general runabout. While out on an errand for them, Brodny spots a man who is the double of John Steed. Brodny realises that the agents could use him – a seedy male model named Webster – to impersonate Steed and gain access to the conference. Emma sees the agents setting up a deal with Webster at the Embassy, and guesses what is afoot. She tells Steed about his double, but he does not seem to take her warning seriously. After being schooled in Steed's speech, dress and mannerisms, Webster goes to a cocktail party dressed as Steed, where it is arranged that he sees Emma. She soon sees through him, and the agents forcibly detain her. One of the Embassy staff, Ivenko, is blamed for the failure of the plan and, in desperation, he phones Steed with the offer of vital information in exchange for political asylum. A rendezvous is arranged in the Embassy grounds. However, the agents have wired Steed's apartment 'for sound and when Ivenko appears for the meeting, the agents send out a radio-controlled midget submarine which shoots him dead just before Steed arrives. Lethal model machines are a macabre hobby of Colonel Psev. Trussed up in the corner of a room, Emma believes she is about to be rescued when she sees the familiar face of Steed at the window, but instead of freeing her he declares himself to be the impostor, Webster. The agents are now satisfied that their man can pass the test and order him to dispose of the real Steed at his flat, and then go to the conference and secure on microfilm some top-secret documents. They hear Steed's death over the transmitter planted in his apartment, and soon Webster returns

with the vital microfilm. Emma breaks free and demands the microfilm at gun point. Webster, however, disarms her and stresses that he will only give the film to Colonel Psev. The agents now reveal that there is no Colonel Psev. The elusive spy is in fact all four of them, and the name made up of all their initials. Webster now hands over the film and hurries Emma away. Once outside, Webster reveals himself to be the real Steed, who turned the tables on Webster earlier. The agents, however, discover the truth before Steed and Emma can leave, and using a complex panel board, they send a model spitfire after the couple. Steed manages to bring it down with his revolver. Undaunted, the agents release a model bomber. Now out of ammunition, Steed discovers that the portable radio transmitter in the Bentley is tuned to the same frequency as the agents' control device. He diverts the bomber's path and brings it round on the Embassy. The agents themselves now fall victim to their own miniature bomb.

who tries to stop them. Emma overpowers him and Steed gives him a hearing aid, which immediately frees him from the plant's influence. While Steed and Peterson battle to save Dr Sheldon from the plant, Emma goes to collect the acid plant-killer, but the plant surrounds her and in the struggle she loses her hearing aid. Now the plant's slave, Emma battles with Steed to stop the plant's destruction. After a tense struggle, the acid is thrown onto the plant, which dies, releasing Emma from its deadly spell.

Steed and Emma use hearing aids so they can't hear the call of a strange plant, in The Man-Eater Of Surrey Green.

TOO MANY CHRISTMAS TREES

By Tony Williamson

John Steed	**Patrick Macnee**
Emma Peel	**Diana Rigg**
Brandon Storey	**Mervyn Johns**
Dr Felix Teasel	**Edwin Richfield**
Janice Crane	**Jeannette Sterke**
Martin Trasker	**Alex Scott**
Jenkins	**Robert James**
Jeremy Wade	**Barry Warren**

Music by Laurie Johnson
Directed by Roy Baker
Produced by Julian Wintle

STEED is plagued by a vivid recurring nightmare. Featured as a corpse in this frightening dream is a one-time colleague, Freddy Marshall, with whom Steed shared exclusive knowledge of top-secret information. Steed's dream becomes reality when he learns of Freddy's sudden death in mysterious circumstances, his mind having collapsed from too much strain. To cheer him up, Emma invites Steed to a festive house party given by eccentric publisher Brandon Storey, a man obsessed with Dickens. But at Brandon's home Steed finds himself in identical surroundings to those of his dream. Unwittingly, Emma has led Steed into a trap; it is revealed that two other house guests, Trasker and Wade, are exerting dangerous, telepathic influences on Steed's mind. Their previous experiment with Freddy Marshall has misfired. Apparently unaware of the plot, Steed in induced into a deep sleep by the mindbenders, and into a *Tale of Two Cities* nightmare in which Steed is Sydney Carton, taunted at the guillotine by a dark, mysterious woman. As the blade crashes down, Steed awakens in a state of shock – heightened by the arrival of another guest, Janice Crane, the dark beauty of his dream. Storey holds a Dickensian-style Christmas Eve party in fancy dress. Emma is given an Oliver Twist outfit, while Steed gets the Sydney Carton clothes of his dream. At the height of the celebrations, Storey announces that Janice will do a mind-reading act, and she selects Steed as her assistant. However, it is really one last attempt by the mind-benders to extract the secret information from Steed's mind. As the game progresses, Emma becomes increasingly alarmed by Steed's strange behaviour and deliberately drops a glass of wine to shatter the spell. Wade, full of misgivings about his part in the experiment, is on the point of talking to Emma when he is murdered. Emma, believing that Steed is fast approaching a mental collapse, turns in desperation to another guest, Dr Teasel. She begins to suspect that Teasel is also involved, but no

Oliver Twist and Sydney Carton attend the Dickensian party held by Brandon Storey, in **Too Many Christmas Trees.**

In fine style, Emma throws Omrod, the crooked landowner, to the ground, in a scene from **Silent Dust.**

sooner has she knocked him out than she learns that Steed has been a willing victim all along, and that Teasel was working with him. Together, they had hoped to learn the motives behind the mind-benders and the identity of the mastermind. Now Steed – once again his debonair self – and Emma must stand alone against the sinister trio. They hunt down the mind-benders and after an all-out fight in a hall of distorting mirrors, Brandon Storey himself is revealed as the brain behind the plot, and Steed's deadly nightmare is laid to rest.

SILENT DUST
Strictly For The Worms

By Roger Marshall

John Steed	**Patrick Macnee**
Emma Peel	**Diana Rigg**
Omrod	**William Franklyn**
Juggins	**Jack Watson**
Mellors	**Conrad Phillips**
Croft	**Norman Bird**
Miss Snow	**Joanna Wake**
Clare Prendergast	**Isobel Black**
Sir Manfred Fellows	**Charles Lloyd Pack**
Quince	**Aubrey Morris**

Music by Laurie Johnson
Directed by Roy Baker
Produced by Julian Wintle

WHEN whole areas of the countryside are laid to waste, and birds and beasts die by the hundred, Steed and Emma are called in to investigate. Steed is taken to an area of desolation at Manderley which is under War Department control, and a Minister tells him it was caused by Silent Dust, an organochlorine fertilizer which went wrong – killing instead of replenishing. Emma meanwhile meets a birdwatcher named Quince and she questions him as they walk along the country lanes. A gamekeeper, Mellors, orders them away from the area with a double-barrelled shotgun. Omrod, the owner of the land, appears on horseback and sends Mellors about his business. Eyeing Emma admiringly he invites her to join him at the next hunt. Steed is introduced to Sir Manfred Fellows, and learns that the man in charge of the Silent Dust project, Prendergast, was sacked years ago. Fellows tells Steed that the man had a daughter, Clare, who may be able to help. Steed visits her and finds that she is bitter about the treatment her dead father received. When Steed has left, Clare is joined by Omrod, who has been eavesdropping. Emma is having a drink at the local inn with a rose-grower, Croft, when she notices Quince beckoning her from outside. He arranges to meet Emma that night and leaves. Standing near the bar, listening, is Mellors. That night, Emma arrives to find no sign of Quince – only his broken spectacles suspended on a bush. Returning to the inn, Emma meets Steed. They are discussing the event when a horse trots into the yard. They look out to see the local beauty, Miss Snow, dismounting. She is obviously disturbed because her horse is sick. Steed invites her inside for a drink, but when Omrod and Croft appear she makes an excuse and leaves with the men. Miss Snow, Croft and another man named Juggins, all meet in Omrod's home. They decide to continue to destroy Britain county by county, until

ROOM WITHOUT A VIEW

By Roger Marshall

John Steed	Patrick Macnee
Emma Peel	Diana Rigg
Chessman	Paul Whitsun-Jones
Varnals	Peter Jeffrey
Dr Cullen	Richard Bebb
Carter	Philip Latham
Pasold	Peter Arne
Pushkin	Vernon Dobtcheff
Dr Wadkin	Peter Madden
Anna Wadkin	Jeanne Roland

Music by Laurie Johnson
Directed by Roy Baker
Produced by Julian Wintle

the government deposits £40,000,000 in a Swiss bank. Later, while strolling through the countryside, Steed is confronted by Mellors, still carrying his shotgun. Steed pretends to leave but later returns and breaks into a farmhouse. There he finds a padlocked cupboard and on the floor traces of powder. He puts a sample into an envelope and is about to leave when he hears a gun being cocked. Instinctively he jumps to the side but a shot from Mellors' gun hits him in the shoulder. Concerned at Steed's disappearance, Emma goes to the farmhouse. Forcing open the cupboard she finds the dead body of Quince behind a pile of apples. And lurching towards her is the blood-stained body of Steed. Having recovered, Steed is now invited by Omrod to join the hunt, and Emma is also invited. During the hunt, Miss Snow lures Steed into a corner of the stable-yard and, before galloping off, leaves him to face Croft, who is wielding a vicious-looking scythe. After a few wild slashes, Croft is left floundering in a horse trough. Emma manages to unseat Miss Snow and takes her horse. She follows Omrod and Juggins into a barn where they are piling Silent Dust into containers. Emma holds them at gunpoint but Mellors arrives and jumps her. Emma whips him over her shoulder and makes a run for it – pursued by Omrod and Juggins on horseback. Cornered by Omrod, she throws him to the ground and turns to face Juggins, who is carrying a long horse-whip. But then Steed appears, riding a horse and carrying a For Sale sign nailed to a sturdy wooden post. With a swish of the post, Steed sweeps Juggins into the duckpond. Steed and Emma exchange glances, then Steed picks up Omrod's fallen hunting horn and blows a long, triumphant call on it.

Thundering up on a horse, Steed helps Juggins into the duckpond with the aid of a post, in Silent Dust.

WHEN he suddenly reappears after two years' unexplained absence, scientist John Wadkin is a mental wreck from intensive brain-washing. A government official, Varnals, tells Emma and Steed that Wadkin's state of mind suggests he has been held prisoner in a Manchurian concentration camp. In an attempt to restore Wadkin to his senses, Steed and Emma confront him with his one-time colleague, Dr Cullen, but without success. Wadkin babbles on nonsensically, obsessed by the number 621. Any further progress is thwarted when a gang of toughs make off with Wadkin in a Chinese laundry van, despite a desperate bid by Emma to stop them. The focus now turns on Dr Cullen. A mystery man, Len Pascold, begins making enquiries about him, and this leads Steed and Emma to suspect that Cullen may be kidnapped when he visits London for a conference. Steed and Varnals are in the background when Cullen books into Chessman's Hotel. Significantly, he is given Room 621. Unknown to Steed, when Cullen reaches his room, he is confronted by the mysterious Pascold. The following morning, the man who checks out as Dr Cullen is obviously an impostor. Emma then gets a job at the hotel to help with the mystery. Steed meanwhile learns that Pascold had been attempting to secure Dr Cullen's services on behalf of an American chemical corporation. Pascold, however, suddenly exonerates himself by pestering the hotel management with enquiries about Cullen's sudden disappearance. In fact, Cullen now lies in a concentration camp cell, where he listens in horror to the staccato commands of the Chinese guards outside – and the demented ramblings of Wadkin in the next cell. Emma investigates a Chinese laundry in the basement of the hotel. She finds Pascold dead, in a laundry basket, but suspicion falls on her when she is seen leaving, and she is sent on an errand to Room 621. There, she is soon overcome

by gas fumes. She comes to in the concentration camp, where an interrogator menaces her. Meanwhile in his penthouse above the hotel, sits the owner, Max Chessman, who, because of thin blood, has to live in a super-heated atmosphere, and lives on a severely restricted diet, because of his immense size. He hears that the renowned Monsieur Gourmet is a guest in his hotel, and orders a special epicure's dinner for him. Gourmet is, in fact, Steed, who has adopted the pose in order to avert suspicion. It now becomes apparent to Emma that Chessman is using kidnapped scientists as objects of barter to help him realise his plans for an unbroken chain of luxury hotels around the world. All the scientists were booked into Room 621 and thence transported to the prison camp. Wadkin's temporary escape had been a mistake. Finding Emma missing, Steed breaks into Chessman's penthouse and turns off the heat to freeze the information out of the delicate man. He soon learns that Emma is being held in a room on a disused floor of the hotel. Entering the room, Steed finds it is a perfect replica of Room 621, and the one to which the missing scientists had been deliberately misdirected. Steed discovers a false wall behind a wardrobe. Behind the wall is a passage leading to a block of cells. The concentration camp is actually in the hotel. Various tricks were used to simulate Manchuria and to deceive the inmates. He finds and releases Emma and they combine forces to defeat Chessman's vile plot.

Steed finds himself in a tight corner when two of Chessman's henchmen catch up with him, in Room Without A View.

SMALL GAME FOR BIG HUNTERS

By Philip Levene

John Steed	Patrick Macnee
Emma Peel	Diana Rigg
Col Rawlings	Bill Fraser
Simon Trent	James Villiers
Professor Swain	Liam Redmond
Dr Gibson	A J Brown
Fleming	Peter Burton
Razafi	Paul Danquah
Tropical outfitter	Tom Gill
Lala	Esther Anderson
Kendrick	Peter Thomas

Music by Laurie Johnson
Directed by Gerry O'Hara
Produced by Julian Wintle

STEED and Emma are called to a country cottage near London where a man named Kendrick is suffering from sleeping sickness. He was found, wearing a tropical kit, by a Dr Gibson, who is in attendance as Steed examines the man. Steed shows Emma the native arrow found in Kendrick's back. As they examine it tribal drums begin to throb away across the country. Professor Swain, an expert on primitive tribes, is brought to the cottage and he tells Emma about Shirenzai, a cult peculiar to the land of Kalaya. Shirenzai in Kalayan means The Curse of Sleep. Swain tries to cast a spell to revive Kendrick, but Gibson scoffs at it. Later, Gibson is found in a coma, and round his wrist is the mark of Shirenzai. Steed decides to investigate the Kalayan Ex-Serviceman's Association, run by a Colonel Rawlings. As he leaves the cottage, he is attacked by Razafi, a native, and is saved when the vicious knife he wields sinks into Steed's bowler hat. At Rawlings' home, Steed encounters the native a second time but manages to subdue him. But Steed, in the garden, steps into a spring-type animal trap. Recovering, he finds himself in Rawlings' study, where a lovely Eurasian girl, Lala, is beckoning to him. Reaching out he finds himself at the end of a hunting rifle, held by Simon Trent, who makes Steed change into tropical kit before taking him into an intensely-heated jungle area. The blimp-like Colonel Rawlings arrives and is introduced to Steed. The Colonel, his mind gone, believes he is still in Kalaya. After dinner Trent is visited by Fleming, who, not seeing Steed, begins to tell Trent that the two men are still sleeping. When Trent indicates Steed's presence Fleming leaves. Meanwhile, Emma, still keeping watch on the two sleeping men, begins to read a book on Black Magic and dozes off. Back at Rawlings' home, Steed notices two natives arrive carrying a litter. He tries to leave, but Trent orders him to stay at gunpoint. Next

Simon Trent prepares to show Steed his new breed of tsetse fly, which will devastate Kalaya, in Small Game For Big Hunters.

morning, he rises early and manages to phone Emma. She tells him that Swain has disappeared as well as the two patients. Razafi creeps into the house and tells Steed to meet him in the garden at midnight. There, Steed is startled to find that Razafi has a perfect Oxford accent and is a member of the Kalayan Intelligence Service. He tells Steed that Trent and Fleming have grudges against his country. Razafi then takes Steed to a hut where Kendrick and Gibson are sleeping. Suddenly Lala springs out and stabs him, before running off. Trent appears, takes some papers out of Razafi's pocket and congratulates Steed on killing a spy. He then takes Steed to a laboratory and explains how he and Fleming have bred a new kind of tsetse fly immune to all known insecticides. They will take thousands of them to Kalaya, where they will breed in their millions and desolate the land. He and Fleming will then take over the country. Trent hears Lala and calls to her. Steed prepares to run, but Lala turns out to be Emma in a sarong. Steed fights with Trent and Emma runs off with the canister of tsetse flies but is cornered by Fleming and Swain – the brain behind the plan. Emma is saved by Steed swinging through the trees Tarzan-style to her rescue. In the cold, drizzly English day outside they open the canister and let the rain fall onto the flies – washing away the deadly plans of Swain and his henchmen.

THE GIRL FROM AUNTIE

By Roger Marshall

John Steed	Patrick Macnee
Emma Peel	Diana Rigg
Georgie Price-Jones	Liz Frazer
Gregorio Auntie	Alfred Burke
Arkwright	Bernard Cribbins
Ivanov	David Bauer
Aunt Hetty	Sylvia Coleridge

Music by Laurie Johnson
Directed by Roy Baker
Produced by Julian Wintle

STEED returns from holiday to find a shapely blonde impersonating Emma. He follows her to a theatrical agency and, when questioned, she explains her real name is Georgie Price Jones, and she got the job after answering a newspaper advertisement. They search the agency, and find the body of the agent – with a large knitting needle protruding from his back. Two other men were present when Georgie got the job, but when Steed tracks them down, they have also been killed with knitting needles. A cheque – part payment of Georgie's fee – with three signatures leads to three more bodies and three more knitting needles. Georgie now recalls that her Emma Peel outfit came from a theatrical costumiers, Jacques Brothers. They find three of the brothers dead, but the fourth manages to gasp, 'Auntie... Auntie did it,' before dying. At that moment, an old lady arrives carrying a bag of knitting. She says that she is Auntie Hetty, favourite auntie of the brothers. She then tells Steed that the needles could only have come from the Arkwright Knitting Circle, and she takes him to the circle where Steed meets Mr Arkwright, who complains that the needles were stolen from his storeroom. On the way out, Steed meets Colonel Ivanov, a Russian agent, coming out of Art Incorporated – the next office. Steed waits until he has left, then returns to the Circle, where through a ventilation shaft he hears a voice order the elimination of Mrs Peel. Meanwhile at her apartment, reading a book on self-defence, Georgie doesn't see the heavily-veiled old woman enter carrying the now familiar knitting needles. When attacked, Georgie puts the book to good use, before escaping into the kitchen. Posing as an art connoisseur, Steed visits Art Incorporated, saying that he was recommended by Colonel Ivanov, but he cannot see the boss. The boss, however, has observed Steed, and orders his investigation. Later that day, Steed returns and breaks into the storeroom. He is discovered by the owner, Gregorio Auntie, who says that his organisation can get hold of anything – for

THE 13TH HOLE

By Tony Williamson

John Steed	Patrick Macnee
Emma Peel	Diana Rigg
Reed	Patrick Allen
Colonel Watson	Hugh Manning
Adams	Peter Jones
Jackson	Victor Maddern
Collins	Francis Matthews
Professor Minley	Norman Wynne
Man on TV screen	Richard Marner

Music by Laurie Johnson
Directed by Roy Baker
Produced by Julian Wintle

Steed and Emma discuss the strange cult of Shirenzai, peculiar to the land of Kalaya, in Small Game For Big Hunters.

Steed introduces Mrs Peel to Mrs Peel, after the real Mrs Peel has been released from her cage, in The Girl From Auntie.

STEED and Emma's investigations into the murder of a colleague lead them to the Craigleigh Golf Club. There they decide the people they will have to watch are scientist Dr Adams, Collins the club pro, Jackson the caddy master and two members named Reed and Colonel Watson. Emma plays solo behind Reed and Adams up to the 13th hole. While they are playing on the green, she waits below. Suddenly a driverless caddy car plunges down the hill towards her and she just escapes. But Reed and Adams have completely disappeared. Steed meanwhile searches the club office and finds Reed's bag, containing a .303 rifle covered like a club, and a box of ammunition. Steed meets Emma in the bar and then Adams and Reed appear. Suddenly the lights begin to flicker, before going out. When they come on Adams and Reed have gone. Steed and Emma search independently for them on the course, even though it is dark. Emma is attacked by Collins, whom she subdues. As they are talking, a golf ball strikes Collins on the forehead and kills him. As she crawls away, Emma notices that she is on the 13th green. Across the course she sees the outline of a strange vehicle with what appears to be a gun turret jutting from the front. She eventually finds the vehicle in the staff office. It is a caddy car with a large telescope mounted in the front. Inside the cart are charts and maps of stars and constellations. Reed and Jackson enter and she hides behind a desk. Reed says he has been drawn against Steed in the club tournament and he tells Jackson that he must win, by fair means or foul. Jackson produces a gun which fires golf balls by compressed air and Emma realises that this is how Collins was killed. During the tournament, Emma hides on the course and helps Steed to win. Reed stalks off the green in disgust. Emma now joins Steed and as they talk, a golf ball strikes Steed, who falls to the ground. A specially-padded golf cap saves his life, and undeterred, he arranges to play the next

a price. Steed offers to buy Mrs Peel, but Auntie tells him that her sale is already contracted. Steed and Georgie lay a trap for Ivanov, and once cornered, he admits he is Mrs Peel's purchaser. Steed arranges for his expulsion and once again offers to buy Mrs Peel. Auntie, however, still refuses to sell to Steed directly and arranges an auction instead. The bidding is fierce, but Steed's offer outbids them all. As Steed and Georgie are about to leave, the veiled old lady arrives with proof of Steed's real identity, and only quick action from Georgie prevents Steed from receiving one of the deadly knitting needles. As Steed battles with Gregorio Auntie, the old woman rushes off to kill the real Emma. Dispatching Gregorio, Steed follows. He finds her at the Knitting Circle and reveals her to be a man. The killer now tells Steed how to get to Emma. Steed, with Georgie in tow, arrives in time to see Emma struggling with the receptionist to get the keys to the cage in which she is a prisoner. Emma finally wins. Released from the cage, Steed now introduces Mrs Peel (Georgie) to the real Mrs Peel.

round of the tournament – this time his opponent is Adams. Emma rings the Royal Observatory to check on the photographs she has taken of the astral charts. One chart shows a spaceship, Vostok 3, orbiting the earth. It is timed to be over England at four o'clock that afternoon. She goes to tell Steed but is captured by Reed. He then takes her to the 13th green where he moves a switch hidden in the grass, which parts to reveal a chamber below. Underground, the Colonel is watching a screen, on which thousands of miles away, men are seen waiting for Adams to arrive and pass on his scientific secrets by satellite. Steed and Adams meanwhile arrive at the 12th hole, where Adams asks Steed to hole out while he looks for a lost ball. Suspicious, Steed leaves his ball on the lip of the hole and sends another ball across the green to knock it in. There is a tremendous explosion, watched with glee through a periscope by the occupants of the underground shelter. The door opens and Adams walks in – followed by Steed. After a furious fight, Steed and Emma soon round up the gang but in the ensuing mayhem, the Colonel escapes – only to be brought down by a beautifully-driven ball from Steed.

THE QUICK-QUICK-SLOW DEATH

By Robert Banks Stewart

John Steed	Patrick Macnee
Emma Peel	Diana Rigg
Lucille Banks	Eunice Gayson
Ivor Bracewell	Maurice Kaufmann
Chester Read	Larry Cross
Peever	James Belchamber
Bernard	Colin Ellis
Willi Fehr	Michael Peake

Music by Laurie Johnson
Directed by James Hill
Produced by Julian Wintle

WHEN Willi Fehr, a foreign agent, is involved in a road accident, the body of a man is hidden in the pram he was pushing. Having gained nothing from interrogating Fehr, Steed and Emma have to rely on two small clues they find on the body. Emma goes to check out a tattooist's, while Steed, convinced that the man's evening suit was hired, finds the hire company. Emma learns that the dead man's name was Peever. Steed finds the costumiers, but the assistant is murdered as he searches for the information in the back room of his shop. In the meantime, Willi Fehr has been shot while trying to escape. Steed goes to an address provided by the manager of Peever's bank, and narrowly escapes death when he opens the door – it is false and above a building site. Following up another clue, Emma visits the Terpsichorean Training Techniques – a dancing school run by Lucille Banks, and gets a job as an instructress. One of the first students she meets is introduced as Mr Peever. Emma decides to find out if he is genuine, and leaves a pair of the dead man's shoes in his locker. When Lucille sees Peever trying on the shoes she hurriedly takes them from him. Steed meanwhile visits the tattooist's shop, but he arrives too late to save the man, who has been shot. Before dying, the man tattooed a message on the skin of a large garlic sausage, reading 'The killer has a rose tattoo on his right wrist'. Emma is trying to become friends with Peever, but he says he will soon be graduating. Knowing him to be an atrocious dancer, Emma asks a fellow instructress what's happening. She is told that certain students are chosen for graduation, they receive a diploma, then disappear. Believing that he will get a lead at the dancing school, Steed enrols as a student. He tells Lucille that he is quite alone in the world, and she decides that he warrants her own personal attention. Emma learns that a man called Bernard has given all the students dancing shoes. Before she can visit him, however, he is given a face-lift – with a bowl of quick-setting plaster. At the school, Lucille tells an accomplice to inform someone called The Commander that Steed will be their next victim. At the Gala Dance, Steed tells Emma that he suspects the school is being used to infiltrate foreign agents into the country. Each agent, he says, assumes the identity of a lonely student who is then disposed of by Lucille and her friends. Lucille announces a dancing competition, and tells everyone to don masks. She insists on partnering Steed, and slowly guides him towards a large display unit, behind which is an agent waiting to take his place. Steel realises what's happening and manages to signal to Emma – whose partner, Bracewell, has a rose tattoo on his right wrist. Working in perfect unison, they manoeuvre their partners until Emma manages to get Bracewell behind the display unit. She emerges with a different partner. In a game of change-your-partners, Steed joins up with Emma and together they make for the door. They find their way blocked by Lucille, Peever, and The Commander – alias Read, the school musical director. With a quick-quick left and right, The Avengers soon overcome the group and dance out of the school.

Mrs Peel tells Major Robertson that she wants to lead a more exciting life, when she and Steed meet **The Danger Makers.**

THE DANGER MAKERS

By Roger Marshall

John Steed	Patrick Macnee
Emma Peel	Diana Rigg
Major Robertson	Nigel Davenport
Dr Harold Long	Douglas Wilmer
Col Adams	Fabia Drake
Peters	Moray Watson
Lieut Stanhope	Adrian Ropes
RAF officer	Richard Coleman
Gordon Lamble	John Gatrell

Music by Laurie Johnson
Directed by Charles Crichton
Produced by Julian Wintle

WHEN General Woody Groves is killed in a crash, after apparently taking part in a chicken-run, and Gordon Lamble, Head of the Chemical Warfare Establishment, is injured while trying to scale St Paul's, Steed and Emma are briefed to find out what's going on. They visit Harold Long, consultant to the Psychological Warfare Department, who says that there have been a number of such inexplicable cases recently. Leaving Emma to keep an eye on the injured Lamble, Steed visits General Groves' Battalion Headquarters. There he meets Major Robertson who tells him he cannot understand why the General should have taken part in such a dangerous stunt. At the hospital, Emma and Long discover Lamble on the narrow ledge outside his window. Long stops Emma from helping Lamble, and soon he returns to his bed unaided. Later, a noise from Lamble's room attracts Steed's and Emma's attention. They enter the room and find Lamble dead. Following another clue, Steed visits Wing Commander Watson of the RAF but arrives in time to see him put a high-speed jet through a series of crazy stunts. One of them goes wrong, and the plane plummets to the ground. On Steed's instructions, Emma introduces herself to Major Robertson. She convinces him that she wants a more exciting life. Steed's suspicions are soon justified when Robertson acts favourably to Emma. Steed receives a phone call from a Lieutenant Stanhope of Groves' Battalion, who claims he has important information. When Steed arrives he finds Stanhope dead. He also finds a postcard of an army museum called Manton House. He goes there and meets the owner, Colonel Adams – an elderly ex-women's army officer whose only interest is military history. He also meets the sinister Peters, who talks to Steed as if he expects him to know all about the secret society of which he claims membership. Major Robertson tells Emma that he knows of a place where she will find the excitement she craves –

A TOUCH OF BRIMSTONE

By Brian Clemens

John Steed	**Patrick Macnee**
Emma Peel	**Diana Rigg**
John Cartney	**Peter Wyngarde**
Lord Darcy	**Colin Jeavons**
Sara	**Carol Cleveland**
Horace	**Robert Cawdron**
Willy Frant	**Jeremy Young**

Diana Rigg's wardrobe designed by John Bates
Music by Laurie Johnson
Directed by James Hill
Produced by Julian Wintle

Emma makes her first appearance as The Queen of Sin, with spikes and snake, at the Hellfire Club in A Touch of Brimstone.

AN important diplomat from the Eastern bloc is held up to ridicule before a television audience of millions and a massive oil deal is cancelled when the Sheik is made to look like a monkey. National prestige, not to mention big business, is in danger and The Avengers are ordered to take a closer look. Steed tells Emma that other hoaxes, such as plastic spiders in the Ambassador's soup, and something quite outrageous in a diplomat's bed, have been played. The only suspect is the Honourable John Cleverly Cartney, and Steed tells Emma to investigate. From the outset, Cartney is attracted to Emma. Believing her story about collecting for charity, he immediately donates a thousand guineas, and invites her to dinner. At dinner, their conversation is interrupted by the arrival of Lord Darcy and while the men are talking quietly, Emma searches Cartney's desk. All she can find is a diary with the entry 'Today – 4.30 – Friendship'. In the meantime, Steed searches Lord Darcy's office, and finds several pairs of scissors — all made of rubber. As he is leaving, he is interrupted by Horace, Darcy's manservant, but Steed overpowers him and makes his escape. Steed is puzzled by the rubber scissors, until Emma tells him of the entry in Cartney's diary. Steed and Emma tear across London to the newly-built Hall of Friendship, but arrive too late — another hoax has been played, this time with more serious consequences. While performing the opening ceremony a VIP has been electrocuted by a current passing through the ribbon. Emma goes to see Cartney again, while Steed goes in search of Lord Darcy. He finds him drunk, and sets to work on him. He soon confesses to his part in the hoax, but insists that he didn't know that murder was intended. Apparently, such jokes are part of the rules of the Hellfire Club. Emma attends the next meeting of the Hellfire Club at Cartney's home, and sees that it is an exact replica of the infamous 18th-century organisation, and all the

members wear Regency costume. In the company of her host, she is forced to watch as two men fight before the members. Suddenly an agitated Lord Darcy arrives, and accuses Cartney of duplicity and murder. Cartney calmly orders a meeting of the Superior members and they, with Darcy, withdraw. Later, as they stand over the coffin containing Darcy's mortal remains, Emma tells Steed that she is sure that he was murdered by the 'Superior' members of the Hellfire Club. Steed makes immediate arrangements to join the club. At the next meeting, Steed is introduced to Cartney, who is suspicious of Steed, and makes him take a number of tests. Afterwards Steed pretends to leave but eavesdrops, and hears Cartney tell the others that their next coup will be so outrageous that the whole country will be up in arms. It will occur during the next evening's Gala meeting. At the meeting, Steed sees two members carrying a sedan chair. Emma follows them deep into the catacombs beneath the house, where they unload a box of high explosives. Hurrying away to find Steed, she meets Cartney who tells her that he has something special planned for her. Meanwhile, Sara, Cartney's ex-girlfriend, tells Steed of a number of secret underground passages beneath the house. One, she says, leads directly to the government-owned Calverstone House. Their conversation is interrupted by the arrival of Cartney who introduces 'The Queen of Sin'. It is Emma, dressed in a corset and boots, and carrying a live snake! Dancing with her Steed suggests that Cartney is going to blow up Calverstone House, where three foreign Prime Ministers are staying. His fears become greater when Emma reminds him that the original Hell Raisers were dedicated to overthrowing the government. Steed is suddenly exposed when Horace, Darcy's manservant, recognises him. A member called Frant challenges him to a duel, and as they fight, Emma slips away, followed by Cartney. In the catacombs Emma makes short work of the men guarding the explosives, but she is confronted by her host carrying a gun. Suddenly she hurls the rapier she is holding at him. As she stands over Cartney's dead body, Steed races in. Together they board an 18th-century coach and exit laughing.

Manton. Believing Steed to be a member of the organisation, Robertson tells Emma that the society is called The Danger Makers, and that members only live for the excitement of mortal danger. He adds that he will arrange for Emma to be initiated. For her test, Emma has to negotiate a metallic ring along live electrical poles — one slip spells instant death. It is no sooner over when the principal of the society appears — it is Harold Long. Steed is unmasked and he and Emma are thrown into a cell where Long tells them that he formed the society when he discovered that many ex-servicemen craved danger as a drug addict craves a fix. With such men, he says, he will fulfill Operation Grand Slam — the theft of the Crown Jewels. Steed and Emma manage to break free and Steed challenges Long to a fight. Long, however, tries to escape through the test room, but becomes entangled in the complex of wires and poles and is electrocuted. Another case successfully completed Steed and Emma depart in a go-kart.

WHAT THE BUTLER SAW

By Roger Marshall

John Steed	Patrick Macnee
Emma Peel	Diana Rigg
Hemming	Thorley Walters
Benson	John Le Mesurier
Group Capt Miles	Dennis Quilley
Maj Gen Goddard	Kynaston Reeve
Brig Goddard	Howard Marion Crawford
Vice Admiral Willows	Humphrey Lestocq
Sgt Moran	Ewan Hooper
Barber	David Swift
Reeves	Norman Scace

Music by Laurie Johnson
Directed by Bill Bain
Produced by Julian Wintle

Major General Goddard tells Steed of his son's treachery in failing to join the Cavalry, in What The Butler Saw.

IN search of information, Steed visits his barber, a known double agent. The man says that one of three men – Admiral Willows, Brigadier Ponsonby-Goddard or Group Captain Miles – is selling secret defence plans. Steed settles back while the barber sees to another customer. His peace is soon shattered when the barber's body slumps beside him, a pair of scissors sticking out of his back. The rest of the shop is empty. Dressed in full naval rig and sporting a beard, Steed visits Admiral Willows, who is obsessed with horse racing. At Brigadier Ponsonby-Goddard's home, Steed, now in army uniform, meets the Brigadier's semi-senile father, Major General Goddard, who accuses his son of treachery. Before Steed can substantiate the old man's charge, the Brigadier himself arrives. When Steed mentions the accusations, the Brigadier says the charge is a result of his failure to join the cavalry regiment as all his forebears had done. As Steed leaves he overhears Reeves, Goddard's butler, arranging on the telephone to meet someone in the Brigadier's study that night. From one of Group Captain Miles' aides, Steed learns that the officer is dedicated to his work. Only one thing shares his attention – girls! After arranging for Emma to meet Miles, Steed returns to the Brigadier's home but arrives too late. The butler is dead. Steed manages to withstand a savage attack by Reeves' killer, but cannot prevent the murderer's escape. Operation Fascination is begun by Emma. She arranges for photographs of herself to be planted all over Miles' house and office. Everywhere he goes, Emma's likeness is staring at him. Soon Miles is fascinated to the point of desperation! When they finally meet, Miles invites Emma to dinner. When Steed hears that the replacement for the dead Reeves has come from the Butler's and Gentleman's Gentlemen Association, he enrols as a student. The principal is Hemming – butler to Group Captain Miles

– who says his work at the Association is part-time. Hemming is pleased with Steed's progress, but another instructor – Benson, butler to Admiral Willows – isn't so happy. He has seen Steed somewhere, but cannot think when it was. Steed learns that Hemming has refused a handsome offer to leave Miles' staff. Later Benson catches Steed searching the laundry, where he has found Hemming taking a bath – in an electric washing machine! Benson tells Steed he knows he is a fake, but offers him the chance of making a great deal of money as Hemming's replacement on Miles' staff. Steed accepts and starts work in time to welcome Emma to dinner. Emma needs all her wits about her to deal with the amorous officer, but with Steed's help – he repeatedly interrupts – she manages to hold Miles at bay. At the same time, she discovers that Miles is actually very honest, and is bored playing the gay lover. While Miles is away at a conference, Steed is told to spill wine over Miles' uniform as soon as he returns. Mystified, Steed follows his instructions, and taking the uniform to the kitchen, he is met by Benson who orders him to hand it over. With Emma's help, Steed follows Benson to the B&GG Association. After a search, they find three torn uniforms – one naval, one army and one RAF – and three tiny tape recorders. They realise that the missing tapes must contain the defence secrets. They continue to search, but are caught by Benson and Sergeant Moran – an army barman from the Three Services Club – who admits to being the ringleader. As Benson is about to kill them, a bugle call rings through the building, and they hear General Goddard's order to charge. In the confusion that follows, Steed disarms Benson while Emma takes care of Moran. After the battle, the General explains that he became suspicious when he saw Benson with his son's uniform. A job well done, Steed and Emma take off in an army helicopter.

THE HOUSE THAT JACK BUILT

By Brian Clemens

John Steed	**Patrick Macnee**
Emma Peel	**Diana Rigg**
Professor Keller	**Michael Goodliffe**
Burton	**Griffith Davies**
Withers	**Michael Wynne**

Music by Laurie Johnson
Directed by Don Leaver
Produced by Julian Wintle

WHEN Emma is told that a mysterious Uncle Jack has died and left her his country house, she goes to inspect her new estate. Puzzled by her good fortune, Steed calls Mrs Peel's solicitor. His fears are confirmed – the man denies all knowledge of Emma's Uncle Jack or any legacy. Quickly Steed makes a second call to his friends. Emma's journey is interrupted by a strange character called Withers, who is dressed in a scout-master's uniform and begs a lift, saying that he will be satisfied with Emma's destination. Mrs Peel finds the house dark and empty. Papers are strewn over a desk in the study. They are sheets of her solicitor's writing paper, and bear evidence of forged signatures. A telephone rings, but when she answers it all she hears is asthmatic breathing, before the line goes dead. As she hurries from the study, she is terrified to see that the hall has disappeared. In its place is a kind of perpetual motion machine with corridors leading off in several directions. Turning back to the study, she finds that it, too, has been replaced by corridors. Meanwhile, Steed decides to follow Emma to the house. Emma is now finding that whichever way she turns, she ends up in front of the perpetual motion machine. When she finds a scout's shoulder patch, she is convinced that Withers is her captor, and tries to escape. Suddenly the silence is broken by strange noises – a sinister laugh, the shuffling of feet, the tinkling of a music box. Desperate now, Emma starts to run, and finds herself back in the study. Lying on the floor is Withers, dead. Emma examines the door, and finds a small plug in the frame. She presses it and the whole room starts to spin. When it stops, she is in another room, and sees a huge photograph of herself. Under it is a sign reading 'Welcome to an exhibition of the late Emma Peel'. A strange voice tells Emma that she will find the answer to the riddle in the exhibition. Searching, she finds newspaper coverage of her life – her take-over of her father's empire after his death, her success, and the dismissal of Professor Keller, the company's automation expert, with whose plans for the replacement of

men by machines Emma had disagreed. Suddenly Emma recognises the voice. It is Keller's! He tells Emma that she is prisoner within a house that is a huge machine. It is, says Keller, the justification of his theories. Trying to escape, Emma breaks into what appears to be a machine room, and sees a man she thinks is Keller. After a ferocious fight, she finds that he is another prisoner – terrified, emaciated, and completely mad. She attempts to interrogate him but learns nothing. Suddenly he attacks her with a shotgun. She manages to divert the shot, and knocks him out. Then she sees that where the shot has damaged the wall the outline of a door is revealed. Quickly, she breaks into what is apparently the central control room, to be greeted by Keller's voice, and his face on a large screen. The voice tells her that her discovery will do her no good – the voice she hears is a recording, and Keller is dead. Breaking through the screen, she finds the body of Keller inside a large glass case. The voice tells her that the house is a vast indestructible machine from which she can't escape – a machine that will tend to her every need and still be functioning when she herself is quite mad. Release will only come when she uses the key provided to gain access to a special suicide box. After a brief hysterical outburst, Emma forces herself to think logically and goes in search of the madman. He gives her shotgun shells, from which she makes a bomb. Then the man makes another attack, but is killed when he falls into the suicide box prepared by Keller for Emma. Using the bomb, Emma stops the giant computer that controls the machine. A door quietly opens and Emma leaves the room to find a worried Steed waiting in the hall. As they ride away on a tandem, Steed explains that Withers was a friend of his, sent to keep an eye on her.

A terrified Mrs Peel finds herself in the central control room of The House That Jack Built.

A SENSE OF HISTORY

By Martin Woodhouse

John Steed	Patrick Macnee
Emma Peel	Diana Rigg
Richard Carlyon	Nigel Stock
Dr Henge	John Barron
Grindley	John Glyn-Jones
Professor Acheson	John Ringham
Duboys	Patrick Mower
John Pettit	Robin Phillips
Millerson	Peter Blythe
Allen	Peter Bourne
Marianne	Jacqueline Pearce

Music by Laurie Johnson
Directed by Peter Graham Scott
Produced by Julian Wintle

WHEN James Broom is found slumped across the front seat of his car on a lonely forest road with an arrow in his back, John Steed is sent to investigate. Broom, an economist, was author of the visionary Europa Plan to eliminate world poverty. When Steed arrives, he finds Richard Carlyon, Broom's right-hand man, rummaging through the boot of Broom's car. He emerges with Broom's briefcase. Carlyon tells Steed that Broom was on his way to a university when he was murdered. The briefcase offers no more clues, except that it is full of papers, all headed 'St Bodes'. Steed decides to call in Emma. He wants her to lecture at St Bodes. Emma soon establishes herself and after hearing a history lecture given by Dr Henge, she notices a group of students led by the insolent and cynical Duboys. Enquiring among the staff, she learns that Duboys is a brilliant student, and his insolence is put down to Rag Week high spirits. Emma is unconvinced, and her first meeting with Duboys and his gang strengthens her suspicions. Among the papers in Broom's briefcase, Steed discovers a thesis entitled Economics and a Sense of History, bearing the college crest but no author's name. A neo-facist argument, it is diametrically opposed to all Broom stood for. Broom was on his way to see an enemy, not a friend. In the hope of discovering the author, Steed arrives at St Bodes and meets the friendly university archivist, Grindley. Dr Henge has discovered that Steed is not a member of the faculty and has no right to be there – a fact that has not gone unnoticed by Duboys. Steed's investigations are hampered further when Grindley is found dead. That night Steed visits Carlyon, who lives in a caravan on the edge of a wood, and whom Steed believes will be the next target. He is right – they are soon attacked. Arrows whizz by the caravan they are hiding under. Steed draws his gun and the assailants flee.

Emma goes to the fancy dress Rag Night Ball, which has Robin Hood as its theme, in **A Sense of History.**

But they leave a clue – a photograph of Marianne, the girlfriend of a member of Duboys' clique. Next day, Steed corners Marianne and her boyfriend, Pettit, who agrees to help unmask the real leader of the group, the man who gives Duboys his orders. That night, Pettit dies when some heavy library shelves fall on him. The following day Carlyon, Emma and Steed are invited to the Rag Night Ball. It is in fancy dress and the theme is Robin Hood. At the ball, Marianne, disillusioned by Pettit's death, reveals that an attempt will be made on Carlyon that evening. Their leader will arrive as Friar Tuck, then they will dispose of Carlyon quietly. Once he is dead, the Europa Plan is finished and Friar Tuck and his Merrie Men will have changed the destiny of Europe. Steed's plans are thrown into chaos when three Friar Tucks arrive. However, Steed and Emma discover the author, and their real protagonist. It is Grindley, who feigned his death in order to avert suspicion. A furious battle breaks out from which Steed and Emma emerge the victors, then the successful pair ride merrily into the sunset on a motorcycle and sidecar.

HOW TO SUCCEED... AT MURDER

By Brian Clemens

John Steed	Patrick Macnee
Emma Peel	Diana Rigg
Mary Merryweather	Sarah Lawson
Sara Penny	Angela Browne
Gladys Murkle	Anna Cunningham
Henry Throgbottom	Artto Norris
Joshua Rudge	Jerome Willis
J J Hooter	Christopher Benjamin
Sir George Morton	Kevin Brennan
Jack Finlay	Robert Dean

Music by Laurie Johnson
Directed by Don Leaver
Produced by Julian Wintle
Diana Rigg's wardrobe designed by John Bates

WHEN ten top city executives are murdered within a few days, Steed is puzzled. The only link is the prominence of the victims in commerce, but that alone could hardly be the motive. Embezzlement is ruled out after the murder of Sir George Morton when Steed checks with Morton's accountant, Joshua Rudge, that everything is in order. The murder of executive Jack Finlay gives The Avengers a lead. In the car in which Finlay's corpse was discovered, there is a heavy scent of perfume that reminds Steed of Rudge's office. He searches the office that night, but is attacked and knocked out. Meanwhile, Emma collects a sample of the perfume in a foot-pump and takes it to the perfumier J J Hooter. He identifies it as one of his exclusive lines and promises to prepare a list of customers for Emma that afternoon. When she returns, Hooter is dead and his secretary, Gladys Murkle, has taken charge of the business. She refuses to help Emma. Steed now discovers that each of the victims had a complex office system only understood by their secretaries. In each case, the executive's death meant promotion for the secretary. Once again, Steed calls at Rudge's office. His secretary, Sara, explains that Rudge is away on holiday and she is in charge in his absence. Steed introduces himself as a millionaire who is looking for a part-time secretary to help him set up a new business. Sara accepts the bait. Meanwhile, Emma becomes a secretary to Mary, formerly Sir George Morton's secretary. Following her one night, Emma discovers that Mary attends a keep-fit class run by Henry and Henrietta Throgbottom. Emma tells Steed and next day joins the class, while Steed unearths an interesting fact – Henrietta Throgbottom died in 1939. Emma soon impresses Mary with her efficiency, and is invited to attend the advanced classes. She soon discovers

HONEY FOR THE PRINCE

By Brian Clemens

John Steed	Patrick Macnee
Emma Peel	Diana Rigg
Ponsonby-Hopkirk	Ron Moody
Prince Ali	Zia Mohyeddin
Arkadi	George Pastell
Vincent	Roland Curram
Grand Vizier	Bruno Barnabe
B Bumble	Ken Parry
Ronny Wescott	Jon Laurimore
Postman	Reg Pritchard
Bernie	Peter Diamond
Eurasian girl	Carmen Dene
George Reed	Richard Graydon

Music by Laurie Johnson
Directed by James Hill
Produced by Julian Wintle
Diana Rigg's wardrobe designed by John Bates

Emma takes a break from the keep-fit class run by Henry and Henrietta Throgbottom in **How To Succeed . . . At Murder.**

Mrs Peel abandons her usual clothes for those of a Middle Eastern dancing girl in **Honey For The Prince.**

RONNY Wescott — a colleague of Steed's dies of gun-shot wounds in Steed's flat. Before dying, he tells Steed that the files on the case are in George Reed's flat, and that Reed, a fellow agent, is also dead. Steed visits the flat, but it has been broken into and Steed, caught unawares, is attacked. He fights with the intruder, who flees. The intruder has burnt all the files. Searching the flat further, Steed finds a jar of honey in a cupboard. Back at his apartment, Steed discovers a present from Reed, posted before his death. It is a jar of honey from B Bumble & Company. Dispatching Emma to Bumble's, Steed returns to Reed's flat, where he discovers that Reed was a member of QQF. Quite Quite Fantastic Inc is run by one Ponsonby-Hopkirk. Its purpose is to create people's fantasies, with the aid of theatrical devices, which they can then live. From further enquiries Steed discovers that Ronny Wescott was also a client of QQF. His fantasy was to be chief eunuch in a harem. Meanwhile, Emma learns from B Bumble, a honey specialist, that the Bahrainian Embassy is a major customer. After leaving the shop, however, an attempt is made to kill her. She soon despatches her assailant and returns to the shop. She finds Bumble dead, but his killer has left a clue — an application form to QQF. Steed has now discovered that Wescott's current assignment was to protect a Bahrainian Prince Ali, together with his full entourage, on a visit to London to sign over oil concessions in return for military protection. Obviously his assassination would give the contract to rivals! They hurry to QQF, only to find that Ponsonby-Hopkirk has been shot while staging the fantasy of the assassination of the Prince. Knowing that an assassination is being planned, but with no details, Steed decides to visit Prince Ali.

that the keep-fit school is a cover for a group of modern-day suffragettes intent on the elimination of all men. The group meets in a room at the gymnasium. Henrietta is the leader but never actually attends the meetings. Instead, she is represented by photographs of her when she was a ballerina, and a life-size doll sitting in an alcove. The doll speaks, and the voice seems to come from the alcove. Henry is present, but the women treat him as a menial. Just at Emma is about to be accepted into the group, Gladys Murkle enters and recognises her. The group now have a new problem — they have never killed a woman before. Meanwhile, Sara makes an unsuccessful attempt on Steed's life, but through his expertise in the art of tickling Steed forces her to reveal all about the group. He hurries to the gymnasium and arrives in time to rescue Emma, liberate Rudge — who had been held by the women because of his accountancy skills — and expose Henrietta as Henry. He formed the group in the bitter memory of the way businessmen ruined his late wife's career. The illusion of her voice had been simple ventriloquism.

Striking up an immediate friendship with him, Steed discovers that all the Prince's wives love honey and, as a favour, he has ordered forty man-size jars of it for them. Steed cannot examine the jars because the honey is in the Prince's harem and no man can enter. Steed is invited to dine with the Prince that night. Suspecting that the attempt on his life is to be made that evening, Steed takes Emma along, dressed as a Middle Eastern dancing girl. The Prince is well pleased with her dancing and when Steed offers Emma for his harem, the Prince glady accepts and she is led away. Once there, she immediately begins to search for the assassin. Meanwhile, Prince Ali, excited by the thought of Emma, decides to retire early that night. Steed tries desperately to stall him, but fails. As the Prince enters the harem, Emma spots the assassin about to plunge a dagger into the Prince's back. She throws her new husband to one side and attacks the assassin. The noise of the fighting alerts the harem guards and they rush in to protect the Prince. In gratitude, he offers to grant Steed anything he wishes. He chooses Mrs Peel and he and Emma ride happily away on a magic carpet.

Diana Rigg, as Mrs Emma Peel, wore clothes which could be avant-garde, op art, feline, or just plain feminine. It was all part of her considerable charm.

Diana Rigg wears TV, Jean Varon's black wool coat with white sleeves, designed by John Bates for the fourth series.

Above: Steed joins his partner Mrs Emma Peel in wearing elegant evening dress, in a scene from the fifth series.

Left: Diana Rigg wears a catsuit in Courtaulds Celon stretch jersey, designed by John Bates of Jean Varon.

Opposite page: Diana Rigg models Alan Hughes' silk and chiffon lounging pyjamas, with a couple of friends.

Right: Diana Rigg wears a shiny PVC trouser suit with matching hat and gauntlet gloves, also made of leather.

Patrick Macnee/Diana Rigg
1967-68

'Mrs Peel - We're Needed'

ONE evening, as Emma Peel sat watching television (actually a snatch of the cybernauts episode!) in her penthouse flat in Hampstead, the screen went blank. Assuming that there was something wrong with the set, she half rose to adjust it, when a flicker from the screen caught her eye. The next second the familiar features of John Steed were beaming at her from the television. 'Mrs Peel – we're needed!' he announced, and so began another episode of *The Avengers*.

By now, *The Avengers'* reputation had grown and it had a world-wide audience of over 30 million viewers in 40 countries. Unfortunately, it had still not sold in the important American market, although two American networks had seen a number of episodes and expressed interest. It seems that they were not yet ready for such an extreme series, with its very British flavour. Then, while the series was in production, another problem arose.

It had been decided to produce the first film series in monochrome, partly because Britain and other countries were still transmitting in black and white (though America was moving rapidly into colour), and partly to save money. About halfway through the series, however, the American company NBC announced they were going over entirely to colour. The other networks, ABC and CBS, would clearly have to follow suit.

ABC were concerned that if their product was going to recover its production costs, it had to achieve an American sale quickly, while there was still a market for a monochrome show.

Racing against time, they decided to take over the sales effort themselves and their managing director, Howard Thomas, and another director, Bob Norris, flew to New York for discussions with the two networks which had earlier shown interest. They were offering two things. Either if a network would buy the first 13 episodes in monochrome, they would immediately order the second 13 to be made in colour, or that if a network would buy the first series, ABC would give them an option on a second, colour, series, which would go into production immediately after the completion of the first 26 episodes.

After meetings in London and New York, Bob Norris secured a sale on the second proposal to the American Broadcasting Company, and *The Avengers* had the distinction of being the last television series to be sold to an American network in black and white. ABC took up their option on the second (colour) series and ordered two more series, making 83 episodes in all.

Of even more distinction was the fact that *The Avengers* became the first British-made television series to be screened in prime time on an American network, coast-to-coast, in the premier fall schedule. (Other British series had been used either as summer or January replacements for unsuccessful American shows.)

The success of the previous series had shown that the qualities which endeared *The Avengers* to its audience were its essential Englishness and its off-beat, way-out humour. The producers kept this in mind when planning the colour series, but this time they added more danger. Steed and Emma would be exposed to every hazard that ingenuity could devise. New twists were added to allow them to send-up villains and thwart their dastardly plots. At the time, ABC believed that the spy cycle was on the wane, so in the new series, *The Avengers* fought the private sector of villainy. No more agents of foreign powers – instead, dangerous madmen with delusions of grandeur.

While plans for the new series were being formulated, Diana Rigg was finding that some of the rewards of being a celebrity were actually problems – being approached in public by strangers, signing autographs, making personal appearances, coping with fanmail. Publicity sessions worried her: she found it difficult to talk about herself or her work unless the interviewer was on her wavelength, or to relax with photographers unless there was a rapport between them.

During the summer recess, Diana, who had been earning £150 a week from the show, declared 'I'm worth at least three times that,' and issued an ultimatum to ABC, that unless she received more money, she would not return to the series. Diana also had plenty to say about working on the show. 'It's the life of a mole,' she said. 'My world is 15,000 feet square, lit by high-voltage bulbs, and smells of cigarettes and make-up. I rarely see daylight and sleep on a camp bed during the lunch break.' Her demands were met and she returned to her life of a mole at £450 a week. (In fairness to Diana Rigg, however, it should be pointed out that she did not return simply for the financial benefits, but more from her loyalty to Patrick Macnee, the show and all those who were involved in it. But she did make it quite clear that this would be her last series.)

On hearing of her decision, Patrick Macnee said 'I'm glad that Diana is staying. She is wonderful to work with and we share a mutual obsession for detail. We deliberately set out to contrive new and different ways of playing two-handed scenes for comedy. We put Emma and Steed in routine situations, like having a meal or playing a game of chess. Then, while serving the soup, we would casually discuss some mastermind's ploy to rule the world.'

Viewers of the previous series seemed to prefer the episodes with a science-fiction theme, so many of the new stories were slanted in that direction. Brian Clemens was reported as saying at the time 'When you are dealing with a make-believe world populated by larger-than-life villains, it is difficult not to get into bizarre situations. The science-fiction thing was unintentional. Ideas were easy. It was more difficult finding writers with an *Avengers* mind. My own technique, when I thought of an idea, was to draw up 12 good dramatic moments and lead in and out of them. I needed 12 for a 50-minute script. If I'd only got six I was only halfway there. And this series chews up scripts at the rate of one every ten days.' Along with Clemens, the most prolific writer on the new series was Philip Levene. Between them, they supplied 20 of the 24 stories.

Once again, ABC decided to change both the fighting and fashion formats. This time Emma would be using kung-fu – a 5000-year old Chinese art of self-defence, based on relaxation rather than the brute strength required for karate, or the

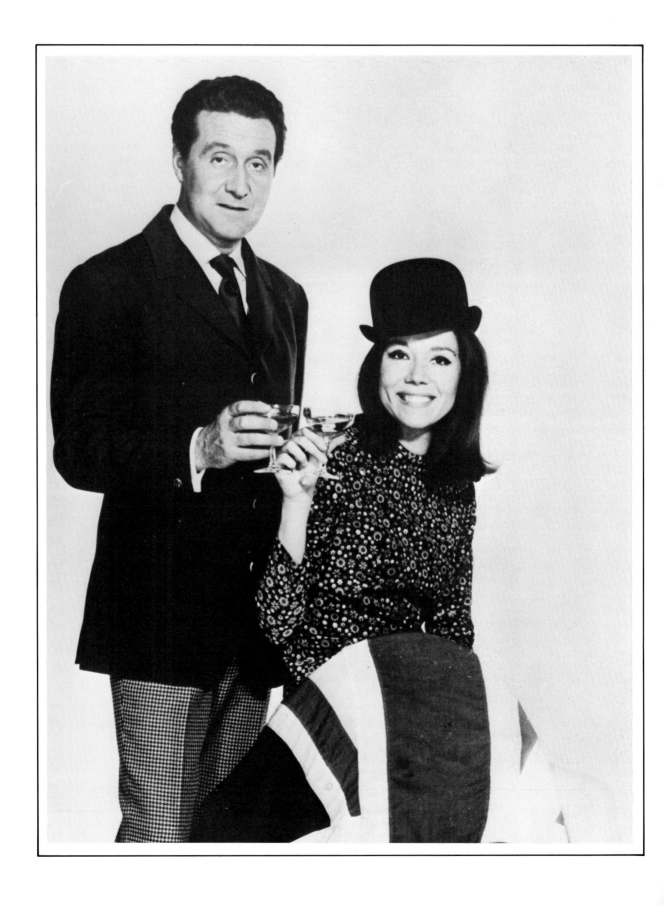

complicated throws and holds of judo. Diana Rigg was coached by stunt arranger Ray Austin for the second time. Austin also taught her the basics of Tai Chi, a series of balletic-type movements which improved her posture, relaxation and breathing.

The (by now obligatory) fashion changes were this time in the capable hands of Alan Hughes. It was Diana Rigg herself who suggested him to ABC. The guiding principle of the brief given to Hughes by the producers was to make Emma elegant and feminine. It seems, however, that Alan Hughes interpreted this as feminine and feline. His Emma in day or evening wear looked beguilingly innocent, but was capable of delivering a knockout blow to any unsuspecting villain. Emma's fighting suits (called by Hughes 'Emmapeelers') were in stretch Crimplene and jersey, with a recurring motif of buckles, links and braiding, but they differed from previous fighting suits by having bootees of the same material to give an all-in-one effect from throat to toe.

'In her Emmapeelers,' said Hughes, 'Emma is like a cat in the night, prowling silently on her secret assignments, ready to strike at anyone who challenges her.' To enhance the feline effect, Mr Hughes also designed several fur coats, including one with a tiger motif. Emma wore boots only with her trouser suits or, in highwayman-style, at thigh length. She wore very little leather, but lots of soft suede in coats, trouser suits and co-ordinates, which alternated skirts with bermuda shorts. Bermudas were also used in chiffon for short evening dresses, but there was a strong Mata Hari feeling about the gorgeously-coloured silk and chiffon dresses and lounging pyjamas, with echoes of Art Nouveau in the flowing curves which dominated the collection.

'All Emma's clothes are made for movement,' said Hughes. 'Skirts are easy, dresses have back pleats, coats have a slim line with back swing. I have designed the whole collection for Diana's particular kind of physical grace, and for the split personality, half warm and womanly, half cool and dangerous,

that she brings to Emma Peel. ABC were surprised to learn at this time that the Americans were very worried about the avant-garde nature of Diana's wardrobe and actually asked the studio if they would change it to conform to American fashion. Thankfully, this request was refused.

The slim lines and physical elegance of Emma's new wardrobe were echoed by the new Pierre Cardin collection for John Steed. Cardin designed all Patrick Macnee's clothes for the series, and introduced two new ideas for him – breast pockets with handkerchiefs, and trousers with a parallel line from knee to ankle to give a slightly more flared effect. Macnee, however, found that his usual Chelsea boots didn't complement the trousers and Alan Hughes designed some new shoes to go with the Cardin suits.

The suits themselves consisted of a single-breasted, chalk-stripe grey, with three buttons on the jacket, and one on the cuff; a pale grey suit with a velvet collar; a coat in heavy silk brocade, with lace ruffles, and a claret-coloured waistcoat. Steed's familiar bowler and umbrella now came in assorted colours to match and complement the new wardrobe.

FROM VENUS WITH LOVE

By Philip Levene

John Steed	Patrick Macnee
Emma Peel	Diana Rigg
Venus	Barbara Shelley
Primble	Philip Locke
Brigadier Whitehead	Jon Pertwee
Crawford	Derek Newark
Bertram Smith	Jeremy Lloyd
Jennings	Adrian Ropes
Clarke	Arthur Cox
Cosgrove	Paul Gillard
Hadley	Michael Lynch
Mansford	Kenneth Benda

Designed by Wilfrid Shingleton
Directed by Robert Day
Produced by Albert Fennell
and Brian Clemens
Executive Producer
Julian Wintle

ASTRONOMER Cosgrove, observing the planet Venus, concentrates so much that he does not notice a nearby glass of beer begin to bubble furiously. A strange high-pitched sound is heard and as the now-hot Cosgrove stares at the glass, there is a blinding flash of light and he falls lifeless to the floor – his hair bleached white as snow. Cosgrove is followed by a second victim, Sir Frederick Hadley. Found lying beside his body are his astro-camera and a note from a friend, Smith. Emma visits Smith, a chimney sweep, who tells her that he and Hadley both belonged to the British Venusian Society. She telephones this information to Steed who is busy developing the film found in Hadley's camera. While they are speaking there is a sudden high-pitched noise. Emma runs into Smith's room, to find his body in the fireplace, his hair and body bleached white. Steed joins the BVS, and meets the secretary, Venus Browne, and her assistant, Crawford. Venus says that with a grant, and contributions from its members, the society hopes to land a satellite on Venus. Although he is accepted as a member, Steed is told that he must have his eyes tested by their optician, Primble. As he leaves, Steed notices a list of members' names on the table – Cosgrove, Hadley, Smith, Lord Mansford and Brigadier Whitehead. Primble tests Steed's eyes. He also claims that invasion from Venus is imminent, and when Steed shows him the photographs from Hadley's camera of a huge fireball, Primble declares this is further evidence. Emma visits Lord Mansford. She arrives to find that he is locked in his vault by a time mechanism. When his secretary, Jennings, opens the door, the dead Mansford lies inside, his body as white as snow. There still remains Brigadier Whitehead who is writing his wartime memoirs. Venus Browne visits him to ask for more money but he refuses to help. Between her leaving and Steed arriving, Whitehead is also given the bleaching treatment. Steed notices a tape recorder beside the body and when he plays it back, hears a strange, high-pitched hum. The tape is taken to the BVS, together with Hadley's photographs. Venus asks Crawford to look at them, and while she and Emma are waiting, an attempt is made on Venus' life too – a statue shatters and the curtains burst into flames. The twinkling light again flashes in the driveway outside. Steed meanwhile decides it is time to observe Venus himself and instals a tailor's dummy, dressed in his own suit, behind Cosgrove's telescope. There is a sudden flash of light and the dummy becomes a mass of bleached and molten wax. Primble then rushes in to say he has seen a strange light coming from the graveyard. Going there, Steed narrowly escapes the light by jumping into an open grave. Primble, meanwhile, is babbling that the Venusians have invaded the Earth. Clarke, a military official, says that the earth in the cemetery is carbonised. This, together with the ultra-sonic hum, indicates a laser beam. Emma searches Primble's home and finds the glittering object – a silvered sports car, with a laser hidden in the bonnet. But Primble arrives with his assistant, Martin, and captures her. They tie her to a chair in Primble's surgery, and focus the laser at her. Steed bursts into the room, knocks out Martin and, using a mirror to deflect the laser rays, tricks Primble into killing himself with the laser. Steed and Emma leave behind their only casualty – Steed's bowler, bleached white by the deadly ray.

Emma is captured by Primble and strapped into a chair, with a laser beam focused on her, in **From Venus With Love.**

THE FEAR MERCHANTS

By Philip Levene

John Steed	Patrick Macnee
Emma Peel	Diana Rigg
Pemberton	Patrick Cargill
Raven	Brian Wilde
Dr Voss	Annette Carell
Gilbert	Garfield Morgan
Crawley	Andrew Keir
Gordon White	Jeremy Burnham
Meadows	Edward Burnham
Fox	Bernard Horsfall
Dr Hill	Ruth Trouncer
Saunders	Declan Mulholland
Hospital attendant	Philip Ross

Designed by Wilfrid Shingleton
Directed by Gordon Flemyng
Produced by Albert Fennell
and Brian Clemens
Executive Producer
Julian Wintle

BUSINESSMAN Richard Meadows awakes to find himself on the grass in the middle of a football stadium. It is completely deserted; he is surrounded by endless tiers of empty seats. Meadows gives way to hysteria and collapses, sobbing like a child. Meadows, along with two companions, both of whom are mental wrecks, is taken to hospital. They are soon joined by Fox, an athlete who has gone berserk at the sight of a mouse in a gymnasium. Steed discovers that all four men were directors of ceramic concerns, and visits Fox's partners, White and Crawley. Crawley can only spare Steed a minute before he is driven away for a business appointment. As the car leaves, Steed stumbles over the body of Crawley's chauffeur and immediately hurries after the departing vehicle. He is too late, however, for the driver jams his foot on the accelerator, and Crawley, who is terrified of fast cars, faints with fear, his mind shattered. A search of Crawley's car reveals a letter from Jeremy Raven, director of a rival company, British Porcelain, suggesting a merger between himself and Fox, White and Crawley – the other sick industrialists. Emma visits White, and overhears White saying he has been approached by a market research organisation, the Business Efficiency Bureau, with a strange questionnaire. Steed meanwhile visits Jeremy Raven. Unfortunately, says Raven, his rivals refused his merger offer, so he has found methods to eliminate their competition. The methods seem to work, for White falls from his office window, frightened by a huge bird which has been placed in his office. Steed visits Raven again and notices a brochure from the BEB in a drawer. Raven explains that he employed them quite innocently, and is horrified to learn

ESCAPE IN TIME

By Philip Levene

John Steed	Patrick Macnee
Emma Peel	Diana Rigg
Thyssen	Peter Bowles
Clapham	Geoffrey Bayldon
Vesta	Judy Parfitt
Anjali	Imogen Hassall
Sweeney	Edward Caddick
Parker	Nicholas Smith
Tubby Vincent	Roger Booth
Josino	Richard Montez
Paxton	Clifford Earl
Mitchell	Rocky Taylor

Designed by Wilfrid Shingleton
Directed by John Krish
Produced by Albert Fennell
and Brian Clemens
Executive Producer
Julian Wintle

S ECRET agent Paxton is hurriedly searching an oppulent country house. The furnishings are modern, apart from five death masks of the Thyssen family through the ages, all remarkably similar. Paxton goes through a door into a corridor which suddenly whirls round — and unconsciousness overtakes him. He wakes to find himself in the same room, now furnished in Elizabethan style. Only one mask remains, and while Paxton stares at it, he is shot from behind. His assassin is the Thyssen of the Elizabethan period. Steed and Emma arrive at Paxton's house, wondering how he came to be floating in the Thames, shot by a 16th-century bullet, when a visitor calls — with a Jacobean dagger in his back! He is holding a scrap of paper containing the message 'Josino — contact in Mackidockie Mews — Monday 12.30 pm' and a drawing of a black crocodile. Both Paxton and Vincent, the second victim, had been trying to discover an escape route through which notorious criminals had been vanishing into thin air. Josino, a ruthless dictator who has recently arrived in Britain, is obviously involved and Steed and Emma decide to keep the rendezvous in the mews. Josino arrives carrying a large toy crocodile. He contacts a girl, Vesta, and exchanges the crocodile for a giraffe. At a nearby toy stall the giraffe is exchanged for a kangaroo with a note in its pocket. After reading the note, Josino visits a barber's shop presided over by T Sweeney and leaves with an elephant, and a large piece of sticking plaster on his cheek. From the barber's shop he goes to an Indian art gallery, and when he leaves, Steed quickly realises that he is following a double! Emma, meanwhile, has been trailing Vesta, and is led into a country field where a man on a motorcycle attempts to

run her down, but he crashes, and the machine bursts into flames. Steed decides to try his hand at escaping and bluffs his way through the mews and into the art gallery. There he meets a beautiful Indian girl, Anjali, who tells him that with the organisation's help, he can vanish from the face of the earth. He leaves the gallery and is escorted, blindfolded, into a waiting car. Emma, standing outside, misses him and follows a double. Steed is taken to Thyssen's home, where Thyssen explains that he has perfected the perfect escape route — a time machine, which enables criminals to escape into the past. He lets Steed try, and he chooses the 18th century and enters the time corridor, while Thyssen's machine registers 1790. Steed wakes up on a couch in what appears to be the same room — with three death masks instead of five, and Georgian furniture. He then awakes to find himself back in the 20th century. He tells Thyssen to book him a one-way ticket into the past. Emma, having discovered that she is following a false trail, eliminates the double and decides that she, too, should sample the escape route. Armed with a toy she has made, she bluffs her way through Mackidockie Mews, but is recognised by Vesta, kidnapped, and taken to Thyssen's home. There, she is offered a visit to 1790. She enters the time corridor and falls asleep. While she lies unconscious, Vesta tells Thyssen who Emma really is and he decides to divert her to another era. She wakes in a Tudor room, searches it and finds Josino's body. Thyssen, dressed as his Tudor ancestor — a notorious sadist — enters the room, followed by a masked executioner. They then prepare to torture Emma by strapping her to the stocks in front of an open fire. Enter Steed, who uses medieval weapons in his fight with the torturers. He releases Emma and explains to her that the time machine was really a series of perfectly furnished rooms in which the victims, having been put to sleep, awakened to apparently find themselves in another era.

that they have been using criminal methods to eliminate his rivals. Raven then visits the BEB, which is headed by Pemberton, whose assistants are Dr Voss and Gilbert, and tells Pemberton that he wishes to break his contract with the Bureau. Pemberton attempts to blackmail him, but Raven leaves and phones Steed with a message to contact him as soon as possible. Raven, waiting for Steed, sees the hairy legs of a spider crawling towards him. There is a terrifying scream and Steed and Emma enter to find the demented Raven surrounded by smashed china. Beside his body is a BEB brochure promising a unique way of building your business up. Steed tells Emma it is time they paid the BEB a visit. Next day Steed tells Pemberton that he is a travel agent wishing to improve his business. He has one rival, a Mrs Peel. What Steed does not know, however, is that his chair incorporates a lie-detector operated by Voss. Pemberton, knowing that Steed was lying, orders Gilbert to follow him. At the hospital, Steed notices that Raven is agitated by a tattoo of a spider on an attendant's arm, and realises what caused his condition. The doctor confirms that the other men had been subjected to things they feared, making them sick with shock. Gilbert tricks Steed into stopping near a deserted quarry, where Steed is almost buried alive by a bulldozer which tips earth on him. Finally, Gilbert himself is killed when the machine crushes him. When Gilbert does not return, Pemberton decides to visit Emma and question her — with a gun. Steed finds Emma's apartment empty, save for a BEB card with the message 'Help' scrawled on the back. Meanwhile, having been unable to discover Emma's secret fear, Pemberton decides to torture her with surgical instruments. Steed arrives to find Emma struggling to escape from the chair in which she is bound. Steed then switches off the lights, and it becomes obvious that Pemberton's secret fear is darkness, for he is soon howling and crying like a baby. Steed releases Emma and she dispatches Dr Voss. Returning to her apartment, it only takes Emma a few minutes to discover Steed's secret fear — the idea that there might be no champagne left.

THE SEE-THROUGH MAN

By Philip Levene

John Steed	Patrick Macnee
Emma Peel	Diana Rigg
Elena	Moira Lister
Brodny	Warren Mitchell
Quilby	Roy Kinnear
Ackroyd	Jonathan Elsom
Sir Andrew Ford	John Nettleton
Ulric	Harvey Hall
Wilton	David Glover

Designed by Wilfrid Shingleton
Directed by Robert Asher
Produced by Albert Fennell
and Brian Clemens
Executive Producer
Julian Wintle

Emma overpowers Brodny, who appeared in two Avengers episodes, Two's a Crowd and The See-Through Man, *shown here.*

Steed and Mrs Peel investigate Vazin's secret room, and discover how he worked his miracles, in The See-Through Man.

WILTON, a clerk in the Mnistry's records office, is amazed to see doors apparently opening by themselves, filing cabinets sliding out, and hearing strange footsteps in the corridor. Then he is knocked unconscious by a blow – apparently from nowhere! When they find a file has been stolen from Wilton's office, Steed and Emma visit Sir Andrew Ford, at his Ministry office. But a mysterious – and apparently invisible – guest, has stolen a secret file from his office. Discovering that both the files dealt with Quilby, an inventor who had been sending useless ideas to the Ministry, Steed visits Quilby, while Emma drives to see Lord Daviot, a retired Ministry official who had previously dealt with the inventor. Quilby and his assistant, Ackroyd, welcome Steed, and he learns that Quilby has invented a formula for invisibility, and when it was rejected by the Ministry, he sold it to the Eastern Drug Corporation for $250,000. Quilby explains that he has lost the formula, but promises he will try to recall it. Emma, having found Lord Daviot taking a bath – in his lily pond – returns home, where Steed tells her of his discovery – and also that top enemy agents Alexandre and Elena Vazin are in town. Their cover is The Eastern Drug Company! Vazin and Elena are staying at the Embassy, and a not very bright Ambassador Brodny is shocked to discover that they have withdrawn $250,000 from the Embassy account. Elena tells him that they have acquired a formula for making men invisible, and that Major Vazin has used it. When Brodny is addressed by the invisible Vazin he faints from fright. Elena receives a phone call from Quilby's assistant, Ackroyd, attempting to blackmail her into silence. She agrees to meet him to talk, and leaves, carrying a gun. Steed arrives at the Embassy and the disturbed Brodny, well aware of Steed's capabilities since their last encoun-

ter during the Two's A Crowd affair, has to speak to him with the invisible Vazin in the room. When Steed mentions the formula, Brodny hotly denies knowledge of it, and Steed leaves, having planted a bugging device. Outside the Embassy, Steed hears Vazin's voice ordering Brodny to destroy the bug, thus confirming his suspicions that Vazin was in the Embassy, heard, if not seen. Meanwhile, Emma has followed Elena, who fails in her attempt to kill Ackroyd. Elena escapes, and while Emma is driving home, she is almost run off the road by a car with an apparently headless driver! Emma picks up the driver's hat, which bears the name Major Vazin. Ackroyd now attempts to blackmail Steed, and arranges a rendezvous. But Vazin gets there first and Steed finds Ackroyd's dead body on a revolving child's roundabout. Steed receives a phone call from Quilby to say that the formula has been found, but when he arrives at Quilby's workshop, he finds the inventor's body on the floor. Then Steed, too, is knocked unconscious – by a headless man! Meanwhile, Vazin decides to put the second phase of his plan into action – the kidnapping of Emma Peel. She is taken to the Embassy, where Elena tells her that they have bought the formula, and Emma is confronted by the invisible Major Vazin. Steed, meanwhile, escapes from Quilby's workshop by mixing some chemicals together and blowing the door off its hinges. Emma escapes from the Embassy, but soon realises that her freedom was planned. She knocks Elena out and is about to search the room when she hears Steed's voice, but there is no one there – Steed is apparently invisible! Chairs move, doors and windows open . . . Steed, in a special room hidden behind the Embassy walls, now explains to Emma how the invisible man worked his miracles. The room contains microphones and television screens that enabled the invisible man to vanish at the touch of a button! Vazin, wearing a specially built-up suit to make him appear headless, enters, and is knocked out by Steed. There still remains Brodny. As he genuinely believes in the invisible man, Steed and Emma feel it would be hard to disillusion him. So the Ambassador is treated to a drenching, from the see-through man, of course, while apologising for allowing Emma to escape.

THE BIRD WHO KNEW TOO MUCH

By Brian Clemens
Based on a story by Alan Pattillo

John Steed	Patrick Macnee
Emma Peel	Diana Rigg
Jordan	Ron Moody
Samantha Slade	Ilona Rodgers
Tom Savage	Kenneth Cope
Verret	Michael Coles
Twitter	John Wood
Cunliffe	Anthony Valentine
Robin	Clive Colin-Bowler
Mark Pearson	John Lee

Designed by Wilfrid Shingleton
Directed by Roy Rossotti
Produced by Albert Fennell
and Brian Clemens
Executive Producer
Julian Wintle

DANVERS, a secret agent, is pursued by a young thug, Robin, and makes his way to a field telephone box. As Danvers desperately tries to contact Steed, Robin fires and Danvers falls dead. Beside his body lies a pile of bird seed from a bag in his pocket. Steed decides that a message may be hidden among the seeds and begins a search. A second agent, George Elrick, is killed when he tumbles into a tub of concrete on a building site where he has been chased by Robin and his partner Verret. Found in Elrick's pocket are photographs of a top-secret missile base, taken from the air, so Steed decides to visit Elrick's partner Pearson, but finds him dying of gunshot wounds. He is only able to whisper that the information about the base is being taken East by a Captain Crusoe. Emma finds an address, Heathcliff Hall, on Pearson's desk. Steed remains at the flat and after a search, finds some photographs of a girl. A moment later she enters the room, and introduces herself as Samantha Slade, Pearson's girlfriend, and Steed persuades her to have dinner with him. Meanwhile, Emma finds that Heathcliff Hall houses an international exhibition of caged birds, organised by one Edgar Twitter and his assistant Cunliffe. They agree to introduce Emma to Captain Crusoe – who is a parrot! But the bird has flown, and its cage is empty. Steed accompanies Samantha to work. She is a model and poses for photographer Tom Savage. Steed, too, does a little modelling – and a little interrogation. While he questions Samantha, Verret arrives, and unseen, slips an impact grenade into Steed's umbrella. Fortunately, Steed discovers the grenade in time, and narrowly escapes death. Deciding that the photographs found in Elrick's pocket could have been taken by a bird, maybe a carrier pigeon, Steed keeps watch at Pearson's pigeon loft, while Emma stays to pose for Tom Savage. Steed's hunch proves correct, for Verret and Robin are soon releasing carrier pigeons which fly over the missile base – all except one, which flies back to Pearson's loft. The pigeon has a miniature camera strapped to its leg, but before Steed can investigate further, Robin arrives and knocks him out. Tom Savage, meanwhile, poses Emma with some very old props, including a parrot in a cage, provided by Samantha. She asks Tom for a copy of the photograph of her and the bird, and takes it to Heathcliff Hall. Twitter and Cunliffe are unable to identify the bird from a photograph, so Emma decides to borrow the bird from the studio. But Verret and Robin are there, and Emma is tied to a chair, facing a loaded gun triggered to go off when Steed arrives. Only quick-thinking by Steed saves his life and he rescues Emma in the nick of time. Emma again visits Heathcliff Hall where Twitter tells her that the parrot's real owner is a man called Jordan. Emma sets off to see him, closely followed by Robin. Jordan explains that his hobby is teaching birds to talk. Captain Crusoe is his prize pupil – a parrot with a remarkable memory, but trained to talk only from a given signal, which is a note on Jordan's special triangle. As Jordan finds the triangle, Robin begins shooting at them from the diving board of a nearby swimming pool. Emma overpowers him, and learns that the parrot has been returned. Steed and Emma return to Heathcliff Hall to search for the missing Captain Crusoe. Emma knocks Twitter out but finds she has the wrong man, when Cunliffe and Verret appear and hold her and Steed at gunpoint. A brief skirmish follows and Verret and Cunliffe are soon overpowered. As Steed and Emma depart, Captain Crusoe cries out loudly – demanding political asylum.

Steed and Mrs Peel are discovered by Twitter, but their feathers aren't ruffled, in The Bird Who Knew Too Much.

Emma is not looking forward to seeing Steed – she will be shot when he appears – in The Bird Who Knew Too Much.

THE WINGED AVENGER

By Richard Harris

John Steed	Patrick Macnee
Emma Peel	Diana Rigg
Sir Lexius Cray	Nigel Green
Professor Poole	Jack MacGowan
Arnie Packer	Neil Hallett
Stanton	Colin Jeavons
Julian	Roy Patrick
Tay-Ling	John Garrie
Peter Roberts	Donald Pickering
Simon Roberts	William Fox
Dawson	A J Brown
Damayn	Hilary Wontner
Fothers	John Crocker
Gerda	Ann Sydney

**Designed by Wilfrid Shingleton
Directed by Gordon Flemyng
and Peter Duffell
Produced by Albert Fennell
and Brian Clemens
Executive Producer
Julian Wintle**

PUBLISHING tycoon Simon Roberts, and his son Peter, sit in their office late one night talking business. After his son has left, Simon pours himself a drink. A few minutes later, the window shatters, there is the sound of beating wings and a huge shadow envelopes the man as he falls dead to the floor. The Avengers are called in and they find strange marks on Roberts' body, as though he had been clawed to death by a large bird. Steed explains to Emma that this is the fourth such death recently, and soon there is a fifth, for Peter Roberts dies in the same circumstances as his father. Steed finds a letter Peter was dictating into his tape recorder, mentioning an author, Sir Lexius Cray. Emma visits Cray, who is also a famous mountaineer. He offers her tea, served by his Tibetan servant, Tay-Ling, who seems strangely interested in newspaper cartoons. Cray tells Emma that one of his books was published by Roberts and that he had tried to cheat him. After Emma leaves, Sir Lexius blows a small whistle and a huge falcon perches on his hand. Emma's enquiries lead her to believe that Tay-Ling is blackmailing someone, so she decides to visit Sir Lexius' home again. When she arrives, however, she is met by Cray, who shows her into the study. There, lying on the floor, is Tay-Ling's body. He also has been clawed to death by some large bird. Sir Lexius discovers that a file is missing from his desk, containing correspondence from a Professor Poole who claims to have invented a special pair of mountaineering boots. Steed and Emma visit Poole, who is dedicated to birds and proving that man can fly. He refuses to talk about his boots however and locks himself

in his study. When Emma peers through the transom, she is amazed to see the Professor hanging upside down, bat-like, from the ceiling. Certain that the next victim will be Damayn, a factory owner who has just sacked thousands of workers, Steed and Emma pay him a visit. But the man has been clawed to death while out shooting. Emma points out that all the victims had been evil, ruthless men. Whatever killed them is selecting its victims carefully, like a winged avenger. She notices a scrap of newspaper lying beside the dead man which shows a cartoon strip called The Winged Avenger – a Batman-like creature which is seen attacking a man in hunting apparel, who looks identical to Damayn. They discover that the cartoon is produced by a cartoonist, Arnie, and a writer, Stanton. Emma visits Poole again and discovers how he is able to hang from the ceiling – a pair of climbing boots with magnetic soles, identical to those worn by the cartoon Winged Avenger. Steed realises that all the deaths so far had been predicted in the Winged Avenger strip cartoon and a search of the cartoonist's office reveals a sketch of Professor Poole – obviously the next person to be murdered. He also finds a second sketch showing Emma walking towards Poole's house. Meanwhile, as predicted, Emma is walking towards Poole's house in response to an urgent call. She enters Poole's study and finds herself confronted by Arnie, dressed in the Winged Avenger costume and wearing the magnetic boots. He has already murdered Poole. Emma hurriedly removes the dead Professor's boots and climbs onto the ceiling, followed by Arnie – now completely mad and believing himself to be the real Winged Avenger. They are struggling on the ceiling when Steed arrives, carrying writer Stanton's story boards under his arm. Steed hits Arnie on the head with the heavy boards (they read 'Pow' and 'Splat'), then with one final lunge, Emma throws him out of the window.

THE LIVING DEAD

By Brian Clemens
Based on a story by
Anthony Marriott

John Steed	Patrick Macnee
Emma Peel	Diana Rigg
Masgard	Julian Glover
Mandy	Pamela Ann Davy
Geoffrey	Howard Marion Crawford
Kermit	Jack Woolgar
Hopper	Jack Watson
Rupert	Edward Underdown
Olliphant	John Cater
Spencer	Vernon Dobtcheff
Tom	Alister Williamson

**Designed by Robert Jones
Directed by John Krish
Produced by Albert Fennell
and Brian Clemens
Executive Producer
Julian Wintle**

STEED and Emma go to the country, to investigate rumours that a ghost has been seen in the private chapel of the Duke of Benedict. Two other investigators also appear – Mandy McKay of FOG (Friends of Ghosts) and Spencer, of SMOG (Scientific Measurement of Ghosts). They are perplexed to find that the local hermit who claimed to have seen the ghost, now denies it, although the local inn-keeper, Hopper, corroborates a story of chapel bells ringing at midnight. The chapel is near the private estate of Geoffrey, 16th Duke of Benedict, a weak character who seems strongly influenced by his estate manager, Masgard. Geoffrey became the 16th Duke when his cousin Rupert was killed, with 30 companions, in the Benedict mine disaster five years before. When Steed seeks permission to shoot on the estate, Masgard says it is impossible, and Steed gets the distinct impression that his presence is not wanted. From a chance remark of Masgard's, he suspects that something is hidden in the Duke's wine cellar. Spencer decides to spend the night in the chapel, having first prepared a great deal of equipment to record any noises. Later, his body is discovered by Steed and Emma – he has been stabbed to death with a sword from a nearby statue. The next night, Emma and Mandy decide to keep watch in the chapel. Soon the hysterical Mandy tells Steed that Emma has been kidnapped – by a ghost! An unsuccessful search is made, and the hermit tells Steed the best place to find Mrs Peel is in the mine, where, he swears, the entombed men are still alive. Before he can say anything more, he is shot. Steed decides to check the mine, and persuades the inn-keeper, Hopper, an ex-miner, to

THE HIDDEN TIGER

By Philip Levene

John Steed	**Patrick Macnee**
Emma Peel	**Diana Rigg**
Cheshire	**Ronnie Barker**
Dr Manx	**Lyndon Brook**
Angora	**Gabrielle Drake**
Nesbitt	**John Phillips**
Peters	**Michael Forrest**
Erskine	**Stanley Meadows**
David Harper	**Jack Gwillim**
Dawson	**Frederick Treves**
Samuel Jones	**Brian Haines**
Williams	**John Moore**
Bellamy	**Reg Pritchard**

Designed by Robert Jones
Directed by Sidney Hayers
Produced by Albert Fennell
and Brian Clemens
Executive Producer
Julian Wintle

WHEN gentleman farmer Sir David Harper and his butler are mauled to death, apparently by a member of the cat family, Steed and Emma are called in. They are helped by a neighbour of Harper's, ex-big-game hunter Major Nesbitt, who confirms that there is no big cat loose in the area. At Harper's farm, devoted to research into new farming methods, Emma is met by the assistant, Erskine. As he shows Emma around, Peters runs in to announce that the prize bull has been killed by a large animal. Erskine is surprised and tells Emma that security on the farm is strict – the whole place is rigged with traps. Steed, Emma and Nesbitt decide to organise a safari to trap the animal, but the only thing they find is the mauled body of Erskine, so they decide to organise a second hunt. While Nesbitt prepares a strong-smelling liquid, guaranteed to attract big cats, Steed and Emma rig up a walkie-talkie set, having first planted miniature microphones around the farm. While they keep watch in the farm grounds, Nesbitt, securely locked inside a cage, watches with his rifle. Hearing a sound on the headphones, Steed follows it to Nesbitt's house, but arrives too late. The big-game hunter is dead, inside the cage! Beside his body Steed finds a small medallion, inscribed with the initials PURRR. Steed discovers that PURRR is in fact the Philanthropic Union for Rescue, Relief and Recuperation of Cats – an organisation providing a shelter for lost cats. It is managed by Cheshire, and his assistants Angora and Dr Manx, a veterinary surgeon. Steed is amazed to find that the committee of PURRR consists of the dead men, Harper, Nesbitt and Erskine. Two other members are Bellamy and Jones. Steed visits Bellamy, but finds him

help him. A third accomplice is Mandy, who insists on tagging along. Together they begin their search in the mine. At the pit-head, the waiting Hopper is attacked by Masgard and his men, who then cut through the cables of the mine lift. In the mine, Steed hears the sound of tapping and discovers a door cut into the rock. Passing through, he is amazed to find a complete street. As he stares at the scene, five chained prisoners appear, led by Rupert, the 15th Duke of Benedict – the man supposedly killed five years before. Before Steed can comment further, however, Mandy, gun in hand, cautions him to move away . . . Meanwhile, Emma is being held prisoner in a nearby cell. Rupert brings her food, and explains that she is in an underground city, and that he and his friends are the sole survivors of the pit disaster. Masgard enters and tells her the city has been built by slave labour and will shortly hold 20,000 men and their families, who will be brought in by submarine. It is a vast nuclear shelter, built to house an army which will take over after Masgard's country has dropped a bomb on Britain. Masgard had organised the whole thing, living underground. He would never have come up if Rupert hadn't escaped and caused the ghost scare in the village. As Emma listens to his story, she sees Steed, escorted by guards, pass her cell window. She realises that he is about to face a firing squad. She overpowers Masgard and fights her way back out of the cell, to find her way blocked by Mandy. Emma soon subdues the ghost huntress, and rescues Steed by turning Mandy's machine gun on the firing squad. Rupert arrives, and tells Steed that there are only two escape routes – the pit-head and the main exit, which has a specially-built lift. They crowd into the lift, and when safely aloft, put the lift out of action. Below, Masgard and Mandy are horrified to realise they are trapped in the mine. . . Above, the 16th Duke of Benedict is horrified to see his so-called dead cousin once again rising from the depths.

lying dead beside his cottage door, his clothes torn to shreds by some enormous animal. While Steed searches the telephone directory for Jones' address, Emma visits PURRR, claiming she has lost her cat. She is shown around the building by Cheshire, who is especially proud of the psycat-therapy, a new form of treatment devised by Dr Manx. As Emma leaves, she spots Peters, from the Harper farm, leaving a van in the courtyard. Investigating, she finds it is equipped like a small caravan, full of food, and secured against possible intruders. Peters and Angora see her searching the van and decide she must be eliminated. Steed meanwhile drives to Jones' home, but again he is too late. He finds the man lying dead on the floor, accompanied only by his pet cat. The cat is wearing a PURRR medallion, and as it leaps from Steed's arms, the medallion falls to the floor. Steed notices that it contains a complicated miniature circuit. Emma is rather taken aback to receive a visit from Cheshire, who brings her a Siamese cat to replace the one she has supposedly lost. It is also wearing a PURRR medallion which, she discovers, is a miniature receiver, containing an electrophone which can transmit brain waves capable of turning an ordinary cat into a ferocious killer. Steed decides to search PURRR but, having despatched Peters and Cheshire on entry, he is captured by Angora and Manx. Manx tells him that they intend to overthrow the entire country. Each cat wearing a medallion will attack at a given signal, while Manx and Angora stay secure in the van. They decide to leave, and tie Steed to a chair, surrounded by the deadly cats! Emma, meanwhile, visits PURRR, taking the Siamese cat with her. She arrives in time to rescue the struggling Steed and switch off the transmitter relaying the deadly brain waves. Manx and Angora, unaware of what has happened and still believing that their cats are potential killers, notice Emma's Siamese cat in the van with them. Manx is so terrified that he drives the van off the road and into a tree. The only survivor is the cat, which emerges from the van without a scratch.

THE CORRECT WAY TO KILL

By Brian Clemens

John Steed	Patrick Macnee
Emma Peel	Diana Rigg
Olga	Anna Quayle
Nutski	Michael Gough
Ivan	Philip Madoc
Ponsonby	Terence Alexander
Percy	Peter Barkworth
Algy	Graham Armitage
Merryweather	Timothy Bateson
Hilda	Joanna Jones
Winters	Edwin Apps
Grotski	John G Heller

Designed by Robert Jones
Directed by Charles Crichton
Produced by Albert Fennell
and Brian Clemens
Executive Producer
Julian Wintle

WHEN two top enemy agents are found dead, suspicion falls on John Steed and Emma Peel. Steed manages to convince Nutski and Ivan, representatives of the other side, that he and Emma are not to blame and they decide to join forces to discover the murderer. Then, a third agent is murdered. Steed, accompanied by Nutski's assistant Olga, leaves for an address which Grotski (one of the dead men) is known to have visited. Ivan and Emma, following another clue, arrive at the surgery of a chiropodist called Merryweather who, with his assistant Hilda, examines Emma's feet. When she leaves the surgery, Ivan has vanished. Steed and Olga find themselves at a shop which sells umbrellas and raincoats. Winters, the owner, denies Steed's accusation that he sold an umbrella to the dead Grotski, but then Steed notices Ivan's body in a packing case. The case is carried away by four bowler-hatted gentlemen – all perfect replicas of Steed. He and Olga follow them to an establishment called Snob, a finishing school which teaches young men how to become complete English gentlemen. The proprietor, Ponsonby, says he has never heard of Grotski, and the packing case which Steed followed now contains only umbrellas! Olga, however, remembers seeing a second, identical, packing case in the umbrella shop, addressed to Merryweather, the chiropodist. Meanwhile, Merryweather and Hilda are examining an umbrella which is really a complicated radio. The four bowler-hatted thugs enter with the packing case containing Ivan's body, and while they are arguing about its disposal, Steed and Olga arrive outside the surgery. Olga enters and is captured by the thugs. Emma now joins Steed but they find the surgery

empty, save for the bare-footed body of Merryweather. Olga is taken to Winters' umbrella shop and bundled inside a packing case. Nearby lies the dead body of Winters. Emma goes to summon Nutski, while Steed returns to the umbrella shop. He arrives just in time to see the bowler-hatted men about to remove the packing case. Swiftly, he changes places with one of the men. They reach Snob and Steed manages to release Olga. But they cannot escape, for Ponsonby and his pupils are outside in the corridor. Meanwhile, Nutski refuses to leave for Snob with Emma, so she sets off by herself. By the time she arrives, Steed and Olga have been discovered and are being held at gunpoint by Ponsonby and his thugs. Emma overpowers Hilda and, donning a fencing mask, prepares to fight her way to Steed and Olga. As she enters the room, the boss arrives. It is Nutski, who has been selling the secrets to the highest bidder – a profitable business until Grotski discovered the truth. With Emma's help, Steed and Olga are released and together they round up the gang, then leave for a celebration drink – vodka, of course.

Something evil is afoot, so Emma follows a clue to Merryweather, when The Avengers discover The Correct Way To Kill.

NEVER, NEVER SAY DIE

By Philip Levene

John Steed	Patrick Macnee
Emma Peel	Diana Rigg
Professor Stone	Christopher Lee
Dr Penrose	Jeremy Young
Dr James	Patricia English
Eccles	David Kernan
Whittle	Christopher Benjamin
Sergeant	John Junkin
Private	Peter Dennis
Carter	Geoffrey Reed
Selby	Alan Chuntz
Elderly gent	Arnold Ridley
Young man	David Gregory
Nurse	Karen Ford

Designed by Robert Jones
Directed by Robert Day
Produced by Albert Fennell
and Brian Clemens
Executive Producer
Julian Wintle

WHEN a corpse walks out of a mortuary, Steed and Emma investigate. They meet a man named Whittle, who claims to have given the dead man a lift in his car and later, Steed and Emma are astonished to witness the corpse involved in a second accident with Whittle's car. This time, however, they are certain that the man is well and truly dead, but Emma realises that there is no sign of blood. An ambulance arrives, and takes the body away but the dead man comes alive and, smashing open the ambulance doors, escapes into the countryside. Emma and Steed visit a local pub where a workman tells them of a man who miraculously survived the shock from a 100,000-volt pylon. They are later joined by an army sergeant, who tells of a stranger who walked onto the nearby army firing range and appeared to be unaffected by machine-gun fire. Believing that the events are linked in some way to the missing man, Steed and Emma set off to search for him. Emma arrives at a lonely cottage. She is searching the premises and fails to see the man arrive. He attacks her, and although she fires at him from point-blank range, the bullets seem to have no effect on his tough skin. He is about to strangle her when the driver of the ambulance, Dr Penrose, arrives with two assistants. They throw a net over the man and carry him away, leaving Emma unconscious on the floor. Later, the still-dazed Emma finds a diary on the floor. It belongs to a Professor Stone and on one of the pages are the words George Eccles – Ariel Cottage. Steed locates Dr Penrose and follows him to the Neoteric Research Unit, which is engaged in top-secret govern-

EPIC

By Brian Clemens

John Steed	Patrick Macnee
Emma Peel	Diana Rigg
Stewart Kirby	Peter Wyngarde
Damita Syn	Isa Miranda
Z Z Von	
Schnerk	Kenneth J Warren
Policeman	David Lodge
Actor	Anthony Dawes

Designed by Robert Jones
Directed by James Hill
Produced by Albert Fennell
and Brian Clemens
Executive Producer
Julian Wintle

ment work, under Professor Stone. Posing as a security officer, Steed bluffs his way into Stone's office and is astonished to find that Professor Stone is, in fact, the man for whom they have been searching. Emma meanwhile visits Ariel Cottage and meets George Eccles, an amateur radio enthusiast. He tells her that Stone has accused him of interfering with the research unit's radio equipment. He demonstrates the method used to tune into the unit's frequency. At the same moment, Stone is suddenly taken ill and rushed into the experimental section of the unit. Leaving the cottage, Emma hears a crash and, dashing back to investigate, finds Eccles has been strangled. His radio equipment lies smashed on the floor. Meanwhile, Steed is shown plans of the research unit by Professor Stone. Steed asks about a section on the plan unmentioned by Stone. He is told that it houses the unit's experimental section, which is top secret. Even Steed would need special clearance to enter it. Later, Steed returns and convinces Stone that he has obtained the necessary clearance. Under protest, Stone offers to allow Steed into the experimental section. He leads Steed through a series of sliding doors into a special chamber, where Steed is astounded to find two Professor Stones – one human, one a replica! Stone informs him that the replica is a duplicate – not a robot, but a computerised double capable of thinking by itself. Stone says great minds need never die: they could be stored inside a duplicate's brain and used for the benefit of future generations. Returning to the pub, Steed meets Penrose and, suspicious of his strange mannerisms, follows him back to the research unit. They are met by Stone who tells him he has been following another double – Penrose, too, is a duplicate man. Steed is taken into the experimental section, where he finds Mrs Peel, locked in a cell with the real Professor Stone and the real Dr Penrose. Steed has been led into a trap! Confronted by the duplicate men, The Avengers are faced with a battle to the death. Steed produces a small transistor radio and quickly tunes it to the frequency which gives the duplicates their power. Before he can use the radio, however, Stone knocks it from his hands. The two duplicates now try to strangle the agents, but Emma retrives the radio in time to overload and stop the duplicate men. Then a sliding panel suddenly springs open to reveal – Emma and Steed. As they stare at the doubles, Emma lifts the bowler on the duplicate Steed. The word 'reject' is stamped on its forehead.

A YOUNG actor is interviewed for a film part by three Hollywood veterans – director Z Z Von Schnerk and his two stars Damita Syn and Stewart Kirby. Damita decides the actor is perfect, so Kirby shoots him – with a gun, not a camera! In response to an anonymous call, Emma and Steed drive to the countryside. The road is deserted except for an elderly vicar. As they drive past him, the vicar (actually Kirby, a master of disguise) photographs them with a camera concealed in his bicycle. The journey is fruitless and, back in his flat, Steed replays the tape recording of the anonymous caller, but fails to recognise the voice. Kirby shows Von Schnerk and Damita his photographs of Emma and the director insists that she must star in his next epic. Emma is kidnapped by Kirby and taken to a deserted film studio which is surrounded by a high, electrified fence. When she wakes up she thinks she is in her own flat until, opening the door, she finds herself in a mews. Venturing further, she comes to a vast studio floor snaked with cables and huge arc lamps. She sees a limousine parked nearby, containing a bridal headdress with an invitation to the wedding of – Emma Peel! Church bells ring and Kirby appears, again dressed as a vicar. She chases him away and arrives at another set with a hearse and a coffin, which bears her own name. A headstone in a nearby graveyard is also inscribed Emma Peel. Suddenly, all the lights are switched on, and then she sees a figure sitting on a chair. To her relief, it is Steed. She goes up to him then realises, to her horror, that it is the corpse of the young actor, dressed in Steed's clothes. Kirby reappears, now dressed as an undertaker, and tries to strangle her. She fights him off but is knocked unconscious. As she lies on the floor, Von Schnerk arrives ready to film another scene for his new epic, *The Destruction of Emma Peel*. Emma recovers

consciousness to find herself in a cinematic nightmare, in which she is attacked and shot by a cowboy in a Western saloon; fired at with a machine gun during a First World War setting; and shot at by a Red Indian. Then an elderly extra, in policeman's uniform, arrives. He visits the studio to relive old memories. Before he can help Emma, however, he is shot down by a Chicago gangster. Meanwhile, Steed has recognised the voice on the tape recording as that of Kirby and dashes to the studio. He arrives in time to find Emma has been tied up by Kirby and Damita, and placed on a platform that is moving slowly but relentlessly towards a huge circular saw. Steed overpowers Kirby and Damita and rescues the helpless Emma, saving her by inches. Von Schnerk, having witnessed the scene, and the destruction of his own plans, shoots himself.

Emma sees her whole life flash before her when she becomes a star of a film about her life – and death – in Epic.

THE SUPERLATIVE SEVEN

By Brian Clemens

John Steed	Patrick Macnee
Emma Peel	Diana Rigg
Hana	Charlotte Rampling
Mark Dayton	Brian Blessed
Jason Wade	James Maxwell
Max Hardy	Hugh Manning
Freddy Richards	Leon Greene
Joe Smith	Gary Hope
Jessel	Donald Sutherland
Kanwitch	John Hollis
Stewardess	Margaret Neale
Toy Sung	Terry Plummer

Designed by Robert Jones
Directed by Sidney Hayers
Produced by Albert Fennell
and Brian Clemens
Executive Producer
Julian Wintle

Emma saves the day when she fights Wade – who is dead but won't lie down – on the deserted island in The Superlative Seven.

Hana Wilde holds Emma at gunpoint, while Mrs Peel explains Steed's motives in going to the party, in The Superlative Seven.

THE scene is a huge, bare gymnasium. Ranged along one wall is a line of men and women. Enter Kanwitch, Jessel and Toy Sung, a huge oriental wrestler. At a given signal, Toy Sung and one of the young men begin to fight. The young man soon overcomes his huge opponent, and as the wrestler remains on his knees, coughing, a girl steps forward. They fight, and again Toy Sung loses. This time, however he is killed with a sword. But Kanwitch is not satisfied and insists on one final test. Steed receives an invitation to attend a fancy dress party, held by the explorer, Sir George Robertson. Dressed as one of Wellington's officers, he sets off, to find that the party is being held on board a private aeroplane! Steed meets his fellow guests, and the plane takes off. They are soon horrified to discover that there is no pilot. The controls are operated automatically and cannot be turned off. Talking amongst themselves, they discover that they have each been sent a false invitation. They have been brought together for a purpose – but what is it? Each of them is an expert in some field. As well as Steed, there is Freddy Richards, a professional strongman; a bullfighter, Joe Smith; fencer, Max Hardy; big-game hunter, Jason Wade; war hero, Mark Dayton; and Hana Wilde, a pretty girl who is an expert shot. The aircraft lands and they find themselves on a small deserted island. Not entirely deserted, however, for Kanwitch and Jessel, well hidden, watch their every move. The seven make their way to a crumbling house. Inside, they find a table set for a meal, and at each place a weapon. At the back of the room are six coffins, and as they stare at the empty caskets, Kanwitch's voice is heard through a loudspeaker. He tells them they are part of an experiment.

One of them has been trained to be a lethal unbeatable opponent and in order to pass the test, he, or she, will have to kill the others. Hana taps a nearby suit of armour and the body of Toy Sung falls to the floor. They decide to search the island, while Steed remains at the house. Suddenly, a cry is heard and they return to find Richards' body in a coffin, his neck broken. They realise that Smith is not with them – at the same time, Smith is killed with a pitchfork hidden in an old wagon. They set out again and search the undergrowth. Jessel is pleased with his protegé's progress, but Kanwitch insists on the test being fully completed. Before his country will finance Jessel's methods, they must have complete proof. The next victim is Hardy. Steed finds him lying at the bottom of a ravine, with a sword in his chest. Dayton and Hana appear, and Dayton thinks Steed may be the killer. Back at the house, they find the bodies of Hardy and Wade, in two coffins. Dayton knocks Steed unconscious, and he and Hana leave for the aircraft. But while he is working on the controls, Dayton is garotted by an unseen attacker. Hana and Steed are now the sole survivors, it seems, but suddenly a third person arrives. It is Emma, who has landed by parachute from a fighter plane which followed Steed's plane by radar. Emma explains to Hana that Steed knew the invitation was forged, as his host was in South America. Steed, recovering from the knockout blow, is pouring himself a drink when one of the bodies steps out of the coffin! It is Wade, who confesses that he is the killer. They fight, Steed with a spear, Wade with a rapier. Eventually Steed throws the spear into Wade's chest, and he stumbles off. Emma and Hana return to the house, but then Steed and Hana are both knocked out by Wade. Just as he is about to shoot Steed, Emma knocks the gun from his hand and makes him unconscious with a kung fu hold. They now realise that Wade was two identical twins, both playing the same deadly game. Kanwitch, too, realises that he has been double-crossed, but Jessel shoots him and prepares to escape. As he leaves, a shot rings out. It is Hana, who has recovered, and as Jessel reaches for weapon after weapon from the table, Hana shoots them from his hands. Jessel is eventually handcuffed by Steed – much to the dismay of Hana, who admits that she was just beginning to enjoy herself.

A FUNNY THING HAPPENED ON THE WAY TO THE STATION

By Bryan Sherriff

John Steed	Patrick Macnee
Emma Peel	Diana Rigg
Ticket collector	James Hayter
Crewe	John Laurie
Groom	Drewe Henley
Bride	Isla Blair
Salt	Tim Barrett
Admiral	Richard Caldicot
Warren	Dyson Lovell
Attendant	Peter J Elliott
Lucas	Michael Nightingale
Secretary	Noel Davis

Designed by Robert Jones
Directed by John Krish
Produced by Albert Fennell
and Brian Clemens
Executive Producer
Julian Wintle

STEED and Emma arrange to meet another agent, Lucas, at Norborough station. While they are waiting, Steed explains that Lucas had been tracking down a gang of troublemakers. The train arrives, but Lucas does not appear, and although they search the compartments, they find no trace of him. They do not know that he got off the train some miles back down the track, at a derelict station which he was led to believe was the one he wanted. A search of Lucas' cottage reveals two things: his body (with a note 4.4.67 in the pocket) and a photograph, which Emma recognises as that of a passenger on the train. Steed recognises him, too – it is Salt, a clerk at the Admiralty. Posing as a journalist, Emma visits the Admiralty and interviews Salt's boss. She thinks Salt may be passing on top-secret information, and they decide to test her theory by passing on a false story. Steed has been checking the train timetables, and realises that the 8.10 to Norborough stopped down the line at one point. He and Emma visit the derelict station, Chase Halt, and meet railway enthusiast, Crewe, who has bought the station and intends to live there. They also find a station name-plate reading Norborough. Steed decides to travel on the next 8.10 to Norborough. Among his fellow passengers are Salt and a honeymoon couple. Steed notices the dining-car attendant pass Salt a note, which he intercepts. It reads 4.1.67. This turns out to be a reserved seat, which Salt takes. But although Steed watches him, Salt makes no suspicious move, and when they reach Norborough, Salt takes the next train to London. The information that Emma has leaked is passed on, but when it is discovered to be false, Salt is killed. His murderer is the young bridegroom from the 8.10

train. Beside Salt's body, Steed finds a pile of railway tickets, all first-class returns from London to Norborough. Each of them has a hole punched through the middle, the size of a micro dot. Steed also discovers a tape recording, which is apparently that of a train. Emma takes the tape to Crewe, who cannot recognise it as being any train he knows. But, he tells her, some trains do have a strange sound – particularly the 8.10, which always interferes with his radio. Once again the honeymoon couple travel on the 8.10. Aided by the ticket collector, they are busy installing a bomb in one of the carriages – a carriage that will be used by the Prime Minister on his visit to Norborough the next day. Crewe's observation that the tape recording cannot possibly be that of a train, leads Steed and Emma to suspect a code, and they set out to break it. They discover that it spells out a name, Durbridge. It is a station on the Norborough line. That night, the 8.10 carries two extra passengers. Emma sits opposite the young bride who is in seat number 4.1.67. Steed drinks coffee in the restaurant car. At the rear of the train, the car attendant and the ticket collector sit in a special control carriage, filled with electrical apparatus and radio computers. They are checking every minute detail of the Prime Minister's progress. Steed is recognised by the ticket collector, who captures him and takes him to the special carriage. There, he is told of the bomb, set to explode in 15 minutes' time, as the train reaches Durbridge. Emma has also been recognised by the bride, but after an intense struggle, she manages to evade the girl, by making her way along the outside of the train to the guard's van. She arrives just in time to save Steed from being shot. Together they round up the gang and try to shut down the computer, but fail. Steed eventually saves the day by ripping the leads from the equipment. The Prime Minister saved, Steed now wonders how he will cope with life as Sir John.

The young bride is not thinking of her honeymoon in A Funny Thing Happened On The Way To The Station.

SOMETHING NASTY IN THE NURSERY

By Philip Levene

John Steed	Patrick Macnee
Emma Peel	Diana Rigg
Mr Goat	Dudley Foster
Miss Lister	Yootha Joyce
Beaumont	Paul Eddington
Webster	Paul Hardwick
Sir George Collins	Patrick Newell
Gen Wilmot	Geoffrey Sumner
Gordon	Trevor Bannister
Martin	Clive Dunn
James	George Merritt
Nanny Roberts	Enid Lorimer
Nanny Smith	Louise Ramsay
Nanny Brown	Penelope Keith
Dobson	Dennis Chinnery

Designed by Robert Jones
Directed by James Hill
Produced by Albert Fennell
and Brian Clemens
Executive Producer
Julian Wintle

WHEN agent Dobson is found dead in the home of General Wilmot, Chief of Defence, The Avengers are called in. Wilmot explains that vital defence secrets have been stolen, and that these secrets had been entrusted to only three men, apart from himself – Sir George Collins, son of the Attorney General, Viscount Frederick Webster, DSO, and Lord William Beaumont. All of them come from the noblest of British families. Steed and Emma decide to visit Beaumont first, and ask Collins and Webster to be there too. But when they arrive, Beaumont is acting like a two-year-old. Disgruntled, Webster leaves, followed by Emma. Later Beaumont recovers to tell Steed that he had a strange dream in which he was back in his childhood. He remembers his old Nanny Roberts, and a bouncing ball. He produces a photograph of himself as a child, with Nanny Roberts, and a rubber ball at their feet. Meanwhile, at home, Webster thinks back to his own youth, and looks out some old photographs. His nanny was also Roberts. Emma arrives to find Webster hallucinating, clutching a rubber ball marked Martin's Toyshop. Emma discovers the butler's body in the cellar, and an unseen attacker tries to kill her with a pike from a nearby statue. When she returns to the drawing-room, Webster is fast asleep and the ball has gone. They now have two leads. Emma follows one to Martin's Toyshop and Steed visits a school for nannies, run by one Nanny Roberts. Martin, the toy shop owner, refuses to sell Emma a ball, when she spots a box of them in the shop. He tells her they are produced specially for GONN – The Guild of Noble Nannies.

Meanwhile, at GONN, Steed meets Miss Lister, Nanny Roberts' assistant, who says the old lady is too ill to receive visitors. Steed poses as an old charge of hers, but when he eventually sees her, it is only for a few seconds in a darkened room. Miss Lister tells her partner, Gordon, that it is time to deal with Sir George. At the same time, Emma realises he is in danger and hurries to his home. She is seen by Gordon who attempts to run her over, but although she escapes, she is not in time to prevent Sir George from becoming mesmerised. Miss Lister and Gordon check their records and find that Nanny Roberts never had a charge called Steed. Accordingly, Steed finds a bomb in his kitchen. Emma meanwhile returns to the toy shop, but finds that Martin has been killed by a lethal jack-in-the-box. Steed discovers that Nanny Roberts also brought up General Wilmot, and he leaves for the General's home. He soon realises that he is being followed. Emma searches the GONN offices and finds Nanny Roberts a weak, helpless prisoner. She also finds Gordon, and knocks him unconscious. She next sees a box of rubber balls and, examining one, is immediately transported into a strange, dreamlike nursery world. At the General's home, Steed is explaining that he believes that the General will be the next victim on Nanny's list, when a rubber ball bounces through the window. Wilmot picks it up and immediately begins to act like a child. Miss Lister and Goat, one of her tutors, enter. He is disguised as a nanny. Assuring Miss Lister that his special drug, which is absorbed by the skin, never fails, Goat produces a map of the British Isles, and makes Wilmot mark off the names of secret missile bases. Steed, who has picked up the rubber ball, pretends that he, too, is drugged, but then they notice that he is wearing gloves. Goat tells Wilmot to kill Steed and Emma, for by this time she has recovered and joined them. But in the ensuing fight, Goat loses his blonde wig and Wilmot, still a child in his mind, and realising Goat is not his real nanny, shoots the impostor.

THE JOKER

By Brian Clemens

John Steed	Patrick Macnee
Emma Peel	Diana Rigg
Prendergast	Peter Jeffrey
Ola	Sally Nesbitt
Strange young man	Ronald Lacey
Major George Fancy	John Stone

Designed by Robert Jones
Directed by Sidney Hayers
Produced by Albert Fennell
and Brian Clemens
Executive Producer
Julian Wintle

WHEN Emma publishes a successful book on bridge, she is invited to spend a weekend in Devonshire with a fellow-player, Sir Cavalier Rousicana. Steed stays at home, with a badly bruised leg from a fall. He does not want to ruin Emma's weekend by being an invalid – or by telling her that Prendergast, a vicious criminal who was jailed on Emma's evidence, has broken out and is in London. When Emma arrives at Sir Cavalier's home, she is welcomed by his ward, Ola, a fey young woman with strange ways, who says her host has been delayed in London and will return later. The old rambling house contains antiques, and many decorations showing playing cards, including a huge card serving as a door to an upper storey. After Emma has dined in a huge candle-lit room and surrounded by life-size playing cards, Ola is suddenly called away to a friend who has been taken ill in the village. She borrows Emma's car, and drives off, leaving Emma alone – or so she thinks. A search of her room reveals little but a pile of old gramophone records, all in German, all the same tune, My Love, My Tender, Beautiful Rose. As she begins idly wandering through the rest of the house, she hears the doorbell ring and answers it. The caller is a young man who tries to scare Emma, and will not reveal the purpose of his call. But he does point out that the telephone wires have been cut. Meanwhile Steed has discovered that his fall was no accident, and finds a trip device hidden on the staircase. He also finds out that Sir Cavalier has been out of the country for some time. When a friend of Steed's picks up a playing card from the floor, and is killed by a poisoned blade attached to it, Steed is certain that someone – Prendergast? – is out to kill The Avengers. He leaves for Devon at once. Emma, alone in the house, begins to suspect that there is someone else there. She finds her room full of roses, the phone rings although the wires are cut, and then she hears a blood-curdling scream. She

WHO'S WHO?

By Philip Levene

John Steed	Patrick Macnee
Emma Peel	Diana Rigg
Lola	Patricia Haines
Basil	Freddie Jones
Major 'B'	Campbell Singer
Tulip	Peter Reynolds
Krelmar	Arnold Diamond
Daffodil	Philip Levene
Hooper	Malcolm Taylor

Designed by Robert Jones
Directed by John Moxey
Produced by Albert Fennell
and Brian Clemens
Executive Producer
Julian Wintle

Steed and Mrs Peel find Hooper, who appeared to be stretching his legs when he died, in Who's Who.

HOOPER, an agent of Floral (a secret department of British agents run by Major B, a green-fingered, flower expert, who codenames his agents after types of flowers), strolls through a deserted warehouse to keep a rendezvous with John Steed. Suddenly, two figures emerge from their hiding place and shoot the agent dead. They leave the body propped up high above the ground, but with his feet on the floor – his legs are elongated by a pair of wooden stilts! Hooper's body is discovered in this ludicrous position by Steed and Mrs Peel, who notices the manufacturer's name, Hi-Limba, pinned to the side of the stilts. Steed tells her that Hooper's codename was Rose, and immediately sets out to locate the Hi-Limba address. Steed's search is made that much easier, when the two assassins, Basil and Lola, erect a sign bearing the name Hi-Limba Products Ltd outside the building in which they lie in wait for him. When Steed arrives, he is knocked unconscious and carried into a back room where Krelmar, an enemy agent, waits beside his new invention – a machine which can transfer the mind, soul and psyche from one person to another. The agents intend to use the machine to transfer Basil and Lola's personalities into the bodies of Steed and Emma. They will then be the perfect double agents, able to infiltrate any government department without suspicion. Steed and Basil are placed side by side under the machine and Krelmar begins the transfer. The remarkable result is that Steed (now with Basil's personality) rises from the machine to plant a loving kiss on Lola's lips! Emma undergoes the same process with Lola, leaving the two assassins (now outwardly Steed and Emma) to set out to begin their reign of havoc and mayhem on Britain's spy network. The bodies of Basil and Lola – now with the personalities of Steed and

Emma – are chained to a supporting post and left under Krelmar's guard. In rapid succession, agents Daffodil, Poppy and Bluebell are all killed by the new and deadly Steed. (Their behaviour gives a novel twist to this Avengers story, as the formerly imperturbable Steed smokes cigars and nuzzles Emma's neck, while the cool and untouchable Emma chews gum and swings her hips to beat music). In a desperate bid to stop the mayhem caused by their clones, Steed and Emma escape – only to be trapped by agent Tulip, and taken to Major B. Though continuing to protest their innocence throughout the interrogation, Major B is convinced that, though their briefing was thorough, it was only a cover, and they are placed under arrest pending trial. They soon escape and, finding a clue to the assassins' whereabouts – a small box of migraine pills, given to Basil by Krelmar – they race to the premises. Emma knocks out Lola, and both are put under the machine. Though Steed attempts to reverse the process, he cannot recall how to operate the machine, and leaves to search Krelmar's office for the instructions. He is spotted by Krelmar who, having knocked Steed unconscious, enters the machine room and finds Emma and Lola. Believing that Steed has managed to reverse the transformation, he reverses the process. After a few seconds, a smiling Emma, now fully restored, rises from the machine and hits Krelmar in the jaw. At that moment, Basil arrives and attempts to kill Mrs Peel but Steed, having recovered consciousness, bursts into the room. After a hectic battle, Basil and Steed are placed beneath the machine and their personalities reversed. A few moments later, when the Floral agents, led by Major B arrive, they are astonished to find the three agents bemused, and trussed up in a corner. Exit a smiling Steed who, when passing through the door in advance of Emma, has to be reminded 'Manners, Steed.'

rushes outside and finds a dummy, dressed as a man, inside the young man's car. When she returns to the house, someone has turned off the gas under the kettle. Suddenly she hears voices calling her in a whisper, then the gramophone record begins playing upstairs. She begins searching the house, and finds the young man in a rocking chair. He is dead – and she is locked in the house with his murderer, who continues to call her in a soft, coaxing voice. She finds him in the dining room, seated beneath a huge reproduction of the joker card. When she reaches for the candle she recognises him as Prendergast. He is completely insane. He tells Emma that he intends to kill her, for he once loved her but she handed him over to the police. Prendergast has Ola as an ally, and she wants to see Emma killed. Finding her gun is loaded with blanks, Emma throws it at the girl, they fight, and Emma knocks Ola out. But Prendergast has enormous strength and Emma finds she is powerless against him. Suddenly, though, they hear the German song ring out again, and Prendergast is horrified to see the huge joker card move menacingly towards them. Terrified, he collapses onto the ground. Emma looks enquiringly at the card, which turns out to reveal Steed. He has come to offer her a lift home!

THE RETURN OF THE CYBERNAUTS

By Philip Levene

John Steed	Patrick Macnee
Emma Peel	Diana Rigg
Paul Beresford	Peter Cushing
Benson	Frederick Jaeger
Dr Neville	Charles Tingwell
Professor Chadwick	Fulton Mackay
Dr Russell	Roger Hammond
Dr Garnett	Anthony Dutton
Conroy	Noel Coleman
Rosie	Aimi MacDonald
Hunt	Redmond Phillip
Cybernaut	Terry Richard

Designed by Robert Jones
Directed by Robert Day
Produced by Albert Fennell
and Brian Clemens
Executive Producer
Julian Wintle

EMMA and Steed are invited to the home of Paul Beresford, a rich art dilettante. There, Steed receives a telephone call saying that a scientist, Dr Russell, has disappeared, shortly after Professor Chadwick vanished. Steed and Emma make their apologies and leave, and as they do so, Beresford presses a button hidden beneath his desk, which opens a sliding panel in the wall. In walks a cybernaut, carrying the latest victim, Dr Russell, on its back. The scientist is taken to an underground cell, where shortly afterwards, Beresford and his aide, Benson, visit him and the other captive scientist, and we learn that they now plan to kidnap electronics expert, Dr Neville. Together they programme the robot with Neville's cardiograph, and the cybernaut goes off to fetch him. Neville is waylaid outside his office and brought back to Beresford's home. Emma and Steed return to Beresford's house, and Benson is worried that the cybernaut, due back any minute, will be seen by them. However, just as Steed is about to enter Beresford's home, he hears of Neville's disappearance on his car telephone, and he and Emma drive away — missing the cybernaut's return by seconds. Beresford now informs the three captives of his plan to get rid of Steed and Mrs Peel by the most gruesome and protracted means possible. Their part in the plan will be to devise the means of doing so, and he offers them £100,000 in cash as part payment for their task. Russell is revolted by the idea and tries to escape, but he finds his way is blocked by the cybernaut which, with one deadly swing of its arm, kills him. Dr Garnett is the next to go, his door being smashed down by the cybernaut's fist. His scatter-brained blonde secretary, Rosie, is struck too, after she has mistaken it for a male visitor. She tells Steed 'His eyes were all misty with desire'. Later that day, Benson makes Dr Garnett and the other scientist watch Emma paying another visit to Paul Beresford, through a two-way mirror. Beresford and Benson listen-in when Steed receives a telephone call from Conroy giving him the address of Hunt, Dr Clement Armstrong's lawyer when he was alive. Armstrong had been responsible for unleashing the cybernauts two years earlier, and had met his death during an attempt on Steed and Mrs Peel's lives. Fearing that Hunt may reveal him as Armstrong's brother, Beresford dispatches Benson and the cybernaut to dispose of Hunt. Steed arrives at Hunt's home, but discovers that the cybernaut has got there first. It is still in the room and knocks Steed unconscious. Meanwhile, Beresford is making advances to Emma, and tries to persuade her to stay overnight, but she declines and leaves. We next see her trying to help Steed recover from the cybernaut blow. Dr Garnett now presents Beresford with a bomb he has made. It unexpectedly goes off in Beresford's face and Garnett escapes. Beresford soon recovers and sends the cybernaut to bring the scientist back. It finds him in Steed's flat, where Emma is tending Garnett's wounds. She is thrust aside like a toy and the robot leaves with the dazed Garnett over his shoulder. Chadwick and Neville, meanwhile, have discovered an ideal way of getting rid of Emma and Steed, for which they need information about their victims' skins. They obtain the required information from a bronze bust which Steed and Emma handled in Beresford's flat. They also photograph Steed's clip-on watch and then duplicate it in the workshop. Inside the watch they install a mechanism which will make Steed Beresford's puppet when he wears it. Chadwick is forced by Beresford to test the watch device on Dr Garnett. It works perfectly, although Garnett is killed when Beresford meddles with the controls. Delighted by the results, Beresford now makes the scientists install a second device in a jewelled bracelet-watch, which he later gives to Emma, asking her to wear it at their next meeting. Benson breaks into Steed's flat and manages to exchange the watch device with Steed's watch. Arriving home, Steed and Emma find the place ransacked. Steed is disturbed, but fails to connect the break-in with Beresford. They then prepare for the evening date at Beresford's home. Beresford, awaiting his guests, now puts the control mechanism

Emma is tending Dr Garnett's wounds in Steed's flat when she has an unwelcome visitor, in Return Of The Cybernauts.

into action, before Steed has put his watch on. Emma, wearing the jewelled watch, now becomes Beresford's puppet. She jumps into her car and almost runs Steed down as she drives away. He follows her in the Bentley, unaffected by Beresford since he has left his watch at home. Emma now arrives at Beresford's home, completely under his control. He decides to use her like a cybernaut to knock out Steed. Later, however, when Beresford tries to make Steed wear a watch containing a control device, Steed manages to get it onto the wrist of the cybernaut, whereupon the robot runs amok, finally killing Beresford. Emma is released when Steed smashes the watch she is wearing, and together they soon handle Benson and the scientists. Steed adjusts the watch control mechanism to immobilise the cybernaut, and finally Emma pushes it over with her little finger.

DEATH'S DOOR

By Philip Levene

John Steed	Patrick Macnee
Emma Peel	Diana Rigg
Boyd	Clifford Evans
Stapley	William Lucas
Lord Melford	Allan Cuthbertson
Becker	Marne Maitland
Dr Evans	Paul Dawkins
Pavret	Michael Faure
Saunders	Peter Thomas
Dalby	William Lyon Brown
Haynes	Terry Yorke
Jepson	Terry Maidment

Designed by Robert Jones
Directed by Sidney Hayers
Produced by Albert Fennell
and Brian Clemens
Executive Producer
Julian Wintle

A CROWD of reporters burst into a conference ante-chamber and face Stapley and Pavret, two government men, who are awaiting the arrival of Sir Andrew Boyd, chairman of the conference and head of the British delegation. Pavret speaks of a rumour that the British may withdraw from the talks. Sir Andrew Boyd arrives, but he stops short at the door to the conference room and refuses to enter. Lord Melford, Steed and Emma meet in Boyd's study, and Steed learns from Stapley that he has covered up Boyd's lapse by saying he had a sudden attack of migraine. Steed promises to collect Boyd that evening and make sure that he attends the next conference. Boyd's doctor gives him some pills, and the highly-disturbed Boyd is left alone. As Dr Evans leaves the study, he begins to rub his neck and soon falls into a deep sleep. In his bedroom, Boyd also rubs his neck and falls asleep. Steed arrives to take Boyd to the conference, and as they leave, Boyd looks for a button missing from the coat of Dalby, his butler. Travelling to the conference in Steed's Bentley, Boyd talks about an escaped lion – 'The last thing I saw before I died'. At the conference hall he really *does* die, by leaping in front of a moving car. Over the entrance to the hall, Steed notices a large stone lion, reminiscent of the one Boyd had mentioned. Steed meets Emma in his flat and they discuss Boyd's strange death. Later, Steed reassures Melford, who tells him he is confident that he will be able to attend the conference in Boyd's place. That evening, Melford gets a sudden irritation at the back of his neck, which he rubs. He asks Stapley for a morning call, and dozes off – it is then that his nightmare begins. He is taken to the conference with menacing incidents

dogging him as he goes. Faceless men torment him, Stapley appears in his dream with his face slashed, and the sequence ends with the conference room chandelier crashing down on him. Later, Stapley wakes Melford, wearing a piece of sticking-plaster on his face, and when Steed arrives and tears off a sheet on his office calendar, revealing Friday 13th – the date in Melford's dream – Melford is in a highly-disturbed state. However, Melford is clearly relieved to find there is no out-of-order sign on the lift door – another item of his dream. But on the way to the conference, several more of the dream's details *are* confirmed. Becker opens the door exactly as he had done in the nightmare, at which point Melford cracks, and will not enter the conference chamber. Steed and Emma tackle Melford and Dr Evans respectively about the Minister's dream. Steed can only discover that Melford thinks he is having genuine premonitions of death. Emma learns nothing from Dr Evans. That night, Steed keeps watch in the room next to Melford and Emma waits outside in her car, keeping in touch by radio. In his room, Melford once again rubs his neck and falls into a deep sleep, and another nightmare follows. Emma is slow to react to Steed's summons – she appears to be recovering from a drugged condition – but Steed is relieved when she finally arrives. They decide to go over the route to the conference together, and find that various items from Melford's dream are revealed even to them. From photographs given him by Steed, Melford identifies the man at the door in his dream as Alfred Becker, an observer from the Eastern bloc. Meanwhile Emma is seen discovering the lift being put out of action, as required in Melford's dream. Her observer informs Jepson, one of the conference wreckers. Later, Jepson waylays Emma in Steed's flat, and after a fight, he is killed on a sword. From his body, Emma removes a Yale key to the Temporary Storage Company in W4. Steed meanwhile waylays Becker, who is practising on a private shooting range in his house. Steed manages to kill Becker by making some holes in the wooden target, and lodges a bullet in them, which he fires by hitting the percussion cap with a stone. Steed also finds a Temporary Storage tag on the body. Emma visits the Storage Company and discovers an air-gun with which the conference wreckers have drugged Boyd, Melford, Steed, Emma and Dr Evans, so they can carry out their deception undis-

It all seems like a bad dream in Death's Door. *In this scene, Emma deals with Haynes, an assistant attaché.*

turbed – carrying off Boyd and Melford's bodies to the warehouse, then rigging reality to fit their dreams. Steed meets Emma in the conference room and together they confront Stapley with his guilt, and rip off his plaster to show he has feigned the cut on his face. Emma throws Haynes, an assistant attaché also in the plot, and Stapley dies when a stray bullet slices through the cord holding the chandelier, bringing it smashing down on his head, as in Melford's dream.

THE £50,000 BREAKFAST

By Roger Marshall

John Steed	Patrick Macnee
Emma Peel	Diana Rigg
Glover	Cecil Parker
Miss Pegram	Yolande Turner
Sir James Arnell	David Langton
Mrs Rhodes	Pauline Delaney
Judy	Anneke Wills
Minister	Cardew Robinson
First assistant	Eric Woofe
Second assistant	Phillippe Monnet
Rhodes	Richard Curnock

Designed by Robert Jones
Directed by Robert Day
Produced by Albert Fennell
and Brian Clemens
Executive Producer
Julian Wintle

Diana Rigg brought a feline grace to the character of Mrs Peel, and dispatched her assailants with ease and style.

Classic Avengers clothes – Patrick Macnee has his familiar bowler and umbrella, and Diana Rigg wears her Emmapeelers.

RHODES is driving along a country road, chatting amicably to a ventriloquist's dummy by his side. Operating the dummy, Rhodes makes it ask him where they are going this time! Charlie, the dummy, answers that they are bound for Zurich. Suddenly Rhodes is forced to swerve to avoid hitting a haycart ahead of him. He crashes the car and ends up in hospital, where the X-rays reveal that he has a stomach full of diamonds worth £50,000. Steed and Emma pick up the dummy from the wreck and return it to Rhodes' wife, who keeps a shop that sells dummies. Mrs Rhodes tells them that her husband has recently been flying to Switzerland every few days to perform at the Alex Litoff Homes there. She is unconcerned about her husband's serious injuries, and will not visit him in hospital. When Steed and Emma have left, Mrs Rhodes turns to her white Borzoi dog, Bellhound, and murmurs 'Visit Dusty! I should laugh!' The scene changes to a funeral for a black Borzoi dog called Dancer, held in the Happy Valley Resting Place, a pet cemetery. The chief mourner, Glover, tells the officiating cleric that Alex Litoff is paying for the funeral. Emma meanwhile learns from a Treasury official that Litoff is a wealthy industrialist and financier who came to London from Armenia in the 1930s, and is now a shy little man who is alleged to have his heart set on a knighthood. If he left London, many would go with him, and the Pound would be in difficulty because of the outflow of cash. Steed decides to visit Litoff at his penthouse, and is received by Glover who has the black Borzoi with him. He is then introduced to Miss Pegram, Litoff's formidable assistant, who supervises two junior assistants, both hard at work in the business section. She tells Steed that Rhodes has simply stolen the diamonds, and that

he is just an employee, as she is. She will have nothing to do with Steed's offer of £5000 for the diamonds, but says she will put it to her chief, and asks him to call back the next day. That night, Miss Pegram's first assistant enters the hospital, disguised as a doctor, and gives Rhodes a fatal injection of poison. The only lead Steed can get at the hospital is that blonde Borzoi hairs have been found on Rhodes' suit. Later, the first assistant steals Rhodes' car from a garage, and has it crushed in a breaker's yard. Steed now shows Emma some old newsreel film of the mysterious Alex Litoff, but she is unable to pinpoint him. He shuns the public eye and never grants interviews – a fact which irritates Miss Pegram, for she would like some credit for her achievements. Steed returns to Litoff's penthouse and Miss Pegram says that her chief says he can have £4000 for the diamonds, which Steed accepts. On his way out, he meets Sir James Arnell, Litoff's doctor, and also Glover, whom he questions about Rhodes' death. He asks if Rhodes had anything to do with the dog Dancer, and Glover discloses that as well as the black one, there is a blonde dog called Bellhound. We next see Miss Pegram talking to Mrs Rhodes. She tells her that her husband, a dog lover, did not get rid of Bellhound as he was supposed to. Later, as a result of the information being passed on, the first assistant visits Mrs Rhodes, kills her, and removes the dog. Dr Arnell has told Steed that Litoff is suffering from heart trouble, but Emma has learned from his niece, Judy, that he has kidney disease. Emma searches Arnell's car but is attacked by the first assistant, who has passed Bellhound onto Glover. Emma throws the man, who falls awkwardly and dies. Steed joins her and learns that, according to the doctor's files, Litoff has heart trouble. Steed also finds more blonde Borzoi hairs on the dead man's body. Later he finds Mrs Rhodes dead in her shop, and when a kennel man calls for Bellhound, Steed pays him to go away. Steed breaks into Litoff's bedroom via the window, and tears away the newspaper covering his face. It is Glover – with Sir James Arnell at his side holding a gun. Meanwhile Emma is told by the minister at the dog cemetery, that a dog named Bellhound was buried there recently, though the dog was black, not blonde. Back at Litoff's penthouse, Steed learns from Glover how the plotters propose to benefit from concealing the financier's death. Glover stands to make £11,000,000

DEAD MAN'S TREASURE

By Michael Winder

John Steed	Patrick Macnee
Emma Peel	Diana Rigg
Mike	Norman Bowler
Penny	Valerie Van Ost
Alex	Edwin Richfield
Carl	Neil McCarthy
Benstead	Arthur Lowe
Bates	Ivor Dean
Danvers	Rio Fanning
Miss Peabody	Penny Bird
First guest	Gerry Crampton
Second guest	Peter J Elliott

Designed by Robert Jones
Directed by Sidney Hayers
Produced by Albert Fennell
and Brian Clemens
Executive Producer
Julian Wintle

Emma fights for her life when she is attacked by one of Litoff's henchmen, in **The £50,000 Breakfast.**

Emma is handcuffed to the steering wheel of a racing car simulator, and is having a shocking time, in Dead Man's Treasure.

but will not accept that Litoff has been murdered. When Steed accuses them of plotting the deaths of Rhodes and his wife, both Glover and Sir James deny complicity in this. At the dog cemetery, Emma learns that it is Litoff who is buried there, not Bellhound. Glover, paying his last respects, sees her and when she arrives at the penthouse dressed as a kennel-maid to collect the dogs, she is tied up with Steed. Miss Pegram, hearing that Litoff's body has been found, plans her escape in the financier's private plane. She decides to kill Emma and Steed before she leaves, but Glover and Sir James are opposed to this. As they are arguing, Steed and Emma manage to escape and Emma soon takes care of the murderess, while Glover and Sir James decide to come quietly. Back at Steed's flat, Emma leaves Steed wondering what to do with the two Borzois he finds waiting there.

A CAR driven by agent Bobby Danvers is pursued in a night chase by another car, that of Carl and Alex. Danvers shakes off his pursuers by turning into the grounds of Benstead's open driveway, and he enters the house by the French windows. He then puts the small metal despatch box he is carrying into a red treasure chest he finds in the room, addresses one of the invitation cards he finds on a desk to John Steed, Esquire, and departs. He drives past Carl and Alex again, who have turned back after realising they have lost him. Emma joins Steed in his flat. He is worried because Danvers is already an hour late. The mortally-wounded agent finally arrives and before he dies, tells them he has hidden the despatch box in a red treasure chest. He does not say where. Carl and Alex, who have trailed Danvers to Steed's flat, listen at the window. They also overhear Steed telling Emma of an invitation he has received to attend Sir George Benstead's car rally. Steed and Emma go to the rally, and discover that Benstead is a car maniac, who practises car-racing on a Brands Hatch simulator he has rigged up in his home. Steed takes Benstead off to have a drink, leaving Mrs Peel to search alone. In the study she distracts Carl, who is looking for an invitation for himself and Alex. She fights the masked intruder, but is unable to prevent his escape, armed with an invitation to the rally. Next day, Carl and Alex are amongst the guests attending the function. Steed mentions the treasure chest to Benstead, not realising that this is the trophy in the car treasure hunt, which Benstead won't show to anyone. Steed continues to ask about the chest while Benstead plays with the simulator. Suddenly, he receives an electric shock from his apparatus and dies. Steed has only one clue – Bates was at the voltage control in the next room but, when questioned, the man can reveal nothing of value. Carl finds the dead Benstead, and later discovers from Alex that neither of them are responsible for his death. Even they are puzzled by this strange turn in events. Steed orders Bates to begin the treasure hunt as if nothing had happened, telling the guests that Benstead is unwell upstairs. Alex knocks out Mrs Elston, the partner to whom he has been assigned, and grabs the envelope containing the first clue, 'The vaults at Mithering'. Carl tackles his partner, Miss Peabody, and joins Alex in their red Jaguar, to be the first away. The cars roar off. The race is complicated by the contestants changing the directions of the signposts, adding sugar to petrol tanks and scattering spikes on the road. Mike, with Emma as his passenger, reaches the house first and forces her to drive faster and faster in the racing car simulator, increasing the voltage in order to force her to give away a clue to the treasure. Meanwhile, Carl and Alex come to grief, their car spinning off the road, through a gate and into a tree. Steed drives on to the house, getting there in time to save Emma from Mike, whom he knocks out after a prolonged fight. He disconnects the shock equipment before Emma is aware that she is safe, giving her a few anxious moments. They then solve the last clue, 'What a shocking place to hide treasure', and find the missing chest – under Emma's driving seat in the racing car.

YOU HAVE JUST BEEN MURDERED

By Philip Levene

John Steed	Patrick Macnee
Emma Peel	Diana Rigg
Unwin	Barrie Ingham
Lord Maxted	Robert Flemyng
Needle	George Murcell
Rathbone	Leslie French
Jarvis	Geoffrey Chater
Shelton	Simon Oates
Chalmers	Clifford Cox
Hallam	John Baker
Morgan	Les Crawford
Nicholls	Frank Maher
Williams	Peter J Elliott

Designed by Robert Jones
Directed by Robert Asher
Produced by Albert Fennell
and Brian Clemens
Executive Producer
Julian Wintle

*What will be the blackmailer's next move?
Mrs Peel and Steed ponder the question in a
scene from* You Have Just Been Murdered.

*In a spectacular river fight, Emma traps
Morgan and forces him to take her to
Needle, in* You Have Just Been Murdered.

TWO mock attempts are made on the life of millionaire Gilbert Jarvis, but each time the handsome blond assailant does not go through with the assassination. First he fires an unloaded gun at Jarvis, then attacks him with a dummy dagger. Each time he leaves a visiting card reading 'You have just been murdered'. Jarvis contacts Steed and says he will talk about the matter at a party held in the home of George Unwin, another millionaire. Jarvis, however, does not turn up at the party and Steed phones him at home, where we see that Jarvis is *really* being murdered, by Shelton, the good-looking assassin. Jarvis answers the phone but does not speak to Steed, who leaves the party to investigate. Steed finds Jarvis shot, and evidence that he had been trying to protect himself with elaborate locks on his doors. While Steed is away from the party, Lord Maxted, a banker, tells Emma that Jarvis had recently asked him for £1,000,000 in cash from his account. When Rathbone, another millionaire, hears that Jarvis has been murdered, he reacts with apparent fright and leaves the party, followed closely by Emma. She finally reaches him through an array of guard dogs, armed men and locked doors. She tries to discover why he is so afraid, without success. Later we discover that Rathbone has also been terrified by four mock attempts on his life. The last was a mock poisoning, which his tormentors managed to stage despite his elaborate precautions. The next millionaire to receive the treatment is George Unwin, whom Shelton terrifies with a pantomime of murder by shooting, again leaving the visiting card. Maxted, the banker, learns that Rathbone wants £1,000,000 in cash to pay off his blackmailers, and tells Emma.

She then follows the man to a stream where he drops the case of money into the water. Here Emma meets Nicholls, another good-looking hireling of the (as yet) unseen mastermind. She finally impales him on a scythe. Shelton now increases the pressure on Unwin. First he nearly runs him down against a wall, and then stabs him with a harmless knife. Finally he fires an arrow at him – with a rubber sticker on the end. Then, a telephone caller tells Unwin to watch his television set that night. On screen as promised, the mastermind (a man called Needle) tells Unwin how he must take the £1,000,000 to Bridge Farm and what to do with it. Unwin contacts Maxted about the money. Steed follows Unwin to the farm, using a bleeping device attached to the case. At the farm Emma is waiting under the bridge and manages to catch Unwin's case before it hits the water. She then traps Morgan, another of Needle's henchmen, by floating the case to him. Emma then overpowers him and forces him to take her to Needle's headquarters. But Morgan misdirects her to a caravan, where Shelton fells her with a karate chop. She is then taken to Needle's headquarters, which are hidden beneath a haystack. Meanwhile Steed catches up with Unwin, who tells him he has put a bomb inside the case. Steed manages to track the case via the bleep device, and the men find themselves at the haystack. While they search for an entrance, Unwin is knocked out by one of Needle's henchmen, who in turn is flattened by Steed. Shelton investigates the disturbance, and Steed drops on him from the top of the haystack, and gets into the headquarters. He releases Emma and together they round up the gang. But they are unable to prevent Needle from escaping with the case in a van. Needle's plans are finally thwarted when the bomb goes off and the van is blown up.

THE POSITIVE-NEGATIVE MAN

By Tony Williamson

John Steed	Patrick Macnee
Emma Peel	Diana Rigg
Cresswell	Ray McAnally
Haworth	Michael Latimer
Cynthia Wentworth-Howe	Caroline Blakiston
Mankin	Peter Blythe
Maurice Jubert	Sandor Eles
Miss Clarke	Joanne Dainton
Charles Grey	Bill Wallis
Receptionist	Ann Hamilton

Designed by Robert Jones
Directed by Robert Day
Produced by Albert Fennell
and Brian Clemens
Executive Producer
Julian Wintle

GREY, an electronics expert, is working at his drawing board in the Ministry of Science when an intruder in a pin-stripe suit and wellington boots enters, points a finger at him, and blasts him into the back wall. When the body is found embedded in the wall, Steed and Emma are called in. They discover that Grey's papers, though securely locked in a safe, have been burnt to a crisp. From Cynthia, Grey's private secretary, Steed learns that the papers related to the lately abandoned Project 90, on which Grey had been working with Bryant, Mankin, Jubert and Creswell. The intruder, Haworth, next arrives at Jubert's electronics company, and on his way in to Jubert, gives Miss Clarke, his secretary, a bad shock from the filing cabinet. She falls to the floor unconscious. Emma discovers both the unconscious secretary and the dead Jubert. He has been hurled back with prodigious force through both a door and a wooden cupboard. Miss Clarke tells Emma of the strange electronic crackling that accompanied the intruder, and as Emma leaves the office she sees a van that has brought Haworth departing. Meanwhile, Steed visits Risely Dale, where the scientists worked on Project 90, and investigates a small black van he finds there. It has a small generator working inside, and when he grips the door handle, he receives a violent electric shock and is thrown to the ground. Emma, who also visits Risely Dale, finds Steed dazed, and the van gone. They bump into Creswell, the leader of Project 90, who arrives bearing a shotgun. Steed stops Emma from fighting with him, and suggests that they go to his house to discuss what has happened. Emma stays behind to have a closer look at Risely Dale. Creswell tells Steed that the research team had been working on broadcasting elec-tricity by radio waves, when the project was shelved and Creswell retired. Suddenly the French windows crash open, and all the lights are dimmed. The light in the room increases in intensity, and Creswell says unconvincingly that it must have been a fireball. Steed, however, discovers a boot print outside, and Emma appears, saying she has seen a blue light approaching the house through the trees, and heard the sound of faint electrical crackling. They also discover a handprint, buried deep in the back of a tree. Steed returns to the Ministry of Science and persuades Cynthia to show him the rest of the files on Project 90, but they discover that these, too, are charred to ashes. Steed next visits Mankin, who tells him about the possibilities of broadcast power. As he leaves, the driver of a black van focuses the sights of an electric broadcasting apparatus, hooked to a generator in the van, on Steed's car. The car is given a charge of electricity and Steed is forced to crash it to escape. Mankin goes to Risely Dale, and discovers the black van. He telephones Steed to say that something strange is going on, but no sooner has he hung up than the man in rubber boots traps and electrocutes him along a metal wire fence, simply by touching it! Emma arrives and discovers Mankin's body. The murderer, after administering the shock treatment to Emma, escapes in the van. Emma is left unconscious beside the body of Mankin. Steed visits Creswell, who is taken aback because he is expecting some-one else. Haworth arrives and, having first removed the rubber boots, joins them. He thinks he has left Mrs Peel dead at Risely Dale and receives a surprise when she soon joins them. As they leave, Emma falls to the ground. The fall, however, was feigned, and Emma now has a trace of the make-up from Haworth's collar. They later discover that the make-up is a mixture of non-conducting oil and aluminium dust and acts as an insulating barrier. Haworth later raids Emma's flat, and she is shocked into unconsciousness and taken to Risely Dale. There she is forced to record her voice, making it appear to Steed on the phone that she is summoning him. Creswell then encases her in silver foil from head to foot, so that they can charge her with electricity from which she is insulated, like Haworth. Creswell hopes to electrocute Steed when he attempts to rescue Emma. However, when Steed arrives, he is wearing rubber galoshes. In the ensuing mayhem, Haworth and Creswell both die, Haworth when one

On the whole, Steed and Mrs Peel found their encounter with The Positive-Negative Man *quite electrifying!*

of his earthing boots is removed, Creswell by falling through a window. Outside Steed and Emma pay the penalty of their contact with electricity. Both become magnetised – Steed to the Bentley, Emma to the lid of a dustbin.

MURDERSVILLE

By Brian Clemens

John Steed	Patrick Macnee
Emma Peel	Diana Rigg
Mickle	Colin Blakeley
Hubert	John Ronane
Dr Haynes	Ronald Hines
Prewitt	John Sharp
Jenny	Sheila Fearn
Croft	Eric Flynn
Forbes	Norman Chappell
Banks	Roger Cawdren
Miss Avril	Marika Mann
Maggie	Irene Bradshaw
Higgins	Joseph Greig
Jeremy Purser	Geoffrey Colville
Chapman	Langton Jones
Miller	Tony Caunter
Morgan	John Chandos
Williams	Andrew Laurence

Designed by Robert Jones
Directed by Robert Asher
Produced by Albert Fennell
and Brian Clemens
Executive Producer
Julian Wintle

OUTSIDE a pub at the sleepy village of Little Storping-in-the-Swuff, Hubert and Mickle, two local rustics, are playing dominoes and quaffing ale, when suddenly a man bursts onto the scene, pursued by another man, who shoots him dead. The rustics continue their game, and the village sleeps on. Emma introduces Major Paul Croft, whom she has known since she was a little girl, to Steed. Back from his overseas posting, Croft has bought a house at Little Storping, and his batman, Forbes, has gone on ahead to tidy things up. Forbes is staying at the local inn, and is told by Jenny Prewitt, the landlord's daughter, that some kind of event will happen soon, at twelve o'clock. Forbes wants to leave, but the locals insist that he has another drink with them. Minutes later, a man arrives and is given a package, containing a shotgun, by Prewitt, the landlord. The man goes outside and apparent gunshots are heard. The man returns and gives the package back to Prewitt. Mickle and Hubert pass off the incident as a car back-firing. The next strange event occurs when Forbes enlists the aid of Mickle and Hubert to unload things at Croft's new home. The pair unaccountably begin to destroy valuable china and furniture. Emma insists on driving Croft to his house, and on the way they pass a limousine driven by Samuel Morgan. At the village, Croft identifies a local man, Frederick Williams, to Emma as they pass the pub. Williams was once an important financier, whose crash was caused by the man they had passed earlier, Samuel Mor-

gan. Croft says it seems strange to see both men on the same day. Croft is furious when he finds his possessions smashed and sets off for the pub to find Forbes. He is not there, and the locals say they have never seen him. Croft next goes to the library, supervised by the attractive Miss Avril, who is arguing with Morgan. As he enters, Croft pots Williams with an unsilenced gun trained on Morgan from behind the bookshelves. Miss Avril points to the 'Silence' signs, and Williams produces a silencer before calmly shooting Morgan dead. As Croft backs to the door, he turns and finds himself confronted by Mickle, with a gun, and Hubert, holding a sickle. Emma, searching the grounds of Croft's house, finds a sickle lying in the grass. Searching further, she finds the dead body of Forbes, with what looks like a sickle wound in his back. Then someone throws a large block of wood at her, knocking her out. She comes to in the pub, where she is in the care of Dr Haynes, with Prewitt and his daughter Jenny in attendance. They try to convince her that her car has skidded, and indicate the car resting on the grass verge, but Emma insists that Dr Haynes goes with her to the house where she has found Forbes' body. At the house, the mess has been removed, and Forbes' body has gone. There instead is the gardener, Higgins, who claims that he has been there all the time, and has no knowledge of Croft buying the house! Emma goes to collect her car but finds Mickle leaning on the bonnet. She notices that he is wearing Croft's wristwatch and, now suspicious, returns to Dr Haynes and says she will take up his offer of pills to help with her delusions. At his surgery, Emma gives up her pretence that something is wrong with her, and threatens to summon the police. Banks, the local policeman, arrives in a squad car, but as Emma is about to tell him of the strange events, she notices that he is wearing bright, un-policeman-like socks. Banks leaves, and Emma tells Haynes that the policeman is bogus, but he threatens to commit her to hospital. He then pulls a gun on her as she attempts to escape. While he calls the exchange operator, Maggie, and orders her to call an emergency meeting, Emma knocks him unconscious. As she is leaving, she notices a private room off the hall. Inside are the bodies of Forbes and Croft. Finding the village deserted, she goes into the pub and breaks open a cupboard to find millions of pounds in cash bundled in there. Meanwhile, the townsfolk are attending a meeting in the library. Haynes bursts in with the news that Emma

Emma is always very well-dressed, but a helmet is not quite the thing to wear to a party, in Murdersville.

has escaped and they rush off to find her. They spot Emma leaving the pub and give chase. Pursued by the whole village, she escapes into the fields. Mickle pursues her in a helicopter, and she is knocked out by the machine's skids. When she comes to, she is confined and chained in the village museum, along with the village's former vicar, police sergeant, local magistrate and the telephone exchange girl. They tell Emma how the village got into its present state. When a murder was once committed there in broad daylight, the rich murderer bought the town's silence for £1,000,000. Since then, the townsfolk have become greedy, and have let it be known that they would kill people discreetly and silently in the privacy of their village for a fee! The four now imprisoned with Emma were the only dissenters. Emma is discovered and taken to the witch's ducking pool where she eventually agrees to reveal who else knows of their plans. She is allowed to ring the other person, her husband John. This is obviously Steed, who drives to the village and tests the reaction of Prewitt and Jenny by shouting out 'Emma Peel'. They are startled and Steed knocks them out. He then moves on to the museum and is freeing Emma, when Haynes, Mickle, Hubert and Prewitt arrive. In the fast and furious fight that follows, Emma and Steed soon put paid to the villains — Emma by grabbing and wearing a medieval helmet throughout the fight, and Steed by wielding a broad sword and smiting the poor unfortunates over the head with it. In the final scene, Steed and Emma enter the library and, with custard pies from the craft exhibition, pelt the rest of the townsfolk into submission.

MISSION...HIGHLY IMPROBABLE

By Philip Levene

John Steed	Patrick Macnee
Emma Peel	Diana Rigg
Shaffer	Ronald Radd
Susan	Jane Merrow
Prof Rushton	Noel Howlett
Chivers	Francis Matthews
Col Drew	Richard Leech
Josef	Stefan Gryff
Gifford	Nicholas Courtney
Sgt Gerald Bancroft	Kevin Stoney
Sergeant	Peter Clay
Corp Johnson	Nigel Rideout
Blonde	Cynthia Bizeray
Brunette	Nicole Shelby
Henrick	Nosher Powell
Karl	Denny Powell

Designed by Robert Jones
Directed by Robert Day
Produced by Albert Fennell
and Brian Clemens
Executive Producer
Julian Wintle

A ROLLS-ROYCE, registration number GB1, disappears while being escorted into a Ministry testing area. The passenger is Sir Gerald Bancroft, a Treasury official, who is to investigate apparent overspending by the research workers. The car passed the perimeter post and had a motorcycle escort in front and security officer behind, and yet vanished. Steed finds a miniature Rolls there, but Gifford ignores this. While they are talking, they fail to notice that Sir Gerald is in the grass not far away from them, and he is soon scooped up in a net by Dr Chivers. They next discover the tracks of a truck with a worn offside tyre. Steed confirms that the tracks are those of a MT4 military truck, and later we see Chivers getting down from just such a truck. He puts the box he is carrying – containing the miniaturised Sir Gerald – into a dustbin among the rubbish. Chivers then tells Professor Rushton that Sir Gerald will be delayed. Rushton has been overspending on an invention of his, urged on by Chivers. He wants to show it to Sir Gerald, but Chivers insists that the time is not yet ripe. Steed arrives at the administration block and stops to check on a truck parked outside. He is nearly hit by Chivers, who quickly regains his composure, and takes Steed to meet Rushton and his daughter Susan, who is also worried about her father's overspending. Steed asks her for an inventory, so he can find the truck with the worn tyre, but Susan lies and says that the inventory is missing. Gifford, meanwhile, finds the truck in the shed with the Champion MK 39 armoured car. He takes the tiny Rolls with him and realises

that the registration number matches that of the missing Rolls. He rushes to phone Steed, but Chivers enters and turns a reducing device, installed in a truck, on him. Gifford is now also miniaturised – and left looking at a giant telephone. Chivers then turns on a water hose and washes him down a grating. Susan now confronts her father. She says she has lied for him, and insists on knowing why he is overspending on the research grant. She, too, is given a working demonstration of the reducing device. Meanwhile, Chivers tells Shaffer, the head of the East European delegation which have arrived to see the Champion MK 39 demonstration, that he can deliver the vehicle. At the demonstration, Steed becomes suspicious when he identifies Shaffer as a Head of Intelligence he has met before – that time the man was dressed as an Admiral! The visitors are impressed with the MK 39, which emerges unscathed after being fired at by heavy artillery. Leaving the test area, Steed finds the miniature Rolls-Royce lodged in the mudguard of the MK 39. Later, he visits the experimental shed, and when he hears someone coming, hides in the MK 39. Chivers enters and trains the reducing ray on to the MK 39. Pocketing the now tiny MK 39 – and the equally miniature Steed – he drives out of the establishment. Steed takes the MK 39 to Shaffer, who says he is even more interested in the greater prize of the reducing machine. He tells Chivers that he intends to kidnap Susan Rushton to make her father bring the machine to him. Steed, unnoticed by Shaffer and Chivers, crawls out of the MK 39 and manages to telephone Emma, despite his reduced size. He tells her to stay with Susan as she is in danger. Emma then goes to Susan's home, but two of Shaffer's henchmen kidnap her instead of Susan when she is inspecting the latter's car. Shaffer soon realises the mistake. He locks Emma in his study, bound hand and foot, and there she is surprised to find the miniaturised Steed. He helps her to get free, and pushes the key of the study to her under the door, allowing Emma to escape. Steed then jabs the dozing Henrick with a pen-point, and Emma knocks him out. She also manages to throw Karl when he is harpooned by Steed with the same pen. Meanwhile, Rushton has burned his papers on the reducing machine, and he and Susan are forced by Chivers to take the truck out of the testing area. At the house, Emma notices the arrival of the truck as it enters Shaffer's grounds. Shaffer demands a de-

Shhh! A miniaturised Emma warns an equally diminutive Steed to keep quiet in Mission... Highly Improbable.

monstration of the machine, and they select a nearby pavilion to be reduced. When Emma overhears them saying they will bring it back to its normal size, she decides to put Steed inside it. This she does, but is seen, and Chivers reduces Emma herself. Chivers now collects Emma in the butterfly net, and pulls a gun on Steed. He tells Josef to take Steed back to the house while he brings Mrs Peel. But Emma makes Chivers slip on a loose stone and he falls dead, face down into an ornamental pool. Emma now makes her way to the house, where Susan, Rushton and Steed are tied up on the floor. She frees Steed's hands, and he hits Henrick. Rushton, freed by Steed, then restores Emma to normal size. They then turn the reducing ray on the truck, in which Shaffer and Josef are trying to escape, and Steed is able to trap them in his bowler. However, Steed has one problem. He is left with a tiny umbrella with no machine to restore it to its proper size!

THE
FORGET-ME-KNOT

The Forget-Me-Knot *was the only one of the 161 episodes of* The Avengers *to be bridged. For this reason, the episode has been given this spread to itself, and is divided into two halves. The main part of the story falls on this page, and the tag scene is on the opposite page.*

'Hallo, my name's Tara.' Agent 69 peers round Steed's French windows and introduces herself.

By Brian Clemens

John Steed	**Patrick Macnee**
Emma Peel	**Diana Rigg**
Tara King	**Linda Thorson**
Sean Mortimer	**Patrick Kavanagh**
George Burton	**Jeremy Young**
Mother	**Patrick Newell**
Karl	**Alan Lake**

Designed by Robert Jones
Directed by James Hill
Produced by Albert Fennell and Brian Clemens

SEAN MORTIMER, a fellow agent of Steed's who has been missing for two weeks, staggers into the forecourt below Steed's flat. Emma Peel, sitting by the window, spots him as he wanders around aimlessly in the street below. She mentions 'a tall, well-built man, wearing an overcoat' to Steed who, seeing Mortimer wandering below, rushes outside and brings the agent back to his flat. It soon becomes apparent that Mortimer is suffering from loss of memory – he does not even recognise Steed. After continual questioning by Steed, Mortimer manages to gasp 'The organisation – a traitor in the organisation'. Worried, Steed leaves to contact Mother, his superior at Headquarters – a large mansion set in spacious grounds. While he is wandering through the garden, he is attacked and knocked down by a trainee agent, 69, who is undergoing a training session at the house. Her tutor, a military man called George Burton, apologises profusely, saying she has mistaken Steed for someone else. Meanwhile, Karl and Brad, two thugs who have trailed Mortimer to Steed's flat, attack Emma and Mortimer. They fire a memory-killing dart at Emma and leave her unconscious, then carry Mortimer's body to the sidecar of their waiting motorcycle. Back at Headquarters, Steed, waiting for Mother to arrive, is somewhat surprised to see a tall, well-built, auburn-haired girl in a mini-suit enter the room through the French windows. She introduces herself as Tara, and seems surprised when Steed doesn't add a 'Ra-boom-di-ay' to her name. Steed then realises that she is the same trainee agent 69 who had earlier knocked him down. She goes on to inform Steed that she recognises him, and that his name crops up everywhere in training. She gives him her address and telephone number on a piece of paper, which he stores in his shoe. Their conversation is interrupted by the arrival of Filson, another agent, who then directs Steed into Mother's office. Mother suggests that Steed returns to his apartment and brings back Mortimer who, because he has been missing for more than two weeks, is now on Mother's wanted list. When Steed arrives, he finds that Emma has no recollection of ever having met Mortimer. Disturbed by her condition, Steed decides to take her back to Headquarters. On the way they are waylaid by Karl and Brad, who ambush Steed's car and kidnap Emma. Steed is left lying in a ditch, with several memory-killing darts in him. Before he passes out, he overhears one of the thugs mention The Heights, a familiar place to Steed. Having lost his memory, Steed wakes up in hospital, but some sense of urgency makes him break out of the place and, finding Tara's address in his shoe, he drives to her flat. She helps to restore his memory by giving him the address of his own flat. Steed, now fully recovered, heads for Mother's headquarters, and arrives to find that his name has been added to Mother's wanted list. He also finds George Burton, the man in charge of Tara's training, waiting with a gun! Steed manages to persuade him to drive him to The Heights, where he expects to find the hideout of Karl, Brad and the rest of the opposition. Arriving at The Heights, Burton pulls a gun on Steed and reveals that he is the traitor in Mother's section. The quick-thinking Steed manages to overcome him, however, and with the help of Emma and Sean Mortimer – who have been battling the villains inside the hideout – and Tara King, who has by this time found her way to the showdown, they round up the thugs in a fast and furious finale of flying fists and karate kicks.

Top: Trainee agent 69, soon to be better known as Tara King, finds her instructor in the training grounds.

Above: Cornered, Emma Peel uses a dart gun in self-defence in a scene from The Forget-Me-Knot.

THE newspaper headline reads 'Peter Peel Alive. Air ace found in Amazonian jungle ... Wife Emma waits.' Steed is on the telephone, saying he has seen the newspapers and will need a replacement as soon as possible. Sadness lines his face. The door to his apartment is suddenly flung open by an excited Mrs Peel, resplendent in a yellow trouser suit. They discuss the newspaper story, and Emma says that her husband will be arriving in the mews in a few minutes. Emma crosses to Steed and places her hand on his chest. Memories of past adventures fill her mind and with a half-smile she says 'Always keep your bowler on in times of stress – and a watchful eye open for diabolical masterminds!' She leans towards him and kisses his cheek, then silently turns and heads for the door. Steed gazes at the retreating figure. 'Emma!' he softly calls. A quizzical look crosses her face as she realises that he has used her first name. 'Thanks!' Mrs Peel looks sadly at him, gives one last smile, and leaves. On the staircase outside Steed's apartment she notices Tara King coming through the front entrance. Tara spots Emma and asks, 'Excuse me, Apartment 3?'. With a coy smile, Mrs Peel points upwards. 'At the top of the stairs,' she answers. 'Thanks,' says Tara, as the two pass each other. Mrs Peel pauses and looks back at her. 'Ahem,' she calls. 'He likes his tea stirred anti-clockwise.' With her index finger she mimes a stirring motion. Tara, looking confused, mimics the stirring motion. 'Yes,' says Emma, nodding. Steed, upstairs, is gazing sadly out of his window. In the mews, he sees Mrs Peel cross to a waiting car, beside which stands – *Steed*? Bowler-hatted, impeccably dressed. Steed stares in amazement at the resemblance. He watches Mrs Peel climb into the car. She looks lovingly at her husband then, with one final look in Steed's direction, the couple drive away. Steed's thoughts are broken when Tara walks in. 'Mother sent me,' she begins. 'Tara –.' 'Ra-boom-di-ay,' smiles Steed.

'Always keep your bowler on in times of stress – and a watchful eye open for diabolical masterminds!'

A shot from the tag scene, where Emma hands over responsibility for taking care of Steed to Tara.

As well as Steed's regular colleagues in The Avengers, *there were other women who appeared in the various series and helped him.*

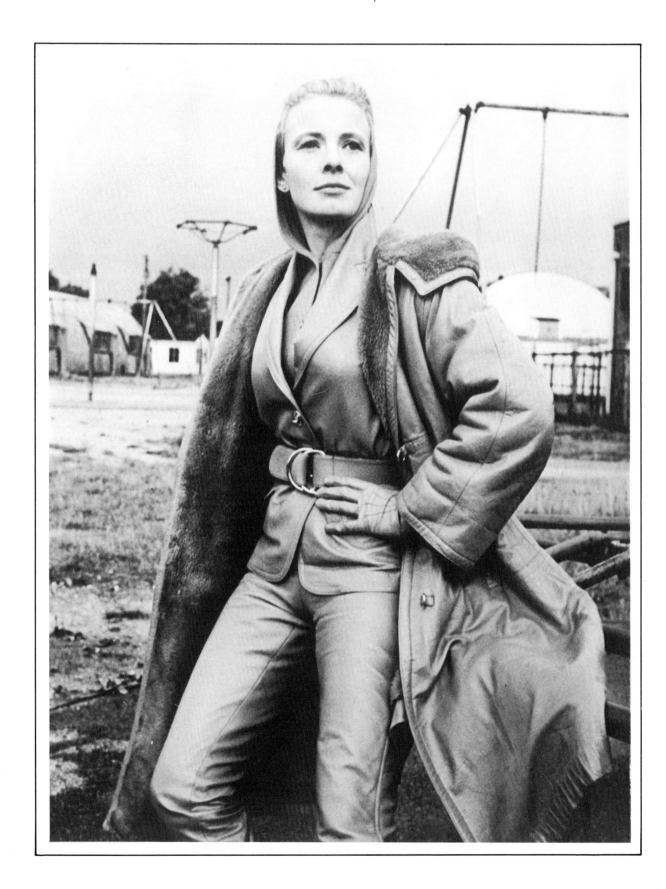

Left: Elizabeth Shepherd was to play the part of Mrs Peel, but the producers then changed their minds.

Top left: Venus Smith helped Steed in the second series of The Avengers. She is shown here in a scene from School For Traitors.

Left: Ingrid Hafner played the part of Carol, Dr David Keel's receptionist, in the first series of The Avengers.

Above: In the sixth series, the part of Rhonda, Mother's assistant, was played by Rhonda Parker, who was 6 ft tall.

Right: Jennifer Croxton, as Lady Diana Forbes-Blakeney, helped Steed to solve the case of Killer. It was her only appearance.

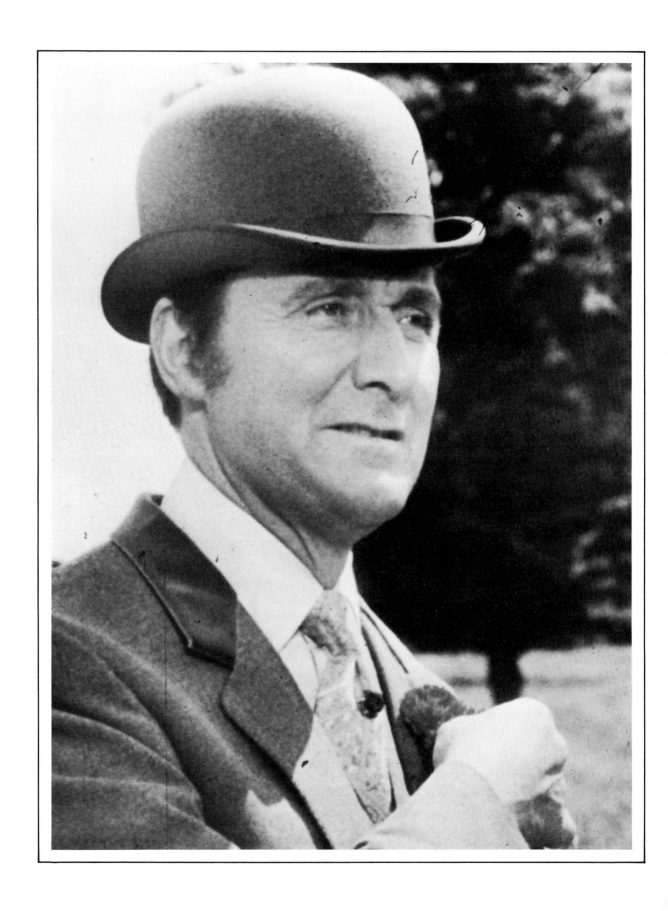

Patrick Macnee/Linda Thorson
1969

'Tara, Ra-boom-di-ay'

The colour series proved to be a big money earner worldwide. Foreign sales were in excess of £5,000,000 and the show was being screened in over 70 countries. In May 1967, Diana Rigg was nominated for an American Emmy (television's equivalent of the Oscar) – it was eventually won by Barbara Bain of *Mission Impossible* – and voted Actress of the Year by the 16 European countries screening *The Avengers*.

The success of the show had led to discussions about making a feature-length film of *The Avengers*. Sadly, though, it never materialised.

After filming on the colour series was completed, Diana Rigg left the show. In a later interview she said, 'Television is so immediate. Within a week of appearing in my first Avengers story I was recognised by 90 per cent of the viewing public. A week after I'd left, I was unrecognised by 90 per cent of the public.'

After screening the colour series, the ITV network repeated the 26 Rigg black and white episodes. (It's ironic, but until Channel 4 began to re-run them at the end of 1982, British viewers had only seen the Rigg colour episodes once in colour. That was in 1970, only a few months after the introduction of colour, when very few people had colour sets.)

Contrary to popular belief that the American influence on the show was becoming more pronounced, I have been reliably informed that the American Broadcasting Company never tried to dictate the show's format.

However, as they had contracted in advance of production to take the next series, they obviously had an interest in what they would be getting, and (as with Hollywood productions), they would ask to see scripts and occasionally express some views on minor points – just as their British counterparts (ABC and later, Thames) would do in England. They even sent a man to London to work closely with the production team.

But everyone associated with the show in England (fully aware of the financial importance of the American purchase and the significance of selling the series to America) was always willing to listen to what the Americans had to say.

It was at this time that ABC (having become Thames Television) felt that, though the show had been highly successful and had style, it was becoming more extreme.

They felt that a move backwards to reality would help to prolong the show's success, and as this would have to be achieved mainly in the writing, John Bryce (formerly story editor and then producer of the Blackman series) was appointed producer of the new series, and Brian Clemens and Albert Fennell left the production team.

Unfortunately, for a number of reasons, this arrangement did not work out and, as ABC were committed to deliver the series for American and British telecast dates, Clemens and Fennell were asked to return as joint producers, with almost total control.

One thing they had no control over, however, was the choice of Steed's new Avenger girl. During their absence, Linda Thorson had been signed to play Tara King.

Neither Clemens nor Fennell believed that Linda was the right choice. As Clemens said later, 'She was fresh out of drama school, and didn't have the necessary experience to handle a star role in a major series. But the shows had been pre-sold to the American market, and there was no time to recast the part.'

Tara King (the name Tara was Linda Thorson's own choice) was the daughter of a prosperous farmer, and had all the skills associated with the outdoor life. At her expensive finishing school, she had learned how to glide, ski and fly, and had acquired the sophistication of the young international set. She was a warm, feminine and sexy woman, with an exuberant and jaunty approach to her adventures with Steed.

There was a bond between the two principals not in evidence previously. Whereas the hallmark of Steed's relationships, both with Cathy and Emma, was haughty, well-hidden respect, the bond of friendship with Tara was frequently sealed with a kiss and a cuddle.

Unlike Steed's earlier partners, Tara was single.

'It was my idea,' said Linda at the time, 'to make Tara single. Steed's other aides had been married. They suggested it might seem immoral for a single girl to be shown having breakfast with a man in his flat. I told them it seemed far more immoral for a married woman to be doing that with another man.

'Before this series, you never really saw a girl making much of a fuss of Steed. But in this series, I kiss him now and again, and look at him devotedly. We took the sex relationship for granted. By the mid-1960s the Pill was part of life, so we took it for granted that Tara, and Emma before her, slept with Steed, but simply didn't dwell on it.'

There was to be no new fighting technique for Tara. No judo, karate or kung fu. Instead, she would rely more on feminine guile than muscular skill. Tara would hit her opponents with a straight right-hander, her handbag, or whatever was at hand that might be used as a weapon. She would even give the occasional scream for help!

Ray Austin, stunt arranger on the two previous Diana Rigg

series, had left the show to work on ITC's *The Champions,* and Joe Dunne, who had worked as *The Avengers* fight co-ordinator with Austin on the previous series, took over the role of guiding Linda Thorson through the rough stuff she would encounter during the stories.

Two men were responsible for designing Linda Thorson's Avenger outfits: Harvey Gould and Alan Hughes.

Harvey Gould was a successful coat and suit designer. In fact, he was so successful that he only had time to create the clothes for the first six stories, making a total of about 30-40 garments. He said 'I thoroughly enjoyed working on *The Avengers,* but it was very time-consuming, and I just had too much to do. Linda is exactly the sort of girl I've had in mind for my ready-to-wear designs – curvy, pretty and feminine. The clothes for the series are designed to bring out her tremendous sex-appeal. There are lots of cut-out backs, plunging necklines, and billowing sleeves. Obviously they have to be very practical, too, but Tara doesn't go in so much for the karate bit. She tends to hit people with her handbag rather than tying them in knots.'

Clothes for the remaining 27 stories were created by Alan Hughes, the man who had designed Diana Rigg's second screen wardrobe. When asked what special considerations there were when designing clothes for a series like *The Avengers,* Hughes replied 'The key word is movement. It's basically an active series, so the clothes have to be active, too. Yet for this particular heroine, Tara King, with her essentially feminine character, the clothes must not be harsh. I think a good example of the combination of action with femininity comes in my design for the brown gabardine pancho-culotte outfit.

'Of course, the series is shot in colour, so I must think in terms of this at all times. Not just the avoidance of horrible clashes with such flamboyant sets as Tara's flat, but also in the manner in which colour is transmitted to the television set. I have to know how each colour actually comes over on the screen. And sometimes colours can appear differently during interior scenes shot under strong studio lighting than in scenes set outdoors.'

It wasn't only Tara's coats and dresses that Hughes designed. His job was a full-time one, designing hats, scarves, gloves, handbags, shoes – even stockings.

'I must create an outfit as a whole,' he said. 'Not a hodge-podge of separate units. Every single colour and shade has to blend perfectly.'

The designs included a brown double gabardine waistcoat and culotte set with striped brown skirt and brown silk cravat; a red hussar maxi-coat with silk square, and accessories, including bronze gloves and matching knee-length boots; a Levi-style fighting suit in pale mustard, with white shirt, cravat and beret; a maroon wool coat with black hat and boots; and a purple satin dressing-gown trimmed with pale blue ostrich feathers.

In a later interview, Linda Thorson said 'During the shooting of the show, I was 10½ stone and had problems. I was too fat for karate, too breathless for the fight scenes, and too busty for the love bits. They had to pour my 39-inch bosom into 36-inch sweaters so that Patrick Macnee could get near me.'

During the summer break, Patrick Macnee gave a press interview in which he said 'I thought of leaving after Diana went, but as I've always believed that once you start something, you should see it through to the end, I stayed. I was feeling pretty jaded and beginning to look like Methuselah. I had a double-chin and' (indicating his waistline) 'my stomach was out here. Well, I ask you, how could I carry on with the show looking like that? I cut down on smoking and visited my doctor, who gave me some pills to help me cut down on food, and now I'm down from 14 stone to 12.'

The weight loss meant that all Patrick's Avenger suits had to be taken in at the seams to suit his sprightly figure.

Macnee's weight problem was not shared by the second newcomer to the show, Patrick Newell. His vital statistics were 50-50-50. Newell had been signed to play Mother, John Steed's superior.

The introduction of Mother to the series was almost by accident. In January, producer Brian Clemens asked Patrick Newell to play John Steed's chief as a small cameo part, in the episode *The Forget-Me-Knot.*

The first episode of the Thorson series was shown in America on 20 March 1969, and the character of Mother was so successful that ABC telephoned Clemens the next day and demanded that Newell be put under contract.

Mother was crippled when he was blown up in the prime of his Secret Service career. Unable to walk without the aid of special straps and ladders suspended from the ceiling, and in constant pain from his injuries, he was not the kindest man to work for. He often carried a stick, which he used as much to strike his colleagues as to support himself.

Mother was forever turning up in the strangest of places. In one story, *False Witness,* Steed boards a London bus and finds the upper level has been transformed into Mother's office. In another, he comes across the huge man and his telephones in the middle of a field of buttercups, and in a later story, Mother and his office equipment are floating in the middle of a swimming pool!

Patrick Newell was quoted as saying 'It is probably the best break of my career. Although it's not much fun having everyone call me "Mother", the part is so good that it is worth it. Like Steed, Mother is terribly British. He spends most of his time drinking champagne out of silver tankards and saying things like

"Good show, old boy". In addition, he is irascible, ruthless and has a dislike bordering on hatred for organisations like MI12 and MI15. He's a real character – the best I've ever played.'

Another semi-regular character (she didn't arrive until a third of the way through the series) was Rhonda, Mother's statuesque assistant. Her role also came about by accident.

Twenty-one-year old Rhonda Parker, a 6ft tall Amazon with a 39-25-37 figure, was booked as an extra. Her role called for her to walk onto the set in the scene where Steed finds his chief sitting in the swimming pool.

The scene was set up, and Rhonda (wearing a white swimsuit) walked onto the set. As she arrived, Patrick Macnee and Patrick Newell stopped what they were doing and just gaped at her.

Rhonda was hired on the spot to play the part of Mother's regular assistant for the rest of the series. No fashion problems for her, though, as she was mostly seen wearing white boxing shorts or tight-fitting sweaters!

One other member of the Secret Service department that Steed worked for was introduced in the episode *Stay Tuned*. This was Father. (Well, *someone* has got to look after the department during Mother's absence.)

Father was a middle-aged, blind colleague of Mother's. She was more gentle than her opposite number, but just as perceptive – she only had to feel the lapel of Steed's jacket to know he was still using the same tailor. Father appeared only once, and was played by Iris Russell.

Steed's address in this series remained the same but, with the arrival of Tara, the production team really went to town on her flat.

Set designer Kenneth Tait gave her a brand-new apartment. The flat, 9 Primrose Crescent, was a mixture of modern and antique design.

It contained two primitive paintings, two pendant Chinese lanterns and a collection of shop signs: spectacles from an optician's; a giant boot from a shoemaker's; a padlock from a locksmith's (that hid a spy-hole in her front door); a bearded bust of a Turk from a snuff and tobacco shop; a wooden horse's head, from a French meat shop; plus two giant gold-plated letters, TK on one wall, and NO on another.

A fireman's pole meant she could get from her upper landing to the ground floor at top speed.

The rooms were furnished with shocking-pink carpets; blue grey, mauve and Imperial Chinese yellow panels; a couch in orange, green and yellow, with curtains to match; and scatter cushions in a mass of colours. There were a dozen period telephones – through which Tara had to search when one of them rang. A wooden postbox was converted into a drinks cabinet. There was even a glass-panelled door with a stained-glass bird in it from an old pub.

Terry Nation, creator of the Daleks for the popular *Doctor Who* series, joined the writing team and was later to become script supervisor.

A man who had contributed to every major filmed television series in the country, Terry Nation said of the programme, 'Although an *Avengers* script is such a distinctive thing, it still covers a wide range of stories, from the straightforward detection tale by way of the horror variety, to the most zany comedy thriller. Yet at the end of the day, the programme takes itself very seriously. Our villains and heroes are never sent up, and remain serious.'

Once again, the title theme music was revamped. It now started with a frenetic staccato drumbeat and progressed to a more exuberant version of the familiar *Avengers* theme. Laurie Johnson explained the need for the change.

'We thought the new series ought to reflect the times we live in a bit more. So we generally jazzed it up, adding the sound of gunfire and a lot more percussion and brass. When Tara King came into the series I decided to superimpose a counter melody over the existing title music at the point at which the face of the new character appeared on the main titles. This counter melody I then used and developed in the incidental score where appropriate.

'Unlike many television series, *The Avengers* does not contain the same music throughout. In fact it is doubtful that anyone has even noticed the music that accents the action. If it has been noticed, then I haven't done my job well. Good scoring should be unobtrusive.'

One other change in format was the addition of the tag scene – the closing minutes of each episode, in which Steed and Tara were seen in a short, self-contained scene. The idea for this (and the tinkling piano accompaniment) was apparently suggested by executive producer, Gordon L T Scott.

The producers asked Diana Rigg to appear in the first Thorson story, and after spending a week vetting the script, Diana consented to film a brief appearance in *The Forget-Me-Knot*, in which she would tender her resignation and hand over the role to Linda. The cross-over scene was restricted to a 30-second encounter on the staircase leading to Steed's flat, making this the *only* bridged series.

Shooting began on the series at Elstree Studios during the summer of 1968.

GAME

By Richard Harris

John Steed	Patrick Macnee
Tara King	Linda Thorson
Bristow	Peter Jeffrey
Manservant	Garfield Morgan
Professor Witney	Aubrey Richards
Brig Wishforth-Browne	Anthony Newlands
Averman	Alex Scott
Dexter	Geoffrey Russell
Student	Achilles Georgiou
Manager	Desmond Walter-Ellis

Designed by Robert Jones
Directed by Robert Fuest
Produced by Albert Fennell and Brian Clemens

Steed and Tara discover Dexter's dead body. He is clutching pieces of a jigsaw which are part of a deadly Game.

Mother sits by a swimming pool, surrounded by telephones. He has the knack of turning up in the most unlikely places.

IN the home of a man called Bristow, a strange game of snakes and ladders is in progress. Bristow throws a six, moves his marker, and then we see Dexter, the victim of the deadly game. He climbs a ladder to a trap door marked 'Reward', opens it, and is bitten by a snake. He falls to the floor, dead. Bristow's man-servant idly watches, then calmly serves tea. Later, Steed discovers Dexter's body on a children's roundabout. He tells Tara he is an old army comrade. Strangely, the dead man is clutching a handful of jigsaw pieces. Steed explains to Tara that it is the second death of this type in recent weeks. Another of his army colleagues, racing driver 'Cootie' Williams, was found in identical circumstances the week before. Tara takes the jigsaw pieces to a games shop but the manager is unable to help. She doesn't see Bristow's man-servant in the shop, keeping an eye on her. The next victim is the financier Henry Averman, who is chloroformed in his flat and taken to Bristow's home. Averman is forced to play a mad game of 'Stock Market', which he loses. He then dies when Bristow won't let him take his heart pills. The financier also ends up on the roundabout, jigsaw pieces in hand. Adding the latest pieces to her puzzle, Tara has now assembled the picture of a house. It seems as though the killer is giving them a clue, and playing a kind of game. Steed recalls another army friend, Brigadier Wishforth-Browne, and visits him. But he can't think of anyone who served with them and now bears a grudge. Wishforth-Browne is the next participant in Bristow's deadly game, and is invited to Bristow's house for dinner. Now, for the first time, we see Bristow's face, which has had plastic surgery. He makes Wishforth-Browne play a game of toy soldiers, at which he does very well — until Bristow shoots him with a toy cannon. When Steed and Tara keep a dawn appointment with the Brigadier on a military parade ground, they are startled to see Wishforth-Browne's body advancing towards them, propped upright in a field car. Steed now realises that the four dead men were all part of a tribunal which court-martialled one Sergeant Daniel Edmund in 1946, for black market activities in Germany. Edmund was believed killed while trying to escape from detention. Ex-Major Witney is the fifth member of the tribunal, but Steed and Tara are unable to contact him. He is already in the clutches of Bristow, who devises a word game for him, which he fails to solve. Witney, like the others, ends up in the children's playground. Steed now realises that he was the sixth, and last, member of the tribunal. Bristow now sends his man-servant, to kidnap Tara. She is abducted after being chloroformed in her flat. Steed later discovers the signs of the fight and pursues his enquiries with more urgency. The manager of the games shop is now able to identify Tara's completed jigsaw puzzle as being a picture of the home of games king Bristow, a leading jigsaw manufacturer. Steed goes to Bristow's home, and is astonished to find that he is expected. Bristow has actually been playing a macabre game with Steed, of which the deaths and jigsaw pieces were a part. He now sets Steed his game, which he calls 'Super Agent'. Steed is given only six minutes to beat a number of obstacles and save Tara, who is now a captive in a giant hour-glass. She will suffocate unless he completes the course. He first defeats a Japanese wrestler, then opens a safe in 60 seconds. He then gets safely out of a six-sided room — five of the doors are booby trapped — and then negotiates a tunnel in which a steel blade slices through his bowler. He is rewarded with a gun and six cartridges, only one of which is live. He then has to take on six assailants. Steed quickly solves the problem of finding the live bullet by repeatedly firing at Tara's hour-glass. She is then free to help him defeat his adversaries. Armed with his half-bowler, Steed prevents Bristow's next obstacle, which is a razor-edged card. Steed deflects it with the steel-lined bowler brim back at Bristow, who is killed. Tara, meanwhile, takes care of the manservant. In the last scene, Steed stacks the odds against Tara in a dice game he has invented, called 'Steedopoly'.

THE SUPER-SECRET CYPHER SNATCH
Whatever Happened To Yesterday?

By Tony Williamson

John Steed	Patrick Macnee
Tara King	Linda Thorson
Peters	John Carlisle
Maskin	Simon Oates
First Guard	Alec Ross
Jarret	Clifford Earl
Vickers	Donald Gee
Ferret	Ivor Dean
Betty	Anne Rutter
Myra	Angela Scoular
Second Guard	Lionel Wheeler
Davis	Anthony Blackshaw
Lather	Nicholas Smith
Webster	Allan Cuthbertson

Designed by Robert Jones
Directed by John Hough
Produced by Albert Fennell and Brian Clemens

JARRET, an agent, runs for his life from the Cypher headquarters building, pursued by an armed man dressed in white overalls, gas mask and bowler. Other men in overalls block Jarret's way as he desperately tries to escape, but finally he is gunned down. The guards at the establishment pay no heed to what has happened and Jarret's body is bundled into a van bearing the sign Classy Glass Cleaners and driven away. Mother tells Steed that MI12 have lost Jarret, and their department has been asked to find him. Steed's enquiries begin with Webster, the director of the Cypher HQ, whom we have seen briefly in the opening scene, witnessing Jarret's death. But when Steed shows him a photograph of Jarret, Webster denies all knowledge of him. Tara is sent to Jarret's flat with Ferret of MI12, and they find the agent's body lying in a window seat. They also find, hidden in a pen, a rolled-up page torn from a calendar, bearing the date of Jarret's death. As they search the flat, they fail to notice Maskin, dressed as a window cleaner, watching them from across the street. Meanwhile, Webster continues to deny that Jarret was ever at his establishment, and Steed, suspecting he is lying, picks up Jarret's lighter-cum-camera from a desk. Steed, together with photographer Peters, joins Tara and Ferret at Jarret's flat. Peters says he will develop the apparently ordinary pictures the agent took of the Cypher establishment. When he is in his darkroom, Maskin, the window cleaner, shoots him from outside the window. Steed and Tara are quickly on the scene. They find the charred remains of the

photographs, but Steed has the negatives from which to prepare more prints. From these they see the Classy Glass Cleaning van, which they immediately connect with Peters' murder – the assassin must have used a ladder. Ferret decides that after the murders they must have someone inside the Cypher building and Tara is nominated. Steed, meanwhile, visits the Classy Glass Cleaners. Charles Lather, in charge of Classy Glass, tells Steed that his firm has not visited the Cypher establishment for months. They used to have the concession, but gave it up as uneconomical. When Steed leaves, he is followed by Maskin, in one of the firm's vans. Maskin uses a ladder to smash Steed's windscreen and the car is driven off the road. Steed, however, escapes uninjured and when he regains consciousness, he tells Mother to send Ferret to help Tara, whom he now believes is in danger. At the Cypher building, Webster sends Tara to fetch the 'Q' Cypher file. As she finds it Tara is alarmed to see a Classy Glass Van pull up outside. When Ferret arrives, he is amazed to see there are no guards at the gate. Driving to the main entrance, he is attacked by one of the Classy Glass men, and suffocated with a cleaning leather. Tara, watching from the window, can see the body of Ferret, but she just stares blankly. In the next scene, the Cypher establishment is back to normal. Ferret's body has been removed and the guards are working normally. Tara, however, is puzzled that she forgot to fetch the file for Webster. When Steed arrives, she is sure that Ferret has not been there. In fact, she feels that the day did not happen at all. Together they visit the Classy Glass Cleaning yard, where they discover Ferret's body. They also see Jarvis and Vickers, two of the staff, as they take the body away in a van and dump it at Ferret's home. Next day, Tara returns to Cypher, keeping in touch with Steed by walkie-talkie. Later, Steed discovers something strange in one of the photographs taken by Jarret. Meanwhile, Vickers and Jarvis are leading another raid on Cypher. They cut the telephone lines, and knock out the guards with vapour sprays they carry with them. They also introduce the knock-out vapour into the ventilation shafts of the building, and a voice – on a dictaphone – tells the staff it is a perfectly normal working day, while the raiders photograph all the documents in sight. From the picture of Myra, taken by Jarret, Steed notices that the girl is holding a match which is burning down to her fin-

Tara King and Steed play chess, while wondering what the next move will be in **The Super-Secret Cypher Snatch.**

gers. Puzzled, Steed goes to Classy Glass, and bursts in on Jarvis and Vickers at their work. Tara eventually joins him in a hectic fight, at the end of which Steed meets Lather, the boss of Classy Glass, at gunpoint in Webster's office. Tara saves him by impaling Lather to the wall with a ladder. Later on, Steed decides to try his hypnotic powers on Tara, but sends himself to sleep instead. Tara orders her hypnotised partner to take her for an expensive dinner.

YOU'LL CATCH YOUR DEATH
Atishoo, Atishoo, All Fall Down

By Jeremy Burnham

John Steed	Patrick Macnee
Tara King	Linda Thorson
Colonel Timothy	Ronald Culver
Butler	Valentine Dyall
Glover	Fulton Mackay
Matron	Sylvia Kay
Mother	Patrick Newell
Dexter	Dudley Sutton
Preece	Peter Bourne
Dr Fawcett	Charles Lloyd Pack
Maidwell	Henry McGee
Camrose	Hamilton Dyce
Farrar	Bruno Barnabe
Janice	Fiona Hartford
Seaton	Geoffrey Chater
Georgina	Jennifer Clulow
Melanie	Emma Cochrane
Padley	Willoughby Gray
Herrick	Andrew Laurence
Postman	Douglas Blackwell

Produced by Albert Fennell and Brian Clemens
Directed by Paul Dickson

RALPH Camrose, FRCS, is attending to a patient when Preece arrives, travelling in a Rolls-Royce but dressed as a postman, to deliver a letter. As the patient leaves, Janice, the receptionist, gives Camrose the envelope. It is empty, but makes Camrose sneeze violently and he finally chokes to death. Receiving the news of Camrose's demise, Mother tells Steed and Tara of the deaths of other ear, nose and throat specialists, and asks them to investigate. Steed visits the scene of the crime, while Tara is sent to see Padley, an ENT man who is a friend of Steed's. Steed finds the empty envelope and wonders why it contained no letter. At Padley's, Preece, the fake postman, delivers another apparently empty envelope, which sets Padley sneezing, and he soon chokes to death. Tara, sitting in the waiting room, is powerless to prevent his death. Steed finds out from the envelope manufacturers, Maidwell and Pugh, that the envelopes left with Camrose and Padley are of their cream-wove bond, and that a nursing academy recently bought 10,000 in a single order. Tara visits Seaton, another ENT man, but he is unable to explain his colleague's deaths and soon, he too, encounters one of Preece's envelopes. This time, however, Tara spots the Rolls departing and gives chase, but she loses the car in a country lane. Dexter, the driver of the Rolls, and Preece, decide to follow Tara back to Steed's flat, where they chloroform her with a perfume spray. Steed, posing as a moneyed philanthropist, visits

the Anastasia Nursing Academy, which bought the envelopes. He learns from the Matron that the academy send out about 50 letters a week. Arriving back at his flat, Steed finds Dr Fawcett, of the Institute of Allergic Diseases, waiting for him. Fawcett explains that Tara made an appointment to talk to him about the deaths of Padley and Seaton. They find the empty perfume spray, suggesting what has happened to Tara. Steed returns to the nursing academy and discovers a suspicious letter from Colonel Timothy of Walsingham House. Steed also sees a room full of girls busily typing addresses on envelopes. He pays Colonel Timothy a visit, and finds that he runs a private clinic with an assistant, Dr Glover. Steed tells them he is looking for advice for the Steed Foundation, which is considering endowing the Anastasia Academy with funds. Timothy says to have nothing to do with them, although Steed notices there are Anastasia nurses working in Timothy's cold-cure clinic. Steed is concerned when Timothy admits he has written to Padley and Seaton for their co-operation on cold-cure research, without success. And he leaves quickly when he discovers a notice on Timothy's desk to contact Herrick, another ENT man at Padley and Seaton's consulting rooms. Unknown to Steed, Tara is now confined in the cold-cure clinic. Preece and Dexter are already on their way to kill Herrick, who is in his car, and sneezes himself off the road to his death. One of the envelopes is now posted to Steed. However, Steed opens it wearing a face-mask as a precaution. Dr Fawcett examines the envelope and explains that the tiny quantity of powder in the envelopes is concentrated cold virus, sufficient to kill anyone exposed to it. He also tells Steed that all the dead ENT men had been working on an anti-allergy drug, which would make them the rivals of anyone able to produce the powder. Meanwhile, Tara explodes her way out of her deep-frozen prison and into a tunnel, which leads to the main area of the clinic, dominated by a huge replica of a nose. Tara is listening to Matron, Preece and Dexter inside the nose when she sneezes and gives herself away. She is recaptured and told by the gang that they intended to use her as a guinea pig in one last, dangerous, experiment. That night, Steed is also captured by Colonel Timothy and his butler, when he makes a second visit to Walsingham House. Although Steed is held at gunpoint by the Colonel and his butler he soon discovers that the Colonel is not

It could be said that Steed has a nose for trouble. It certainly stands him in good stead in You'll Catch Your Death.

responsible for the lethal envelopes. This is confirmed when the Colonel himself receives one of them. He does not open it, however, because of what Steed has told him. Steed now enlists the aid of the Colonel and his butler in finding the real culprits. At this moment, Tara is being prepared for a test of Dr Glover's new lethal serum, capable, she is told, of killing millions. Glover means to gain power by selling to the highest bidder. Steed and the Colonel arrive in time to free the distraught Tara, but Glover escapes down the tunnel behind the huge nose to the deep-freeze room. He is about to throw the deadly phial of virus at Steed, when Steed forestalls him by throwing the deadly envelope of powder sent to the Colonel. It hits Glover in the face, and he immediately begins to sneeze and then chokes to death, falling out of the nose. Tara catches a terrible cold, but Steed preens himself on not having one. He does, however, suddenly develop one, and ends up producing a foot-bath just like Tara's.

SPLIT

By Brian Clemens

John Steed	Patrick Macnee
Tara King	Linda Thorson
Lord Barnes	Nigel Davenport
Peter Rooke	Julian Glover
Dr Constantine	Bernard Archard
Himel	John G Heller
Petra	Jayne Sofiano
Kartovski	Steven Scott
Frank Compton	Iain Anders
Swindin	Christopher Benjamin
The Butler	John Kidd

Directed by Roy Baker
Produced by Albert Fennell and Brian Clemens

THE stringent security of the Ministry of Top-Secret Information is badly shaken when agent Frank Compton is suddenly murdered in the executive rest area of the Ministry's rural retreat. It seems impossible that anyone could have penetrated the security screens, and in fact the murderer is agent Harry Mercer, who also works at the establishment. He shoots Compton after a voice on the telephone asks for someone called Boris – an enquiry which causes a sudden change in Mercer's personality. The handwriting on his report changes suddenly to an extrovert scrawl, his hand gnarls and his left shoulder slopes. But after the murder he appears to resume his own personality, and he himself raises the alarm, as if he has really forgotten what he has just done. When Steed and Tara arrive at the Ministry, they are joined by Lord Barnes at the scene of the crime. Tara picks up the report that Mercer was writing, and notices the sudden scrawl. Steed takes another call for Boris and Mercer reacts as before. Steed notices the gnarling of the hand, but Mercer explains it away as the result of an accident during the Berlin episode of 1963. This gives him away, as Steed knows full well that Mercer was not involved in this. Steed and Tara consult a graphologist called Swindin, who tells them that Mercer's report indicates two distinct personalities at work; one is a brutal, hard-living extrovert, and the other a reliable agent. The former sounds to Steed like a man who *was* involved in the Berlin episode of 1963, an enemy agent called Boris Kartovski. Steed asks Colonel Rooke, in charge of security at the Ministry, to find him a sample of Kartovski's handwriting. Mercer, overhearing Rooke mentioning Boris' name again, immediately begins his personality change, and when Rooke leaves the room, Mercer is so much invaded by the

other personality that he even does a wild Cossack dance. Mercer now telephones Dr Constantine at Nullington Hospital, asking for help. Dr Constantine and his colleague, Himel, confer, and agree that their experiment has gone wrong. They decide that they will now have to use another subject, and they ring Lord Barnes, asking if Boris is there. The same personality split begins to affect Barnes. In this condition, Lord Barnes goes to the Ministry and shoots Mercer. The only clue is that Mercer has left a note reading 'Help Me', with the 'Me' in the extrovert scrawl. Steed also discovers that Mercer was recently admitted to Nullington Private Hospital. Steed visits Nullington, and Dr Constantine tells him that Mercer was a routine minor accident case. Steed then discovers a link with Lord Barnes, who had also been admitted to Nullington recently. He visits Barnes, who is still in the other personality, and he attacks Steed with a knife. Steed escapes death, but he has not seen the face of his attacker, who quickly leaves the room. Moments later, Lord Barnes rushed in and he, like Mercer, seems to have forgotten what he has done, and has reverted to his normal personality. Tara discovers from Swindin that the 'Me' section of the note is similar to Kartovski's handwriting, given to Steed by Rooke. It is also like a specimen of Lord Barnes' writing stolen by Rooke during his investigations. Tara and Rooke are now convinced that Barnes is involved, and therefore Steed is in danger, because he is on the way to see Barnes, who has called him for help. Torn by his personality split, Barnes handcuffs himself to an object in his room, but even this does not prevent him eventually leaving to visit the hospital. Once there, however, he reverts once again, and returns home. By this time, Rooke and Tara have got there, and before Steed can intervene, Rooke shoots Barnes, claiming that he is Kartovski. This Steed strenuously denies, saying that he himself shot Kartovski in the heart, in Berlin in 1963. Kartovski is lying in the Nullington Hospital surrounded by heart and lung machines. Constantine and Himel have kept him alive because no other agent has such a good mind. They can transfer his personality to another man's brain, using the ten per cent of the brain that lies dormant. Steed's bullet from 1963 lodged in the Russian agent's left side, causing those given his mind to limp and develop a gnarled hand. They next try to use Tara as Kartovski's mind-carrier. They fake an accident, and

Steed manages to rescue Tara just in time, before her brain is fused with that of Kartovski, in Split.

take her to the hospital for the fusion with Kartovski's brain. But Steed is on their trail and manages to get into the hospital, free Tara, and send her to fetch Rooke. But he is another victim of the transferred mind, and although he struggles between his two personalities, he attacks Tara when she enters the Ministry. Steed dashes in to save them both, just in time. The last scene shows Steed with a limp and an injured hand, making Tara suspect him of having the treatment. But, Steed has just taken one knock too many in his recent fight.

WHOEVER SHOT POOR GEORGE OBLIQUE STROKE XR40

By Tony Williamson

John Steed	Patrick Macnee
Tara King	Linda Thorson
Jason	Dennis Price
Pelley	Clifford Evans
Loris	Judy Parfitt
Ardmore	Anthony Nicholls
Tobin	Frank Windsor
Baines	Adrian Ropes
Anaesthetist	Arthur Cox
Keller	Tony Wright
Jacobs	John Porter-Davison
Jill	Jacky Allouis
Betty	Valerie Leon

Directed by Cyril Frankel
Produced by Albert Fennell and Brian Clemens

Sykes attempts to stop Steed reaching Tara, who is getting cheesed off by the whole affair, in False Witness.

In fancy dress, Tara discovers Baines, who has been shot dead in his flat in Whoever Shot Poor George Oblique Stroke XR40.

COMPUTER research worker Baines calls in his colleague, Tobin, when George/XR40, a computer, suddenly goes wrong at a Ministry of Technology research establishment. Then Jacobs, an intruder, breaks in while they are away and shoots George, nearly finishing him off. Dr Ardmore, a cybernetic surgeon, is called in and he conducts an operation to save George. Steed stays for the operation and Tara goes with Baines to this flat to fetch the set of equations which, when fed into George, made him go wrong. But Jacobs has got there first and he shoots Baines. Back at the research establishment the operation progresses, and George coughs up some computer tape which appears to condemn Sir Wilfred Pelley, George's creator, as a traitor. Steed visit Pelley, and is received by Jason, his butler. Pelley, however, refuses to attend George. He is not even keen to talk and seems to be drunk. Tobin gives Steed a file on Sir Wilfred then, when left alone with George, he again sabotages him, this time by pouring acid into George's 'mouth'. Dr Ardmore decides to give George a 'brain' transplant from an earlier model of George named Fred MKIII. Steed visits Pelley and tells him of this, but Pelley still refuses to attend the operation. During his visit, Steed notices a woman's fur coat hanging in the hall. The coat belongs to Loris, who appears to dominate Pelley. She tells Jacobs to follow Steed to Baines' apartment and kill him there. Steed, however, has set this up, and he makes a dummy which the would-be killer shoots, and Jacobs dies in the ensuing fight with Steed. Steed next sends Tara to Sir Wilfred's home, disguised as his long-lost niece, Prunella, whom he has not seen since she was a child. Meanwhile, Loris and

Pelley have learned that Jacobs' attempt on Steed's life was not successful. Tara visits Pelley's home, and introducing herself as Prunella, and tells Jason, Pelley and Loris that she would like to stay for a few days. She discovers that Loris has a strange hold over Pelley, induced by drugs, and also that food is being taken to someone in the basement – perhaps the top man? Meanwhile, the 'brain' transplant on George proceeds. It is no sooner completed, when Tobin makes a last attempt to sabotage the operation, by snipping some electric cables. Steed notices and prevents Tobin from doing any serious damage. Tara is now revealed as an impostor by Jason, the butler, who then declares himself to be an impostor, too. He is, in fact, the ring-leader of the plot to get secrets from Pelley. Meanwhile George has been repaired, and out of his 'mouth' come the words which Pelley has been trying to convey to them – that he is being drugged and interrogated daily against his will. This proves that he is not the traitor. Steed rushes to Pelley's home, where he knows Tara will be in danger. He told her to trust Jason, whom George has now revealed as the real traitor. The gang tell Keller, one of their henchmen, to burn Tara alive in the summerhouse, but when he gets there, Steed is waiting. Tara and Steed then return to the house and rout the opposition. Steed later tries out a recipe supplied by George for the world's most devastating cocktail. Finally the mixture explodes, and Steed decides it should remain on the secret list.

FALSE WITNESS

By Jeremy Burnham

John Steed	Patrick Macnee
Tara King	Linda Thorson
Land	Rio Fanning
Melville	Barry Warren
Brayshaw	John Atkinson
Penman	Peter Jesson
Lord Edgefield	William Job
Mother	Patrick Newell
Rhonda	Rhonda Parker
Dr Grant	Arthur Pentlow
Gould	Larry Burns
Little Man	Jimmy Gardner
Sloman	Dan Meaden
Sykes	John Bennett
Plummer	Michael Lees
Sir Joseph	Tony Steedman
Amanda	Terry Eliot
Nesbitt	Simon Lack

Designed by Robert Jones
Directed by Charles Crichton
Produced by Albert Fennell and Brian Clemens

STEED'S department is in trouble. They are losing agents and suspect that one of their own men, Melville, may be working against them. Melville, keeping a lookout for his colleague, Penman, who is photographing a notebook in a Rolls-Royce in an underground garage, fails to warn him of the danger when the chauffeur arrives. Shot by the chauffeur, Penman staggers away. Steed keeps a rendezvous with Mother, on top of a double-decker bus which has been stripped and furnished as a sitting-room, with his secretary, Rhonda, in attendance. Mother tells Steed that they have lost two men trying to prove that a peer of the realm, Lord Edgefield, is blackmailing security and Foreign Office personnel. As they talk, Melville boards the bus. He does not report the shooting of Penman, and is sent with Steed to look after Plummer, the star witness in the case against Lord Edgefield. Meanwhile, the badly-wounded Penman, after hiding the film he has taken in a dustbin, arrives at Steed's mews flat. Before he dies, he warns Tara that Melville is a traitor, and tells her the whereabouts of his film. Steed and Melville arrive at Plummer's flat, too late to assist him in a brush with an intruder. They look over the flat but nothing seems to have been disturbed except the fridge door, which is open. Plummer is only too willing to testify against Edgefield, who was responsible for his brother's suicide. All three have coffee, Steed taking his black, the other two white, and leave for the office of Sir Joseph, who is compiling the case. Lord Edgefield, who

has been summoned to be confronted by the witness, is ushered into the room by Amanda, Sir Joseph's secretary. But Plummer, under questioning, completely contradicts everything he has said before. Edgefield leaves, gloating. When Steed returns home, he finds the contents of several dustbins piled high in the room. But Tara has found the film, and passes Penman's final message on to Steed. They inform Mother, who sends Tara to question Plummer and discover why he changed his evidence. Steed's mission is more hazardous. He must go with Melville and discover, the hard way, whether he is a traitor. Leaving Melville to keep guard outside a nearby telephone box, Steed enters Lord Edgefield's flat. Occasionally calling to Melville on a portable transmitter, he begins to probe Edgefield's wall safe. Steed manages to escape approaching danger by seconds when Melville fails to warn him that an intruder has entered the flat. He then rushes outside and knocks Melville to the ground. But Melville is adamant that he warned Steed, and denies that he is a traitor. Steed takes Melville to Mother, and the suspected traitor is strapped to a lie-detector by Dr Grant. Steed and Mother question the agent and are astonished when Melville tells apparent lies, because the graph indicates that he is not lying. The real test comes when Steed asks Melville if he worked with him that evening. Melville replies in the negative. Yet according to the graph he is telling the truth! Tara finds her assignment equally puzzling. While searching through Plummer's flat in his absence, she knocks over a bottle of milk, which is lapped up by Plummer's pet dog. Afterwards, even the dog lies, by barking at a non-existent intruder! Tara later hides from a real intruder, Lane, dressed as a milkman, who, after placing a bottle of milk in the fridge, leaves on a milk float bearing the sign Peter Pan Dairies. Tara follows in her car. At the dairy, Lord Edgefield is paying off Sykes, who has manufactured and arranged the deliveries of the strange milk. Sykes is then given a new customer for the milk round. Using an intercom, Sykes tells the bogus milkman, now returning with Tara in pursuit, to make a detour. The new customer is Sir Joseph. Tara watches the delivery to Sir Joseph, then continues to follow the milk float. Steed gives Sir Joseph the list of blackmail names he stole from Edgefield's safe. Sir Joseph then telephones each of them, and the last one, Nesbitt, agrees to testify. He is brought to Sir Joseph's office

and tells him what he knows. But before the confrontation with Edgefield, Sir Joseph asks his secretary to serve three coffees. Tara investigates the dairy, but is cornered by the bogus milkman. After a fight, she finds the milk vat room, where she sees an employee, Sloman, mixing a colourless liquid with the milk. As he leaves, Tara checks the milk vat, but Sloman re-appears with Sykes. In the ensuing fight, Tara and Sloman end up in the vat of milk. She manages to knock him out but, in the process of doing so, her head is pushed under and she swallows some milk. Covered with milk, she escapes to a nearby telephone where she conveys a strange message to Sir Joseph – 'This is very important. I *don't* want to warn you . . .'. Sir Joseph, Steed and their witness discuss the strange message over coffee. When Lord Edgefield arrives, both Nesbitt and Sir Joseph reverse their testimony and exonerate Lord Edgefield . . . Only Steed makes sense, but he has been drinking black coffee. Steed is the next to receive a delivery from the bogus milkman. But Tara recognises him, and rushes out to the milk float to stop the man, only to be thrown to the ground. She immediately runs back to the apartment and knocks a glass of milk out of Steed's hand. Strangely, she does not know why. Tara, unable to warn of the dangers in the milk, goes to the dairy and begins to smash all the bottles she finds there. But she is caught by Sloman and Sykes and forced into a butter-making machine. Steed has the milk analysed and, discovering it contains an hallucinatory drug, sets off for the dairy. The butter machine is about to churn when he arrives, and he is astonished to find Tara with milk oozing around her waist. He subdues Sykes and Sloman with cartons of yoghurt, and then opens the butter machine to rescue Tara. A large slab of butter pops out with a smile on its face. Later on, Tara is showing Steed her new outfit. He is rude – then she notices the half-empty glass of milk beside him.

ALL DONE WITH MIRRORS

By Leigh Vance

John Steed	Patrick Macnee
Tara King	Linda Thorson
Watney	Dinsdale Landen
Sparshott	Peter Copley
Barlow	Edwin Richfield
Col Withers	Michael Trubshawe
Mother	Patrick Newell
Pandora	Joanna Jones
Miss Emily	Nora Nicholson
Carswell	Tenniel Evans
Miss Tiddiman	Liane Aukin

Directed by Ray Austin
Produced by Albert Fennell and Brian Clemens

STEED is under house arrest at Mother's headquarters, because Steed has been spending time recently at Carmadoc Research Establishment, and secrets have been leaked from there. Mother has sent Tara to investigate, together with a very serious trainee agent named Watney. There, they meet the establishment's security chief, Major Sparshott, who sits in the security area surrounded by strips of silver foil. A flare of light hits the foil as they go, with Sparshott, to the main part of the building, where the establishment's research is revealed to be connected with harnessing the power of the sun. The flaring light is associated with the ability of Markin, a radio operator, to overhear their conversation as Sparshott tells them of the death of a local resident named Guthrie. Markin overhears Tara say that she would like to visit Guthrie's home. From Miss Emily, Guthrie's housekeeper, Tara learns that Guthrie was interested in astronomy, and was friendly with radio-astronomer Williams. He had also, recently, told her to smash everything shiny in the cottage, including the mirrors. Markin again overhears their conversation. Tara arrives at Williams' home, and finds the man dead. He has been strangled by Gozzo, a huge man who is still there and whom Tara fights. After a furious brawl, Gozzo is left impaled on a scythe. As Tara leaves, she picks up an envelope on which Williams has written a complex equation before he died. Returning to the research establishment, Tara enlists the help of Professor Carswell to decipher the figures on the envelope. He tells her that they are a table of light intensities. Watney meanwhile is investigating the research team. Seligman arranges to meet him outside in the clearing, and Sparshott follows Watney as he goes to keep the rendezvous. Both are too late to prevent Seligman from being shot. The voice of Markin calls Selig-

man to a shaving mirror hanging from a tree. This is then shattered by the bullet which kills Seligman. As he dies, he tells Watney 'It was all done with mirrors'. Tara now investigates a lighthouse owned by Colonel Withers. He says he did not know Guthrie or Williams. Through Withers' telescope, Tara sees the arrival of Pandora Marshall, a pretty young woman, at the lighthouse. Yet Withers does not know who she is, and asks his secretary, Barlow, and Kettridge, another of his staff, to find out. As she leaves, Tara just misses seeing Markin (the window in the stair wall hides his secret radio room). She does, however, notice his smouldering cigarette in the stairway. Barlow behaves strangely as he receives Pandora, who has come to the lighthouse to interview Colonel Withers. She has arranged her accommodation with Barlow, but he does not seem to know about it. Pandora knows the man to be an impostor, for she has met Barlow before. She creeps out of her room and up to the lamp-room, where she discovers that the telescope hides a device which can both transmit and receive sound over vast distances. The sound travels on a beam of light which flares over the object at which the telescope is aimed. Before she can tell Tara, however, she is taken prisoner by Kettridge and Barlow. Tara is examining the cliff edge where Guthrie fell to his death, and they force Pandora to lure her to the cliff face. Then Kettridge drives his motor-cycle at her. Tara falls into the sea below, and when Watney and Sparshott arrive, they assume she is lost. They telephone the news to Mother, who reluctantly tells Steed of Tara's death... Tara, however, is not dead. She crawls on to the rocks and then makes her way to the lighthouse. She then disposes of Kettridge and discovers the secret of Markin's telescope device and knocks him out, after discovering the secret radio room. There, she finds Pandora, the real Colonel Withers, and the real Barlow, all bound and gagged. Pandora explains that the telescope is a retro-meter and the Colonel confirms that the impostors have been using it to steal information from the research establishment. The fake Barlow finds the unconscious Kettridge as Tara surprises and knocks cold the fake Colonel in the lamp-room. Downstairs they overhear Tara using the speaking tube on the retro-meter to contact Watney. She just manages to make contact before she is attacked by two more heavies who have come up from below. One of the thugs is

Trapped in the lighthouse and facing death, Tara prepares to fight for her life in **All Done With Mirrors.**

killed by his own gun, and the other falls down the stairs after being thrown through the door by Tara. She then disposes of Markin and Kettridge. Barlow, however, corners Tara in the lamp-room, but she is saved when Watney arrives and slams the lamp door into Barlow's back. Moments later, Steed arrives, only to find that Tara has handled the heavies in her own special game of 'Solo'.

LEGACY OF DEATH

By Terry Nation

John Steed	**Patrick Macnee**
Tara King	**Linda Thorson**
Sidney	**Stratford Johns**
Humbert	**Ronald Lacey**
Baron Von Orlak	**Ferdy Mayne**
Dickens	**Kynaston Reeves**
Farrer	**Richard Hurndall**
Zoltan	**John Hollis**
Ho Lung	**Leon Thau**
Gorky	**Tute Lemkow**
Oppenheimer	**Peter Swanwick**
Slattery	**Vic Wise**
Winkler	**Teddy Kiss**
Dr Winter	**Michael Bilton**

Designed by Robert Jones
Directed by Don Chaffey
Produced by Albert Fennell and Brian Clemens

Steed arrives at Tara's flat just as the unfortunate Gregor falls onto the dagger and dies, in Legacy Of Death.

KILLERS are on their way to murder elderly Henley Farrer for the ornate dagger in his possession. But Farrer, who has lived his life surrounded by trappings of the Orient, has found a way to elude his assassins. He hands the precious dagger to his servant, Zoltan, telling him to take it to John Steed. Then Farrer steps into a prepared coffin, and within seconds his pulse has stopped. Sidney Street, a large fat man, and his colleague Humbert Green, a small sad-faced man, arrive to take possession of the dagger, which is engraved with a falcon's head. They find Farrer in his coffin, but no dagger. Zoltan is already on his way to Steed. He finds Steed at his home, trying to master a line-controlled model aeroplane. Zoltan hands the ornate dagger to him, refusing to give any information, save that it is a legacy. One of the many cut-throats seeking the dagger, Gorky, is eavesdropping. Another, Slattery, waits across the street as Tara drives up in her car. Wearing full evening dress, she has dropped in on Steed between parties. Before she leaves, Steed hands her the dagger and asks her to research into its background. As Steed intercepts Gorky at his letter-box, the cut-throats outside are joined by Oppenheimer, and a mysterious elevating truck. After drinking Steed's champagne, Gorky offers him £1,000,000 for the dagger. Before he can add anything further, he is shot from the elevated truck outside the window. Steed calls a doctor. Meanwhile, Tara takes the dagger to a Chinese curio shop. The proprietor, Ho Lung, is strangely excited when Tara shows him the dagger, and when she leaves, he makes a hasty telephone call to his accomplice, Gregor,

who soon joins the growing number of thugs after the dagger. At Steed's apartment, Oppenheimer has intercepted Doctor Winter, and takes his place to examine Gorky. At gunpoint, he attempts to force Steed to reveal the whereabouts of the dagger, but Slattery bursts in and they shoot each other. Street and Green are the next to call. Bemused by the pile of bodies, they fabricate a story of sentimental attachment to the dagger, but leave when Steed tells him he has given it to a friend. Meanwhile, Tara has used the dagger as a coat-hook on the wall of her apartment, and content that it is safe, decides to take a bath. She is surprised by Gregor and a fight breaks out. When Steed arrives, he is in time to see Gregor fall to his death on the dagger, which has been removed from the wall during the fight. As the two agents ponder the strange attraction of the dagger, cars arrive outside with more men after the dagger. Machine-gun bullets shatter the window as Street and Green eliminate their rivals with a well placed grenade. During all this, Steed and Tara have slipped out of the rear entrance and escape, rendering another villain unconscious as they go. In his pocket they find a slip of paper containing a solicitor's address. Now pursued by a vast number of cars and motorbikes, they drive off to hide the dagger in a secret place, known only to Steed. Tara then leaves to investigate the Chinese curio shop and Steed heads for the solicitors mentioned in the slip of paper. Before Dickens, the solicitor, can unearth the source of the dagger's bequest to Steed, he is also shot through the window from the elevated truck. The assassin is Zoltan, Farrer's assistant. Meanwhile, at the curio shop, Tara is captured and tortured by Von Orlak, a one-armed Prussian in a wheelchair, and his midget henchman, Winkler, while Ho Lung looks on. Street and Green take over the torture, which is a feather duster on Tara's feet. Unable to withstand the dreadful torture, Tara agrees to disclose the whereabouts of the dagger. She manages to turn the tables, however, and under similar torture, the two villains reveal that the dagger is the key to a secret treasure. At the solicitor's, Steed has made the same discovery. Driving to Farrer's home he meets Tara accidentally, and they discover that the reflected pattern from the shaft of the dagger matches the mosaic on the floor. The blade itself fits into a slot on the floor. The lights come on and they find them-

selves surrounded by all those wanting the dagger, who have now decided to form a consortium. Green reveals that they are all after a priceless black pearl, which is the largest in the world. But it is not under the floor. Henley Farrer (still alive, having only taken a drug to simulate death) steps from his coffin and reveals that he has the pearl. The legacy to Steed was just a trick to ensure that he could possess the pearl in peace. All Farrer's enemies are now under one roof, and Zoltan steps forward to mow them all down with a machine gun. In the melée that follows, Farrer is killed and the pearl falls into a glass of wine. It dissolves, leaving the villains to go sadly on their way and Steed and Tara to drink the world's most expensive glass of wine.

NOON-DOOMSDAY

By Terry Nation

John Steed	Patrick Macnee
Tara King	Linda Thorson
Farrington	Ray Brooks
Grant	T P McKenna
Baines	Griffith Jones
Lyall	Lyndon Brook
Kafta	Peter Bromilow
Mother	Patrick Newell
Rhonda	Rhonda Parker
Perrier	Peter Halliday
Sunley	Anthony Ainley
Hyde	John Glyn-Jones
Carson	David Glover
Cornwall	Lawrence James

Script Editor Terry Nation
Directed by Peter Sykes
Produced by Albert Fennell and Brian Clemens

STEED is recovering from injuries sustained during a recent case. His leg is in plaster and, needing crutches, he is recuperating at a special convalescent home for agents. Tara decides to visit him, and the taxi-driver is astonished when she asks to be dropped in the middle of nowhere. But Tara, armed with a large bunch of flowers, pushes her way through hedgerows, barbed wire, an electrified fence and a minefield (both turned off for her visit) and finally arrives at the secret sanatorium. She is greeted, and vetted, by a guard, Cornwall, who then re-activates the defences by turning a key in a device like a parking meter. Steed is delighted by Tara's visit, especially as the flowers conceal a bottle of vintage champagne. As they chat, Cornwall is ambushed by two hired guns, Kyle-Farrington and Norman Grant, and killed with a farming implement. Tara gives Steed his post, and he explains that his leg injury was caused by stepping into a cucumber frame while pursuing a suspected saboteur. Tara also meets Dr Hyde, and Sir Rodney Woodham-Baines, another patient, who has both his arm and neck in plaster. Steed opens a letter containing a ticket for the opera, dated 19 June 1961. The date, seven years ago to the day, is familiar. Steed puzzles over it for a moment, then realises that on that date he sent Gerald Kafta, head of Murder International, to prison at noon. Now he is out and bent on revenge! Tara tries to contact Mother's headquarters, but finds the telephone lines are dead. Farrington and Grant have cut the wires. Roger Lyall, another patient, takes Tara to use the radio transmitter, only to find that it, too, is wrecked. They decide to separate and search for Cornwall. Tara enters the hospital grounds and is only inches away from stepping on a land

mine, when a French patient, Jules Perrier, with an eye-patch and his arm in a sling, saves her. The sundial in the grounds moves slowly towards noon. Tara discovers the dead body of Cornwall hanging from a rope, in the barn. As she turns to leave, a mysterious intruder knocks her down. Recovering, she goes outside to find Perrier in the grounds. Meanwhile, at a nearby deserted railway station, Farrington and Grant are practising their skills with knife and gun. Tara and Steed discuss their plight and she remembers that Cornwall had a key to activate the defence system. Who has it now? Hearing shots, Tara runs into the gardens to a well, at the bottom of which lies the dead body of Dr Hyde. His assistant, Carson, obviously works for the other side, and proves his guilt by trying to gun her down in the garden. But Tara grapples with him, and he is accidentally shot with his gun. Before he dies he tells her that he threw the system key away. As the sundial approaches noon, the two hired killers prepare to meet their leader, Kafta. Tara meanwhile questions the four patients in the sanatorium and three of them give their reasons for not helping in the defence of the crippled Steed. The Frenchman says he works only for France, Sir Rodney claims he is a pacifist, and Lyall is obviously suffering too badly from battle fatigue. The only one who offers to help is Edward Sunley, who is so incapacitated by bandages that he is only able to act as lookout. As Farrington and Grant meet their leader's helicopter, Steed tries to lock Tara in a cupboard for her own safety. But she knocks him out with the vintage champagne bottle. As the clock strikes 12, Tara sets out to do battle for Steed. Kafta, Farrington and Grant arrive for the kill in classic Western style on horseback. Tara soon finds herself cornered by Grant in the barn. She outwits him with a bale of hay on the end of a rope, and then shoots him. Sunley, keeping a lookout, saves Tara from Farrington's knife by dropping a flower vase on him. Tara then uses his knife with deadly effect. With one bullet left in her gun, she and Kafta pin each other down and it is checkmate. But the mortally-wounded Farrington recovers enough to knife Tara'a sleeve to a wall, giving Kafta the upper hand. Steed, having regained consciousness, staggers out on crutches and shoots Kafta with a spear gun concealed in a crutch. Steed, now fully recovered, takes Tara a present – his plaster cast. It is full of presents: champagne, pearls, a hat, parasol – and a sundial.

LOOK (STOP ME IF YOU'VE HEARD THIS ONE) BUT THERE WERE THESE TWO FELLERS

By Dennis Spooner

John Steed	Patrick Macnee
Tara King	Linda Thorson
Maxie Martin	Jimmy Jewel
Jennings	Julian Chagrin
Bradley Marler	Bernard Cribbins
Marcus Pugman	John Cleese
Lord Dessington	William Kendall
Seagrave	John Woodvine
Brig Wiltshire	Garry Marsh
Miss Charles	Gaby Vargas
Cleghorn	Bill Shine
Sir Jeremy Broadfoot	Richard Young
Merlin	Robert James
Fiery Frederick	Talfryn Thomas
Tenor	Jay Denver
Escapologist	Johnny Vyvyan
Ventriloquist	Len Belmont

Designed by Robert Jones
Directed by James Hill
Produced by Albert Fennell and Brian Clemens

SIR Jeremy Broadfoot, head of the Land and Development Company, is alone, working late in his office. Two men, 'Merry' Maxie Martin and Jennings, move through the building towards him, stopping to change into music-hall entertainer's dress as they go. Maxie Martin shoots him with a silenced gun, then he and Jennings make a crazy music-hall dancing exit. Steed and Tara are called in. Tara finds a magician's wand and Steed a footprint of enormous size made by the clown shoes of Maxie Martin. The killers are inmates of Greasepaint Grange, a variety artistes' rest home, and there they receive their instructions to kill from Mr Punch in a Punch and Judy theatre. Mr Punch praises their successful killing of Sir Jeremy and urges them onto their next victim, another director of the Capital Land and Development Company, Thomas Randolph Cleghorn. Martin and Jennings kill him with an iron bar when he is duck-shooting, and this time they leave a red ping-pong ball false nose at the scene. This makes Tara suspect that the killer could be a vaudeville clown. She asks Marcus Pugman, who keeps a register of copyrighted clown make-ups, to help her find the red-nosed comedian. Steed meanwhile tells the board of the company (who are building the government's new underground seat, for Ministers to use in a wartime emergency) the line they are taking. Strangely, this information seems to get to Mr Punch. He reprimands Maxie and Jennings for leaving pieces of their make-up behind, and gives them their next victim, Pugman, who has Maxie's make-up on file. He is killed just as he is about to tell Steed and Tara on the phone that he has found the clown make-

HAVE GUNS...WILL HAGGLE

By Donald James

John Steed	Patrick Macnee
Tara King	Linda Thorson
Col Nsonga	Johnny Sekka
Adriana	Nicola Pagett
Conrad	Jonathan Burn
Spencer	Timothy Bateson
Crayford	Michael Turner
Lift Attendant	Robert Gillespie
Giles	Roy Stewart
Brad	Peter J Elliott

Designed by Robert Jones
Directed by Ray Austin
Produced by Albert Fennell and Brian Clemens

up they are after. They arrive to find him dead in his office, but, fortunately, he is holding an egg painted with Maxie's make-up. Brigadier Wiltshire is the next director to die, meeting a grotesquely funny end when he detonates a comical-looking bomb, labelled 'bomb', in his car. The Brigadier is killed when it really does blow up. Lord Bessington, however, the next victim, escapes from a custard pie of suffocating gluey material thrown at him by Maxie in his boardroom. Miss Charles, his secretary, arrives in time to help Bessington to recover. From Bradley Marler, Maxie's gag-writer, Steed discovers that Maxie was a vaudeville star of the now-closed Gladchester Palladium. Lord Bessington says that the theatre was taken over and closed down by the Capital Land and Development Company. Marler is the next to go, knifed by Maxie on the instructions of Mr Punch. He is left dying, but manages to phone Steed and say that he has written down Maxie's present address. When Steed arrives at Marler's office, however, he finds the place piled high with screwed-up pieces of joke scripts. After a long search, he eventually finds a piece of paper bearing the address of Greasepaint Grange. Tara, meanwhile, is sticking close to Lord Bessington, but this does not prevent Maxie from killing him in broad daylight. He is disguised as a tree, and when Tara is investigating what she rightly thought was a tree moving, Maxie strangles him. Tara gives chase, but she is tricked and captured by Maxie when he does another quick change and arrives dressed as a policeman. Under arrest, she is taken to Greasepaint Grange. Steed decides to visit the rest home dressed as 'Gentleman Jack, a smile, a song, and an umbrella'. Meanwhile, Tara is in the process of becoming the first woman to be burnt in half, by ex-vaudeville magician, 'Fiery' Frederick. Steed arrives, but finds the place closed, so he breaks in and finds 'Fiery' Frederick in the throes of warming up Tara. He disposes of the magician in typical style and releases Tara. They then dress up as two halves of a pantomime horse and join the meeting Mr Punch is holding in the main hall. Eventually, the meeting ends and a pantomime fight breaks out, which The Avengers win, revealing Mr Punch to be Seagrave, the last of the directors of the company. Later on, Steed does a fast quick change, like 'Merry' Maxie, when Tara turns up in a lovely evening gown, ready to go to the opera. However, it takes him three attempts to find the right attire.

FOUR men carry out a raid on a Government Ordnance Factory. They leap over the perimeter fence with a trampoline they have brought with them, then they signal with a knock on the warehouse door to Crayford, their contact inside the factory. Crayford lets them in, then encourages them to fake a struggle with him. They knock him unconscious, and leave with several crates of FN rifles of a new top-secret type, the FF70. Tara King goes to the scene of the break-in, and bounces on the trampoline. She and Steed have come to investigate the raid, which means that 3000 of the new rifles are now off the secret list. Meanwhile, in the garden of English-rose Adrianna's house, Conrad, her brother, stalks and kills Smith in a weird rifle testing duel which ends with Adrianna coolly inviting her victorious brother Conrad to come in for tea. Smith's body is dumped in a reservoir, and Steed and Tara are on the scene when it is dredged up. Steed gets the bullet from the dead man's body, but needs the help of ballistics to prove whether it is fired by an FF70 or not. He sends Tara to find out, while he calls on Colonel Nsonga, an African military man newly arrived in the country. He is well-known to Steed, who believes, rightly, he may have come in search of the rifles to back up his struggle for the Presidency of a newly independent African state. Adrianna visits Nsonga in his room, but does not yet name a price for the rifles. Steed, hiding in the hotel phone booth, sees Adrianna, Conrad and Nsonga leave, and when they are gone, he bribes the lift-operator to take him up to Nsonga's room. Picking the lock with a credit card, he searches the room and finds some money in Nsonga's safe. As he leaves, he accidentally knocks over a tailor's dummy wearing military uniform. But he gets away just as Nsonga and Giles, his servant, return. Tara, disguised as a blonde, visits the ballistics establishment, and there Crayford sees her give Spencer the bullet,

taken from the dead Smith for testing. Crayford phones Conrad who asks him to deal with Tara, and she is ambushed as she leaves. The thug tries to retrieve the bullet, but Tara escapes after a fast and furious car duel. Tara, now back to a brunette, tells Steed that the bullet was fired from an FF70. Steed tells her about the money he found in Nsonga's safe and that he is having a uniform with presidential insignia made, which shows his ambitions. Handing her a blonde wig, Steed suggests that she take a closer look at the Ordnance Factory. Meanwhile, Steed visits Nsonga again, this time meeting him as he knocks Giles out. Steed confuses Nsonga by telling him that he, too, is a gun-runner, for the Colonel's own President. When Tara reaches the factory, she interrupts a second raid – this time for ammunition – by Conrad's men, but she escapes. Conrad, however, kills Crayford, then pursues Tara back to her apartment. There, he attacks her and takes her off in his car to Stokely House. Steed visits Tara's flat, and finds the signs of a struggle. He returns home and discovers from his answering service that Adrianna has invited him to Stokely House. Nsonga has told her that Steed is in the market for guns. As Steed arrives at the house, he just misses being killed by a shot from Giles. Conrad, noticing the servant, shoots Giles before he can fire a second shot at Steed. Before the gun auction begins, Adrianna holds a demonstration, in which two men duel with the FF70s. One finally kills the other. Then she surprises Steed by bringing in Tara, to duel with Conrad. Steed manages to hold up the proceedings during the auction, but his bid is beaten by Colonel Nsonga's. Nsonga then orders the duel to commence. Steed moves off from the group to try to help Tara with a friendly shot, but Tara, rather than going for her gun, sneaks up behind her opponent and knocks him cold. She and Steed then escape. Steed, following Tara, comes across a hut in which he finds the FF70 rifles. He lights a fuse to blow them up, not knowing that Conrad has captured Tara, tied her up and left her in the hut. Steed finds her in time, however, and after a struggle kills Conrad and frees Tara. The hut explodes and one of the FF70s falls on Nsonga's head, killing him. Afterwards, Steed, having anticipated the arrival of an exotic gift from the grateful President for sorting out the Nsonga business, is more than surprised when he finds a large jungle cat growling at his door.

THEY KEEP KILLING STEED

By Brian Clemens

John Steed	Patrick Macnee
Tara King	Linda Thorson
Baron Von Court	Ian Ogilvy
Arcos	Ray McAnally
Zerson	Norman Jones
Captain Smythe	Bernard Horsfall
Mother	Patrick Newell
Verno	Arthur Howell
Golda	Bill Cummings
Smanoff	Frank Barringer
Bruno	William Ellis

and Hal Galili, Nicole Shelby, Rosemary Donnelly, Gloria Connell, Michael Corcoran, Ross Hutchinson, Reg Whitehead, Anthony Sheppard, Angharad Rees, George Ghent

Directed by Robert Fuest
Produced by Albert Fennell and Brian Clemens

Steed is strapped down so that a mould can be made of his face in They Keep Killing Steed.

A WRECKED car in a disused quarry conceals the entrance to an underground headquarters, where a group of men are hatching an imaginative plot. Using a scientific method, they intend to provide one of their agents with a replica of John Steed's face. Then, as Steed, the agent will infiltrate a peace conference with a bomb. However, when Arcos and Zerson finish their first experiment, it is not perfect. Arcos now decides that they must have the real Steed and make a mould from his face. Steed and Tara are asked to be official observers at the peace conference and they book into an hotel, thinking they can have a rest. They have a light-hearted incident when a Baron Von Curt knocks at their door and asks Tara to pose as his wife so that he can escape the advances of two young women. Steed receives a phone call from a Captain Smythe of Security, and is kidnapped as he climbs into a taxi. He is taken to the quarry headquarters and Arcos and Zerson explain their plan to make a cast of his face. Then, by injecting their agent's face with a special serum, the man will assume every detail of the mould. Steed is then strapped to a concrete base and the agents proceed to make the face mould. Arcos decides that Nadine, one of the five agents available, will impersonate Steed. A labelled mould and syringe are placed in a special case, ready to be delivered to him. But Steed escapes, locks the gang out of their headquarters, and before being recaptured, places four more labelled moulds in the case. Arcos then gives the case to another of the gang, Bruno, to deliver to Nadine. Bruno, reading the labels, innocently delivers the Steed kits to all five agents. Meanwhile, Tara finds a useful ally

in the Baron. As they visit Mother in a bizarre underwater capsule he is testing for the Navy, the five agents inject themselves, put on their masks and become John Steeds. One dies in the process, but the other four make their way to the peace conference, where on seeing each other, they begin to fight. The sole survivor then places a percussion bomb under the gavel to be used by the chairman. Arriving at the conference hall, Tara and the Baron find — and keep on finding — dead Steeds. Only when their fingerprints don't match those of the real Steed is Tara reassured. Steed manages to escape and reach the conference just in time to snatch the deadly gavel from the chairman's hand and throw it through the window. In the garden, Tara accepts the fake Steed as her real partner and is narrowly saved from death at his hands by the Baron. Joining them, Steed sets off in his car to trap the villains in their quarry hideout, and Tara and the Baron follow him in hot pursuit. Steed arrives to find that Arcos has become another Steed double in an effort to escape. Steed attacks him and they fight over a gun. Meanwhile, above ground, Tara and Von Curt win a spectacular sword fight and rout the rest of the villains. One of them, Zerson, recovers before dying and returns to the underground shelter where he shoots Steed, who staggers from the fight into the waiting Tara's arms. But is it the real Steed, or the bogus one? As a second, smiling, Steed steps out of the shelter, Tara has the answer. Only the real Steed would smile under such circumstances. In the final scene, Steed and Tara are sunbathing in deckchairs with the sea in the background. The camera then pans back and reveals sunlamps and a travel poster on the wall. They are in Tara's apartment — Mother has cut short their holiday and sent them home. Outside, it starts to rain.

Tara King raises her hat to the camera. The only one of Steed's colleagues to be single, she had a more open relationship with him.

THE INTERROGATORS

By Richard Harris and Brian Clemens

John Steed	**Patrick Macnee**
Tara King	**Linda Thorson**
Col Mannering	**Christopher Lee**
Minnow	**David Sumner**
Caspar	**Philip Bond**
Mother	**Patrick Newell**
Blackie	**Glynn Edwards**
Rasker	**Neil McCarthy**
Mallard	**Neil Stacy**
Norton	**Neil Wilson**
Mr Puffin	**Cardew Robinson**
Captain Soo	**Cecil Cheng**
Naval officer	**Mark Elwes**
RAF officer	**David Richards**

Designed by Robert Jones
Directed by Charles Crichton
Produced by Albert Fennell and Brian Clemens

WHAT appears to be an ordinary dentist's waiting-room is actually being used for torture and interrogation – part of a brilliantly conceived plan to extract information from secret agents. Lieutenant Roy Caspar is strong enough to withstand the torture imposed by Colonel Mannering, Blackie, Captain Soo, and their associates, yet they manage to extract the names of his two most important contacts, Wilson, an archer, and Izzy Pound, a one-man band. Both men are shot by Blackie. After interrogation, Caspar is released. Believing it is part of the test, he refuses to tell Mother and Steed what has happened to him, even when they confront him with the dead bodies of Wilson and Pound. Afterwards, Colonel Mannering has him shot when Caspar asks awkward questions. The next agent for interrogation is Minnow. He too is told by Mannering and associates that the interrogation is part of a test set by Mother's organisation to discover their breaking point under torture. Tara and Steed, following the trail of the missing agents – who always seem to take his toothbrushes with them – are too late to save Minnow's prime contact, Fillington. He is shot while playing football. Tara does, however, save the second contact, Puffin. Like Caspar, Minnow returns and acts as though nothing has happened. But Steed and Mother show him photographs of his dead contacts, and he finally realises that the interrogation was not part of a training course. Yet he still denies that he broke down while under pressure. Minnow does not know where the interrogation took place, but recalls that he was given a pigeon to release, should anything

go wrong. Steed follows the pigeon in a helicopter. Just as well, because another agent, Mallard, is now under torture, and Tara – who has played a phoney taped message from Mother – has also gone willingly to undergo the interrogation course. In the bar at the interrogation establishment, where agents are allowed to relax, Tara gains some insight into how the agents unwittingly leak their secrets. When congratulated by Colonel Mannering on withstanding interrogation and passing the test, they are plied with drinks and eventually tell what they know. But not Tara. She overpowers Captain Soo after noticing that Mannering's cigarettes are the same brand as the butts she saw in the homes of the dead agents. When Steed arrives, Mannering tells the assembled agents that he is an intruder breaking into the building as a security test, and there will be merit points awarded to the one who shoots him with the pistols, loaded with blanks, he provides. Steed, however, soon overcomes two of Mannering's henchmen with his bowler, and then turns to face the agents. To protect him, Tara leaps in front of them, but she is unable to convince them that they have been duped, until she tells them to aim their guns at Mannering. His nerve breaks and he ducks – only to be hit over the head with a firm tap from Steed's steel-lined bowler. Later on, Steed is seen interrogating Tara, but it is simply to make her disclose the vital ingredient of her delicious soup.

Colonel Mannering, played by Christopher Lee, visits Tara in The Interrogators. *Lee often appeared in* The Avengers.

Patrick Macnee lost so much weight for the final series that the seams of all his suits had to be taken in!

Linda Thorson wears an outfit designed by Alan Hughes and made of silk, for an episode in The Avengers.

THE ROTTERS

By Dave Freeman

John Steed	**Patrick Macnee**
Tara King	**Linda Thorson**
Kenneth	**Gerald Sim**
George	**Jerome Willis**
Pym	**Eric Barker**
Palmer	**John Nettleton**
Mother	**Patrick Newell**
Rhonda	**Rhonda Parker**

Frank Middlemass, Dervis Ward, Harold Innocent,
Toni Gilpin, Amy Dalby, John Stone, Charles
Morgan, Harry Hutchinson, Noel Davis, John Scott

Designed by Robert Jones
Directed by Robert Fuest
Produced by Albert Fennell and Brian Clemens

AT the Department of Forestry Research, Sir James Pendred is fleeing for his life from two gunmen. He finds sanctuary in his office, and throws the bolt on the heavy wooden door. Suddenly, the wood dissolves, leaving only the metal fittings. Two men, Kenneth and George, are framed in the doorway and without emotion, George shoots Pendred. Steed and Tara discuss the murder with Mother, in an office built completely of polythene. Sir James Pendred, it seems, had telephoned the Prime Minister before he was shot, claiming he had information of national importance. Mother sends Steed to Pendred's office, while Tara goes to the dead man's apartment. She arrives in time to see Kenneth and George about to shoot Pendred's man-servant, and although she stops them stealing a photograph, she is unable to prevent the servant's death. The photograph shows Pendred with four other boffins. Meanwhile, a pencil has dissolved in Steed's hands at Pendred's office. Puzzled, he decides to seek the advice of Reginald Pym, a leading expert on timber decay. He finds Pym, one of the men in the photograph, probing a woodworm-ridden beam in a church tower. When Steed shows him the remains of the decayed pencil, Pym is strangely silent and tells him he is busy. Tara visits Professor Palmer, who is nurturing young trees at the Institute of Timber Technology. He is able to identify the other men in the photo and reveals that they had recently made a startling discovery while researching fungi, but he has taken an oath not to reveal it. Before he can say more, he is killed by a knife thrown by Sandford, a gardener working nearby. Steed and Tara are also too late to save Pym's life. Kenneth and George arrive at the church and dissolve the woodwork in the bell-tower, bringing the giant bell crashing down on the timber expert. Tara and Steed discuss the three remaining men in the photograph. They are Mervyn Sawbow, an antique dealer, Forsythe, who is in Africa, and Wainwright, the managing director of Wainwright Timber Industries. Steed finds Sawbow faking antique furniture but the man is unable to help him and he leaves. Tara calls at Wainwright's timber yard, where she meets Sonia, his receptionist and Mrs Parbury, a solemn-looking colleague of Wainwright's. Together they lead her to a coffin. Inside lies Wainwright. They explain that he died of overwork. As Tara leaves, Sonia and Parbury are joined by Kenneth and George. Sonia then phones Sandford, the gardener, and orders him to kill Tara. He blocks the road with a large truck and stops her car, then tries to kill her with an axe. Tara outwits him, but to her astonishment, Sandford escapes by driving his car through a wooden farm gate – which suddenly disappears! Steed hears that Forsythe, the other man in the photo, is returning home, and he goes to his house to wait for him. Forsythe fails to arrive, but not so Kenneth and George who, to the amazement of Forsythe's mother, dissolve a piano which falls on Steed while they escape. Tara now follows Sawbow in her car, and is in time to see him killed – after digging his own grave – by Sandford and his huge friend, Jackson. The two thugs spot Tara and she hides in a nearby wooden hut – which suddenly dissolves around her! Jackson knocks her cold, and she is taken to Wainwright's timber yard and chained to a chair by Sonia and Sandford. Once alone, Tara manages to burn off her chains with acid. She disposes of Sandford, on guard outside the room, and is about to leave, when she is cornered by Wainwright, now very much alive, with a gun in his hand. Forsythe, back from Africa, manages to overcome Jackson, who has been sent to waylay him, and arriving home, meets Steed. He then reveals that he and the others had been working on a mutation of dry rot that was highly contagious. He also reveals that Wainwright cannot be dead, as he telephoned him offering a job. Wainwright, meanwhile, is telling Tara the details of his plan. He is going to rot the whole of Europe unless the main powers pay him

In Invasion Of The Earthmen, *Linda Thorson wore a blonde wig – her hair colour varied considerably throughout the series.*

£1,000,000,000. Armed with a spray-gun taken from the dead Jackson, Steed arrives in time to save Tara. Using the wood-dissolving spray with both deadly and comical effect, he overcomes the villains and brings the building crashing down around their ears. In the final scene, Tara is ticking off her shopping list as Steed prepares a gourmet meal – Steed's crushed omelette of mushroom. Alas, Tara has forgotten the mushrooms. Steed, fortunately, is able to produce a giant mushroom grown by Professor Palmer.

INVASION OF THE EARTHMEN

By Terry Nation

John Steed	Patrick Macnee
Tara King	Linda Thorson
Brett	William Lucas
Huxton	Christian Roberts
Emily	Lucy Fleming
Bassin	Christopher Chittell
Trump	Warren Clarke
Sarah	Wendy Allnutt
Grant	George Roubicek

Designed by Robert Jones
Directed by Don Sharp
Produced by Albert Fennell and Brian Clemens

BY the side of a remote English country road, agent Bernard Grant cuts his way through a high wire-mesh fence and finds himself looking at three teenagers in semi-military uniform in a disused quarry. Emily Wade is flashing a signal lamp at the sky, Rodney Trump is shooting stars with a sextant, and Huxton is operating a radio transmitter. Suddenly, a giant boa-constrictor grabs Grant. The three teenagers note his plight but instead of helping, they simply laugh out loud. Huxton and Trump are watching from their jeep as Steed and Tara arrive at a country hotel. In Grant's room, Steed finds a prospectus for the Alpha Academy, which he was investigating when he disappeared. Tara, looking through the window, notices that the insignia on the jeep outside is the same as the one on the prospectus. They decide to visit the Alpha Academy and the jeep follows them. From behind the closed gates, they notice groups of teenagers strolling around the grounds. They finally gain entrance, and are shown into the headmaster's room where, posing as parents interested in sending their 18-year-old son to the school, they meet Commander Brett, the headmaster. As they leave, Steed takes an interest in the classrooms and Tara even manages to get into one, where she sees a strange helmeted spaceman. As she does so, Huxton rabbit-punches her from behind and she falls to the floor unconscious. Huxton later explains to Steed, who has been brought back under escort, that Tara stumbled and hit her head. Back in their car, The Avengers give the jeep the slip and return to the school. Getting into the grounds via the wire fence used by Grant, they begin to search the quarry. When they are almost killed by a booby-trap of falling rocks, they decide to split up and investigate separately. In the quarry Tara finds a radio-active canister and a human skeleton. Then, she finds another of the helmeted space crea-

tures, and has a narrow escape when a scorpion alights on her hand. Fortunately, she is able to knock it off. Steed meanwhile has penetrated the school buildings and enters the cryobiology store-room, where he finds dozens of cocooned bodies of young people. Back at the quarry, Tara saves Huxton from Bassin, another student, who is about to crush him from above with a huge boulder. All she gets in return for her warning cry, however, is an arrow from Huxton's bow – which fortunately sticks in her jacket sleeve. In the Academy, Steed enters another room and accidentally activates a powerful wind current, which swirls him up into the centre of the room. He manages to reach a switch and return to the floor of what appears to be a weightlessness-simulating room. As he leaves, he notices a dark tunnel at the far end of the passage outside. Tara, meanwhile, is in a state of anxiety for she is now faced with another of the space creatures – with a group of the Alpha teenagers in support. She loses consciousness, and they carry her away. As Steed leaves the Academy, he finds Bassin prowling in the grounds. He overpowers him and learns that the young students at the Academy are being trained by Commander Brett, for the conquest of outer-space, and will take over the new territories of space when inter-planetary travel becomes feasible. Tara learns exactly the same from Brett in his office, from which she is trying unsuccessfully to escape. Bassin tells Steed that the students have to run the gauntlet of the tunnel, to come face to face with their secret fears. Brett is so impressed with Tara's instinct for survival that he releases her – sending his students off in pursuit 60 seconds later as part of their survival training. Huxton now finds Bassin, left bound and gagged by Steed, but this time they do not attempt to kill each other. Huxton explains that there is a security condition red alert, and together they set out in search of their joint enemy, Steed. Tara soon finds herself trapped by a space creature and, knocking it to the ground, she removes the helmet to discover that there is an ordinary human being inside the suit. With the aid of a map he found earlier, Steed locates a bolted door in the quarry, and enters the darkness of the tunnel hidden behind it. Tara also finds herself in the tunnel. She enters it from the corridor hotly pursued by the group of students. But they pull up at the tunnel's entrance and refuse to follow her. Emily, the group leader, decides to report

Tara edges into the narrow section of the tunnel, hotly pursued by the Alpha students, in Invasion Of The Earthmen.

to Brett. In the tunnel, Tara is faced with one danger after another. First she has to ward off an attack by giant rats, then she is bitten by some leeches. Finally, she enters a narrow tube section in which she is sealed when large metal doors close ahead and behind her, and spiders drop through a hole in the grating. Crushing spiders as she goes, she finally manages to break through the doors. Brett, meanwhile, is following her progress through the tunnel when he spots a second figure on his radar screen. It is Steed, making his way towards Tara from the quarry entrance. Brett orders the students to head them off and block their progress. Emily's group enter from one end, Trump's from the other. But Steed is facing dangers of his own. He just misses being caught in a man-trap when his umbrella tip is snapped off by it, then he has to negotiate a stretch of acid that looks like water, by jumping over it. He finally meets the distraught Tara, and when the students meet in the centre of the tunnel, Steed and Tara have vanished – into the ventilation shaft. When Steed and Tara get out, they seal off the shaft, and block both ends of the tunnel. Steed then puts Huxton and Bassin out of action with his bowler. Tara then knocks out Brett, who is leaving his office to deal with her and Steed personally, being disappointed with the performance of his troops. Later on, Steed shows Tara a hip-throw, which she, in return, uses on him. He then tells her that Whitehall has taken over the school, and the deep-frozen students have been resuscitated and show no ill-effects.

KILLER

By Tony Williamson

John Steed	**Patrick Macnee**
Tara King	**Linda Thorson**
Lady Diana	**Jennifer Croxton**
Merridon	**Grant Taylor**
Brinstead	**William Franklyn**
Clarke	**Richard Wattis**
Mother	**Patrick Newell**

Harry Towb, John Bailey, Michael Ward,
James Bree, Michael McStay, Anthony Valentine,
Charles Houston, Jonathan Elsom, Clive Graham
and Oliver Macgreevy

Designed by Robert Jones
Directed by Cliff Owen
Produced by Albert Fennell and Brian Clemens

*When Tara takes a well-deserved holiday,
Mother decides to give Steed a new partner,
in* Killer.

*Lady Diana Forbes-Blakeney, from Special
Services, helps Steed discover who is killing
his fellow agents, in* Killer.

SOMEONE, or something, is depleting the ranks of Steed's fellow agents. Trouncer, a double-agent, has found out that the killer is Remak (Remote Electro-Matic Agent Killer), a computer programmed for murder. And in Remak's lair, a factory from which there is no escape, Trouncer is fighting for his life. Steed, waiting for Trouncer to arrive at his apartment, receives a visit from Tara. She explains that she is taking a well-earned holiday and, kissing him on the cheek, leaves. Outside Steed's apartment, Merridon and Brinstead, two employees of the Remak organisation, lie in wait for Trouncer. As he arrives, they shoot him from their car and drive away. Trouncer's dying words to Steed, are 'Remak... killer... Polly... tell Mother'. Steed arrives at Mother's headquarters, to find him giving a lecture in a room full of blackboards and maps. He sits in a rocking-chair, as do the rest of the agents in the class, save for one, a beautiful young woman called Lady Diana Forbes-Blakeney. Mother links the word Polly with a recently-discovered body, wrapped in *poly*thene, tied with ribbon, and found in a churchyard. He assigns Lady Diana, from Special Services, to help Steed. When the body of Wilkington, the architect of Remak, is found similarly wrapped in the same churchyard, Steed and Lady Diana go to investigate. Clarke, an expert from the forensic department, tells them that the man was clubbed, poisoned, shot, spiked, stabbed, strangled and suffocated to death. Steed discovers that his neck has also been broken! Wilkington's identity is revealed by his wrist-watch, but Merridon and Brinstead have watched the scene and reach Wilkington's house first. Lady Diana arrives in time to fight – in an unusual balletic style – with Brinstead. He escapes, leaving only charred remains of Wilkington's papers. Steed meanwhile tackles the source of the

pink ribbon which tied the corpses. The proprietor of Fancy Frills and Packaging Limited tells him to return later, but when Steed has left, Merridon strangles the proprietor with one of his own ribbons. As Mother and Lady Diana piece together Wilkington's papers, three other agents are lured, one at a time, to a disused village, erected as a film set. There, another Remak man, Paxton, sends them on to a pub at Lower Storpington with his dying breath. (He feigns death – once with a knife in his back, then from an arrow in his chest, and finally with a sword in his stomach.) At the pub the agents are met by Brinstead and sent to the factory, to be murdered by Remak. Lady Diana gets a lead to the factory where she meets Ralph Bleech, partner of the dead Wilkington. He tells her that his partner was an electronics expert working on an advanced computer at Lower Storpington. Bleech, however, knows more than he reveals and immediately leaves to blackmail the men behind Remak. But at the factory he himself becomes another victim and is pushed into a murder room by Brinstead and Merridon. His gift-wrapped body is then dropped by helicopter into the same graveyard as before. Steed and Lady Diana close in on the factory, crushing Brinstead on the way with a large log which they roll down a hill. They enter the factory from different ways, and Steed runs the gauntlet of the murder rooms, pitting his wits against his computer adversary. He successfully avoids death by arrow, horizontal guillotine (which cleaves his bowler in two), crushing, garrotting and electrocution, before being joined by Lady Diana. He then feigns death at the hands of a remote-controlled gun, and as his jacket is whisked away to be gift-wrapped, he and Lady Diana follow it and find Merridon operating the computer. In the ensuing fight, Merridon meets his death in one of his own murder rooms, and before they leave Lady Diana sets the computer on a course of self-destruction. Steed arrives back at his apartment and has difficulty entering because Tara has sent him so many postcards. Tara is waiting for him, her arm in a sling. Writer's cramp, she explains. She also has a present for him, an inflatable dinghy concealed in a small box. When it is released...

THE MORNING AFTER

By Brian Clemens

John Steed	Patrick Macnee
Tara King	Linda Thorson
Merlin	Peter Barkworth
Jenny	Penelope Horner
Brigadier Hansing	Joss Ackland
Sgt Hearn	Brian Blessed
Major Parsons	Donald Douglas
Yates	Philip Dunbar
Cartney	Jonathan Cartney

Designed by Robert Jones
Directed by John Hough
Produced by Albert Fennell and Brian Clemens

IN the hands of John Steed, a bowler and an umbrella can be as deadly as a machine gun. So he seldom carries a firearm. But as Steed hides in his apartment, waiting for a visitor to arrive, he startles Tara by producing a pistol. He explains that Merlin is one of the most cunning, dangerous and charming spies of them all. Steed has lured him to his flat to capture him before he can sell the newly developed sleep capsules he has stolen from a secret establishment. Merlin — actually a quadruple agent — lives up to his reputation. He bursts through the door, and in the resulting mêlée a gas capsule is smashed and all three fall to the floor unconscious. When Steed awakens, he discovers a whole day has passed. He tries to phone headquarters, but there is no answer. And when he goes out into the normally busy street, he finds it deserted. Returning to his apartment, he finds Tara still sound asleep, but Merlin is almost awake, so Steed decides to hand him over to the authorities alone. Handcuffed to each other they set off in the vintage Rolls until they find their way blocked by abandoned vehicles. Continuing their journey on foot, they arrive too late to save a man, Cartney, from being shot by a military firing squad led by Sergeant Hearn. Steed and Merlin are nearly shot themselves, but escape when Steed grabs Sergeant Hearn, and uses him as a shield. From reporter Jenny Firston, and her photographer Yates, whom they discover hiding in a van, they learn the truth of the situation. Martial law has been declared, and the population evacuated because a nuclear bomb has been discovered beneath a trade commission building. With everyone on the streets being shot on sight, Steed is concerned that Tara may wake and go outside. So, placing Merlin on his honour not to escape, he unlocks the handcuffs and with Jenny and Yates sets off to warn Tara. Sergeant

Hearn, however, has set a trap for them and in the resulting fight, Yates is killed, Merlin escapes, and Steed and Jenny are captured. Tara, meanwhile, wakes and sets out to find Steed and Merlin. She arrives in time to rescue Steed and Jenny from the firing squad they are now facing, but Merlin has come back to help too, and accidentally puts Tara back to sleep with one of the gas capsules. From the captured Hearn, Steed learns that Brigadier Hansing, who is supposed to be defusing the nuclear bomb, is in fact masterminding a scheme to hold the government to ransom. Disgusted at being made redundant by a computer, he invented the story about the bomb as an excuse to substitute bribed men for the real troops, and is now in the throes of placing a real nuclear bomb in the trade commission building! Steed and Merlin join forces to overcome the Brigadier, his Adjutant Major Parsons, and their phoney troops. Using the gas capsules, they put the Brigadier's gang out of action. After a long, drawn-out fight, Steed puts Merlin on his best behaviour and allows him to go free. As Jenny leaves to file her story, Tara wakes and asks if anything exciting has happened. Later, Steed opens the door to his apartment to find Tara holding a box she has found on his doorstep. The box, from Merlin, is empty. Then Steed receives a phone call to say that Merlin has broken into a secret establishment and stolen some luminous dust. Realisation dawning, Steed switches out the lights — the empty box is glowing.

Tara finds the sleeping figure of Sergeant Hearn in a scene from The Morning After.

Lady Diana Forbes-Blakeney was the most aristocratic of all of Steed's up-market female colleagues.

In the churchyard, Lady Diana imperiously dangles Wilkington's fobwatch in Steed's face, in Killer

THE CURIOUS CASE OF THE COUNTLESS CLUES

By Philip Levene

John Steed	Patrick Macnee
Tara King	Linda Thorson
Earle	Anthony Bate
Gardiner	Kenneth Cope
Stanley	Tony Selby
Doyle	Peter Jones
Janice	Tracy Reed
Flanders	Edward de Souza
Burgess	George A Cooper
Dawson	Reginald Jessup

Designed by Robert Jones
Directed by Don Sharp
Produced by Albert Fennell and Brian Clemens

TWO men are apparently investigating a murder which has been committed in the Dulwich flat of Herbert Dawson. A chalk outline indicates where the body would lie, but the body is missing! Suddenly, Dawson arrives home, and Earle, one of the two men, shoots him, firing his gun through a polythene bag. The two men depart, leaving Dawson's body lying in the chalk outline on the floor. Steed commiserates with Tara in her apartment. Her leg is in plaster following a mishap on holiday. He explains that he cannot stay long, since he has an appointment with Ministry sleuth, Sir Arthur Doyle, who sports a deer-stalker hat, smokes a meerchaum pipe, and has a (female) assistant called Watson. Doyle has picked up all the carefully-laid clues at the Dawson murder and he suspects a friend of Steed's, press tycoon Sir William Burgess. Doyle suspects that Burgess might be the owner of a Rolls-Royce seen leaving the scene of the crime, with the registration number partially identified as CLU. Steed is asked to check out Burgess' story. Steed questions his friend and is disturbed to see that Burgess has a button missing from his coat. A similar button was found in Dawson's flat. Also during the interview, the mention of Dulwich seems to shake the man so much that he miscues a shot on the billiards table. He smokes Havana cigars, and the butt of such a cigar was found at the scene of the crime. However, Burgess has a strong alibi when he mentions being helped out after a breakdown on the A4 by the Motor Rescue Service, at the time of the murder. (Later Steed discovers that the MRS have not recorded the breakdown and the matter will take some time to check.) As Steed leaves, Earle, Dawson's killer, enters and begins a game of billiards

with the distraught Burgess. Earle and Gardiner, his partner in Dawson's murder, get into a lift with financier Robert Flanders, and manage to take his handkerchief and a button from his coat. Then, when Flanders goes for a drive in his white Jaguar, the two men pick up an identical car. Flanders' car soon breaks down on the road in the same way that Burgess' did. Earle then dresses in Flanders' clothes and allows a passing cyclist to see him. He then takes a rifle, which he and Gardiner have brought with them, to a nearby cottage where he shoots a man named Scott. This is to pin the Scott murder on Flanders, who is meanwhile being helped after his breakdown on the A4 by a Motor Service Rescue patrolman. Doyle reports Scott's murder to Steed, and points out that the clues point to Flanders being the killer (as intended by Earle). Steed says he knows the financier through his sister, Janice, so Doyle asks him to check Flanders' alibi. Steed discovers that Flanders also had a breakdown on the A4 at the time of the murder, but when he finds a .275 calibre rifle missing from Flanders' cabinet, a rifle of the type used to kills Scott, he is suspicious. Flanders, however, tells him the rifle is at his hunting lodge. Steed leaves and just misses the arrival of Earle, who now shows Flanders how he has been set-up with Scott's murder. Even the Motor Rescue man, Stanley, who was part of the plot, will not establish his alibi for him. Earle then extorts a valuable Valesco painting from Flanders. As he leaves with the painting, Janice notices him and goes to her brother's study to find the Valesco missing. Gardiner now menaces Burgess and tries to extort a painting from him, but Burgess refuses. He phones Steed and says he lied about the Dawson murder, and now wants to make a clean breast of things. But before Steed can get to him, Earle menaces Burgess again, saying that the police, having found Dawson's murder weapon, are on the way to pick him up. Before Steed can intervene, Burgess is arrested and charged. Doyle is convinced that Burgess is guilty, but Steed believes that it is all too neat. And he is encouraged further when Janice calls to tell him that Scott was sacked from Flanders' firm for fiddling the books. Janice also tells him that a man has removed a valuable painting from her brother's collection. When questioned, however, Flanders won't discuss it. Earle now puts further pressure on Flanders for another painting, and Janice once again sees Earle and Gardiner removing

the painting. She follows them to Earle's cottage, but as she is phoning Steed for help, Stanley, the MSR man, finds her. When Steed arrives, Earle and his entourage have flown, leaving a cross-bow trap for Steed to walk into. He foils it by wearing a breast-plate which he has taken from a suit of armour in the hall. Steed goes to Flanders' house and is astonished to see that the paintings have been restored. Janice backs up her brother's story that nothing is amiss. Only later when Steed returns to look at Flanders' rifle does the real story break. Flanders disturbs Steed as he removes the rifle, which Steed points out as being the wrong one. The real one has been removed in order to frame Flanders. Janice cracks first, then persuades her brother to tell Steed how the frame was worked. Earle now decides to use the framing technique on Steed himself. He and Gardiner remove a glove, umbrella and bowler from Steed's Rolls, then tamper with the car so that it will break down. Stanley arrives, but Steed knocks him out. He then discovers a photograph of Tara among Stanley's possessions, which suggests that she may be next for the framing technique. He phones Tara, but before he can warn her, the line goes dead. Earle is with Tara already, and cuts the wires. Steed rushes to Tara's apartment. Tara meanwhile, fighting for her life, squirts the contents of her hot-water bottle into Earle's face, then knocks him out with a pair of skis. Steed arrives in time to dispose of Gardiner, then, rather ignominiously, he trips over the furniture and hurts his leg. In the last scene, Steed is an invalid, with the fully-recovered Tara playing the ministering angel. She produces champagne — and for Steed, a yard of ale in a special elongated glass.

WISH YOU WERE HERE

By Tony Williamson

John Steed	Patrick Macnee
Tara King	Linda Thorson
Charles Merrydale	Liam Redmond
Maxwell	Robert Urquhart
Basil	Brook Williams
Parker	Dudley Foster
Mother	Patrick Newell
Kendrick	Gary Watson
Mellor	Richard Caldicot
Vickers	Derek Newark
Brevitt	David Garth
Miss Craven	Louise Pajo
Mr Maple	John Cazabon
Girl	Sandra Fehr
Rhonda	Rhonda Parker

Designed by Robert Jones
Directed by Don Chaffey
Produced by Albert Fennell and Brian Clemens

TARA'S uncle, Charles Merryvale, is being held prisoner in a holiday hotel, while his captors take over his vast business empire. It is a prison with no visible restraint, but Parker, the manager, and Mellor, the waiter, prove it is just as effective when Merryvale's friend, James Brevitt, attempts to walk out. He slips on a highly polished step and breaks his leg. Concerned that Charles has not returned from his holiday, Maples, the family retainer, calls on Tara King. He explains that Stephen Kendrick, the company secretary, has taken over the business. When Kendrick appears and produces a postcard reputed to come from Tara's uncle, Steed and Tara pretend to believe him and leave. But Tara visits her uncle at the hotel shown on the postcard – and finds that she too is a prisoner at the hotel. She sees Brevitt try to escape again but this time he is knocked down by a car. Trying to escape herself, Tara finds her car won't start, and then a window-cleaner drops a bucket of water on her. Her wet dress is taken away to be dried, but when it is returned it has a large burn mark on it. Steed meanwhile visits Mother, whom he finds suspended by a parachute harness in a room full of photographs of agents. Another agent, Basil Crighton-Latimer, Mother's nephew, is in attendance, practising with a golf club. After Basil chips a golf ball into Mother's drink, he is sent to assist Tara, while Steed is told to go in search of a missing agent. Meanwhile, at the hotel, Tara has stolen a chambermaid's dress and gone to look for Brevitt, the man knocked down while trying to escape. She finds him dead in his room, but when she and her uncle take a bonafide guest, Maxwell Greene, to see

the body and prove they are being held prisoner, it lashes out at them. Vickers, one of the captors, has changed places with the corpse. Maxwell says he will go for help, but soon limps back with a story that he fell on a roller skate. Over a game of croquet, Tara, Maxwell and Uncle Charles discuss their plan of escape. Enter Basil, with a huge collection of luggage and holiday paraphernalia. He finds Tara's uncle bandaged in bed, after trying to escape in a visiting laundry van. He was unceremoniously returned through the laundry chute! At first Basil refuses to believe that they are being held prisoner. Then he tries to leave, but his car tyres are flat, and a pot of red paint is dropped on him. As Stephen Kendrick arrives to see Parker, the manager, Basil, now wearing a waiter's uniform, tries to escape while playing ball with Tara in the grounds. Once on the road, however, he is lured into a trap by a girl in a bikini. Mellor knocks him out. Basil is returned to the hotel, and he, Tara, Maxwell and Uncle Charles barricade themselves in the hotel kitchen and cut off all food, water and electricity supplies, to make the real hotel guests leave. Then, Maxwell produces a gun and reveals that he is the mastermind behind the hotel prison. Maxwell is knocked out by Basil with two large wooden butter-patters, and then Basil signals to the rest of the gang with a flashlight, making them believe that Maxwell has the upper hand. He then turns off all the hotel lights and, under cover of darkness, they render the rest of the gang unconscious, one by one, with frying pans. Maxwell, now recovered, is the last one to succumb. He escapes and runs to his car but finds the tyres are flat. As he passes the hotel, a pot of red paint is dropped on his head, and his demise is completed after he slips on a carefully-placed banana skin! Steed arrives at the hotel as Basil and Tara are shaking hands. Then Tara visits Steed. He whispers to her that he is being held in his flat against his will. Tara pledges herself to tackle the hidden culprit – and Steed goes off smiling. Leaving her holding a baby, which then starts to cry . . .

Steed discusses The Curious Case Of The Countless Clues with Sir Arthur Doyle, a Ministry sleuth.

Tara is trapped in a holiday hotel with her Uncle Charles and another guest, Maxwell Green, in Wish You Were Here.

STAY TUNED

By Tony Williamson

John Steed	Patrick Macnee
Tara King	Linda Thorson
Proctor	Gary Bond
Lisa	Kate O'Mara
Mother	Patrick Newell
Father	Iris Russell
Wilks	Duncan Lamont
Collins	Howard Marion-Crawford
Sally	Denise Buckley
Kreer	Roger Delgado
Dr Meitner	Harold Kasket
Travers	Ewan Roberts
Taxi driver	Patrick Westwood

Designed by Robert Jones
Directed by Don Chaffey
Produced by Albert Fennell and Brian Clemens

When Mother goes on holiday in Stay Tuned, *Father steps into the breach – but Father, of course, is a woman!*

STEED is about to leave for a holiday. He puts a carnation in his button-hole and picks up his luggage. But as he opens the door he is confronted by Proctor, who then knocks him out. We come back to a scene identical to the first. Except that when Steed goes to take a carnation, the vase is full of withered flowers. This time, as he tries to leave the apartment, it is Tara King who confronts him. She convinces him, with some difficulty, that he has already had three weeks' holiday. And that he sent postcards and even phoned Mother from Paris and Rome. Opening his luggage, Steed finds that all his clothes have been used, and there is even a present for Tara. Dr Meitner, the Department's psychiatrist, tells him he is suffering from a form of amnesia, but Steed still has his doubts and decides to visit his chief. But Mother is away, and Father is looking after the Department. Father is a gentle, middle-aged, blind woman who surrounds herself with objects which are nice to touch. Everything in the room has an interesting texture, shape or smell – sculptures, ornate door knobs, collages and flowers. Steed persuades her to remove him from the active list and reduce his security rating to third class. Back in his apartment, an extremely worried Steed tries hard to recall the last three weeks, but can only remember the grinning face of an oriental. After driving around London in a taxi, Steed eventually comes to a street that seems vaguely familiar. Paying off the cab, he walks down the street until he is surprised by Proctor, who again knocks him out. Steed is again in his apartment, preparing for a holiday, until, with astonishment, he sees the vase of dead carnations and recalls what has passed. When Tara arrives, she finds Steed in a state of mental disintegration. Steed next goes to see Travers, a forensics expert, who is examing his car. Travers assures him that even if Steed did not take a holiday on the Continent, the car most certainly did – it even has French petrol in its tank! Steed returns, brooding, to his home. When the doorbell rings, he finds an attractive girl waiting for him. She introduces herself as Sally Unstrutter, and explains that she has called to apologise for colliding with his car a fortnight ago – in London! Sally restores Steed's faith in his sanity and when he goes to the street where the accident took place, he sees the smiling oriental face he recalled. It is a brass door knocker. Later, he drives Tara to the house, but the knocker has gone. Inside the house are Kreer, Proctor, Wilks, and Lisa, gloating over their successful plan. It appears that Kreer has hypnotised Steed and is conditioning him to kill Mother. Steed and Tara decide, separately, to break into the house and investigate its contents. Tara arrives first and after a fight, Kreer is impaled on his own sword-stick. Proctor and Lisa capture Tara, however, and through post-hypnotic suggestion, tell her that Proctor has been erased from Steed's mind and that he is unable to see him. When Steed breaks into the house, Tara accuses him of killing Kreer. What Steed does not see is Proctor standing with a gun at his head, in case Tara should disobey. Father sends one of her agents, Collins, to follow Steed when he goes back to the house. But Proctor shoots Collins. Steed, not seeing Proctor, imagines that he may have killed the agent himself. Taking a gun with him, Steed goes to see Mother, who has now returned. Tara, meanwhile, escapes after overpowering Lisa and Wilks, and sets off to stop Steed before he can kill Mother. Steed's finger is tightening on the trigger as she arrives. She knocks the gun from his hand, and then explains the whole mystery. Steed is now able to see Proctor, who has been shadowing him. With a blow that matches the ones he's received from the thug, he knocks Proctor cold. It is now Tara who is performing the pre-holiday ritual previously enacted by Steed. He arrives and at her apartment offers her a holiday in the sunshine, but Tara turns it down – only to discover that the job was in Bermuda!

TAKE ME TO YOUR LEADER

By Terry Nation

John Steed	Patrick Macnee
Tara King	Linda Thorson
Stonehouse	Patrick Barr
Mother	Patrick Newell
Captain Tim	John Ronane
Cavell	Michael Robbins
Major Glasgow	Henry Stamper

and Penelope Keith, Hugh Cross, Elisabeth Robillard, Michael Hawkins, Sheila Hammons, Bryan Kendrick, Raymond Adamson, Mathew Long, Cliff Diggins, Wilfred Boyle

Designed by Robert Jones
Directed by Robert Fuest
Produced by Albert Fennell and Brian Clemens

FOR The Avengers, it is a case with a difference. This case is an ingenious device, slightly larger than a briefcase, which is being used by the other side to carry stolen secrets. Steed and Tara must follow it, as it is passed on by a chain of enemy agents, and find out for whom it is intended. The case has a mechanism which enables it to talk, and this it uses to startling effect while it is in the hands of an agent named Shepherd. When Holland, one of Mother's men, breaks into Shepherd's room to steal it, the case cries 'Stop thief!' Shepherd emerges from the bathroom to shoot Holland, with a blade fired from a clarinet. Steed and Tara follow the next link in the chain, Howard Trent, to an airfield. Steed has filled the area with concealed agents – even one masquerading as a scarecrow – but the next contact surprises them all. It is an Alsatian dog! In the resulting confusion, Trent falls from his motorbike and is killed. Steed, however, manages to grab the case. He takes it to a warehouse where he finds Mother sitting in a fork-lift truck, driven by his secretary, Rhonda. Without the keys possessed by the agents in the chain, the case will self-destruct if opened. Major Glasgow, a forensics expert, X-rays it and declares it is a security expert's dream. Its contents include a tape recorder, an explosives charge, an elaborate key mechanism and £500,000 – the final pay-off for the mastermind. Tara finds a key hidden in one of the studs on the dead Trent's leather jacket. When she turns it in the case, a recorded voice tells them the next contact is at the Cremone Hotel. At the hotel the case tells Steed to place it in a wardrobe and wait. But he fails to realise the wardrobe has a false back, and as he lies on the bed, the case is stolen by its new envoy,

Condon. Tara saves the day by hiding in the back of Condon's car and knocking him out after he has turned the key and triggered off the taped information about the next contact. Substituting herself for Condon, she takes the case to its next rendezvous, a ballet school. There she meets teacher Audrey Long, a child of six called Beryl, and her lollipop-sucking contact, a little girl in a fairy outfit, called Sally Graham. When Steed arrives and is hit on the head by Audrey, Tara fights with her and finally knocks her out. They then bribe Sally for the key to the case, which is hidden in the star of her fairy wand. The case announces that their next contact will meet them at a telephone box. Mother meanwhile receives a visit from Colonel Stonehouse, head of a rival department. Mother, it seems, is suspected of leading the chain of agents who are stealing the secrets. At the telephone box Tara is met by Cavell, who is at first inclined to mix business with pleasure, until Steed steps in and overpowers him. Tara gains details of Cavell's next contact by pretending to escape, and they leave Cavell tied up as they take the case to Captain Tim, one of the world's leading karate experts, who they find practising at a judo school. Unfortunately, the agent Tara has replaced was reputed to be the only person in the world who could beat the Captain in a fight. And the karate expert decides to put her to the test. Steed ends the fierce fight by reaching through the door and hitting Captain Tim on the head with his steel-lined bowler. The Captain, believing Tara has dealt him a secret blow, gives her the key to the case. Shepherd, the killer with the clarinet, is the next contact. As he fights Steed, he reveals that this time there is no metal key – only a sonic note on a tuba. Shepherd is killed in the struggle, but Steed finds the key note, by sitting on a set of bagpipes! At the luggage-loading bay at Kings Cross station, The Avengers deposit the case, and are astonished to see two men arrive carrying similar cases. Tara follows one, Jackson, and buries him under a pile of timbers, only to find she has been following a decoy case. She is trapped in a church crypt as the case begins to emit poison gas, but escapes by using the case's self-destructing device to blow off the crypt door. Steed, who is following the other man, Williams, is astonished when he takes the case to Mother! But he refuses to believe that his chief is a traitor and overpowers Williams. Then he and Mother wait to see who comes to collect the case. It is Colonel

A smart tap from Steed's bowler convinces Captain Tim that Tara is the girl for him in Take Me To Your Leader.

Stonehouse. Tara arrives in time to place a booby-trapped case in the Colonel's car, and he is gassed. In the final scene, Steed and Tara wait for someone to arrive. Their visitor turns out to be a dog. In his mouth is a mini skirt, and Steed, smiling, sets off to find the owner.

A Publicity shot of Linda Thorson taken before the beginning of the sixth series of The Avengers.

FOG

By Jeremy Burnham

John Steed	Patrick Macnee
Tara King	Linda Thorson
President	Nigel Green
Travers	Guy Rolfe
Mother	Patrick Newell
Carstairs	Terence Brady
Sanders	Paul Whitsun-Jones
Maskell	David Lodge
Fowler	Norman Chappell

and David Bird, Frank Sieman, Patsy Smart,
Virginia Clay, John Garrie, Bernard Severn,
Frederick Peisley, Stanley Jay, Arnold Diamond,
William Lyon Brown, John Barrard

Designed by Robert Jones
Directed by John Hough
Produced by Albert Fennell and Brian Clemens

WHEN two foreign delegates at a disarmament conference are murdered as they walk through the foggy London streets, there is all the makings of an international incident. But the murderer seems to be re-creating the Gaslight Ghoul murders which took place in 1888. Wearing a top hat and cape, and carrying a sword-stick in a cricket bag, this modern Jack the Ripper even makes his escape in a hansom cab. Steed and Tara meet Mother, who is navigating his Rolls-Royce through the dense fog in nautical fashion, with Rhonda at the helm. They are assigned to investigate the murders and visit the scene of the crime in time to glimpse a man named Osgood, wearing a similar outfit to the murderer, leaving the scene. He escapes but leaves behind his cape and sword. Tara takes the cape to a theatrical costumiers, where Fowler, the proprietor, identifies the owner. Steed visits a master cutler, Maskell, with the sword to discover who owns it. Both agents then meet at the home of the owner of both – Osgood. The landlady, Mrs Golightly, tells them that Osgood is out, wearing his Gaslight Ghoul outfit. When he returns, Steed and Tara pounce on him. But he is not the killer. Opening his cricket bag they discover only a flask of coffee and sandwiches. Osgood turns out to be a member of the Gaslight Ghoul Club, formed to investigate the unsolved murders committed by the killer. As Steed and Tara leave and are about to get into their car, a blood-curdling scream is heard. They rush back to Osgood's flat, where they find him dead, an obvious victim of the Gaslight Ghoul. With a fake diary in which Steed's Great Aunt Florence recorded an eye-witness account of a hither-

to undiscovered Gaslight Ghoul murder, Steed manages to gain membership of the exclusive club. The headquarters are an eerie Victorian mansion, set in an imitation Victorian street. In the clubroom Steed meets the President, Sir Geoffrey Armstrong, and five bearded members. Mark Travers, secretary of the club and the possessor of a warped sense of humour, takes him to see the club's Black Museum. The museum's curator, Wellbeloved, says that several knives are missing from the collection. Meanwhile, Tara, having broken into the club's rear entrance, is searching through Sir Geoffrey's office. She learns from papers that Sir Geoffrey was once a surgeon. And in a a dimly-lit, fog-filled street, the Gaslight Ghoul strikes again. Valarti, another member of the conference, is the victim. Sir Geoffrey returns in time to discover Tara looking through his files and collection of scalpels. They fight, and Tara knocks him out with a chair and escapes. She returns to her flat and, opening the door, is confronted by the Gaslight Ghoul! It turns out to be Steed, wearing his new club uniform. Steed leaves to check on the safety of the three remaining members of the conference. But on arriving at their hotel he learns that one of them, Haller, has gone for a walk. Rushing out into the foggy street, Steed manages to save him from the Gaslight Ghoul. He leaves Haller at his apartment, armed with an arsenal of weapons, and under the protection of Carstairs, an agent from another department who is helping him on the case. Tara is checking on the hansom-cab that is always heard leaving the scene of the murders. She visits Sanders, proprietor of the only hansom-cab firm in London, but she is unable to prevent him from being murdered by the Ghoul, who escapes after bowling Tara over with a wheel. An invoice, bearing Sir Geoffrey's name, leads her to his home. Steed is already there, but before they can enter, however, they see someone leave in Sir Geoffrey's car. Tara follows in Steed's vintage Rolls, while Steed stays to search Sir Geoffrey's study. A figure suddenly lurches out of the dark at Steed. It is Sir Geoffrey. He has been stabbed by the real Ghoul, who has stolen a file containing the professions of the conference members. Steed now has a clue to the identity of the Ghoul, for he remembers that Travers has an armaments business, and it would be in his interest to sabotage the disarmament meeting. Hindered by the wheel of the hansom-cab, which threatens to fall off,

Steed and Tara, suitably dressed, set out to find the Gaslight Ghoul, but the London streets are full of Fog.

Steed clatters his way to the Gaslight Ghoul Club to save Tara, who is already feeling the point of Travers' blade in the Black Museum. As Steed arrives, Travers uses swords from a showcase as spears and hurls them at him, but Steed deflects them with his sword. As he finally knocks Travers out, he discovers that the deflected swords have narrowly missed Tara and are embedded in the wall around her. The fog outside is clearing, and Mother and Rhonda, still navigating their car like a boat, are able at last to confirm their bearings. They have taken a wrong turn and are in a railway tunnel! Back at Tara's apartment, the fog has returned, both outside and inside. The air conditioning unit has gone wrong. As they stumble about the room, Tara wonders what has happened to Mother and Rhonda. They soon find out. There is a roar of an engine and Mother and his secretary whizz straight through the apartment in their car. It seems that Tara has left the front door open!

HOMICIDE AND OLD LACE

By Malcolm Hulke and Terrence Dicks

John Steed	Patrick Macnee
Tara King	Linda Thorson
Mother	Patrick Newell
Harriet	Joyce Carey
Georgina	Mary Merrall
Col Corf	Gerald Harper
Dunbar	Keith Baxter
Fuller	Edward Brayshaw
Rhonda	Rhonda Parker

Designed by Robert Jones
Directed by John Hough
Produced by Albert Fennell and Brian Clemens

This scene appeared in Homicide And Old Lace, *but is actually part of* The Great, Great Britain Crime.

IT'S Mother's birthday. And to celebrate the occasion he pays a visit to his two ageing aunts, Harriet and Georgina, who present him with a brace of duelling pistols. As well as being his most ardent fans, they have also seen practically every spy film ever made, and are consequently familiar with the jargon of the underworld. So that they beg him to tell them an inside story about the workings of his department. Mother embarks on the story to end all stories. Embellished by some of the best fights from the Avengers series, and by Mother's own vivid imagination, he tells his two aunts how Steed and Tara thwarted the crime of the century – The Great, Great Britain Crime. Intercrime, the opposite of Interpol with whom Steed had battled before (helped by Mrs Catherine Gale), is an alliance of the international underworld. And they are aiming high. In one swoop they are going to steal every single art treasure in Britain, including the Crown Jewels. It appears that in a national emergency, Colonel Corf, head of security, is given a code word on his hot line from the Prime Minister, and immediately every art treasure in the country is secured in a hidden underground ware-house, and replicas substituted. Dunbar, head of Intercrime, plans to gain possession of the code word – changed every 24 hours – and use it to get all the art treasures in one place. Then he will move in with his men. Mother, however, gets wind of the plot and sends Steed and Tara to infiltrate the gang. This Steed achieves by robbing an Intercrime gang of £3,000,000 worth of diamonds that they have just stolen from a Bond Street jewellers. Thus gaining their respect, he introduces Tara, who proves her worth by beating the world's best safe-cracker in a safe-breaking contest. The double-agent Avengers then visit Colonel Corf, and under cover of a security check, Tara cracks his safe and photographs the code which will actuate the withdrawal of every item of Britain's heritage. Intercrime's Chinese operative, Osaka, taps Colonel Corf's hot line and enables Steed to pass on the codeword to Operation Rule Britannia, ostensibly run from the Prime Minister's office. Corf then calls in all the art treasures in Britain. Even the throne is removed from Buckingham Palace. Dunbar, however, suspects The Avengers and leaves Tara behind as a hostage when they go to raid the vaults where the treasures are stored. Tara escapes from her captors and tries to warn Colonel Corf of the imminent raid. But he will not believe her, and she is forced to hide when Dunbar's gang arrive. Between them, she and Steed overpower the whole gang. Steed and Tara are later having a drink with Mother, with Rhonda in attendance, when Steed says that he has never heard Rhonda speak. He persuades her to talk – only for Mother's voice to issue from her mouth. Mother, it seems is practising to be a ventriloquist!

Linda Thorson models one of the designs specially created by Alan Hughes for her part as Tara King.

LOVE ALL

By Jeremy Burnham

John Steed	**Patrick Macnee**
Tara King	**Linda Thorson**
Martha	**Veronica Strong**
Bromfield	**Terence Alexander**
Sir Rodney	**Robert Harris**
Mother	**Patrick Newell**
Thelma	**Patsy Rowlands**

and Brian Oulton, Frank Gatliff, Ann Rye, Zulema
Dene, Peter Stephens, Norman Pitt, John Cobner,
Robin Tolhurst, Larry Taylor, David Baron

Directed by Peter Sykes
Produced by Albert Fennell and Brian Clemens

FOUR important civil servants, Tait, Fryer, Roxby and Sir Rodney Kellogg, are attending a top-secret meeting in a Whitehall Ministry. All have one thing in common – they seem incredibly prone to love at first sight. This is unfortunate, for the first person they see is a frowsy-looking charlady scrubbing the corridor outside. And she is in the pay of the enemy. After the meeting, Sir Rodney embraces the charlady, Martha, and she extorts the secrets of the meeting from him. When Metcalfe, a young man from security, overhears them, Martha orders Sir Rodney to shoot him with her gun. Steed keeps a strange rendezvous with Mother at an underground cricket school. Nonchalantly walking along the road reading a newspaper, he falls down an open manhole, landing safely on a mattress. He finds his superior playing cricket, with Rhonda bowling and Tara looking on. They discuss the security leaks and Mother assigns the two agents to the case. Sir Rodney, meanwhile, is under arrest following the murder. But he escapes and makes his way to Martha's home. Without her charlady disguise, she is an attractive young woman. Sir Rodney persuades her to elope with him in his Rolls, but after they have driven a short distance, she shoots him and joins an accomplice, Bromfield, in another car. At the scene of the crime, Tara recognises the scent of a rare perfume in the Rolls-Royce and visits the manufacturers, Bellchamber Brothers. From them, Tara receives a list of the rich clients the perfume had been sold to, but Martha (in her charlady disguise) has been listening and makes Bromfield send one of his henchmen to get the list from Tara. In the ensuing fight at Tara's apartment, the man accidentally shoots himself and the list is charred to ashes. At the Ministry, it is Roxby's turn to succumb to Martha, soon after he receives a strange book. His colleague, Tait, gets a book, too – , and

immediately declares his passionate devotion to a policewoman who has come in to give him a parking ticket! An engraving on a ring taken from the dead thug in Tara's apartment leads Steed to the Casanova Ink Company, where he finds author Rosemary Z Glade, a man, dictating a book to his attractive secretary, Thelma. In the printing room he sees Bromfield, Martha and a large, tough woman called Athene. Steed distracts their attention and steals a copy of the books they are printing. Before he can read the book in his apartment, Steed is attacked by Fryer, the fourth civil servant, who is the latest to fall for the charlady. She has told him that Steed is a rival for her affections. After knocking him out, Steed looks at the book and finds a mechanism in the back which shines through a hypnotic pattern of microdots on the pages. Under magnification, they reveal the message 'You will fall in love with the next person you see'. Tara, alas, has been reading a similar book in Tait's office. And the next person she sees is Bromfield. He tells her their love has no future and orders her to leap through the window. Fortunately, Steed arrives in time to knock out Bromfield and save Tara, but she, in turn, wishing to avenge the man she loves, attacks Steed, who is forced to give her a gentle tap from his bowler. Steed then dismantles the mechanism from the books and sticks 12 of them on his jacket and waistcoat. As Athene, Bromfield and Martha advance menacingly with their guns, it is love at first sight. Tara, recovering from the bump, also catches sight of Steed's coat and joins the queue for his affections. As Steed's Rolls glides off into the darkness, it is full of admirers arguing their claims to him.

It's just not cricket when a dastardly plot makes four civil servants very prone to love at first sight in Love All.

GET-A-WAY

By Philip Levene

John Steed	Patrick Macnee
Tara King	Linda Thorson
Col James	Andrew Keir
Rostov	Vincent Harding
Major Baxter	William Wilde
George Neville	Terence Langdon
Paul Ryder	Neil Hallett
Lubin	Robert Russell
Ezdorf	Peter Bowles
Professor Dodge	Peter Bayliss
Peters	John Hussey
Bryant	James Bellchamber
Magnus	Barry Lineman

Directed by Don Sharp
Produced by Albert Fennell and Brian Clemens

THREE Russian agents, Rostov, Lubin and Ezdorf, are sent by their bureau to kill three British agents. They are, however, caught by the British and confined in a tightly-guarded monastery, held by the British Army. Rostov escapes by knocking out one of the security personnel, Major Baxter, and bolting from his cell. Once recovered, Baxter searches, but finds no sign of the prisoner. Nor does anyone else, as Rostov makes his way to the East Wing, from which there is no escape. Although apparently cornered there, he appears to vanish completely and get clean away. Steed, Tara and a couple of agent friends are meanwhile enjoying a reunion dinner party at Steed's apartment. George Neville and Paul Ryder are the two guests. They were among the targets of the attempted Russian Great Assassination Plot. The party ends, and as Neville walks home, Rostov suddenly emerges as if from nowhere to kill him, and disappears just as quickly. Hearing the shots, Steed and Tara look out into the street, but they see nothing. Steed complains of the administration slip in not letting Neville know that Rostov was at large, but is told that Colonel James at the monastery was not apparently aware of the nature of the Great Assassination Plot. Steed decides to investigate the monastery, and while he is there, talking to Ezdorf, who has not yet divulged his target, Lubin suddenly escapes. He, like Rostov, appears to vanish into thin air. Steed tells Tara to go to the flat of Paul Ryder, who is Lubin's target. But she is too late. Lubin shoots Ryder just before she gets there, and then apparently vanishes. All Tara finds is a trail of red footprints, caused by Lubin accidentally knocking over a tin of red paint during his escape. Steed and Tara check the contents of Lubin's cell, and Steed is puzzled by the

Lizard brand vodka they find there, because he believed that Lubin was a teetotaller. Colonel James, however, confirms that Lubin started drinking while at the monastery. Checking the remaining agent, Ezdorf, he tells Steed that he is gratified that his friends have succeeded in their missions, and also that Steed will be his target when he escapes. Puzzled that the men have escaped from what seems to be an impregnable place, Steed goes to see Professor Dodge, the technologist who designed the monastery's security system. Dodge is concerned that his brainchild has failed and together they visit the monastery. After a check of the system, however, Dodge is flummoxed, and can offer no explanation for the escapes. Steed, however, finds a clue – a copy of Bryant's Natural History Magazine, like the one found in Lubin's cell. Page 25 of Rostov's copy is missing. Tara is sent to visit Peters, a civil servant, who shows her the files on the three Russians. All three agents had the Roman numerals CXVIIIVIIIV written on a piece of paper hidden in their shoes. Although the cypher men fail to crack the code, Tara by chance discovers that it means page 25 in a certain issue of Bryant's Natural History Magazine, a copy of which she has in Steed's apartment, taken from Lubin's cell. The issue number is CXVIIIVI, and the page is IIV, or 25. Tara phones Bryant for another copy of the issue, because Lubin's has page 25 missing. However, Lubin has got to Bryant before her and kills him. Then, with the aid of Magnus, a heavy, he makes his escape – apparently straight through a window, five storeys up. Tara, however, finds an intact copy in Bryant's office. On page 25 is an article on lizards, which seems to connect in some way to the Lizard trademark on the vodka bottle found in Lubin's cell. It also bears the name and address of the Magnus Importing Company, which matches the name on the van Tara saw leaving Bryant's premises. Steed pays the Magnus Importing Company a visit and finds crates of Lizard vodka in a warehouse. As Steed leaves, Magnus is preparing a bottle for special delivery to Ezdorf. Intercepting it, Steed himself delivers the package to Ezdorf, and lets it be known that he is hot on the trail. Tara, however, makes the real breakthrough. In conversation with Peters, he tells her about his pet chamelons, which change their colour to match their background. Meanwhile, in his cell, Ezdorf pours the contents of the Lizard vodka bottle down the sink, un-

screws the top and removes some liquid. This he pours onto his tracksuit, and its colour changes to merge with the background. He then escapes, throwing the prison officers into confusion. Ezdorf then meets Magnus and arms himself to kill Steed. Meanwhile, Colonel James warns Tara that the Russian has escaped and is on his way to eliminate Steed. Tara drives to his flat. Steed, however, has discovered the secret of the vodka bottles, so when he gets home and finds Ezdorf waiting, he is able to make himself invisible and he takes the Russian, who has bound and gagged Tara, by surprise. In the last scene, an invisible Steed wreaks havoc on Tara as she desperately tries to fix the curtains.

Ezdorf, who has chameleon-like qualities, takes Tara by surprise in Steed's flat, in **Get-a-Way.**

THINGUMAJIG

PANDORA

By Terry Nation

John Steed	Patrick Macnee
Tara King	Linda Thorson
Inge	Dora Reisser
Teddy	Jeremy Lloyd
Kruger	Iain Cuthbertson
Truman	Willoughby Goddard
Major Star	Hugh Manning
Dr Grant	John Horsley
Brett	Edward Burnham
Stenson	Vernon Dobcheff
Pike	Russell Waters
Philips	Michael McKevitt
Williams	Neville Hughes
Greer	John Moore
Bill	Harry Shacklock

Designed by Robert Jones
Directed by Leslie Norman
Produced by Albert Fennell and Brian Clemens

AN attractive archaeologist, Inge Tilson, and her colleague Greer, are excavating some Stone Age remains beneath a village church that is being rebuilt, when they discover several passages. And in one of the passages is 'It'. Greer is working separately from Inge, when he hears a slithering sound, then a soft bleeping, that is both electronic and animal. Suddenly the organ upstairs mysteriously begins to play and there is a blinding flash of light. Inge finds Greer's body, with a small burn mark in the middle of his forehead. In the dust behind him, he has traced the word 'It'. The vicar of the church, the Rev Shelley, seeks the help of Steed, who was his wartime colleague. While Steed investigates the church grounds, Tara visits an electronics expert, Professor Truman, to get his opinion on Greer's lamp, which was badly damaged when he was killed. The Professor, a constantly-sneezing snuff-taker, tells Tara that the lamp has been subjected to a white-hot discharge of electrical energy. Two other finds from the tunnel – some sand which has fused into glass and a necklace which has become molten – seem to indicate the same thing. Meanwhile, Major Star, an officious and overbearing member of the excavation team, tries to track down the mysterious killer in the catacombs below. But he and an elderly deaf man, Reston, are both killed. Brett, a third member of the team, who witnessed their deaths, is in a trance when rescued. Later Brett is wakened from the trance by the sound of the church organ and dies when he goes to investigate. Steed is at the church when Pike, a local angler, rushes in to report that all the fish in the stream are floating dead on the surface. The stream is dredged and a myste-

rious sealed box discovered. Steed is unable to open it and decides to send it to Tara so it can be examined by Professor Truman. Before he can do so, however, he first has to foil an attempt to steal it by Kruger, a large man with a foreign accent. Kruger then reports to Stenson, a representative of a foreign power, that he has been unable to recover either of the two deadly boxes that he has developed for them. He apparently lost them after crashing his van into a quarry. Tara meanwhile has received the box and shown it to Professor Truman. But he can make nothing of it. Later, when an X-ray of the box is developed, he phones Tara to say that the box is lethal. But he is too late. The deadly black box is already slithering towards her. Tara now plays a deadly game of hide and seek, and by the time she gets back to the phone, nearly every piece of furniture in the apartment is scorched. On the phone, the Professor tells her the box recharges itself on the electricity in the room, so Tara throws off the mains switch, plunging the flat into darkness. She finally manages to halt the progress of the box by throwing every electrical appliance in the room at it. She then administers the coup-de-grâce with a cascade of foam from bottles of champagne. She rushes to the church to save Steed from the other box in the catacombs below. But Steed is already in the catacombs, doing battle with Kruger as well as his deadly invention. Kruger reveals that he intends to release thousands of the boxes all over the country to devour the electricity and wipe out the population. The meglomaniac is about to shoot Steed when the box makes its presence heard. But instead of destroying Steed, it attacks and kills its inventor, and Steed manages to overcome it with the help of an arc welder.

By Brian Clemens

John Steed	Patrick Macnee
Tara King	Linda Thorson
Mother	Patrick Newell
Rupert Lasindall	Julian Glover
Henry Lasindall	James Cossins
Murray	Reginald Barrett
Juniper	John Laurie
Miss Faversham	Kathleen Byron
Hubert Pettigrew	Anthony Roye
Uncle Gregory	Peter Madden

Directed by Robert Fuest
Produced by Albert Fennell and Brian Clemens

IT is a bizarre scene from another era. In the corner of the room a phonograph blares out a rag-time tune of the 1914-18 period. And even the conversation between Rupert Lasindall, and his brother Henry, as they sit at the heavy Victorian dining table, is dated. Rupert is in the uniform of an Army Captain of the First World War, and he tells his brother that he will soon be recalled, as the Kaiser has launched an offensive on the Somme. 'But they cannot call me before tomorrow, so I shall not miss your wedding', he says, turning to Pandora, who sits at the head of the table. Pandora stares back blankly. Pandora is a dummy! The elaborate charade is part of the brothers' plans to prise a hidden fortune from their insane and senile Uncle Gregory. They have recreated Pandora, the beautiful girl who jilted him in his youth. The next step is to capture Tara King and brainwash her into believing she is Pandora. Tara is lured to an antique shop to see a rare clock, and is chloroformed by Henry, while Rupert looks on. Steed, having invited Tara to lunch, is concerned when she does not arrive. He visits the antique shop, only to be told by Murray, the proprietor, that he was out to lunch when Tara was supposed to have called. The next occurence is unprecedented. Instead of Steed visiting his chief, Mother actually calls on him! Mother explains that his latest office was in a balloon and communications had become difficult. Steed shows Mother a piece of paper which fell from Tara's assailant's pocket. It contains the words 'Fierce rabbit'. Mother is astonished. He explains that Fierce Rabbit was the code-name of the British agent in Armentières during the First World War! From the government file on Fierce Rabbit, Steed learns that the operative was named Simon Juniper, and goes to the clock shop where he now works. Juniper, however, tells him that the code-name

REQUIEM

By Brian Clemens

John Steed	**Patrick Macnee**
Tara King	**Linda Thorson**
Miranda	**Angela Douglas**
Firth	**John Cairney**
Wells	**John Paul**
Mother	**Patrick Newell**
Murray	**Denis Shaw**
Rista	**Terence Sewards**
Barrett	**Mike Lewin**
Jill	**Kathja Wyeth**
Bobby	**Harvey Ashby**
Vicar	**John Baker**
Rhonda	**Rhonda Parker**

Designed by Robert Jones
Directed by Don Chaffey
Produced by Albert Fennell and Brian Clemens

was used twice before he inherited it. Later Juniper visits a previous Fierce Rabbit – the brothers' weird and sinister Uncle Gregory (who is heard but not seen). And in the Victorian house, a terrified Juniper dies mysteriously. The brothers and their grim servant, Miss Faversham, attempt to brainwash the captured Tara. But, although dressed in Pandora's clothes, heavily drugged, and continually told that she is Pandora, she tenuously clings to her real identity. In an attempt to sidetrack Steed, Rupert and Henry place a skeleton in Tara's car and set fire to it, then place Juniper's body nearby. Mother breaks the news of her death to Steed, who refuses an offer of compassionate leave and continues on the case with renewed fury. He receives a visit from another Fierce Rabbit, Hubert Pettigrew who, after exhausting the contents of Steed's cocktail cabinet, tells him that the third Fierce Rabbit is Gregory Lasindall. Meanwhile, the brothers continue to brainwash Tara and she finally believes that she is Pandora. Wearing Pandora's wedding dress, she is taken by the brothers to meet their terrifying uncle. Faced by his lost love, Uncle Gregory tells them his fortune is hidden behind the picture of Pandora on the wall. In his haste, Rupert slashes away at the painting with a knife, only to discover that he has destroyed a priceless Rembrandt beneath Pandora's portrait. His furious brother, Henry, struggles with Rupert, and the strain is too much for their uncle, who has a heart attack and dies. Finally, Steed breaks into the house and, with his trusty steel bowler, finishes off the brothers and Miss Faversham. Later on, Steed has apparently got a headache. On the table nearby is the rare clock that Tara had been searching for in antique shops. It bears a label to Steed. But when Tara arrives, he pleads with her to take it back. She soon discovers why when it starts to chime – in tones that would rival those of Big Ben.

THE inscription on the wreath, propped on the grave, reads 'In loving memory of our dear Mother – the finest chap we ever knew. Died suddenly – explosively – RIP'. Among the mourners sits Tara King in a wheelchair, both legs in plaster, sustained only by pain-killing drugs. John Steed's department, it seems, is at its lowest ebb. But back to the beginning. Two thugs, Rista, and Murray, are waiting in an underground car park for Miranda Loxton, key witness in a court case against Murder International. But Miss Loxton and her bodyguard have been to a fancy-dress party and when their car arrives they are dressed as a tramp and a bewigged dame. The thugs mistakenly shoot the bodyguard (dressed as the dame) and Miranda escapes in her car. Mother sends Steed to guard Miranda and he takes her to a house in the country until the hearing. Cleaver, another agent, acts as decoy by dressing as Steed and placing a dummy of Miranda beside him in the passenger seat of Steed's Rolls. At the house, Steed and Miranda spend the time by enacting famous Army and Naval battles. But Miranda inevitably defeats Steed, for most of her ancestors were famous military strategists. Steed suggests a game of chess – his uncle was a chess Grand Master. Alas, he is defeated again. Miranda's aunt was a Grand Mistress. Only when they turn to Ludo does Steed show signs of superiority. Meanwhile, Tara is kidnapped by Rista and Murray and overhears them planning a booby-trap for Mother in Steed's apartment. She escapes, but has been so heavily drugged that she arrives outside Steed's apartment too late to stop the tragedy. She recovers consciousness to find her legs

covered by debris and two ambulance men carrying Mother's body away. Major Firth and Dr Wells tell her that her legs have received multiple fractures and they place her under sedation. She awakens in what appears to be a hospital, with her legs in plaster. A nurse called Jill, and Major Firth's assistant, Lieutenant Barrett, are in attendance. They tell her it is vital that they trace Steed, for he too is in danger. His gold pencil contains a bomb. But Tara cannot remember the whereabouts of the house. In the hope of jogging her memory, she asks Firth and Dr Wells to see agent Cleaver, but when they arrive he has been killed. Later when she asks them to take her to Mother's funeral. They agree, but insist on tranquillising her to make the journey more comfortable. When they return, Tara wakes up and sees Murray, one of the two men who held her prisoner, at her bedside. She recognises a tattoo on his arm, and tells Major Firth, who shoots the man. The incident jogs Tara's memory, and she recalls that there is a cannon weather vane on top of Steed's childhood home – the house in question. After Firth and Barrett leave to look for the house, Tara notices that one of her plaster casts is cracked. Breaking it open, she finds her leg is unscathed. Outside her room, she discovers that the hospital is actually a house, and in it is a mock-up of Steed's apartment in which Mother was supposed to have been killed. Investigating further, she finds the room in which she was earlier held captive by Rista and Murray. Realising that all the people in the house are impostors, and that Steed is now in danger, she escapes, overpowering Wells and Jill on the way. She finds Mother alive and well in Steed's flat, and together they devise a plan to construct a replica of the house that Firth and Barrett are looking for. When the two men come across the house with a cannon weather vane, they enter and are soon disposed of by Rhonda, Mother's assistant. She shows, for the first time, a dazzling display of speed and precision fighting. Tara later visits Steed and find him busy studying his family tree. He discloses some startling facts. One of his ancestors, Steed-the-Ready, dominated three shires in the Dark Ages. Another, Sir Steedalot, was one of King Arthur's knights. Finally Steed finds what he has been looking for. 'As I've always suspected,' he tells an enthralled Tara, 'I have Royal blood!'

TAKE-OVER

By Tery Nation

John Steed	Patrick Macnee
Tara King	Linda Thorson
Grenville	Tom Adams
Laura	Elisabeth Sellars
Bill	Michael Gwynn
Circe	Hilary Pritchard
Sexton	Garfield Morgan
Lomax	Keith Buckley
Groom	John Comer
Clifford	Anthony Sagar

Designed by Robert Jones
Directed by Robert Fuest
Produced by Albert Fennell and Brian Clemens

Steed packs his shooting gear as he prepares for his Christmas holiday – which he takes in February – in Take-Over.

AN elegant limousine shudders to a halt on a lonely country road. It appears to have engine trouble, and two of the occupants alight to investigate, leaving a handcuffed man, apparently their prisoner, in the back of the car. But it is a put-up job and the men, Fenton Grenville and Lomax, exchange secret smiles as their prisoner slides out of the car and makes his escape. It is an ideal test for a secret weapon which will help them sabotage a peace conference of foreign ministers, to be held at nearby Critchley Manor. For as soon as the fleeing man is out of sight, Grenville lights a cigar with a lighter, and the fugitive drops dead with a cloud of smoke gushing from his throat. With the aid of their mysterious weapon Grenville, Lomax, Sexton, and the beautiful Circe, take over the country cottage of Bill Bassett, in order to train a long-range rocket gun on Critchley Manor. Bassett, his wife Laura, and their servant, Groom, are gassed. Circe performs an operation on their throats. Then, to ensure the co-operation of Bill and Laura, their captors allow Groom to escape and kill him from afar with the aid of the lighter. But the gang have not reckoned on John Steed. He and Bill were prisoners-of-war together and, because they lost track of time while in captivity, they later discovered that they had celebrated Christmas in February. As a result, Steed has visited Bill and Laura for a February Christmas ever since. When he arrives, Bill introduces his captors as business colleagues. He has no choice, for Grenville tells him that he and his wife both have phosphor-bombs implanted in their throats, which can be detonated with the specially adapted lighter! Steed, however, quickly suspects that something is wrong, and after beating Grenville in a record contest of 'Guess the musician', Grenville challenges him to a shooting match. The wager is a hundred guineas for the first kill of the day. Unfortunately, Grenville intends the first kill to be Steed, and in a duel of wits and guns next day, Steed is wounded in the temple and, only escapes by convincing his enemies that he has died in some quicksand. Then he passes out. He is found by Hatch, one of the security men who has been drafted into the area for the peace conference, and is put on a London-bound ambulance for questioning. When he recovers consciousness and hears the men talking about the conference, he remembers everything. He knocks the men out and turns the ambulance back towards Critchley Manor. Meanwhile, Bassett receives another surprise visitor – Tara King. She is soon overpowered by Grenville and the gang, but breaks her bonds before Circe can operate and put a bomb in her throat. Grenville, however, forces Tara to drop her gun by threatening to detonate the bombs implanted in Bill and Laura's throats. Tara is then bound and gagged and left in a spare room while Lomax goes upstairs to fire the rocket gun at Critchley Manor. As Lomax is leaving, Steed arrives, and with an elastic-band catapult, he fires a phosphor bomb at Grenville, which sticks to his neck. Sexton, realising that he cannot detonate the bombs in the throats of Bill and Laura without killing Grenville too, falters – giving Steed the chance to overpower him and Circe. Steed then releases Tara and they dash upstairs reaching Lomax in time to swivel the rocket gun from its target, and knock him out. Some time later, Tara arrives at Steed's apartment to find him playing a round of invisible golf. But when Tara follows suit with an invisible club and an invisible ball, there is a resounding crash! Invisible maybe, but the ball has broken a window!

Dangerfield's plans go awry when Steed finds him in his special boxing ring with Tara in Who Was That Man I Saw You With.

WHO WAS THAT MAN I SAW YOU WITH

By Jeremy Burnham

John Steed	Patrick Macnee
Tara King	Linda Thorson
Fairfax	William Marlowe
General Hesketh	Ralph Michael
Zaroff	Alan Browning
Gilpin	Alan MacNaughton
Mother	Patrick Newell
Dangerfield	Alan Wheatley
Phillipson	Bryan Marshall
Miss Culpepper	Aimee Delamain
Perowne	Richard Owens
Kate	Nita Lorraine
Hamilton	Ralph Ball
Powell	Ken Haward
Pye	Neville Marten

Designed by Robert Jones
Directed by Don Chaffey
Produced by Albert Fennell and Brian Clemens

FAIRFAX and Perowne, two of Mother's agents, keep a rendezvous with enemy agent Gregor Zaroff, who has something to sell. Perowne finds Zaroff, who kills him, leaving his identity card in his hand. Afterwards, Zaroff reports to Dangerfield, who spends his time in a boxing ring receiving beauty treatment at the hands of his attractive secretary, Kate. As Zaroff gives his report, the mud-pack on Dangerfield's face cracks into a smile and together they drink a toast in champagne – to Tara King! At a secret Whitehall establishment, Tara, wearing a commando-style outfit, goes about her latest assignment – testing the security arrangements of the government's War Room. She breaks in through the back of a sentry-box and overpowers security guards, Powell and Hamilton before taking a lift to the floor which houses the War Room. Inside the room, Gilpin and Pye, two boffins, are explaining to General Hesketh the function of the room's most vital piece of equipment – a black box nicknamed The Field Marshall. This can monitor the flight of every military aircraft in the world, and not only detect whether they are carrying nuclear weapons, but programme Britain's own anti-missile missiles to intercept them. Tara enters the room through a ventilation shaft and attempts to fire her pistol at the box. But a special magnetic field surrounding it locks her pistol solid, and she is overpowered by the guards. Gilpin and Hesketh congratulate her on nearly reaching the security box, and encourage her to keep trying. After all, if she can break the system, so can the enemy. Tara returns to her apartment and finds Steed waiting for her. He

has passed the time away by building a house of cards. He reveals that he devised the security arrangements for the Field Marshall, and then lets her into another secret – he has glued the house of cards together! As Steed prepares to leave, Tara receives a gift of flowers and pearls in the post. Enclosed is a card bearing the initials GZ. She says she does not know the identity of her admirer. Tara's fellow agent, Fairfax, is beginning to suspect that she may be a double-agent, and as he keeps her under surveillance with a cine-camera, he sees Gregor Zaroff waiting outside her flat. He then follows Tara when she goes to a telephone box and picks up a strange envelope. To test the security in the War Room, Tara is taking pictures of secret documents with a miniature camera concealed in her handker-chief. But as she is about to leave, a beam that is sensitive to the chemical compo-nents of film emulsion sets off an alarm, and she is once again arrested by the guards and the camera is taken from her. Unknown to the guards, Tara has a second camera concealed in her watch, and arriv-ing back at her apartment, she develops the film. When Fairfax shows Mother the film he has taken of Tara, and adds that he has seen Zaroff, Mother reduces Tara's security rating to zero minus, and instigates an investigation into her loyalty. Returning to her apartment with Steed, Tara finds one of Mother's agents, Phillipson, going through her room. They fight, but the agent escapes. Later, when Steed next visits Mother, he recognises Phillipson and demands an explanation. Mother is forced to tell him that Tara is under suspicion of selling secrets to the enemy. More impor-tantly, she has breached the War Room and its secrets. Her bank account has been checked – Gregor Zaroff has recently paid her £2000. Steed is given 24 hours to prove her innocence. But when he discov-ers the photos Tara took in the War Room, even he begins to have doubts about her loyalty. The case against her becomes even graver when Steed discov-ers her standing over the dead body of Fairfax with a gun in her hand. Tara is taken to Mother's, where Phillipson pre-sents his case against her, while Steed tries vainly to defend her. But the evidence against her is too strong and Tara is placed in Phillipson's custody pending an official enquiry. Tara, however, escapes and Mother is forced to reduce her rating to zero minus three – she is to be shot on sight! An anxious Steed gets a call to go to

a phone booth in the country, where he finds an envelope. When he returns home, he finds a crate of champagne in his sitting-room, with a note from Zaroff. Tara is lying dead in the next room. As Steed picks up the gun and kneels over her body, Tara sits up. She explains that she has planned the demonstration to show how easy it is to manufacture circumstantial evidence. As they leave the apartment, Steed is knocked out by Zaroff, who then takes Tara at gunpoint to Dangerfield, whom they find still sitting in the boxing ring and being fussed over by Kate. Dangerfield now reveals his plan. They have deliberately discredited Tara and allowed Mother's security to believe that she penetrated the War Room, in order to make it necessary to dismantle the black box and build in new circuits. In the 48 hours this will take, the country will be totally defenceless and foreign rockets will be launched. Meanwhile, a desperate Steed shows the film taken by Fairfax to a lipreader, Miss Culpepper, and from Zaroff's mouthings, she gives Steed a clue about the enemy's headquarters. Steed arrives there just as Zaroff is about to shoot Tara, and using the boxing ring to its full advantage, Steed delivers a knockout blow to Dangerfield's plans. Later on, Tara finds Steed looking over a complex blue-print. While she watches agog, he erects his latest invention – a tower of glasses. He pours champagne into the top glass until it overflows and fills all the other glasses. Steed then proposes a toast: 'To Tara King – whom I never suspected of funny busi-ness for one moment. Well, almost never.'

MY WILDEST DREAM

By Philip Levene

Tara and Steed discover Tobias kneeling beside Slater's dead body, in a scene from **My Wildest Dream.**

John Steed	Patrick Macnee
Tara King	Linda Thorson
Jaeger	Peter Vaughan
Tobias	Derek Godfrey
Chilcott	Edward Fox
Nurse Owen	Susan Travers
Slater	Philip Madoc
Reece	Michael David
Paul Gibbons	Murray Mayne
Dyson	Tom Kempinski
Winthrop	John Savident
Peregrine	Hugh Moxley

Directed by Robert Fuest
Produced by Albert Fennell and Brian Clemens

ALOYISIUS Peregrine, Vice-Chairman of the Acme Precision Combine Limited, is stabbed in his penthouse as he is working on his hobby, mending watches. His attacker is Paul Gibbons, also on the board of Acme. But the killing has taken place only in Gibbons' mind so far. Gibbons is actually shown stabbing a dummy in the office of Jagger, a psychiatrist. Peregine is alive when Gibbons collects a card for his next appointment from Jagger's assistant, Nurse Owen, and then joins him in his chauffeur-driven car outside. At Gibbons' next appointment, Jagger incites him under sedation once again to kill Peregrine, getting him to stab at a dummy which has Peregrine's face. When he has been conditioned, Gibbons goes to Peregrine's penthouse and stabs him to death. Nurse Owen tells Steed and Tara on the telephone that the crime is about to happen. They arrive at the penthouse to find Peregrine dead, and see Gibbons stagger in shock back out of the window, to fall to his death. Steed visits Gibbons' office, but learns little of interest. Tobias, another board member, however, tells him that it seems strange that Gibbons does not appear to have left a diary. The next member of the board to die is Winthrop. Jagger again conditions one of his colleagues, Slater, to do the killing. Tobias, the fifth member of the board, is now under threat from Slater who, after the murder of Winthrop, is sedated and placed under the care of Dr Reece in hospital. Tara investigates Slater's office and finds his diary, but loses it when Dyson, an aide of Jagger's, attacks her and escapes. She tails Dyson but loses him in Marlin Street, where Jagger has his consulting rooms. Later, Slater calls to mind a Dr Jagger while under sedation in hospital, and Tara finds a Dr Jagger listed at 42 Marlin Street. Nurse Owen and Dyson arrive at the hospital and knock out Dr Reece. They

Steed is poised for action, wearing one of his ubiquitous bowler hats and carrying a trusty umbrella.

then take Slater with them, and when they have conditioned him, Nurse Owen phones Steed and tells him that Tobias is in danger in Slater's office. Tara and Steed rush to the Acme office but find Tobias alive. He has shot Slater, after the man went for him with a gun. Steed visits Jagger, who admits that Gibbons and Slater were indeed his patients, and that he taught them to act out their aggressive fantasies in the surgery. He claims, however, that both men came to him too late for him to prevent the real murders being committed. When Steed has left, Jagger decides that the game is up and he must get rid of Steed. He and Nurse Owen decide to use their technique on the agent and they select as Steed's enemy Lord Teddy Chilcott, who has been appearing in scenes throughout being rejected as a suitor by Tara. He has built up a real hostility against Steed, especially when he was caught in Tara's flat. Steed, believing that Tara was being molested by a stranger, hit Chilcott with his bowler. Chlicott is picked up as he is leaving Tara's flat and taken back to Jagger's consulting room, where he is given the conditioning treatment. Dyson meanwhile goes after Tara. But she knocks him out and pockets the key to 42 Marlin Street. Tobias and Nurse Owen are in league, for Tobias drugs Jagger, who is discovered by Tara when she reaches Marlin Street. She realises Steed is in danger when she sees a dummy with his face on it, used in the conditioning of Chilcott. Tara rushes to Steed's flat, and although Chilcott lies in wait for Steed, she manages to warn her colleague by throwing her shoe at the window. Steed quickly discovers and disposes of Chilcott, then he and Tara foil Tobias when he appears for the showdown in the flat. They tug the carpet from under his feet and knock him cold.

BIZARRE

By Brian Clemens

John Steed	Patrick Macnee
Tara King	Linda Thorson
Helen Pritchard	Sally Nesbitt
Captain Cordell	James Kerry
Jonathan Jupp	John Sharp
Happychap	Roy Kinnear
Tom	Michael Balfour
Bob	Patrick Connor
Mrs Jupp	Sheila Burrell
Shaw	George Innes
Charley	Ron Pember
The Master	Fulton Mackay

Directed by Leslie Norman
Produced by Albert Fennell and Brian Clemens

HELEN Pritchard, an attractive London secretary, is found wandering in a daze, miles from civilisation. She is wearing only a nightdress. Captain Cordell, one of Mother's men, deduces that Helen fell, or was pushed, from a passing train. In hospital Helen rambles about a coffin on the train – and a man in it who wasn't dead! In a flashback we see what really happened. During the night Helen went to the luggage van to feed her pet dog and was startled to see a man getting out of a coffin. In the ensuing struggle she fell from the train. Steed and Tara discover that the coffin on the train should have contained the body of a financier called Jonathan Jupp, who was later interred at the Happy Meadows Cemetery. When Tara foils an attempt on Helen's life by Morton, another financier, they discover another strange coincidence. Morton was interred at Happy Meadows Cemetery six months before. And both he and Jupp were on the verge of prosecution for fraud when they died. Visiting the cemetery, Steed and Tara receive another shock. It is commercialised in the worst possible taste, with signs such as 'Get in while the going's good' and 'People are dying to get into Happy Meadows'. The cemetery even gives trading stamps! But even worse, they discover that bodies have a habit of popping in and out of their coffins, even when they are buried – especially in the exclusive area called Paradise Plot. Steed obtains permission to exhume the bodies of Jupp and Morton and finds they are both missing. So too are the bodies of four other men, who all have good reasons for wanting to elude the law. The proprietor, 'Bagpipes' Happychap, and his two gravediggers, Tom and Bob, look on in ever-increasing consternation. Captain Cordell calls on Mrs Jupp, and learns that her husband spoke of taking a holiday with Mystic Tours, which he described as 'a trip to Paradise'. Investigating

Mystic Tours, Cordell tells the proprietor, Shaw, that he is in business difficulties, and needs to get away. Shaw offers him their Paradise Holiday, and arranges for him to have a convenient road accident. As Steed and Tara survey his grave in Paradise Plot, Cordell is very much alive enjoying himself with wine, women and song, in an elaborate complex built beneath their feet. But he is recognised as a spy by Charley, one of Shaw's men, and by the time Steed and Tara have Cordell's grave exhumed, he really is dead! Steed follows in Cordell's footsteps. A visit to Mrs Jupp leads him to Mystic Tours, and a briefcase full of banknotes gains him an interview with the real boss of the tour company – The Master. He is a small wiry man, dressed as an Indian Fakir, who lies in suspended animation on a bed of nails. When Steed gains his confidence, he reveals there is a sheet of glass between his body and the nails! He is a charlatan in all save one thing – he really has found a way of simulating death. A road accident is arranged for Steed, and soon Happychap and the two grave diggers are gazing down at the agent's lifeless body in a coffin. By the time Tara arrives, he has been buried in Paradise Plot. Steed awakens to the sound of music and dancing. He is lying on cushions and being offered grapes by two pretty young women. It now becomes obvious what has happened to the missing financiers, for in the rock formation above his head there are a series of coffin-shaped doors. The bodies can leave and re-enter their graves at will! When a distraught Tara has Steed's coffin exhumed, he tries to attract her attention by sliding a knife through the lid of the coffin, but he is seen by Jupp, Charley Shaw and The Master. Tara, however, leaps through the coffin to his assistance and there is a short but amusing fight, which culminates in The Avengers leading a crocodile chain of prisoners from the open grave. For Happychap, the sight of all the dead bodies coming to life is too much – he faints!

Steed visits the commercialised Happy Meadows Cemetery, where he and Happychap examine a corpse, in Bizarre.

*Mother decides to record Steed's new toy —
a rocketship he assembled himself — for
posterity, in* Bizarre.

*And so the series ended. But not
quite, for there remains the final tag
sequence. As this was the last
Avengers episode, I have
transcribed the whole sequence.*

*Steed and Tara stand overlooking a
control panel. Steed is adjusting
various controls.*

STEED: Like it?

TARA: Very complicated, isn't it?

MOTHER: *(Entering.)* Steed! Tara!

STEED: *(Aside, almost to himself.)* Bom!
Bom! *(Then, aside to Tara.)* Bit
of a squash. *(And directly to
Mother.)* Mother!

MOTHER: I say! Splendid achievement,
Steed. Splendid!

STEED: Well, thank you very much.

MOTHER: Hard to believe you assembled
it yourself.

STEED: Well, the instruction booklet is
very explicit.

MOTHER: Yes, but a thing like this . . . and in
your own back yard.

STEED: *(Chuckling.)* Hmmm!

MOTHER: It must have been expensive?

STEED: Oh, I've saved up a bit. *(Then
wistfully.)* I've always wanted
one of these.

TARA: *(To Mother as he turns towards
the door.)* Well, where're you
going?

MOTHER: Outside.

STEED: Outside?

MOTHER: Yes . . . I want to take a snap of
it . . . for my album.

STEED: Ah! *(Mother leaves, while Steed
continues to adjust the control
panel. Tara is watching
curiously.)*

TARA: *(Flippantly.)* Where do you light
the blue paper?

STEED: *(Chuckling.)* You don't. All you
do is press that button there.

TARA: *(Nonchalantly.)* This one?

STEED: Yeah! *(Tara presses button. Set
vibrates as sound of unleashed
power drowns Steed's cry.)* No!
*(Cut to shot of rocketship
leaving a launch pad, beginning
its ascent. Cut back to Steed and
Tara at rocket's control panel,
Tara looking bewildered at
Steed.)*

TARA: How do you stop it?

STEED: Er . . . *(Chuckles.)* That part of
the kit arrives next week.
*(Mother's voice is heard over
the intercom.)*

MOTHER: Steed! Steed! Steed, I demand
that you bring that thing down at
once!

STEED: *(Feigning indignation.)* Demand?
(A broad grin crosses his face.)

TARA: *Can* you get us down?

STEED: Eventually, yes.

TARA: *(Coyly.)* Eventually?

STEED: There's no hurry . . . *(Long
pause.)* Is there?
(Tag theme gently fades in.)

TARA: *(Seductively.)* None at all.
*(A knowing look passes
between the two of them, and
the tag theme continues to build.
Cut to Mother, seated in his
wheelchair in the middle of a
field. He looks skyward.)*

MOTHER: *(Turning to camera and
addressing the viewers.)*
They'll be back . . . You can
depend on it. *(Then, realisation
dawning.)* They're
unchaperoned up there!
*(Camera pans skyward, gives
way to main title theme and End
credits.)*

*'Can you get us down?' Tara asks Steed
when their rocket leaves the launch pad in
the tag scene from* Bizarre.

THE END?

Linda Thorson continued the tradition of having a special wardrobe designed for her when she played the part of Tara King in the sixth series.

Above: Linda Thorson wears a kimono-style mini dress and blonde wig in a scene from Have Guns . . . Will Haggle.

Right: Tara visits the Acme Precision Company in My Wildest Dream, wearing a distressed leather jacket and culottes.

Above: Patrick Macnee designed several of his suits, including this one, tailored by Bailey and Weatherill of Bond Street.

Left: Another Macnee design: a tan jacket, fawn cavalry twill trousers and a moss-green waistcoat.

Patrick Macnee/Gareth Hunt/Joanna Lumley
1976

And Gambit Makes Three

After the failure of the stage production (it closed after only six weeks), *The Avengers* went into television limbo – at least, as far as the British television channels were concerned. It did, however, continue to appear on American television sceens at regular intervals. Some stations even showed all the 83 filmed episodes on 83 consecutive nights, while other screened four episodes a day!

Almost six years passed then, in 1975, Brian Clemens received a call from a French television and film executive, Rudolph Roffi, asking if Tara King was available to make a champagne commercial for French television. (Linda Thorson was still a big name in France at the time.)

Linda was contacted, as was Patrick Macnee, as a sort of tribute to *The Avengers*, and the commercial was made at Elstree Studios during the summer of 1975.

When Roffi discovered that *The Avengers* was no longer in production, he asked why. Clemens explained that though he and Albert Fennell had always believed that the show would re-appear, one day, they had been unable to interest any British company in financing a new production. Clemens said it would cost over £2,000,000 to produce a new series. In the event, it was to cost at least double that sum.

A few weeks later, Clemens received a second call from France. It was Roffi, saying that he'd raised the money, and asking when production could begin.

Within three months, Clemens, Fennell and ex-Avengers music arranger, Laurie Johnson, had formed a new independent company, The Avengers (Film & TV) Enterprises Ltd. in association with IDTV Paris. Plans were formulated to produce a new series of 26 films under the name of *The New Avengers*.

Knowing that any new *Avengers* series would require the presence of Patrick Macnee, Clemens rang the ex-Avenger at his Hollywood home.

Macnee's acceptance was essential to the show's success for, as Clemens told the press at the time, 'Avenger girls can come and go, but if Patrick Macnee fell down a manhole tomorrow, it would be the end of *The Avengers* for good.'

At first, Macnee was hesitant to accept, and asked for time to consider the offer. 'I didn't believe they were serious,' he said. 'I thought it was some gigantic joke. So I asked them to send some scripts. They never did, but after seeing them, I realised that they were as good as, if not better than, the old Avengers stories.'

Within two weeks, Macnee telephoned to accept.

Faced with the task of finding a new Avengers girl, Clemens auditioned over 300 actresses, and eventually reduced the list of candidates to one dozen.

On 8 March 1976, Nigel Dempster's Diary page in the *Daily Mail* carried the following:

JOANNA SCOOPS THAT SUPER-ROLE AS STEED'S AVENGERS SUPER GIRL . . .

With aspiring hopefuls still clamouring for the female lead in the new Avengers series, which starts production next month, I can reveal that the role has now been filled. The debby-voiced Miss Joanna Lumley, 29, has been chosen to take over the part pioneered by Honor Blackman and subsequently inherited by Diana Rigg and Linda Thorson.

Originally, the new Avengers girl was to have been called Charlie, but prior to filming, Clemens discovered that there was a perfume of that name on the market. Not wishing to spend lavish amounts of money endorsing another company's product, the name was changed.

Joanna Lumley herself is credited with suggesting the new name Purdey – after the most revered and expensive shotgun in the world.

'Purdey will be a stockings and suspenders girl – giving lots of glimpses of thigh,' said Clemens. 'She will be tough, yet vulnerable, with a huge sense of humour. *The Avengers* girls will have gone full circle with Joanna. So much so that she won't have to burn her bra – she can put it back on.'

Press pictures at the time showed Miss Lumley doing just that. Lots of stocking-tops were on view and, in one case, even a garter holster à la Cathy Gale.

Joanna herself said 'I will be a male chauvinist pig's dreams. It will be lovely to play a feminine lady. There have been far too many butch-looking girls in TV recently. I know that men are hung up on stockings, and there will be a glimpse of them in the series,' she said. 'I always wear stockings. They are so much prettier than tights.'

She revealed that before winning the part she had been out of work for six months and was so disillusioned that she was thinking of leaving Britain for America.

At the time, Joanna was sporting a mane of long blonde hair. Before filming began, however – and apparently against studio wishes – she had it cropped into the now familiar Purdey bob.

'It's fine,' said Joanna, 'if you have long, healthy shining hair like Diana Rigg, but look at mine – it's really quite tatty. As I'm going to be leaping about the place and working outside a lot, it's bound to go frizzy, so I thought I'd have it shortened.'

Purdey was to be a girl of the 1980s. Sexy, warm and ultra-feminine. An ex-ballerina, she was born in India, where her father served as a Brigadier in the British Army. She had an international education, including spells at Roedean and the Sorbonne, and lived with her father in many of the world's troublespots.

Her father was later seconded to the Secret Service and eventually shot as a spy. (But we weren't told by which side.) After his death, her mother remarried – a Bishop. An expert shot with all kinds of firearms, Purdey could shoot the pips out of an apple at twenty paces. She was a competent driver and could drive anything, from her own sports car to a motorcycle, extremely well. She learned the Chinese martial art skills while studying in Peking, and became well-versed in the style of fighting modelled on the mysterious and secretive French martial art of Panache – a technique which involves fighting with the feet. Straight-legged kicks, delivered from a wide variety of angles, and a graceful, almost balletic, straight arm jab.

Purdey lived in what she described as 'the biggest bed-sitter in the world'. It was a basement flat in London, gutted and refurbished by her in feminine Art Deco style and colours, right down to the amusing idea of having a bedroom door that was little more than a hanging curtain of beads.

A third member of the team was added to the new format – Mike Gambit. After testing for the part, the role was given to 35-year-old Gareth Hunt. He said: 'I didn't believe it when I heard I'd got the part. Some of my friends had auditioned for it, too. Actors like Patrick Mower were all in with a very good chance. After my television image as Frederick (the butler in *Upstairs, Downstairs),* I bet quite a few people are surprised I beat the natural glamour-boy choices to it. When I heard that Joanna was going to be wearing black stockings and suspenders, I knew she'd be terrific. That sort of thing turns me on far more than the leather gear that Joanna's predecessors wore in the previous series. Gambit will steer clear of romance. The action is too fast to bother with lingering kisses! But, to me, looks say more than actions. I'd like to leave the relationship between Mike and Purdey up to the viewers' imagination. Looks say more than gropes.'

Brian Clemens added, 'There will be more sexual tension between the three stars. But it will be up to the audience to put their own interpretation on it. If you have a dirty mind, it can be dirty. But it can also be watched by your maiden aunt.'

Gambit was said to have risen to the rank of Major on merit while serving in the Parachute Regiment, and was later seconded to the SAS (Special Air Services). He served as a mercenary in Africa and the Middle East, and gained comprehensive knowledge of guerrilla warfare. He wrestled crocodiles in the Congo before returning to something 'with more excitement' – competing in Formula One racing at Brands Hatch. He handled any car with consummate skill and could turn his Jaguar XJS on a sixpence.

Gambit was the 'hard' man of the team. Deceptively quiet, until the situation called for action, when he would move faster than the eye could follow – like a striking cobra. He was experienced in most methods of unarmed combat, adding the skills he was taught in the Army to those learned as Steed's companion-in-arms, with judo and karate high on his list of specialities. He was also an expert shot, pilot, archer and good all-round athlete.

Like Purdey, Gambit's stunning apartment in London was ultra-modern and functional. It had every electronic device invented by man, including a fully automated bed.

Steed's role differed slightly from the original series. He still retained his olde worlde charm and manners. He still appreciated the better things in life – like a good brandy, a 1928 claret, Royal Ascot and the click of leather against willow. He still knew that Britannia rules, and was still sworn to defend her against her enemies. But although he was still the hub of the series, Steed had mellowed. He had the lease on his mews flat, but now preferred to spend most of his time at Steed's Stud, a large house in the country, where he entertained beautiful mature women and bred horses.

The house (in reality Lord Brocket's Georgian manor in Hertfordshire) was set in the countryside – just a push of the accelerator away from London. It was from there that Steed issued orders to minor agents who, in turn, reported back to him at the house. Steed found more time for relaxation, allowing his partners to do most of the legwork, until he himself would become actively involved in yet another fiendish plot by some madman out to rule the world.

The relationship between Steed, Purdey and Gambit was that of partners and good friends. One factor alone welded them together as a team – mutual respect.

The format for *The New Avengers* differed little from the previous *Avengers* stories.

The off-beat, wacky humour was stilll apparent, as were the

bizarre qualities. These included a man whose mere touch could spell death; Nazis alive and well, and living as monks on a remote Scottish island; a man hell-bent on ruling the world . . . aided by flocks of controlled birds of prey; and even Steed's old enemy, the dreaded cybernauts.

Brian Clemens explained: 'The situations are just as fantastic. Mind you, when one learns that the CIA planned to poison Castro's boot-polish, it's difficult to compete with reality. But we're doing just that – and outstripping it. This time, we've carefully framed our stories so that, no matter how mind-blowing the plot, it will remain believable. And that is the big change, if you want to point out the difference! The old series was a humorous spoof, with dramatic undertones. *The New Avengers* is dramatic, with humorous undertones.'

Clemens put the *Avengers'* amazing track record down to a 'happy knack right from the start'. He said 'We were always at least two or three years in advance of our time. It was costume, without being period costume. We even upstaged James Bond, with karate, kung fu, mini-skirts and women's lib, and we managed to stay ahead. This time we mean to top all that has gone before. Audiences have grown more sophisticated, and the successful show must get ahead of them. This is what we've tried to do – to produce a show that is in the 1980s. A show that will seem as fresh as ever, but still stay ahead of its nearest emulators. The production values of the new series *are higher than any other television series in the world*. The use of location exteriors is a 100 per cent improvement. You are going to be seeing a lot of Britain in the new series, but *Avengers* style, weird, bizarre, unusual locations.'

Changes in fashion were not as predominant as in the earlier *Avengers* series.

London-born Catherine Buckley was commissioned to design Purdey's new wardrobe. The creations included: a silk dress, gathered at the waist and tied at the shoulder, with a skirt in pleated chiffon; a kimono in orange, black, green, red and yellow flowerprint silk, with long sleeves and side slits; an evening dress in red, green and blue lurex, with velvet top and lurex dangle pieces attached to large buttons at the shoulder – complete with wrap-over skirt with draw-strings to hitch up

the skirt over the knees for easier movement; black cotton jump-suits, with an Avengers lion motif and the name Purdey trimmed in white and red.

The original intention was to make Gambit a swinger – complete with jeans, bomber jackets, etc. The end product, however, was a very up-to-the-minute man. He wore expensive, well-cut, three-piece suits in a traditional business dark blue pinstripe, and moth-head checks and plain brown gaberdine, worn with smart ties, became the staple items of Gambit's wardrobe.

Steed's wardrobe retained a wide selection of bowler hats, some of which were as useful as they were decorative. One, for instance, had a steel crown, which was ideal for protecting his head from attack and handy for knocking out the opposition. Another had a steel brim, which served as a deadly missile when thrown frisbee-style. A third bowler had a miniature receiver built into the crown. The tightly-furled brolly was also still in evidence – a weapon in itself when used to hook an opponent's arm, or for fending off attacks. The umbrella also doubled as a swordstick, with a thin rapier blade hidden in its shaft. This, coupled with Steed's knowledge of fencing was, like everything else about him, impeccable.

For the new series, Steed would be seen wearing – along with the familiar Edwardian suits – riding breeches, shooting jackets, blazers and sportswear.

Prior to filming, Cyd Child, the series fight arranger, together with Ray Austin (who had held the same position, and directed some of the episodes on the previous *Avengers* series), rigged up a gymnasium in the studio, and Joanna and Gareth were put through a vigorous fitness training schedule.

Both had already been put through a commando training course to toughen them up but, because the producers wanted the gestures in the fight scenes to look completely authentic, Joanna was given an additional hour of ballet training each day, in which every fight sequence was worked out with Austin. Sometimes he would have Joanna's leg held up on a tripod to achieve the right height for Purdey's kicking technique.

Both stars did 90 per cent of their own stuntwork, with doubles being used only when Austin considered the stunt to be too dangerous to risk Lumley or Hunt being injured. Which would, of course, have held up the expensive production.

One other major change was *The New Avengers* theme music. The opening few bars remained the same, a bouncy kettle-drum boom, followed by the familiar strains of *The Avengers* theme, but this soon gave way to a punchier, more military-sounding, disco rhythm.

The production went before the cameras in April 1976, at Pinewood Studios.

Any initial success *The New Avengers* might have had, was sabotaged before it even reached the screen. The ITV network failed to reach agreement on when the programme should be shown.

Some channels opted for Sunday evenings, others for Tuesdays, and the remainder screened the show on Friday nights. (Quite a contrast to the prime-time Saturday evening spot which the original *Avengers* had always been allocated.

Interviewed at the time, Clemens said 'It is total madness. With a proper network showing we could have emptied the streets on our opening night. Now we won't even make the Top Ten ratings chart.' (They did, but in eighth place.) 'It is tragic because *The Avengers* was the best adventure series British television ever made. But isn't that just typical of Britain, to sabotage and to underrate that which we do best?'

The series did, however, receive worldwide orders and soon recovered its production costs.

It seems that the original plan was to film 26 episodes, with a short break following the completion of the 13th episode, before continuing to film the final 13. This, however, was not to be. During the recess, Clemens was contacted by Roffi, one of the French backers, and told 'Purdey is short on lip gloss' and 'Her clothes are dull and drab'.

Roffi, when interviewed by the British press, said: 'We feel that Joanna would come over better if she was like one of *Charlie's Angels*. Much more sexy. Though we're happy with what we've seen so far, we have certain reservations. To us, Miss Lumley's clothes are dull and drab. We would like to see her in top French designs, like those of Yves St Laurent, which should attract everyone, but especially Frenchmen when they see the shows in France. I think, in general terms, the stories could be sexier, more violent also, and still remain sophisticated.'

Parallels can be drawn between this situation and that of the earlier *Avengers* series, when the American buyers put money into making the Linda Thorson series, then promptly began to dictate the show's future format — until the consequences proved disastrous. Seemingly the French were bent on going the same route.

Joanna Lumley, angered by the criticism, blasted back. 'I don't mind anyone saying other women are prettier, and I'm the first to admit that *Charlie's* ladies are lovely. All that sitting around in the Californian sunshine, with dark brown tans that make their teeth look twice as white. I'd like to see an Angel, pale as a lily, crawling round the back lot in Pinewood in March.' (Joanna was apparently being interviewed on a dull, grey Pinewood backlot they used as a television sewer, as she was being bound and gagged for the eighth take.)

'This is nothing,' she said, dabbing a split lip, 'to the two days I spent jumping 30 times into a slimy green pond. It would be a pity if *The New Avengers* had to jump on the bandwagon because of the influences from other programmes. I think it would be madness to model the *Avengers* on the *Angels*. If we copy the Americans, instead of doing our very own British thing, we've had it. I believe we've got to play up the British elegance and lightness of *The Avengers*. That typically British humour that endeared Patrick Macnee and Diana Rigg to the Americans.

'My own dress designer is considered to be sexy and sophisticated by the French. But we did have some problems with the earlier shows because after the first three or four, it was a rush to get the right clothes. This time more thought has gone into it. The French certainly have a way with women's fashions, so there will be a French selection when the series comes back.'

When asked why the stockings and suspenders promised for the first series were never (well, almost never) used, Joanna replied, 'As for the sex, I'm all for the occasional flash of thigh, but how can Purdey justify constantly twitching at her undies? That's why the stockings and suspenders were out — it's just not practical for a secret agent to spend her life with her bum hanging out of her pants, and her cleavage tumbling over a gate.'

Patrick Macnee agreed that more sex and violence could signal the death of the show.

'Ours is a surrealistic Grimm's fairy tale sort of terror,' he said. 'If we start pumping bullets into people's stomachs, we're done for. And it's a joke that the French should ask for more violence when the Americans are so interested in buying the show. They've got the biggest no-no against violence – viewers are even striking against *Starsky and Hutch.*'

Changes were made, however, and as promised, around half of Joanna's new wardrobe for the second season was of French origin. The rest, however, was chosen by Joanna herself. She visited the premises of Betty Jackson, at Quorum, and selected a high-fronted, near-backless slip of black Hurel crêpe, with cupped sleeves, slightly bloused bodice, and a long skirt slit to thigh-level at the sides.

The producers were so impressed that they ordered not just one but four of it for her – the black original, plus ones in vivid ink-blue, cerise-pink, and the fourth in sharp acid-yellow. The wardrobe also featured hacking jackets, knitted check-weave dresses, a blue, three-piece gaucho trouser suit in zig-zag pattern, an off-white, open-sleeved jacket, with matching trousers and boots, worn with shirt and tie, plus various skirts, boxer pants and calf-length boots.

Purdey's hairstyle was changed, too. Gone was the smooth-as-glass mushroom bob. In its place was a shaggy but controlled hairstyle. John Frieda was the man responsible for both the original bob and the new cut.

'When you see girls trotting around Paris, Amsterdam and Johannesburg, all with mushroom heads, it's time to move on,' said Joanna. 'For the new season, I'm having my hair layered.' The hair was layered at the top, and the back and sides allowed to grow to mid-neck level.

'The layering gives it body,' she said. 'It is enhanced by subtle streaking, and Purdey's actions will supply the rest of the movement.'

Other changes were made, to give the second 13 stories their fair share of sexy moments. Purdey's role was made sexier. In one episode she meets and falls in love with an old flame. We even got to see her in bed!

Gambit's character was broadened and developed. He was given a succession of dolly-birds and other female admirers.

Even the formerly untouchable John Steed was revealed as a man with a past – and a romantic interest!

Clemens told the press, 'Purdey very obviously has a love affair. You won't see nudity or anything like that. After all, we have a reputation for being respectable. But it is clear that Purdey is carrying on with somebody. And Purdey's guardian angel – Mike Gambit – will receive more attention. We're strengthening his character, and giving him a collection of girls all to himself.'

Patrick Macnee, however, was unsure about Steed's new, romantic, role. 'When you're in your fifties, however good you look or feel, you've got to act your age.' he said. 'You're not really supposed to start leaping into bed with young ladies on the television screen. It would look ludicrous.'

Clemens placated him and said that Steed's women would be of the mature variety. (Though one or two of Steed's girlfriends *did* appear to be young and trendy!)

'Patrick doesn't think the audience will accept his running around after young girls,' said Brian Clemens. 'There will, however, be some changes, but they will be very subtle. It will take at least six episodes before anyone will notice the difference.'

Largely because the series was being financed by the French and Canadians, the decision was taken to film seven of the episodes on location in the two countries. Three were made in France and four in Canada.

Once again (possibly due to the programme being made by an independent company), the second season's shows suffered the same fate as the first – no network showing by the ITV companies.

This time, *The New Avengers* did not even dent the viewing charts. But it did gain huge international sales and the producers immediately began negotiations to get financial backing for a further series.

On 2 September 1979, the *Sunday People* carried the following (edited) article, by Tony Purnell.

STEED RIDES AGAIN – THANKS TO YANKS

John Steed, television's most successful secret agent, is all set to make a comeback.

Actor Patrick Macnee has his brolly, bowler and buttonhole booked to make another series of The New Avengers *early in the New Year.*

It looked like the end for the Old Etonian hero 18 months ago when no one would put up the cash to make more of the costly adventures.

But now the Americans have come to Steed's rescue.

Producer Brian Clemens explained: 'The show is a big hit in the States and the Americans have agreed to provide most of the finance for another 26 episodes. Other companies over here are also interested and it is now just a case of sorting out who puts in what.'

Patrick Macnee, 57, said, 'I have told Brian I will definitely be available. I have a great affection for The Avengers.'

In the last series, Patrick and Joanna Lumley were joined by dashing Gareth Hunt as Mike Gambit and it put Steed's nose out of joint. Patrick confessed 'I was pushed rather into the background and complained. Gambit was taking over a lot of the stuff that Steed would have done. Changes were made and I was quite happy in the end. The three of us are great friends and there is a wonderful bond between us.'

Both Joanna and Gareth said they would be interested in making more New Avengers.

Brian Clemens said 'It would be nice to have the three together again, but not essential. Avenger girls can come and go, but if Patrick Macnee decided to drop out of the picture, it would signal the end of The Avengers for good.'

CBS in America wanted to inject $140,000, and London Weekend TV (influenced, no doubt, by the success of their joint venture with Fennell and Clemens' Avengers MK1 Productions – The Professionals series) agreed to put up the remaining cash, but that still left about £25,000 short for each episode.

Almost five months to the day of the announcement in the Sunday People, the following appeared in the Daily Mail on 9 February 1980, written by Paul Donovan.

STEED'S A WANTED MAN

The giant American network CBS, which is showing ITVs The Avengers coast-to-coast every Friday night, wants to turn the legendary series into a two-hour feature film.

And the bowler-hatted star Patrick Macnee – who made his first appearance as John Steed 20 years ago – said this week, 'I would be absolutely delighted to do it again.'

Mr Macnee, who spent his 58th birthday on Wednesday flying home to Britain from Bombay after completing a movie, added that he was keeping himself free of commitments after mid-May.

As he spoke, Mr John Redway, the West End agent for both him and Avengers creator Brian Clemens – as well as ex-Avengers star Diana Rigg – was in New York discussing the project.

Said Mr Clemens, 'CBS are showing 13 episodes featuring Diana Rigg which were made around 15 years ago. It was way ahead of its time – and still stands up well today.'

Asked whom he would like as his leading lady in a possible film, Patrick Macnee replied, 'I love Diana Rigg, adore Honor Blackman and have the greatest admiration for Joanna Lumley. It's a profusion of riches, isn't it?'

All that was, of course, some time ago.

I can confirm that a feature-length film script does exist – and has, in fact, been paid for by the American CBS company, but obviously, this also has received the same negative response as earlier plans.

To reiterate Mother's last words from Bizarre, 'They'll be back . . . You can depend on it.'

Personally, I can't wait.

Simon Oates/Sue Lloyd
1971

From Screen
To Scream

In April 1971, almost two years after *The Avengers* faded from British television screens, the media began carrying reports of a new *Avengers* production – a stage show! John Mather, one-time head of the William Morris Agency in Europe, had negotiated with ABC/EMI to obtain the rights to transfer the popular television series to the British stage and, to quote Mather's words, 'Blast the British theatre into the Seventies'.

Mather acquired the services of one-time *Avengers* writer, Terence Feely, and producer/writer of the television series, Brian Clemens, to produce the script for the show.

'The script is ready,' said Mather. 'I now have the difficult task of finding the stage equivalents of the Patrick Macnees, the Honor Blackmans and the Diana Riggs of this world.'

By early May, Mather announced that Simon Oates (who had previously played a trendy, well-dressed scientist in BBC's *Doomwatch* production, and had appeared in several episodes of *The Avengers*) had been signed to play John Steed.

'I was very dubious about the bowler,' Simon Oates said at the time. 'I had the distinct feeling that if I wore the thing in public, a chap might rush up and kiss me.' (No one did – which isn't surprising when you consider that Mr Oates is 6 ft 4 in and a former Army heavyweight boxing champion.)

Kate O'Mara was chosen to play the evil Madame Gerda. She complained that the vinyl suit she had to wear for the role stopped her from sitting down, and creaked as she walked.

The part of Steed's new female partner in the show, Hannah Wild, took slightly longer to fill. It eventually went to blonde actress, Sue Lloyd.

When told that Hannah would have to fight ten girls while Simon Oates threw a villain into the orchestra pit, Oates said to the producer 'Tell you what, why don't I fight the girls and Hannah can have the bloke!'

The following is a slightly edited version of an article printed in the *London Evening News*, 2 July 1971, written by James Green.

NOW THE AVENGERS GO WEST

That sophisticated hokum series, The Avengers, which had the right chemistry of in-jokes and send-ups to become a TV cult, is all set to become a stage show. Directed by Leslie Phillips, using a helicopter, a Bentley, and back-projection on stage, it opens in Birmingham shortly and arrives in the West End on 2 August.

Not, however, with Patrick Macnee as agent John Steed. When the TV series ended, unflappable Macnee took his bowler and carnation off to Los Angeles.

In his place, Simon Oates, debonair and handsome, will bring his own brand of stiff upper lip to the role of Steed.

They have found him a new girl assistant, Sue Lloyd. Her job is to knock 'em out with looks or hooks. To date, four actresses have enrolled as Steed's Girl Friday. I have been interrogating them all . . .

HONOR BLACKMAN, alias Mrs Cathy Gale, Avenger girl MK1. A 5 ft 6 in ash-blonde noted for kinky black leather gear, she says,

'I played Cathy for two years, and the kinky leather thing was an accident. At first I wore culottes but they looked awful. So I changed to tight pants. But when I threw a man over my shoulder they split up the middle, and there I was in front of the camera with my knickers hanging out. So we had another think. I already had leather trousers. Boots to match seemed a good idea, and it all happened from there. As it turned out we were way ahead of fashion.

'Cathy Gale was super for me and I enjoyed my time tremendously. She was an anthropologist originally, you know, and was brilliant at everything. Judo, guns, fencing . . . she could do the lot. We made her a widow because the producers didn't want a love interest with Steed, but as a widow she could flirt and there was always a feeling that someday romance might happen.

'I received some very strange fan mail as Cathy, some of it so weird they wouldn't let me see it. Some people seeing me thumping around in black boots, with no man in my life, and practically carrying a whip, decided that I must be lesbian, and I had some extraordinary offers.'

DIANA RIGG, alias Mrs Emma Peel, Avenger girl MK2. Chestnut-haired, single, 5 ft 9 in and statuesque, she specialised in sci-fi space clothes and sexy second-skin catsuits.

'I had two years as the widowed Emma and I've little idea how she differed from Cathy because I never saw Honor in the part and only saw a few of my own shows. My girl was a great character who used judo among other things to look after herself. She was also financially free.

'Escapist stuff, of course, but really pointing towards the future, because women today have become more realistic and self-sufficient. They are moving in the direction of Emma Peel.'

LINDA THORSON, alias Miss Tara King, Avenger girl MK3. Canadian, another five-feet-niner, unmarried, brown-haired, her trademark was fluffy, pink feminine dresses.

'I had 18 months as Tara and she was the only one of Steed's girls to be single. I used a lot of wigs and changed from blonde to brunette and redhead.

'I decided that she was in love with Steed. Any girl who would risk her life and spend that much time with a man must be in love. I think my interpretation influenced the producers and they let me play it my way.

'Viewers noticed that she was in love with him and, judging by the letters received, Steed's image changed as a result. He seemed to care, too.

'One problem was that fashions were changing and they didn't know whether to put me in minis or maxis. Usually they settled for midis.

'Another difference was that Tara didn't go in for karate but fought more like a girl – scratching, kicking and lashing out with her handbag.

'The part came early in my career, right after drama school. I'm glad I did it.'

SUE LLOYD, alias Hannah Wild, Avenger girl MK4. Unmarried, 5 ft 8 in, reddish-gold hair.

'When I walk out as Hannah Wild, it will be my first time on the London stage.

'I see Hannah as a highly intelligent girl with a certain hardness. Practical, yet with a lot of warmth. She's fond of Steed, but otherwise there's no man in her life. On the action front her accomplishments will include shootings, half-nelsons, and the occasional karate chop.

'Since Kate O'Mara as the villainess is in black shiny leather, they've given me a crimson leather fighting outfit. I also wear a golden leather suit and dusty pink costume.

'Obviously, having had so little stage experience, the first night will be doubly tense for me. What must help is that I did face a studio audience while making His and Hers.

'Some people think I'm a toughie . . . rather like Hannah Wild . . . but I don't agree. If I seem hard that's a cover. Because actually, I'm a big softie. What I've discovered is that the really dangerous girls who need watching are the wide-eyed innocents!'

SIMON, SUE AND KINKY KATE

THE AVENGERS are back with a vengeance, complete with lascivious leather, crude karate and whimsical wit.

The stars of the new spectacular stage version, which opens at London's Prince of Wales Theatre tonight, have all the off-beat appeal that made TV's Patrick Macnee, Honor Blackman, Diana Rigg and Linda Thorsen famous.

The big stage demands a magnified projection of the small screen original, so the cast are more glamorous, more amorous and considerably more kinky.

Consider Kate O'Mara, of the almond eye and moistly pouting lip. She plays the sinister Madam Gerda, in the highest of thigh-boots.

ANGELS

If Madam Gerda represents the forces of evil, who wants to be on the side of the angels?

Well John Steed does, played by virile Simon Oates, of TV's Doomwatch Immaculate in trendy suit, curly-brimmed bowler, tightly furled brolly and well polished shoes, the debonair Oates has obviously coped with the likes of Madam Gerda before.

There's also faithful Hannah, played by luscious Sue Lloyd, to help Steed cope with all contingencies.

Comedy star Leslie Phillips has directed this spoof with a light touch that promises to make the show a winner and Simon, Sue and Kinky Kate established stars.

LESLIE PHILLIPS
He's in charge

The Avengers are back, larger than life

All geared up for action: Sue Lloyd, Kate O'Mara and Simon Oates

PICTURES by DAVID MAGNUS

hen leather fails, cunning Kate resorts to shiny PvC

THE AVENGERS ON STAGE

PRODUCTION CREDITS
Director Leslie Phillips
Producer John Mather
Writers Brian Clemens and Terence Feely
Designer Michael Young
Fight sequences Tim Condron
Mr Oates' suits by Bentley, Perry and Whitley
Miss Lloyd's costumes by Berkely Sutcliffe
Publicity Fred Hift Associates

(Reprinted from the official theatre programme)
Is there anyone, watching television over the last ten years, who has not tuned in and listened to that familiar theme music without a thrill of anticipation? For John Steed is the modern Robin Hood, and we know in advance that he will not come to harm, even though he never made Marion.

Every week we have switched on to Steed and his faithful girl-friends – Cathy Gale, Emma Peel, Tara King – those cynical, leather-clad females who could kiss or chop you according to their moods.

Now Steed and his latest Avenger girl – Hannah Wild – are presented on stage in a fast-moving outrageous comedy, with all the panache and gloss of the imperturable Avengers, but with the sinister and exotic Madame Gerda, leader of the Forces of Evil, and her incredibly wicked gang of beautiful girls.

With the Avengers – anything can happen!

I count myself fortunate to have been present at the première at The Birmingham Theatre, 20 July 1971. For those who missed seeing the show – or those who may have seen it, and would like a memory-jogger – here's a personal review of that first-night performance.

John Mather's promise that the production would have 'a very special look' was not just idle boasting. Nothing was overlooked in an effort to provide the audience with 'something different' in British theatre production and, as Mather had promised, to 'blast the theatre into the Seventies'.

The show had all the off-beat appeal of the successful television series: imaginative sets – 16 in all; colourful, trendy costumes; over 30 dolly-birds. It all helped to give the production an up-to-the-minute look.

The ambitious sets, designed by Michael Young, included a full-scale replica of Steed's vintage Bentley; Steed's luxury penthouse apartment; the top secret Operations Room of MI5; the Brain Room of the Master Computer; Madame Gerda's Academy for Young Girls (complete with scantily-clad nymphets); even a helicopter landing!

Simon Oates, immaculate in his trendy suits, shooting jackets and cuban-heel shoes, made an excellent Steed.

Sue Lloyd, in her red, fawn and off-white trouser suits, made a luscious Hannah Wild, and Kate O'Mara, in her black shiny

PVC suit and thigh-length boots, completed the trio as the evil (though rather too attractive) Madame Gerda.

The plot concerned the efforts of Madame Gerda, and her gang of young students, to overthrow the governments of the world and infiltrate their spy networks.

By using the Giant Computer Brain, Gerda has developed a method of making herself and her girls invisible. Only Steed is immune to her plot and is able to see the girls. This leads Mother to suspect that his prize agent has gone mad, and has Steed committed to hospital.

Needless to say, Steed escapes, only to find that Gerda and her gang have all the world's security ministers in their power.

After numerous battles with the enemy (the scenes in which Simon Oates ad-libbed his fights with his unseen assailants were hilarious), Steed finally convinces his chief that he is sane, and thwarts Gerda's evil plot. But not before he has been court martialled (and we learn that his licence to kill has two endorsements on it!), stripped of his rank of Major (and also stripped of his fountain-pen camera – for photographing fountain-pens!), and undergone various forms of torture (such as being whipped by a half-naked girl while tied to the Giant Computer Brain, which was a giant phallic symbol!).

Yes, the accent *was* on comedy, and Simon Oates and Sue Lloyd shared further funny moments. Steed and Hannah are set upon by three robot girls, and while Hannah tackles two of them, Steed and his assailant fall backwards over a sofa. A few moments pass, during which various articles of ladies' under-clothing are thrown out, followed by a leg, an arm, etc. Finally, Steed emerges, saying 'That's the first time I've ever *un*screwed a girl. Still, she's (h)armless now!'

Plus Simon Oates telling a dying robot to 'Get on with it, man, robots don't have death scenes', and then turning to Sue Lloyd to tell her that 'he died babbling of Green Shields'.

There were also several unscripted funny moments, too. In one, Miss Lloyd hit her opponent over the head with a plastic bottle, and had to stand and watch while it slipped from her hands and bounced across the stage. And Kate O'Mara fell flat on her bottom when the rope ladder she was climbing collapsed.

However, it was the first night (when things are expected to go wrong), and no one seemed to mind, least of all Simon Oates himself, who finished the show with the lines 'Why not come back tomorrow night and see how the show really ends'.

The show ran its scheduled two-week trial run in Birmingham, then transferred to the stage of London's The Prince of Wales Theatre, for a limited engagement. Very limited, unfortunately, since it only ran for a few weeks. (Perhaps The Prince of Wails would have been more appropriate?)

A couple of interesting facts emerged from the show, though. Steed was the youngest of a family of eight – the other seven being girls. And he was christened John Wickham Gascoyne Berresford Steed!

STEED MKIII

If the idea of *The Avengers* on stage strikes you as somewhat bizarre, what could be more strange than our bowler-hatted hero and his female aide appearing on radio?

Believe it or not, that is exactly what happened next in *The Avengers* saga.

A series of *Avengers* radio plays was produced for the South African Broadcasting Company by Sonovision Ltd. The first episode was broadcast in January 1972. Starring Donald Monat as John Steed, and Dianne Appleby as Mrs Emma Peel, the stories were freely adapted from the original Patrick Macnee/ Diana Rigg television scripts. Each episode was 15 minutes long and contained one complete story, or a serialised adventure lasting from five to eight episodes.

The tongue-in-cheek feel of the original television series was achieved by the use of a narrator (Hugh Rouse), whose interjections supplied most of the humorous aspects to each story.

The stories were adapted by Tony Jay and Dennis Folbigge, who also directed the series.

THE AVENGERS MERCHANDISE

One way in which *The Avengers* was promoted was through merchandising. The television production companies, ABC/Thames, earned royalties from the merchandising rights, as did the stars.

The following is a list of *known* items that were issued during the show's life. There are, no doubt, many other items that I haven't listed, such as Steed shooting sticks, an Avengers water pistol, and a board game, because they were only *believed* to exist.

BOOKS

The Avengers by Douglas Enefer, Consul Books 1963
(Featuring Steed and Cathy Gale)
Deadline by Patrick Macnee and Peter Leslie, Hodder & Stoughton 1965
(Featuring Steed and Emma Peel)
Dead Duck by Patrick Macnee and Peter Leslie, Hodder & Stoughton 1966
(Featuring Steed)
The Floating Game by John Garforth, Panther Books 1967
The Laugh Was On Lazarus by John Garforth, Panther Books 1967
The Passing Of Gloria Munday by John Garforth, Panther Books 1967
Heil Harris by John Garforth, Panther Books 1967
(The four Garforth titles were also issued in America by Berkley Medallion Books)
The Afrit Affair by Keith Laumer, Berkley Medallion Books 1968
The Drowned Queen by Keith Laumer, Berkley Medallion Books 1968
The Gold Bomb by Keith Laumer, Berkley Medallion Books 1968
The Magnetic Man by Norman Daniels, Berkley Medallion Books 1968
Moon Express by Norman Daniels, Berkley Medallion Books 1969
(These five titles were published for the American market only)

ANNUALS

TV Crimebusters TV Productions 1962
(Featuring the original Avengers, Steed and Keel)
The Avengers Annual Atlas Publications 1967, 1968, 1969
(The 1967 annual features Emma Peel. The 1968 and 1969 editions feature Tara King)

MAGAZINES

Meet The Avengers Star Special 15, World Distributors 1963
(40 pages, featuring Cathy Gale and Steed, plus black and white photographs)
TVTimes Diana Rigg Spectacular TV Times 1969

COMICS

The Avengers Thorpe & Porter 1966
(68 pages, British, black and white photographs)
John Steed – Emma Peel Gold Key 1968
(This is a reprint of the above)
TV Comic Polystyle Publication
(This ran Avengers strips from 1969 to 1972. The annuals also had text and strip Avengers stories)
Diana
(This girls' comic ran Diana Rigg's life-story in the mid 1960s. In full colour, it was by far the best Avengers comic strip)

TOYS/GAMES

The Corgi Gift Set No 40 1966
This boxed set (complete with interior/exterior drawings of The Avengers) contained die-cast models of Steed's Bentley and Emma's Lotus, plus miniature figures of Steed and Emma. (Some models were issued wrongly coloured, and the Bentley was painted red!)
The Avengers Jigsaw Puzzles 1966
A set of four were issued to tie-in with the Rigg black and white series. Each depicted a scene from one of the episodes.

RECORDS

The Avengers by Johnny Dankworth, 45 rpm, Fontana TF422, 1963
The Avengers and Other TV Themes by Johnny Gregory Orchestra, album, Wing WL 1087, 1961
Kinky Boots by Patrick Macnee/Honor Blackman, 45 rpm, Decca F 11843, 1964
(The above three records are theme music from the Blackman series)
The Avengers by Laurie Johnson, 45 rpm, Pye 7N 17015, 1965
TV Themes includes the Johnson theme, extended play, Pye NEP 24244, 1966
Time For TV by Brian Fahey Orchestra, album, Studio 2/EMI TWO 175, 1967
Theme From The Avengers by Jerry Murad's Harmonicats, album, Hallmark CHM 629, 1969
The Phase Four World of Thrillers by Roland Shaw, album, Decca/SPA 160, 1971
50 Popular TV Themes by Bruce Baxter, album, Pickwick 50/DA 315, 1977
(The above six records feature the Rigg theme)
Themes and . . . by Laurie Johnson, album, MGM/CS 8104, 1969
(Features the original Thorson theme)

THE NEW AVENGERS MERCHANDISE

BOOKS

House of Cards by Peter Cave, Futura Books 1976
The Eagle's Nest by John Carter, Futura Books 1976
To Catch A Rat by Walter Harris, Futura Books 1976
Fighting Men by Justin Cartright, Futura Books 1977
The Cybernauts by Peter Cave, Futura Books 1977
Hostage by Peter Cave, Futura Books 1977
(Unlike the earlier *Avengers* paperbacks, which all contained original stories, the six *New Avengers* books are novelisations of selected *New Avengers* episodes: House of Cards; The Eagle's Nest/The Midas Touch; To Catch A Rat; Dirtier By The Dozen; Last of the Cybernauts . . .?; Hostage.)

ANNUALS

The New Avengers Brown & Watson 1977
The New Avengers Brown & Watson 1978

MAGAZINES

TVTimes Souvenir Extra – The New Avengers, TVTimes 1976
(68 pages of text/photos from *The Avengers/The New Avengers*)

TOYS/GAMES

The New Avengers Mission Kit Thomas Salter 1976
The New Avengers Shooting Game Denys Fisher 1976
The New Avengers Board Game Denys Fisher 1977
The New Avengers Jigsaw Puzzles 1-4, Arrow Games 1976
Purdey's TR7 Plastic Assembly Kit Revell Toys 1979
Gambit's XJS Plastic Assembly Kit Revell Toys 1979
Purdey's TR7 Die-Cast Model Dinky Toys 1978
(Steed's Jaguar was advertised on the box but is believed to be unobtainable)

MUSIC

The New Avengers Theme by Laurie Johnson, single, EMI 2562, 1976
Music From The Avengers/The New Avengers/The Professionals album, Unicorn/Kanachana KPM 7009, 1980

MISCELLANEOUS

There were also satin sheets (based on the exotic bedlinen used by Purdey in the series); *New Avengers* patches, belts, badges etc; plus *New Avengers* marshmallows!

NOTES

CHAPTER THREE

Paul Whitsun-Jones played the part of Steed's superior, Charles, in the episodes *Man With Two Shadows* and *The Wringer*.

Ronald Radd played Quilpie, Steed's chief in *The Outside-In Man*. Unlike Charles, who was seen issuing orders from a Ministry office, Quilpie was a distinctive character. His office lay hidden behind a butcher's shop, where he passed out prime cuts of meat between briefing his agents, who entered through the cool room. This gave Quilpie the opportunity of uttering a typical Avengers line – 'Come into the fridge – there's something that needs to be done'.

The Little Wonders featured Cathy's first screen kiss from her partner. Throughout 33 episodes, the cool and immaculate Mrs Gale remained inviolate to the advances of everyone from eligible business tycoons to the ever-hopeful Steed. Producer John Bryce was finally presented with circumstances in which he could no longer maintain his ban on the kissing of Mrs Gale – a New Year's Eve party, where naturally the ever-gallant Steed would be expected to do just that!

CHAPTER FOUR

At the beginning of *Town Of No Return*, Emma and Steed are already familiar with each other. No mention is made of Cathy's disappearance. However, Cathy Gale is mentioned in *Too Many Christmas Trees*. Steed is opening his Christmas cards and, finding one from Cathy, says to Emma 'A card from Mrs Gale! Whatever can she be doing at Fort Knox?'. (Honor Blackman was filming *Goldfinger* at the time.)

Each of the episodes ended with Steed and Emma departing in various forms of transport, such as hot-air balloons or bubble-cars. Wherever possible, I've described the transport used.

CHAPTER FIVE

Though *The Forget-Me-Knot* introduced Linda Thorson as Tara King, making it the *first* Thorson story, it was actually an unused Rigg episode. Therefore it is the *last* to feature Diana Rigg as Emma Peel, and is credited as such in the official studio files. I have divided the episode into two parts, with the cross-over scene and Diana Rigg's farewell as the introductory passage to the beginning of the Thorson series, but have given the episode its own spread.

In *The See-Through Man*, Warren Mitchell played Brodny, a character he had played in the black-and-white Rigg episode *Two's A Crowd*. If one discounts the usual semi-regulars, this is the only time that a character was used twice.

Philip Levene both wrote and appeared in *Who's Who?* He played the role of Tulip, an agent employed by Major B.

Some of the storylines to this (colour) series and one or two of the earlier (black and white) Rigg series, may differ slightly from the episodes that eventually reached the screen. This is because in each case I've used official scripts or synopses as a working guide. A typical example of this can be found in the synopsis for *Never, Never Say Die*. The version that finally reached the screen has one or two different scenes to the breakdown given here. However, as I believe that most fans of the show would welcome the extra information, I offer no apology for the differences.

One other item of interest came to light during the original breakdowns of the episodes. This is the obvious fact that some stories are strikingly familiar. For instance, *The Correct Way To Kill* is a re-hash of *The Charmers* (Blackman Season 2). If one substitutes a chiropodist for a dentist, and an umbrella shop for a tie shop, one gets a very similar story. *The Joker* has virtually the same plot as *Don't Look Behind You* (Blackman Season 2) and *The £50,000 Breakfast* is almost, but not quite, a re-run of *Death Of A Great Dane* (Blackman Season 1). How strange that one man, Alex Litoff, can die twice! I am, however, reliably informed that such story repetitions are common practice on a long-running television series.

CHAPTER SIX

The first episode, *The Forget-Me-Knot*, was a compilation of some unused Macnee/Rigg footage and some newly-shot Macnee/Rigg/Thorson scenes.

Homicide And Old Lace was a compilation of the unused Thorson pilot *The Great, Great Britain Crime* and previously unused Macnee footage from earlier Macnee/Rigg/Thorson episodes.

Killer was Jennifer Croxton's only appearance in the role of Lady Diana Forbes-Blakeney. A pretty blonde, she resembled a young Honor Blackman. Throughout the story, she wore a leather waistcoat and trousers, à la Cathy Gale. One wonders if she was perhaps testing for the role of Linda Thorson's replacement, had a further series been made.

Although the Thorson series was well-received in Britain, and international sales had grossed over £18,000,000 – with Paris awarding the Macnee/Thorson partnership Le Prix Triomphe in 1970 – the show's success was still dependent on being well-received in America.

For some inexplicable reason, ABC/TV (America) decided to screen the series in direct opposition to the immensely popular *Rowan and Martin's Laugh In* shows, and for the first time, *The Avengers* met an unbeatable opponent – the American television audience ratings.

Faced with such opposition, the show only managed to reach 69th position in the top 100 ratings. Soon after, ABC telephoned Clemens to say that they wouldn't require any further episodes of *The Avengers* after the 33 Thorson shows.

I think that the American decision to give Mother a major role and the laboured comedy that followed, plus the inexperience of Linda Thorson, all helped to accelerate the end of the show. (However, in fairness to Linda Thorson, after a dozen or so episodes, she handled the role of Tara King with conviction, and later matured into a fine actress.)

Though *The Avengers* went on to become the single biggest foreign currency earner of any television series (a record it still holds today), Thames Television couldn't afford the cost of producing the show alone and, unfortunately, the rest is history.